ARENA THIEVES

BY MADISON ZEHRING

The Diamond Game Series
Arena Thieves, Book 1

Cover design by Madison Zehring/Brandy/Artemis Gordon
Map by Madison Zehring
Illustrations by Madison Zehring
Professionally Typeset By Reedsy
Publishing Imprint owned by Madison Zehring

Snow Paw Press Publishing Rights
Name: Zehring, Madison / Author
Title: Arena Thieves / The Diamond Game Series, Book 1
Description: Fantasy / First Edition

ISBNs:
979-8-9958265-0-7 Hardcover
979-8-9958265-1-4 Paperback

Because I would take your place
on the auction stage—Bri, this one's for you.

THE NORTHERN HEMISPHERE

Now, prepare for the auction…
because once you enter,
you may never leave.

CHAPTER 1: RUNNERS

Quiet as a field mouse, I prop my pack onto the chipped bathroom sink as my hands work quickly, rummaging through sparse cabinets in search of necessities. The auctioneers may look for me, but I'll be long gone before they send the guards on their hunt.

There's no turning back now.

Months ago, among the garbage behind the butcher and fishmonger shops, I found a bar of soap I'd been saving for a special occasion. Last night, I decided to use it sparingly on the month-old grease coating my roots. If my runaway journey doesn't warrant clean hair, I'm not sure what will.

My hand hovers above the ivory bar perched on the sink as I contemplate stuffing it in my pack. It's mine, after all, and I'm not sure when I'll find such a rare commodity again.

With a sigh, my hand drops reluctantly. My guilty conscience can't take it from my mother, whether she realizes I'm about to go missing or not.

I twist limp, blond locks into a bun at the nape of my neck without sparing a second glance at my reflection. Calloused hands work from muscle memory, shaping the same tiresome hairstyle, but it's all I know. Besides, I don't have time to try anything flashy or new.

My mother used to have such beautiful hair. Long golden locks flow freely in the aged oil paintings she thinks are a secret, but I found them years ago tucked away in her closet.

I'm sure her younger self would be embarrassed by her state today. Instead of full lips and creamy skin, her cheeks are sunken from self-inflicted malnutrition while thin, pale strands cover her face where beauty no longer lives.

I watched her begin to slip when my father left us for another family. Then she lost herself altogether after the auction took my brothers in a single evening. I haven't known my mother in years. The gray shell of a woman living in her place is simply a ghost waiting to die, and I can't wait around for her anymore.

Swallowing the past, I have no choice but to focus on the future. *My* future.

Unimpressive, dull brown eyes shy away from the mirror, complementing pale skin that's never appreciated the sun and a frail body forbidden to move faster than a brisk walk.

Traitorous body. What would happen if they caught us? What if I need to run away or defend myself? I suppose that's why I have Kole. He'll protect me.

Kole.

My entire reason for deserting my mother and leaving behind the dusty cottage I've known my whole life. The auctioneers would notice if he weren't present, and the King takes great offense to students who try skipping town. The royal guard tracks down every last missing delta like a hound hunting its prey. That prey is met swiftly with their cruel demise. So, the only way out is to run. Far away and for long enough that people wouldn't recognize Kole's face. He's the special one they're after anyway.

The pulse in my neck accelerates at the thought of something happening to Kole. My breath slithers through an anxious throat, threatening to pitch an attack on my asthmatic lungs. That is, until I slip the powdered incense can from my pocket. Shaky hands unscrew the lid as my index finger drives the fine dust to my nostrils.

Relax, I tell myself as instant relief washes over paper-thin lungs. *I've been waiting for this my entire life—a way out.*

Last night, I snuck out to our spot on the grassy hilltop, the halfway point between our homes in the countryside as the mourning doves hummed from afar. Kole wasn't his usual chipper self, crossing his arms instead of holding me in them like he usually does.

"What's wrong?" I had asked him, scooting closer as the sun set its auburn glow across the spring fields below.

Kole sighed while tucking a long strand of dirty blond hair behind his ear. The muscle in his jaw hardened as he tugged at a blade of grass between us.

"It's no use," Kole sighed deeply. I stared at his strong jaw, his sun-kissed skin with a sprinkle of boyish freckles. The sight of him took my breath away. But everything about him tonight exuded negativity, which had me confused. He'd been excited about the auction ever since I could remember.

I ran a hand down his cheek, gently pulling his face, but still, his eyes wouldn't meet mine.

Kole swallowed. "If I show up to the auction tomorrow, there's no guarantee they'll take me. And if I *don't* show up…"

Sadness had tightened around my chest like a vise. I hated to see him so miserable, especially since this was his dream.

His gift changed everything for him. It changed everything for my brothers as well.

"But isn't this what you've always wanted?"

I whispered, remembering Kole's excitement every time he learned a new trick with his delta. The way he makes water move is magical. Unworldly. *Beautiful.* And I know he loves it. So why would he jeopardize the most important day of his life?

I've heard the gift blesses its holder, becoming an intimate part of who they are. I've never known the feeling. Nor will I ever. A delta is born by the time someone reaches adolescence, so by ten years old, most children either have a gift or don't. By twenty-one, they're put up for auction to the highest bidder like cattle in a ring. Make no mistake—the gifted are the ton's unmistakable commodities, and most relish their rare talents.

Kole had nodded slowly to my question, finally rubbing a smooth thumb over my palm. "I've been dreaming about auction day for years. But I only have one shot. They don't let students in a second time, and they'll disintegrate anyone on the spot for an offensive gift."

As always, I offered him a gentle smile to ease his worry, "Your delta could never be offensive. So, you have to make this time count. I believe in you."

I laced my arm through his, pressing closer and holding onto this memory in hopes it wasn't our last. I always knew this day would come. It is the same day that stole my brothers.

The law of the auction has been decreed by decades of kings with no room for opposing discussion. The annual showcase of gifts is a tradition on our side of the world, allowing suits with deep pockets to purchase whatever student shows promise for their cause. Sadly, no amount of little girls sobbing for their brothers will ever bring them back once their train leaves the tracks.

The militant heads of border protection always show up with millions to spend on metalists and shield deltas to ensure the safety of our country, Bachaloria. The Grand Pree Hospital also sends a group of its administration to bid on any healer, weaver, and mender to add to their doctors' staff that encompasses our country.

For people born with a traditional delta like manipulation of metal, they understand their future will most likely be spent within the Bachalorian military, guarding the border from our Enemy In The North. But for someone like Kole, who obtains the power to command water, that gift isn't usually ignored by the most coveted group of bidders—Aegis.

The discerning, highly influential billionaires of the world storm through auction day to collect the most dangerous deltas with a budget that has no ceiling. There are rumors that Aegis hauls students away to a private base for months of grueling training, where most don't make it out alive. Despite this cruel treatment, even the worst healers who stand before the sea of bidders silently pray to be bought by Aegis for the slim chance of becoming a legend.

A rare icon to live within the fabric of eternal history.

A *Player.*

And that's the caveat to the auction. Some try to run to stay away from a life of a forced career, but most stay for that impossibly small chance to become one of the few. The proud.

Kole's dream from the moment he flicked his first droplet has been to acquire the title of Player. He has no desire to guard the border or work in the mines, craving the possibility of becoming something more. I've always admired him for his dream. Even if that meant he'd leave me one day for Aegis just as my brothers did. Their deltas were too powerful to overlook.

Kole shook his head in agitation at my reassurance, seeming irritated that I could possibly be encouraging.

He stood up, abandoning me on the grassy hill, his voice laced with annoyance, "You don't understand, Soria. What if Aegis overlooks me? What if they collect all the hydromancers they're allotted for, and border protection buys me? I don't want to forge knives along the coast for the rest of my life!" Stressed hands flew through his hair as anxious
questions spilled into the night,

"Or… what if *no one* bids on me…"

I should have felt bad for my stirring thoughts. My own selfish desires have always silently hoped for that outcome, no matter how slim a chance. Out of the thousands of students who take the stage, less than a handful ever get to leave without a single bid. If that happened to Kole, it would destroy him. But at least he would be mine forever.

I tucked a loose strand behind my ear, searching for the right words to make him feel better, "Don't overthink this, Kole. You're *amazing.* Aegis would be lucky to have you, and if they can't see that, then screw them."

For some reason, my pitiful blurb of encouragement only added fire to Kole's frustration.

He snapped his head, hovering above me, "Again, you don't understand. The auction isn't about *luck.* It's about raw, unfiltered talent that a bidder wants so bad they're willing to spend hundreds of thousands to stamp their name on it."

I cross my arms, muttering under my breath, "Yeah, like property."

I've never agreed with the auction and what it represents.

Kole's hands found his hips with a furrowed brow, "Don't mock the auction, Soria. You weren't born with a delta. You don't have to worry about failing. You're one of the lucky ones."

I leaped to my feet, facing him in the sunset and ignoring what his beautiful gaze did to me. How dare he tell me I should be fortunate to be born so purposeless. At least if I had a delta I'd use it to never feel the ache of an empty stomach again.

"Don't ever call me one of the lucky ones," I seethed, "You don't know what it's like to eat boiled mushrooms for two months straight. You have everything." Perhaps I let the grief of our last night seep into my curt response because I've never spit back at him like that before.

Kole looked at me then, moving closer to wrap me in his arms as if he'd realized his harsh words.

And then suddenly, it happened. His irritation shifted into optimism within a blink. That was when everything changed.

"*We* could have everything." His eyes sparkled as the idea fired on all cylinders.

"What do you mean?"

"Do you trust me?" Kole whispered, roving between my eyes quickly.

My heart fluttered into a full-on stampede because I knew the words he was about to say. The words we've always dreamed of, but knew the moment we said them seriously, there would be no going back. I couldn't believe it.

I swallowed the nerves in my throat as I nodded my answer and watched a smile creep across his face, matching my own. He cupped my face, "Let's run and start our lives over. Just you and me without the pressure to perform."

My breath caught in my throat, and I scanned every scenario before the excitement could take over, "But if they catch you, they'll kill you!"

"We'll be long gone by then."

"But what about my mom?"

I had asked, my smile fading suddenly. I'd thought about leaving every single day, but I never had the guts to actually do it. Would she miss me? Would she even know I'd left?

Kole squeezed me tighter in his arms, "Your mom doesn't even know *she's* alive. Trust me, she won't miss you."

I almost recoiled then, but the image of my new future kept me clinging onto Kole. *Our* future. So, I pushed away the guilt when the image of my mother's face came to mind.

"But what about *your* family? Your friends?"

My voice lowered thinking about Kole's poor mother, grief-stricken at the thought of losing her only child.

Kole simply tilted my chin to stare into my eyes as if no excuse could loosen the idea of running away, "Nothing will matter so long as I have you, Soria. Say yes."

I couldn't believe he would give up his dream for me. And even more, I couldn't believe he would risk his life to run away with me. That was always *my* dream. And it was finally happening.

The memory from only ten hours ago replays in my mind like a sweet escape as I shove my feet into worn loafers. My eye suddenly catches the most valuable item I own. A chocolate violin case sheathing my delicate instrument. It may be impractical for two fugitives on the run, but I can't possibly leave it behind.

Regrettably, I stop by my mother's bedroom. I let go of the softest exhale, peeking past the curtain to find her sound asleep on that stained cot, a collection of empty bottles littering her nightstand. The sun begins to rise through the cracks in the walls, illuminating the notches in her spine that cut through her sheer, tattered robe.

In this light, my mother looks fragile as her shoulders rise and fall with every breath. Her face only holds this much peace when she collapses in the fetal position, and for a moment, I feel guilt wash over me like a tidal wave as my pack weighs heavy on my shoulders.

But then I remember the time she stole my savings jar, spending every last krona on enough rum to tranquilize a bear, and my guilt vanishes. I was only twelve.

To my mother, I've only ever been an able body who existed within her decaying home. Someone to forget easily, as everyone else in my life has. Everyone, that is, besides Kole.

Tucking the crumpled goodbye note into the windowpane, I creak past the frayed screen door, bidding my home one last goodbye.

I face the moss-covered cobblestones held together by nothing more than tree sap and sheer will, wondering if I'll ever see this place again or the face inside it.

***

I take the usual trail to Kole's house with all but a skip in my step. I always get excited to see him, but now I'll never have to say goodnight and make the half-mile walk back to loneliness.

After today, I'll never say goodnight again.

As I round the side of Mr. Seifson's lamb farm, I wonder if the King's Guards have started preparing the cathedral for the auction yet. There's no doubt that thousands are already lined up behind the fifteen-foot doors, considering the morning round of students have the highest chances of being noticed and they've traveled from all over Bachaloria.

But that won't be my Kole. Not anymore.

We had our plan laid out last night like a beautifully detailed blueprint. The King's Guard will already be on the hunt for runaways, combing the city from the outskirts to catch students who've tried taking off early. No one will think twice about a young couple traveling west to Jurant, one of the most heavily populated cities in Bachaloria. We could become anyone there, hiding in plain sight. *I* could become anyone.

With a wheeze in my chest, I finally reach the top of the hill as the warm sun peeks over the horizon, signaling the rooster from two fields over to scream his morning wake-up call.

Kole's mother will still be working her night job as a waitress and probably won't make it home until lunchtime to get ready for the auction. We'll be long gone by then.

I climb the worn wooden steps to Kole's front porch and eagerly twist the metal doorknob to find it locked on the other side. That's weird.

Setting down my violin case and pack, I squint through the smudged window to find no movement. Not a single trace of life.

Rapping on the door, I'm convinced Kole overslept again.

He always oversleeps. I don't blame him, though. He was probably up all night like I was.

"Kole?" I call out while knocking on the door again.

No answer.

With a hand on my hip, I scan the front porch. I shouldn't be shouting his name for all of Bachaloria to hear, just in case some King's guards linger along the property lines. But where is he?

Kole must have gone into town to retrieve supplies. That's a risky move, but he's calculated and always planning ahead. Whatever he went to retrieve must be essential.

Taking a seat in the old wooden rocking chair on the porch, I conclude he should be back any minute. I can't wait to see the look on his face when he apologizes for being so late. But that optimism slowly starts to fade as the minutes bleed into an hour, and the morning sun beams brightly over the summer fields below. My mind threatens to spin into a frenzy, wondering what could have happened or where Kole went, but I force those thoughts away. There is a perfectly logical explanation for why he isn't here.

Or *is* he?

Gathering my violin case and pack, I follow my hunch, praying the window in Kole's bedroom is unlocked.

Trailing toward the back of the black-stone house, I lean the wood pallet by his window to make a ramp as I've done before, and haul my items up with me, preparing the speech I'll relay if Kole really is still sleeping and didn't hear me yell his name.

I slide up the glass pane with a sigh of relief, tossing my gear onto his bed while awaiting a thudding sound or a grunt from my sleeping boyfriend. But there's nothing. Only the sound of my pack rolling off the mattress and onto the tile floor.

In any case, waiting inside is better than sweating on the hot front porch. Plus Kole's mother always has delicious leftovers.

I peek around his house, sweeping the rooms to ensure Kole hasn't passed out somewhere, only to find his home empty of everyone except me. And a *hungry* me.

Strolling back into Kole's bedroom with a handful of dried apricot slices from the kitchen, I gobble them up without remorse. I'm careful to only take a few, considering Kole's mother has struck me in the past for stealing food to ease the ache in my empty stomach. She's never been a fan of the 'starving girl her son entertains.'

I catch a glimpse of my reflection in Kole's full-length mirror, cringing at my ratty clothes. A dark brown tunic, stained with every possible liquid imaginable sits draped over my body, two sizes too big. And the fitted capris only add to the suggestion that I have never cared about my appearance, considering every young lady my age wears only proper gowns in the public eye of society.

No. Today is special. I can't start my new life in a disgusting tunic.

Throwing open my pack, I dump the contents on the bed, hoping to see something... clean? Formal? But there's nothing besides a wool jacket and mismatched socks.

I grimace at my options until I remember the dress I left in Kole's closet months ago, and I can't help but giggle at the thought, because it's something the proper ladies of the ton would lose their heads over. Kole had gotten the dress for me as a late birthday present, but strictly speaking, the dress didn't stay on for too long that night.

I rummage through the closet until a sliver of red fabric peeks back at me beneath a heap of dirty laundry. Chuckling, I slide into the backless, floor-length red gown, grinning at the dirty loafers peeking below the hem.

This dress is far from the frilly and modest gowns society accepts. Two thin straps support a plunging neckline that dips into a deep V, showing off a pale, flat chest and collarbones that scream *forever malnourished*—but not after today.

Today marks the start of my new life, where I can be anything I want. S*tarving* will never describe me again.

I take in my frail, slim image in the mirror, placing my medicinal can of incense in the dress pocket as I habitually do. One time, I even needed it during a ferocious round between the sheets with Kole, barely catching my breath before going another hour. I bite my lip at the sweaty memory.

Staring down my reflection, I decide the dress is undoubtedly impractical for our journey, and gather my tunic to change back into, trying to maintain patience for this boy. And where are his bags? Are they packed? I hope he's okay.

Tangled nerves start to spiral as I imagine, for some irrational reason, Kole not being okay. What if the auctioneers found out he was planning on skipping town? What if someone caught wind of our plan and locked him up? What if—

The front door swings open, and I exhale the fear away, rolling my eyes at my own hastiness for getting so worked up in the first place. Obviously, he's okay.

"Dammit, Kole Arnson! You scared me to death!" My voice quivers with relief as I pull the straps of the dress back up, ready to hear his laughter at my choice of ensemble. I pluck the violin case from the bed and make my way toward the front room.

"And your bags better be packed! We have to get moving."

I can't hide the smile as I round the corner with a playful hand on my hip, but Kole's nowhere to be found. And the front door sits wide open.

The bright sun fills the front room, warming the floor and the skin along my chest where the deep neckline dips.

An eerie feeling crawls along the back of my spine, thrumming against my neck until I realize something isn't right.

Where is Kole?

"Kole?" I call out slowly, inching toward the door. Curiosity and a pang of fear keep my head on a swivel as I prepare for anything to bounce into sight. I take another step out onto the porch, clutching my violin case in my arms as the hairs on my neck rise to the silence of the farm.

Why is everything so quiet?

I glance slowly to my left to see the same rocking chair sitting idly, untouched. To my right, nothing but a few old terracotta pots with shriveled daisies and weeds stare back at me. Perhaps the wind opened the door?

"The locked door?"

I freeze. For some reason, this voice is not my own. But it came from my head. Maybe that was me?

My hand grazes the pocket where my incense sits while my other palm clutches the worn violin case, finally exhaling with a shake. There's no one out here.

But before I can return through the front door, something comes crashing into my skull, knocking every last thought from my mind and the wind from my lungs. Everything goes black, and my brain sends me into an instant sleep without permission.

CHAPTER 2: THE AUCTION

My head feels so foggy. My lips are cracked and chapped. Why are my lips chapped? Where am I?

Shaky palms scramble for anything familiar to get my bearings, but to no avail. My body is horizontal, throwing my equilibrium off its axis, and for some reason, it feels like I'm moving.

Wait. Am I moving?

A bump tosses me to the side as a painful cry rips from my throat, and something hard digs into my spine. Blinded by darkness, I throw my hand out to find old leather, worn in familiar spots with a familiar rip in the seam above the top clasp. *My violin case!*

Another bump throws me squarely onto the case, and a groan escapes as I try to sit up. The sound of old, rickety wood fills my senses for the first time, reminding me of wheels churning on stone through the square, and the smell of musty, stagnant water hints at the brick tunnel leading into town.

Cerica. The last town I need to be in.

I begin palming the ground madly, searching for a way to get to my feet until I find an odd texture that feels strangely like denim. I cling to the fabric, hoisting myself to a seated position as a bright light blinds me instantly. Gripping the denim with both arms, I squint, all but hissing at the sun like vermin removed from its hiding spot.

My surroundings become painfully clear as squinted eyes adjust, and my heart nearly bursts from palpable, overwhelming fear.

Old wooden planks create this cage of a carriage I find myself in, completed with barbed chicken wire rounding off the top to prevent escape from the bodies inside.

This inhumane cart slides in line with hundreds of carriages pulling into drop off students and their families toward a grand building.

My blood runs cold.

Satin-black pillars line the cathedral that groans with age and sophistication. Every dark brick detailed with golden flecks is a testament to the old money this historic building was crafted with. The polished grand staircase sweeps toward the stone street like a velvet blanket. The staircase that every student walks up for one reason only.

The auction.

My grip tightens around the denim until I look up to find myself clinging to a stranger's leg. A stranger who seems more groggy than me.

Releasing the boy's leg, I scramble backward, squeezing my violin case to my chest as if the harder I clutch, it might get me out of here somehow. I coil into the corner of the enclosed cart, wondering how on earth I got here in the first place.

I can't be in Cerica. I can't be here!

About six other men and women my age sit in this prison on wheels beside me, all coming to the same realization that we're trapped. Vulnerable. And entirely on display for the gawkers making their way into the cathedral.

Peeking past the razor wire enclosing me in this cart, I find several leery and judgmental eyes murmuring amongst themselves as we roll through the cobblestone path, inching closer and closer to the cathedral.

As we pass, voices from the road murmur among themselves, loud enough to send a bout of nausea to my stomach because they shouldn't be talking about me… and yet, they are.

"Don't look, sweetie. Those are the degenerates who tried to run."

"How shameful, honestly."

"Those cowards don't deserve to set foot on the stage."

"I hope they're blasted to oblivion for trying to run."

This has to be some mistake! How did I end up here? What are they going to do to me? I was about to be on the run with…

My eyes grow wide as I whip around, searching desperately for Kole.

Dread unravels as I inspect each person in the carriage, my nails digging into the violin case at a horrific realization.

None of these faces belong to him.

What did they do to Kole?

Jittery palms instinctively reach for my incense powder to ease the wheezing in my throat. I force a deep breath, feeling the instant satisfaction graze my lungs, and shove it back into my pocket as I sit crumpled on the ground.

The pocket… *not* of my flowing tunic, but of a skin-tight, backless, *inappropriate*, scarlet gown. *Shit.*

Another bump along the cobblestone road sends me flying into the side of the prison cart, my hair obstructing my view like a frizzy curtain. The cart rolls past the cathedral entrance toward the backside, out of sight from the public.

The other students trapped with me finally gather enough bearings to begin panicking, conceding their plans to escape have been foiled.

I was trying to escape, but I don't belong here! There are laws against enabling runners, but the offenders are usually fined or shipped for penalty work along the border until their debt to society is paid.

Not sent to the cathedral on auction day.

Without warning, the cart comes to a heavy halt, tossing its passengers to the front and earning every exposed knee a sweltering bruise.

To my horror, the tailgate drops open to the back door of the Black Top Cathedral, revealing four men dressed in sleek, dark uniforms, adorned with a plethora of knives strapped to wide chests. The Bachalorian emblems on their chests tell me they're members of the King's Guard and have no tolerance for nonsense—not that His Majesty would ever entertain such an act.

The closest one with a copper ponytail barks at us, "Thought you all could escape, huh?"

His voice guts me like a wrestling trout, and I can't shake the terror lancing through my body from that twisted gaze with too much power.

The ponytail snaps again, making me wince as I lie here curled up on the floor of the dusty cart, "So here's the rules, dickheads. King Ragnar declared every delta has to be present for the auction. If it were up to me, your throats woulda' been slit on sight for such a treason."

The guard eyes every one of us with an amused leer, "But the king's rules won't stop me from defending myself if one of you's happens to use your delta between now and the time you get on that stage. And you *will* get on that stage. Now, whether or not the bidders decide to blow you's to bits for trying to run is up to them. You're free game to that audience."

His snicker sends me even further into panic. A panic that could stop my heart in an instant with no one to save me. Not even Kole.

"Now get the fuck out!" The King's Guard shrieks and everyone behind me obeys immediately, their body language mimicking petrified rabbits stuck in a snare.

Gathering my violin case with quivering hands, I follow suit by tumbling off the tailgate with as much grace as a one-legged fawn. I land on my case with a painful thud, causing the guards to scoff at my unorthodox outfit for such an occasion.

A guard with a snub nose chuckles, his spit flying too close to my face, "What were your plans today, sweetheart? Waitressing in a brothel?"

"Or stripping in that brothel?" Another one chimes, throwing a finger at my red dress, flashing milky, yellow teeth.

Eagerly, I scramble to my feet, trying my best to keep the tears at bay. I don't think I'd earn any points for sobbing to armed men who already see me as a joke.

The ponytailed man snatches the violin case from my arms, inspecting my possession with ravenous, greedy hands.

Without permission, he rips open the case, ignoring the snap of the metal clasps that keep the tired leather together, and my violin and bow tumble to the ground.

A gasp lodges in my throat as I fly to the cobblestones and scoop up my instrument. This violin is my only reminder of the mundane life I wish I never ran from. I got too bold—too selfish. Why is this happening to me?

A single tear plummets down a burning cheek as I squeeze the violin to my chest, facing the guard with a whimper.

"Why are you doing this? I don't even belong here!"

"That's what they all say. Now, get in line before I force you." He brandishes a knife, and I conclude I have no choice but to line up behind the other students enduring the guard's harassment.

A small girl with tight, curly brown hair and beautiful dark skin shivers in front of me, trying to avoid eye contact with any of the guards poking at the students ahead of us. Her outfit reminds me of something I would typically wear. A stained tunic and hole-patched pants in need of a good wash.

She must not come from money either.

My feet inch closer to her, my arms locking around my instrument so tight I fear the wood may be making an impression on my body.

Nervously, I whisper to the girl, "Hello."

Instantly, the muscles in her shoulders tighten, and her head snaps in my direction with wide, dark eyes.

I inch a little closer, lowering my voice to show I mean no harm, "What are they going to do to us?"

The girl swallows, whispering, "I think they're gonna make us perform… like everyone else."

My mouth goes dry. Perform a delta?

As our little line toward the clipboard grows shorter, I shuffle closer, "But what if I don't have anything to perform?"

"Next!" A burly guard with the clipboard snaps. The girl before me shuffles forward, wringing her palms as she answers his questions in a meek voice.

"Name and delta," the guard grumbles.

She sobers the quiver in her voice, "Hera Bjornsdottir. And… it's glowing."

The guard arches his brow, *"Glowing?"* he repeats, unimpressed.

Hera nods quickly, still wringing her hands to keep the rest of her body from shaking, I imagine. The guard simply rolls his eyes, finds her name on the long scroll, and makes a mark before nodding for her to pass through the dark door.

"Next."

I force my legs to move one step closer toward the clipboard, squeezing my violin tighter.

"Name and delta."

I find myself swallowing as Hera had, nerves sliding up my spine to form trickling beads of sweat on my *very* exposed skin.

Eventually, I squeak, "Soria… Davidsdottir."

"And delta." The guard demands without looking up. I shake my head, wondering how to convey that I don't belong here. But I have a feeling no amount of convincing will get me out of this mess.

"I don't have one."

The guard smirks, still flipping through his scroll of names, "Never heard that one before. I won't ask again, girl."

Before another tear falls, I try to throw a Hail Mary, "*Please,* I promise you I'm telling the truth. I don't have a delta. I never have. Please just let me go home!"

Perhaps it's the pleading in my eyes, or maybe the fact that the guard simply cannot find my name on the roster of every student ever recorded to have a delta by the age of twenty-one.

He sighs while showing a hint of humanity, "Sorry, but you're going on that stage. Nothing anyone can do about it now. Just be lucky they don't have your ma and pa's names."

"Ask my mother! Ask my neighbors. *Anyone.* I'm not special! I'll take you to my mother myself if you just…"

"That's enough, girl."

And with a few strokes of his quill, my name lands on his parchment, along with a firm palm against my back, pushing me toward the door.

Darkness surrounds me like a cloak, and I stumble forward, slamming into a body that might be frailer than mine.

"Sorry!" I whisper, blinking rapidly to adjust to the dim lighting.

"It's okay," Hera whispers, turning toward me, "I hate the dark too."

Ahead of us, I make out several silhouettes shuffling forward in line as guards direct the way. Perhaps they're lining us up to be executed. I can't imagine the bidders would be pleased to see me fumble with my hands on stage, wasting their time. It's not like I can suddenly pull metal bending out of my ass.

"What's your delta?" Hera whispers in front of me, pulling me out of my fear trance.

"I don't have one," I whisper back, feeling that same eeriness as our line inches forward in the dark.

Several guards in pitch-black uniforms begin to move students around as the line merges down the dim corridor, filtering in with the rest of the lot.

Hera peeks over her shoulder in a mutter, "You don't have a delta? How did you end up here?"

I shake my head, feeling like I've been asking myself the same question over and over ever since I gained consciousness, "Your guess is as good as mine."

We continue trudging forward as candlelight flickers every twenty feet, illuminating our surroundings just enough to keep every student on course. From what I gather, behind me stands a tall young man, and ahead of Hera seems to be a boy about her size and perhaps another girl, but everything's beginning to blur together.

My palm finds the smooth surface of my incense can before these thoughts soar to dangerous lengths, wishing I never left my cottage this morning. Babysitting my greedy, deteriorating mother for the rest of my life sounds better than dying in front of a ravenous crowd.

Hera must notice my fear beginning to boil over as I fight hyperventilation, because she turns slightly, a bright smile in the darkness, "I never meant to run, you know."

My throat emits a jagged breath as we travel, thankful for something to take my mind off impending doom.

Hera goes on, her voice remarkably calm considering where we are "My grandma raised me. She always told me my delta was something special. Something for the stars, or whatever. She said any bidder would be lucky to have me and never to run. But I got held up working in the mines too late last night and overslept… by several hours. I suppose someone tipped off the auction folk that I was a flight risk and here I am." Her head drops as we continue walking, and so does my heart.

I shake my head, loosening my grip slightly on the brass fittings against my arms.

"That's not fair. You don't deserve to be treated like a criminal for an honest mistake."

Hera's warm smile flashes over her shoulder again before imparting the most important sentence I've heard in a long time, "Hey, others have it worse, I suppose."

"I'll say," the young man ahead of us twists around, completely invading our conversation, "Ty Yang," he throws out a hand to fully face Hera while walking backward in line, nearly startling my poor new acquaintance, "But my friends call me Grape."

"Oh, um," Hera gingerly takes the boy's hand as he shakes confidently, "Hera. Nice to meet you… I guess."

"It's always nice to meet me. Who's the beauty blond in the dress?"

I feel an eyebrow arch as my arms tighten back around the violin, "Soria."

I murmur, thankful for the buffer of Hera in the middle, "Your name is Ty *Yang?* I know a name like that isn't Bachalorian, as our young typically take our father's name as a surname. And Yang sounds way too close to…"

"The Enemy In The North named me," the boy grins, "My parents adopted me from a fugitive couple taken to detainment from trying to cross our borders. I get asked that a lot. But like I said, you can call me Grape."

"And why do they call you Grape?" My curiosity gets the better of me.

He chuckles as we pass another flickering candlelight, revealing two childish dimples, spiky black hair, and a sprinkle of freckles across olive skin. His cotton vest just barely matches a cream button up, along with loose trousers, and I can't help but think he's not how I'd imagine a grape. He is small, though.

Grape raises both brows as if he's seeing me for the first time beneath the warm glow of the candlelight we pass, "Now that's certainly a long story. But I'll make you all a deal," he nods to Hera and I, still walking backward and surprisingly not stepping on the poor girl ahead of him, "We all make it on Aegis and I tell you my nickname story, shorty shows us her delta and blondie tells me about the viola she has in a choke hold."

I nearly snort as I correct him, "It's a violin."

"And I'll show you my delta right now."

I blink, and before I can ask Hera any questions, her once beautiful brown skin shifts into a golden hue, brighter and brighter until she becomes the sun in the dark and desolate hallway. Her light bounces off the enormous walls of the cathedral, illuminating everything that was once hidden in a beautiful, mesmerizing warmth. Making everything look magical and timeless. All around, people sigh at the beauty until suddenly, it's gone within a second, and I'm left in the dark with a giggling little Hera inches ahead of me.

"Wow. That was amazing!" Grape chimes, slapping his hands on Hera's shoulders as he continues his walk backward.

"Truly beautiful. Your Grandma was right," I whisper, "Any bidder would be lucky to have you."

"Pathetic."

A feminine voice sneers ahead of Grape, not bothering to look back. I can't get a good look at her, but her dark hair sits perfectly styled in a luxurious braid that reaches her hips. A silk blazer sparkles against a frilly lace gown, telling me all I need to know. She certainly comes from money. Bratty money.

Ignoring the mean girl ahead of us, distant chattering begins to pick up, growing louder and louder the further we trail down the long corridor into who-knows-where.

The candlelight becomes more frequent the further we venture, and the mumbling grows in volume. The foul smells of cigar smoke, and fresh wax from recently polished shoes fill my senses. As I look ahead, my heart nearly leaps from my chest. It's the stage.

A warm, unfriendly light beams from the top of a six-foot staircase as the line proceeds in a downward spiral. The bidders sit out of view while I wait at the bottom of our procession, concealed by the sanctuary of the black curtain. But I fear my hiding spot won't last long.

Suddenly, a voice I've only heard squealing about prices for hogs pipes up, causing my heart to race faster than ever.

"Lemme get a five, now four, now five, five fifty, five fifty… *sold!* For five thousand fifty krona to Border Protection."

Hera turns to me as we inch closer to the base of the stairs, "Nervous yet?"

Nodding furiously, I drive more medicinal powder into my nostril as our line grows shorter. If I collapse from an asthma attack, I might be doing myself a favor, but self-preservation won't let me get that far.

A stout man with a permanent frown ushers us to climb the stairs as another student makes their way across the stage. I force my legs to follow after Hera's, praying the heavens save me before I get too far.

Only Hera, Grape, and Mean Girl stand between me and the hungry bidders. I want to throw up.

Now, with a clear view of the stage and who's on it, my heartrate flies, my skin growing clammy for the unknown.

An older man with perfectly styled white hair and a dapper ivory suit stands behind an oak podium with the world's skinniest bugle levitating before him. No doubt his delta creates such an effect, but what's even more menacing is the grim reaper looming a few feet to his right, keeping a trained gaze on the current student for purchase.

Kole has warned me of the reaper before. An odious man built like a stalk of corn with pasty skin and dark, soulless eyes. Students have passed down stories of his terrifying ability to turn anything or *anyone* into ashes with the stroke of a finger. He's terrifying, callous, but more importantly, the reaper is King Ragnar's pet. That fact alone makes him an untouchable creature of the crown.

Though the reaper represents death in its most lucid form, he's the most necessary individual at the auction, according to Kole. He listens to the bidders, weighs their emotions about the delta performing, and strikes down any gift deemed useless, offensive, or some other wild reason the bidders may choose. So, I suppose strolling onto a stage with no delta *at all* could warrant my immediate demise.

My throat clenches as the boy behind me closes in, locking me to the stage. An older woman sits perched on a stool before the curtain breaks, demanding information with impatience.

"Alright, you're next, girlie," the woman mutters to Mean Girl in a husky voice, signaling it's her time to shine, "Name and delta."

Mean Girl flicks a perfectly manicured hand through silky black hair, barely acknowledging the roll-keeper on her stool.

"Sera Jonsdottir. Hallucination."

I barely catch her last word, nearly gasping at the thought of such a rare delta. It almost makes me envy her.

Sera flicks her chin over her shoulder to Grape, "Don't take it personal when the reaper decides you're worthless."

She strolls onto the stage, smiling with perfectly polished teeth as if she's Bachaloria's sweetheart. From what I can hear, the bidders love her already. So much for envying a snake.

"Don't listen to her," Hera mumbles to Grape, earning a cheeky smile from our newest friend, "I'm sure you'll do amazing."

"Yeah, if I..." his voice trails off, "...*Woah.*"

Suddenly, my vision swirls into darkness as if I just blinked, but my eyes are wide open.

I stagger backward into the boy behind me, earning an annoyed huff as he pushes me off him.

"Hera?" I whisper, clutching tighter to my violin, "Hera, can you see anything? What's happening?"

"I can't see a thing!" She exclaims, grabbing my elbow to steady herself. Meanwhile, I hear Grape sighing to himself a mere two feet away, sounding unimpressed.

And all at once, it's like the lights in my mind flick back on, and I can see everything again. My body nearly leaps in relief. Being blinded like that was one of the worst sensations I've felt. It was like a cloud fogged my mind without permission.

The auctioneer's voice picks up before I can relay my disgust to Hera, booming over the enthusiastic audience of bidders.

"Ladies and gentlemen, Sera Jonsdottir, hailing from Prijon University. A rare delta before us, so if there's a time to pull out the big checks, call in the favors, she's the one!" The auctioneer smiles from ear to ear, charming and inviting as he urges the suits to prepare for war amongst their checkbooks. "Let's start the bidding at ten thousand."

"Twenty."

"Fifty!"

The auctioneer raises both brows, smiling wider than ever with a surveying finger at the crowd to keep track, "Fifty now

sixty, seventy, now eighty."

"One hundred."

"One hundred! I see you, Grand Pree! One hundred over here, one ten, now one twenty, one thirty, one forty."

Sera stands with her hands folded behind her back, silky hair wafting over her shoulders, and a gentle smile spread across full lips, aimed at the crowd. She seems more than pleased with the numbers fighting over her.

"*Sold!* To Aegis for one hundred eighty thousand krona! Ladies and gentlemen, Aegis is the group to beat tonight, and they did *not. Come. To. Play!*"

Of course Aegis bought her. I have no doubt their bidders are drooling over such a terrible power. I can't begin to imagine her in that arena.

Out of the corner of my eye, I catch Grape arguing with the roll-keeper in an arbitrary match.

"Young man, you better tell me your delta right now!"

The woman whisper-yells as the crowd begins to settle, ready for their next product of purchase.

Grape waves a dismissive hand, whisper-shouting back,

"I told you, it's a surprise!"

She gives in, throwing annoyed hands in the air while muttering something inaudible to no one in particular.

The auctioneer speaks up, taking back over the room as his voice carries far with his levitating bugle, "Now, ladies and gentlemen, next up is Ty Yang from Emporia College, here to wow you today with…"

He falters a moment as Grape saunters out, nearly swallowed by the vast marble stage.

The auctioneer quickly schools his confusion as the roll keeper offers a helpless shrug out of view, "His delta seems to be a … *surprise."*

Nervous chuckles smooth the embarrassment in his voice, but nothing phases the student standing confidently before a sea of sharks.

But Grape does nothing. He stands there. Doing nothing. And the silence stretches on.

My heart pounds as the reaper eyes his pupil like a meal, preparing to send him to the heavens with one finger stroke.

As the silence stretches further, Grape closes his eyes, listening to the silence. The deafening, awkward silence that makes me believe this was a suicide march.

Before his next breath, Grape shouts at the crowd of bidders, keeping his eyes closed as the room sits in the quiet misery he created.

"What's he doing?" Grape calls out, still focused, "What a joke. Where's he going with this? Someone signal the reaper." His voice is clear and purposeful as he goes on, "Why's he saying that? Did he hear me? Do you think Vidir's cheating on me?"

Far off in a corner of the room that I still can't see, I swear I hear a gasp from a feminine voice. Grape doesn't care. He pops his eyes open just to wink, closing them impetuously to finish his grand performance.

"Is it noise acuity? We'll make them into political statements. How many more deltas can Epsum afford? We've got fifty thousand left for disposal. The king's detainment camps barely hold them in."

That last one did it. The silent room erupts into a maelstrom of gasps and murmurs, all shocked by Grape's echo of what they thought was private. He doesn't bat an eye. He simply bows as if to cue that his entertainment has ended once he revealed something juicy to the audience.

In an instant, the auctioneer takes back over, smoothing the bidders with his charming voice, "Well, well, well! I can see now why Mr. Yang's proposal of his delta was a surprise. You don't come across that type of display for super-hearing very often. Shall we go ahead and start the bidding?"

The auctioneer begins the bidding at four thousand, causing a couple of groups to dispute for a moment until the gavel bangs, followed by the words, *Sold! To Aegis!*

I gasp. He really did it. He pulled off the master of all performances to earn a spot on the most coveted team known to Bachaloria.

Grapes bow to the crowd with a giant, pleased grin, shooting us a wink over his shoulder in the process. He kisses his palms and throws the audience a few cheeky gestures as he strolls the stage, immediately swallowed by the darkness of the curtains on the other side.

The other side. That's all I need to get to… if I don't get blown to bits for offending the bidders before then.

"Name and delta."

The woman on the stool barks at Hera, who responds politely with her title of glowing.

I whisper over her shoulder just before she smooths her tunic down with shaky palms, "You'll do great."

Hera turns to me, her curls bouncing with the movement, "And so will you, *friend.*"

Her warm and contagious smile makes me realize I've never had a friend before. Not one who actually cared to know me, anyhow. Every girl in school only spoke to me on occasion to get to my twin brothers. They were the special ones. I suppose Kole is my friend, but Kole means much more than that, wherever he is right now. And hopefully, it's with Aegis. He *has* to be with Aegis.

I watch my new friend's little footsteps take center stage, masking her worry with another bright smile, but I can tell she's nervous. She has no need. Her gift is beautiful.

"Ladies and gentlemen, next we have Miss Hera Bjornsdottir, a graduate of Keplin, and she's here to show us quite
a special talent, indeed. *Glowing!*"

For some reason, I can't hide the smile that tugs at my lips watching Hera enjoy her moment.

Her skin shifts slightly to a golden hue, but the yellow light cascading over the cathedral's auditorium makes it nearly impossible for her to repeat what was done in the hallway.

She needs complete darkness.

I glance up at the chandeliers, wondering if someone will snuff them out for her just before the crowd grows quieter than when Grape held his audience.

Hera focuses with a deep exhale, letting her delta shine as far as it can while competing with other light, but something is off. No one is gasping at the beauty waiting to unfold. The room feels eerie just before the auctioneer clears his throat gently in his bugle, side-stepping back.

The auctioneer's eyes meet the floor as he relays to the rest of the crowd, "Very well. The decision has been made."

Before I come to my own understanding of what's happening, the reaper, dressed in his cloak of darkness from neck to toe, steps a single foot forward, and the room's temperature suddenly drops ten degrees. Hera cocks her head at him just before he flicks his wrist, and a deafening, merciless noise echoes through my ears, creating a jarring vibration that rattles my skull.

When I look up to see if Hera is just as traumatized as I am, I realize the worst has happened.

There is no Hera. Not even a bouncing curl. There is only a dark smattering of soot right where she stood seconds ago.

CHAPTER 3: AEGIS

My palms fly to my mouth with a horrified gasp and send my violin and bow to the ground. The crash alerts the reaper and the auctioneer across the stage. Their heads snap toward me as I try to comprehend what's just happened, but the shock is so overwhelming I can't think.

I can't move.

Hera was here moments ago, gracing the world with a bright presence and extraordinary talent. Now she's nothing but dust in the wind and a mark on a marble stage. My stomach reels as I struggle to find air through quivering lips.

I swallow the bile in my throat, trying to keep myself from having a full-blown panic attack. Something even more pressing hangs in the balance. My *own* life. The reaper just took Hera's. Who's to say mine isn't next?

"You always hate to see it, folks, but the kids who run pay the price—especially if that gift isn't strong enough to overlook their crime."

The auctioneer feigns indifference, dismissing the fact that a murder just took place before an entire crowd.

Hera's poor grandmother. She'll never know what happened to her granddaughter.

"Hey! I'm not asking a fifth time! Get yourself together, girlie. Name and delta!"

The woman on the stool jabs me in the ribs with her quill tip, pulling me out of my terrified trance with a wince.

Since when did I deserve to get stabbed with a quill? Since when did a poor girl with the gift of light deserve to be obliterated without a second thought?

I look down the scroll-keeper's hawk nose and pointed glare, utterly bewildered. Did she not witness what happened to Hera? She existed seconds ago!

She huffs at my trembling, muttering something to the auctioneer while I gather a rational thought.

"I'm warning you, girl. Give me a damn name, or you'll end up like your friend!" The roll-keeper hisses.

"Soria Davidsdottir. And I don't have a delta." I wheeze.

Not surprisingly, she all but cries out of frustration, raising her fists to mimic choking me.

"Fine! It's *your* funeral."

I stand there frozen, wishing to run somewhere, *anywhere,* as the auctioneer's voice grows strained. But by the way the reaper's eyeing me, I know if I don't move soon, I'll never move again. I don't have time to think about anything but surviving.

Reluctantly, my legs decide to obey, lumbering forward with a trip, only to kick my violin further onto the stage, sending my bow sprawling along with it. Embarrassingly, I scramble for my precious instrument as the bright yellow lights hit me like a boulder to the chest, and suddenly, I'm center stage.

Why is the only noise the sound of my own wheeze?

A sweaty palm flies to my forehead as I squint through delirium and blurry eyes, my heart operating on double time.

Copper-toned bricks line the interior of the grand auditorium, creating a heavenly domed ceiling that hoists several chandeliers in the air, making me wonder who lit every last candle. A mesmerizing mural of the stars gleams from above, giving the impression of a starry night singing its praises for the one beholding the stage.

The floor stretches farther than I can see before the lights blind me, tilting into several raised platforms to view the stage at optimal angles. But amid the beauty of the cathedral, something menacing sits within its center.

Staring back at me with filthy rich hands, clean-pressed suits, and judgmental eyes is the sea of monsters. Or rather, the sea of bidders.

Like a predator watching its prey, every eye fixes me with daunting skepticism. There is a staggering number. There must be hundreds. *Thousands.*

The bidders sit at glass tables, seating five or six, facing the stage with name cards I recognize, such as Grand Pree Hospital, Suron Construction, Border Protection, and several others.

I watch some pick at half-eaten entrees of Bachaloria's finest delicacies as if they hadn't just nibbled on a quarter thousand-krona meal with no remorse. If this weren't the most terrifying moment of my life, my mouth would water at the scent of roasted quail on the tables—but it *is* the most terrifying moment of my life. The auctioneer's distinct voice brings me back to reality as I stand here shaking.

"Now, this may be the first time we've had a student *dress up* for our occasion," the auctioneer chuckles, earning a roar of laughter from the audience at my attire.

If I had Grape's super-hearing right now, I'm sure I'd get an earful of how inappropriate I look. How… *offensive* I come across.

A bead of nervous sweat slides down my spine. I'm about to die.

The auctioneer pipes back up, grateful for a distraction to smooth over the harsh obliteration of Hera, "Now, this here is a Miss Soria Davidsdottir, and I'm assuming, as in the twin Davidsons. You don't hear that famous name just anywhere, folks!" He begins pandering to the audience, but no matter how often he throws the name around, I know I won't be able to produce something they want.

Yep. I'm definitely about to die.

A few people from each table mutter to the bidders next to them. The auctioneer goes on, "And her delta, well… I am being told… *undoubtedly* that Miss Soria does not have one. A fun joke like Mr. Yang, perhaps?" He glances to me with an uneasy smile, hoping for the best.

My petrified gaze darts from him to the crowd, pleading with my eyes for someone to save me, but the longer the silence stretches, the more uncomfortable the crowd grows. No, they are not uncomfortable; they are *impatient.* Impatient with me and my audacity to step foot on the stage.

The auctioneer makes one last feeble attempt to sway the audience, but he doesn't have much to work with, "Miss Soria certainly has a reason for being here today, I'm sure. She'll go ahead anytime now."

The lights are too bright. They're too hot on my forehead. My unraveled hair feels stuck to the side of my neck, trailing down an exposed back to reach my hips as more sweat trickles. I have to get out of here. I have to run. But where?

I beg the auctioneer with eyes wider than saucers, but he drops his gaze with pursed lips, and my heart sinks as he sidesteps to his right, further away from me. Further away from the impending explosion.

The reaper moves an inch, and my heart stops as I stand here, sweating, nauseous, and hopeless. This is the end. Kole, I love you so much.

"Play."

I stifle a gasp at that voice in my mind as it fills every space with an unequivocal warmth. That voice, ancient and profound, is undoubtedly the same as the one who asked me about the locked door. And now it demands me to play? Play what? Play a game?

A fuzzy recollection of clammy palms clutching a violin and bow surface. Play this? Play for them?

I snap to find the reaper has moved closer, and the room drops ten degrees as it had seconds before Hera died. I can't breathe.

The auctioneer sighs, "Very well. The decision has been made."

"Wait! Please, wait!" I screech, throwing my hand out as I back up, panting after each word. The reaper gently cocks his head, soulless eyes flickering as if his patience has run thin for idiotic shenanigans this evening.

My breath hitches as I inch toward the center of the stage, praying to the heavens that this works. It's all I have.

Flimsy hands raise the violin to the crook of my neck, quivering violently as I lift my bow. I stare down the reaper in the hope of leaping far enough to avoid the death he wields.

The room opens up to louder murmurs as I slide the bow across the strings in one determined stroke, choosing the saddest song from my memory, but most importantly, the *first* song to come to mind.

The crowd plunges into silence as I ease the bow across more strings, keeping the melody in harmony as my gaze never leaves the reaper.

I begin to play for my life. Literally.

Every muscle in my arms aches from the agony that this day has brought. My mouth sits as dry as the Tujave Desert, and my legs are only drawing strength from petrifying adrenaline.

But I *have* to survive. I have to see Kole again.

The song's natural melody picks up speed, and my hand works the bow faster, easing into the chorus of the most beautiful lines, which is the title, *My Tears Crave the Sea.* It was always my mother's favorite until my brothers were bought and dragged away. She stopped listening to me play after they were gone. Now, my only listener is Kole as I play most nights to help him fall asleep. If only the reaper will grant me one last kiss from my love—wherever he is.

I love playing. It's a part of who I am, I believe. To me, there's not much that creates *me* in my miserable existence.

Before I know it, my eyes drift downward to focus on the notes, nearly losing myself in the cathartic melody. The horrible day greets me with tangible sadness, and I throw every bit of my fear and anger into the song until I, too, crave the sea.

I crave to be someone, *anyone* I'm not. I crave to leave this life and become someone like my brothers. Like Kole. I crave something more, but until then, I will crave the sea because that's where every last one of my tears ends up.

A fateful breath leaves my throat as my bow lowers, understanding my life hangs in the balance before a merciless audience. But they're quiet. *Too* quiet.

I don't know how long I've been playing, but it must have been for several minutes. Several minutes is much longer than any other performance is allowed. In the distance, I swear I spot a few people drying their eyes.

The announcer's voice carries over the pounding in my head, and my head flies back to the reaper whose gaze is dangerously fixed on me.

"That was certainly… a performance." The auctioneer blinks as if clearing away confusion. The audience lingers in perpetual silence as the auctioneer says, "Though this is quite unorthodox, I suppose I'll open the bidding just in case. Folks, perhaps Miss Soria could be of use for morale, grunt work, or if anything, a pretty bird to sing on your sidelines. Just make sure she isn't dressed like *this!"* The auctioneer winks, earning an eruption of laughter at my expense.

He starts the bidding at eighty krona, feeling the crowd out while I stand here, limply holding my violin as my future unfolds without my say. But at this moment, a single bid sounds better than silence. Silence means death.

"Eighty, eighty, now seventy? Seventy for Miss Soria? Fifty?" The auctioneer surveys the crowd mumbling their passes. Here and there, some turn to the suits next to them, shaking their heads because, of course, this is unreasonable. Who would waste a single krona on a girl playing an instrument? They came here to buy deltas to stack their teams, not waste time messing with some stupid girl in a dress.

"Very well, folks, I've read your mind! But a beauty like this need not be wasted. Let's move on to the next. I hear
he's excellent with light-bending!"

I can't believe the auctioneer's words. I did it.

A bubble of hope rises in my chest as I thank the heavens for finding me a way out. Playing my violin just saved my life, and now I can leave this wretched stage and never look back at this horrible day. As soon as I leave here, I'm visiting the chapel every day in appreciation for sparing my life.

A sigh of relief escapes my throat as I turn on a heel to march past the auctioneer and his cloaked death pet.

I swallow my smile to live another day, focusing on my priorities now that my life is my own again. I need to figure out what happened to Kole. There's no way he didn't get sold to Aegis. He's *amazing,* and I can't wait to see the look on his face when I tell him I, *too,* went on the stage. He'll never believe it. I'm so relieved to be alive I could laugh out loud.

Just before I sweep past the auctioneer, thinking of all the things in life I'm grateful for, a deep voice calls from the audience, nearly stopping me in my tracks. "Ten krona."

What?

I force my legs to keep moving, pretending like I didn't hear that. He didn't mean me. I'm about to be free. Just a couple more steps.

A firm hand grabs my arm with a jolt, preventing any escape off the stage. I glance up to see that perfectly combed white hair tilt toward the crowd.

The auctioneer, keeping me prisoner on stage, calls out to the bidder, "I'm sorry, sir, will that be ten krona for the light-bender?"

The light bender. The light bender!

My chest heaves erratically as I try to tug from the auctioneer's grasp again, but he keeps me by his side.

The bidder pauses in the audience for a long time. *Too long.* My neck cranes slowly toward the deep voice bargaining with my life, hoping he'll register the plea in my eyes and grant me mercy.

The chandelier lights blur my vision as the sweat trickling down my back resumes, and I can barely make out the face sitting at one of the glass tables in the distance. He's surrounded by other bidders in suits who lean in for his next words, and it's clear he runs the show for his group.

From what I can see, the bidder's shoulders are broad. *Really* broad. And massive arms lie folded across an enormous chest in a suit darker than the reaper's. Beautiful, sun-kissed skin sits against a satin-silver collar, along with dark sunglasses obstructing the view of his face and any other features. His voice is what does it. A voice so deep and… sensual. It feathers against my brain in a way I've never felt before. It's addicting.

I blink, realizing my palms almost dropped my violin a second time, sweating as I stand here, still detained by the auctioneer who repeats his question for the dark bidder in the crowd.

"If you meant the next delta, he surely would enjoy a lively competition from—"

"For the girl."

The bidder bellows across the room in a tone that says he's tired of repeating himself.

My breath freezes in my throat as the auctioneer chuckles, not daring to open the rest of the floor to a bidding war when it seems one of the most important buyers has made his claim. His claim on… *me.*

"Very good, then! In my life, I've never seen a delta-less buy, but things switch up all the time here, folks! Who knows, maybe next year we'll throw in a few hearty fellas for fun!" The auctioneer releases my arm as if it's a diseased limb, smiling widely at the audience as the horrible sound of his gavel smacks the wooden surface of the podium. The next words seal my fate without a question.

"Sold! To Aegis for ten krona."

A stranger's rough hand escorts me off stage, throwing me into more hands who now control my life. Fighting them every step of the way, I try to get a glimpse of the terrible man who bought my life, but the only other feature I can see is a hint of a sharp jaw.

Two powerful arms grab mine as I'm forced down another dark hallway, gripping my violin like a lifeline as it becomes harder and harder to breathe. Suddenly, the arms release, pushing me toward a cracked door leading outside. Should I run?

One of the men grabs my forearm tightly, "This may sting a moment," is all he says before something sharp blasts onto my wrist, earning a howl as I fling my arm away, trying to shake off the pain.

The gruff man doesn't bat an eye as he continues, "Follow through the door. Aegis recruits are loading the trains now."

Aegis recruit. Is that truly what I am now?

Without a second thought, I'm pushed toward the exit. A free hand flies to my incense can, forcing another deep breath and concluding that I will most certainly die soon. If the other recruits don't kill me first for taking a spot on their coveted team, running out of my life-saving powder will. I can't imagine where I'm going will have an all-you-need apothecary for asthmatic lungs.

Venturing outside, I find a long row of guards standing shoulder-to-shoulder, preventing any escape as I stumble down the path toward the tracks like a lamb following the road to the slaughter.

Several guards eye me in my gown, but they're the least of my concerns.

Glancing down at the base of my wrist, I'm stunned to find I've been marked for life in ink-black cursive. The letters spelling out *Aegis* stare boldly up at me as if I'm property. A commodity. The equivalent of a farmer branding their steers.

Against my will, as if I have any left, I follow the path lined with guards to find several students lined at the bottom of the hill behind King Ragnar's massive palace walls, awaiting their ride near the pearly train track rails. Most are dressed in business casual pleated pants and modest gowns, overly excited as they wait to start their careers.

Ignoring the pain from the Aegis brand that slowly creeps up my arm, I force more powder up my nose in preparation for an asthma attack.

Quivering legs follow the trail, and my only prayer is to stay invisible for as long as possible.

As I fiddle with the can, the ancient voice in my mind utters something that sounds a lot like a command.

"Hide it."

I almost trip hearing that voice again.

One of the guards on my left straightens his sword handle idly while another stares unbothered in the distance. So, it was definitely *only* me who heard that. But hide what? What did it mean?

The pool of recruits buzzing around at the bottom of the hill shift their narrowed gazes as I arrive, judging my choice of outfit with blatant scoffs and snickers. There must be over one hundred students on the train platform, not counting the hundreds that have probably already caught a train to start their new lives.

"Soria?" A voice I recognize calls, and I've never been so elated to see a familiar face.

Grape skips to me, his grin wide and his vest unbuttoned, briefly glancing over my shoulder, "You seriously made it with no delta? What happened? And where's our little buddy?"

I swallow, looking down as Grape comes to the conclusion himself, running a hand through black, spiky hair, "Well, at least *you're* alive. I want to know every detail. What's that you're holding?"

Grape points to the can I'm palming, and the words halt in my throat.

"Hide it. Do not let them become privy to your weaknesses." The ancient voice thumbs my mind, keeping the same tone but louder against my skull.

And for some reason, I listen, shoving the incense can in my dress pocket faster than a blink.

"Nothing."

Before Grape can ask another question, his eyes grow wide at the students who've suddenly inched closer, closing in on the pair of us. Their bodies shift with dubious intent written across each face until Grape and I stand in a small, intimidating circle with no way out.

Just my luck.

"Well, well. If it isn't the talentless whore who took a spot she doesn't deserve."

The conniving feminine voice comes from Sera Jonsdottir, the mean girl who can blind people without moving a muscle.

She steps to the front of the circle as the other students create a barrier with their bodies, gawking at me like a four-course meal. My hand almost flies to my incense, but I choose to listen to the voice in my head and muscle through the urge to take a medicated breath. Shaky ones will have to do.

I inch toward Grape as if his small frame and super ears can save me, but what I really want is Kole. He would defend me. He would get me out of this mess. I cling to the sliver of hope that I'll see him again once we get wherever the hell we're going. Or I'll die trying to get back to him.

I clutch my violin as Sera runs indignant eyes down my body, preparing myself to bash someone's head in as the circle of students constricts. I've never been one for violence but I fear I have no choice.

Sera licks full lips as a perfectly manicured hand meticulously tucks a black strand of hair.

She means to hurt me. Maybe kill me. But there's nowhere to run anymore.

Fuck trying to escape, I guess. It's clearly not an option right now. I have to figure out how to survive. *Again.*

"Do you think you deserve to be one of us? You're nothing but an embarrassment to our country. You'll get all of us killed in that arena."

Sera plants delicate hands on her hips, tilting her chin, "So I'll make sure you don't get the chance."

In a split second, her dark eyes flash behind me as my throat closes to her threats. Without realizing it, I've retreated enough to find myself plastered against someone enclosing me in the circle.

Before I can jump off the stranger, cold, sharp metal ticks against along my shoulder blades, drawing a sharp pain against my will. My mind realizes what's happened before my body has time to react. The boy behind me has just cut my dress straps, sending the thin fabric covering my breasts to my waist.

With a shriek, I leap away, my violin slamming to the ground once more as my hands split to cover an exposed chest. Tears well as Grape shouts by my side, trying to fend off the hungry, dangerous eyes that close in. They don't intend on stopping at humiliation. They mean to kill us both.

Before Sera commands her cronies on me again, the circle disperses faster than it was formed. The crowd of students fall silent, trying to act busy amongst themselves as I stand here, topless and fighting the urge to cry.

With a wheezy breath, I gain enough courage to look up, hoping for a savior who's taken Sera's place, and my jaw nearly hits the ground as he makes his way down the steep path toward the loading platform. I recognize those dark-lensed sunglasses. It's the bidder who bought me.

Those broad shoulders tower over the guards lining his walk, and for a moment, I would believe anyone who told me those guards were arranged to escort him personally. An entourage of smartly dressed bidders follow his lead, confirming my suspicions that this man runs the show for all of Aegis.

His legs look strong in that midnight suit, commanding a massive frame that demands respect. His presence alone straightens every spine within a mile radius. Even mine.

As he gets closer, my gaze crawls up his body, past a thick neck to focus on that sharp jawline, straight nose, and chocolate-colored closely cropped hair fading upward.

Short hair on men is not the typical Bachalorian style. Long hair demonstrates wealth and intelligence to signal any unmarried woman they are of the highest quality. This man doesn't need long hair to tell any watching eye he's high quality. His presence *exceeds* the notion.

A pale scar cuts vertically through the side of his full, bottom lip, vanishing beneath a shadow of perfectly trimmed stubble. Curiosity nags as I wonder about those damn shades covering his eyes, but I can tell his gaze is unwavering.

He's on a mission. This man is the image of strength and professionalism, and for some reason, he's making a beeline toward… me?

Before I can wipe the drool from my mouth, the massive bidder crosses the platform to stand right in front of me. Or, *above* me. Damn, he's so big.

The bidder stares down through dark, squared lenses as if he's judging everything that I am. What I am, is bare from the navel up, though my hands try their best to cover myself while an audience watches in silence.

Not so subtly, Grape takes a half-step toward me, and by the look on his face, I'd bet every last krona his heart's racing faster than mine—if at all possible.

Several feet away, a nervous voice from a young man I don't recognize tries speaking up, obviously kissing ass to whoever this important bidder is, "Jude Blackwell, it's an honor, sir! Will you be riding with us?"

The bidder, who I suppose goes by Jude, barely acknowledges the recruit murmuring to him.

The bidder's jaw ticks as he responds slowly in that deep voice that does something to my insides, "Do not speak to me without permission."

The recruit recoils immediately, vanishing behind someone else for cover.

He got his answer.

There's no way in hell this important bidder, Jude, whatever-his-name, would ride in an old train crate near the deltas he just paid for. We are nothing more than a number at this point. *Especially* me. Even I can put that together.

Jude's chin tilts as he closes the space between us, glancing over my head as he grumbles my first order, "Fix yourself." Embarrassment flushes my cheeks as the bidder takes an impatient sigh, and I notice his wide frame positioned close to me for cover.

Quickly, I take the opportunity to sling the cut straps over my bare chest and tie them around my neck in a halter-top fashion.

Before I can whisper a thank you, my savior swipes the violin from the ground, leveling his stare as those shades disappear with two fingers, revealing cold, stern eyes. Those… *mesmerizing* and beautiful eyes. They're twenty different shades of dazzling bright blue and silver, creating the most delicate and piercing gaze I've ever seen.

Time seems to slow as tangled emotions trip over themselves in defiance of fascination and lust. My heart thuds too loud for my own good until a swift crack ricochets between my eardrums, severing the confused emotions before they've reached maturity.

The sound of wood and brass breaking shatters my heart because I know the devastating sound. Dazzling-Eyes has just broken my violin into two pieces with his bare hands. There's no remorse in his face as several students make noises approving of his psychological abuse.

"No!" I throw myself to the ground to gather my instrument, but it's too late. My violin lies against the platform pathetically, crushed and broken beyond repair. My prized possession, the object that saved my life from the reaper and my only escape, is now gone. I'll never play again.

I throw the bidder a nasty glare as he turns to his entourage of suits without a second thought for me. In a sudden fit of sheer outrage, I leap forward, ready to strike him as my hand flies, but Grape's arms wrap around my waist tighter than a chokehold, swinging me out of slapping distance.

Heat rises in my chest—a heat that makes me more than furious as a grin tugs on the side of Jude Blackwell's lips.

"What a memorable first fight," the bidder hisses with a creamy, proper accent, flipping his shades back down as if the distant orange sun has any effect on his vision, "But my recruits know better. And by the looks of it, I'll be surprised to see you at breakfast."

Then he turns on his heel, walking through the crowd as they part like the Red Sea for him, delivering all of the attention he commands.

Before I have time to utter a curse, Jude turns to address everyone on the platform in his husky and demanding tone, "May I remind every recruit of the unbreakable law. Murder is forbidden off base. So, every head that was bought had better be attached to a body by the time you arrive. However, *mangled* isn't out of the question." With that terribly specific instruction, he just put a target on my back.

I grab an uneasy breath as Jude disappears past the crowd without a second glance.

Grape mutters beside me, trying his best to lift my spirits, "Damn, Soria. This is going to be a long eight months if I have to keep you from thwacking Aegis's captain every-day."

The moisture leaves my mouth as I fix my new friend with wide eyes.

Of course he's the captain. The most powerful and coveted position someone with a delta could ever achieve in life belongs to him. And if this couldn't get any worse, Kole told me the captain always holds the deadliest delta—a gift so powerful that others would only be on a suicide mission to challenge.

Lucky me, I've just become Jude Blackwell's public enemy number one.

CHAPTER 4: TRAIN RIDE

I glue myself to Grape's side as we wait for our train, trying to keep my breathing steady so I don't resort to the incense burning a hole in my pocket.

A new train arrives every fifteen minutes to haul students to their new homes, and from what I've gathered over the years of Kole daydreaming about his future career, Aegis sits on one of the largest provinces along the south coast. They're the pride and joy of our country, so obviously, Aegis gets its own corner of Bachaloria to thrive in.

The Aegis borders are surrounded by fifty-foot steel walls with several flourishing cities right outside their gates, eager to be close to the world's most coveted celebrities—the players. Achieving that title of *player* is an impossible task that usually ends in death for all of those seeking it, as Kole's told me a million times. So when Jude announced to the entire train platform that I wouldn't last until breakfast, he was undoubtedly correct. I'm not cut out for this.

Nervous fingers pick at my thumb cuticles as I keep my gaze straight ahead to avoid any more trouble. I place my hope in staying hidden behind Grape, though I probably have half a foot on him.

"We're up next, Blondie," Grape mutters with half a smile, for which I'm entirely grateful. He doesn't have to be nice to me, and his favor is probably only extending until we reach the base, but I'm thankful nonetheless. I just hope Kole will be waiting for me once I arrive. There's no way Aegis would pass on his skill if he made it to the auction.

I shove those dangerous thoughts away, forcing myself to focus on staying alive for the next twenty-four hours. One minute at a time.

A giant, silver tin with glass windows resembling mirrors rounds the bend half a mile away with a whistling chime, signaling it's about to enter the train platform. The sun's orange evening hues bounce off our sleek convoy, blinding anyone who makes direct eye contact with the expensive metal.

If this type of lavish transportation is what Aegis moves recruits in who may not live to see the next day, then what could be more magnificent to transport a *captain*? The clouds above?

Grape nudges me as the train approaches, and we head to the quickly forming line of Aegis recruits, each bearing the same permanent tattoo on our wrists.

It becomes evident that the students boarding this train hold themselves higher than others on the platform. Chins tilt to the sky while postures straighten with arrogant attitudes, overindulging in their early fame. I even notice one recruit from our line pick a fight with someone wearing the Border Protection name, claiming they're nothing but glorified grunts. But I know the truth. Without metalists and weavers securing the only entrance into Bachaloria, we'd all be dead.

Every Bachalorian child has been taught in school that the Enemy In The North, Bloodletters, or Seyka, as their nightmarish names are endless, have threatened war for hundreds of years with a mission to steal our women and children for their own means. It's rumored their militia constantly checks for kinks in our border protection's armor, but we keep them at bay with the treaty of the annual Diamond Game to prevent an all-out war.

As Kole has put it before, the Enemy In The North are a vicious and vile people who look to see Bachaloria destroyed. The military keeps the borders secure in case of an attack, but the game keeps everyone in line, or so we've all been taught.

Avoiding as much interaction with people ten thousand times more deadly than me, I keep my head ducked and follow closely behind Grape, who seems concentrated.

A slender-built man sporting a sharp uniform in Bachalorian navy blue scans our wrists with a laser flashing from his pupils, raising the hairs on the back of my neck from such an unnerving delta. I still haven't gotten used to *everyone* having a delta where I'm about to go, not just a few students from my class or a special business owner in town.

I trail Grape closely as we enter the train to find the interior just as marvelous as the exterior. A plethora of red velvet booths sits on either side, each hosting a professional oak table as if we're all here on trade travel. The aisle is lined with an intricately woven cotton rug and candles are mounted on the ceiling in a meticulous fashion. It is the very portrait of wealth.

Our country's emblem of the massive tiger-bear sporting eight points on its crown of antlers adorn every seat, wall, and curtain as if to remind us where we come from. I certainly will not be forgetting.

My body wants to give in to exhaustion and slump into the booth opposite Grape, but right now, I need to breathe more than I need to sleep.

As more recruits file in, some glance around with wide eyes while others regard our surroundings with no more emotion than boredom. Seizing my opportunity, I ask Grape to save my seat so I can finally inhale my medicinal powder without dangerous eyes watching.

I try to avoid the gaze of Sera Jonsdottir and her ever-growing posse of leering boys as I pass their group, though one nearly trips me as the others spit their laughter.

Quickly and quietly, I lock the steel bathroom door to find a toilet enclosed with a half-sized sink, a glass bowl of complimentary ruby mints and a polished mirror to fix my appearance.

I stuff the entire bowl of mints into my dress pocket.

A defeated sigh escapes when I see what everyone else has been looking at all day. Disheveled, long blond hair, tired brown eyes, malnourished collarbones, and a couple of red marks along my forehead from who-knows-what. Not to mention the dress. Worst idea ever.

The pain lingering from the letters seared into my wrist climb higher and higher, seeping over my chest with a hardly bearable heat, but I don't have time to worry about this new condition.

After taking a few medicated breaths to ease the heaviness in my lungs and crunching through several mints, I dip my grimy hands through the sink water and take it to my face. I can't wait to change.

The train begins moving as I finally build the courage to unlock the door, though I wish I could stay in here forever. Thankfully, Sera's miniature army appears too interested in one of the boys moving his tie with his mind to notice me sneak by. But when I find Grape, he's not alone.

Sitting by his side, deep in conversation, is a lean girl with a thick, messy black bun and a frilly blouse that complements her warm brown skin.

As I slide into the velvet booth, the stranger's dark eyes flash to me, and for a moment, I fear I may not be in good company with how she quickly sizes me up. But in an instant, that terrifying gaze disappears, and a wide smile takes place as she cocks her head like a dog in my direction.

"Y-y-you must be th-th-the one everyone's talking about. The girl with "no-no delta," she says slowly, never taking her eyes off of mine.

She's beautiful in a lethal sort of way. But her eyes…they're too inquisitive. Like a viper or a spider deciding my next move before I do.

Gingerly, I nod, shooting a helpless glance at Grape to see if she's safe.

"That's me. I have no idea what I'm doing here," I admit. I spend a few minutes studying the girl as she does the same. My shoulders roll as the lingering pain turns into a dull throb that meets my stomach, and I begin to worry if this is normal.

Grape speaks up, smoothing the awkwardness as he seems good at doing, "Oh, where are my manners? Soria, this is Merry Oskarsdottir. Merry, this is Soria… Dans…dottir? Someone's daughter." He throws a dismissive hand, "There's no creativity with you lot—you're all the same."

"Davidsdottir," I correct with a half-smile, "I thought you could hear everything."

Grape raises a brow for the banter, "As a matter of fact, I *can.* Hyperacusis just takes concentration on what I'm listening for." He smirks while crossing his arms. Merry rolls her eyes at him, giving the impression she's known Grape for a long time. I wonder what her delta is.

"Are you wondering what my d-d-delta is?"

Merry asks, folding her arms on the table between us. I can't help but shrink back, hoping it isn't mind-reading. Those deltas never make it to auction. Anyone with that ability is immediately taken to King Ragnar to be used for high-profile work, whether they want to or not. A girl down my road got taken by a palace guard from our classroom by age twelve. No one saw her again.

I swallow, trying to keep my thoughts in order and not let the girl across me know I find her utterly frightening, but she chuckles at my nervousness. Am I that easy to read?

In one quick sweep, Merry throws her arm out to shake my hand across the table, but as my eyes trail down, I find it isn't an arm. It's a *wing.* A giant, black-feathered wing that lies fully extended as if it belongs to a lion-eagle or some other creature only kept in training prisons or found in the badlands.

Merry begins laughing as Grape snorts, each of them finding my shock amusing.

Carefully, I take her wing in my hand, shaking gently while examining the details of each dark feather.

"You're a shapeshifter?"

Merry nods as her wing peels back into a white-laced blouse sleeve, returning to a normal human hand as if the feathers had been a hallucination.

"N-no-not a very good one, though. I can only d-do rabbits and birds, but I can't f-f-fly yet."

Grape nudges her with an exasperated eyeroll, "You impressed them well enough. Merry had four groups bidding back and forth until Aegis took her for six thousand."

Before Merry can argue the merits of her performance with her friend, a redolent scent prickles my nose in a devastating, mouth-watering way, and suddenly, my stomach reminds me I haven't eaten a bite since those dried apricots. I nearly foam at the mouth at the beautiful aroma of smoked pork.

Certainly better than the mints I've almost finished.

My companions across the table must notice the primal hunger glaze my focus because Grape snaps to get my attention, motioning behind us. To my delight, a cart strolls through the back entrance, stopping at each booth to let every recruit pick their plate, and the back of my wrist meets my chin to wipe away the drool.

I've only ever known quarter-portions and rationing the same tiresome vegetables. I wouldn't let myself take food from Kole's mother after she'd scold him for feeding me, or worse, scold me herself with that hearty right hook.

After what feels like hours, the cart finally stops at our booth, and I nearly gasp at the options before me. Braised pea-duck on a steamed bed of honey-glazed carrots, wild shrimp basted in an orange sauce, fried sirloin with white gravy, and cherry-crusted cream nearly make me faint.

I reach for the duck plate first, my other hand plucking the sirloin greedily.

"Careful."

I nearly drop the sirloin on the table at that voice ricocheting in my brain again. But careful of what? I'm *starving.* I've always been starving. There isn't another word that describes me better.

Ignoring the voice, I decide my stomach craves satisfaction over listening to some weird conscience my brain has created to keep me sane. I decide that if I'm already living on borrowed time, I might as well enjoy a real meal for once in my life. This makes up for all those years of stale rye and wilted gooseberries.

Without thinking, I pile six more plates before me, pulling the duck close with my fork and knife palmed like a wild child, digging in without a second thought. I hardly taste the food as I shove larger bites into my mouth, swallowing mouthfuls. Instant gratification greets me in its most glorious form.

After polishing off my fourth course and downing a third chalice of cinnamon tea, I finally glance up to see Grape and Merry eyeing me as they gently take bites from their singular plates.

"Hungry?" Grape smiles, inspecting the dishes I've nearly licked clean.

"Give her a b-break. She probably hasn't eaten all day." Merry nudges him, keeping her voice low, though her eyes tell me she knows I haven't eaten much all week. She doesn't know that it has been years.

Grape nods quickly, beckoning me closer as I wipe my mouth with the corner of a silk napkin.

"Between you and…well, *you,*" he whispers, peeking over my head, "I wouldn't let certain… *recruits* know how much you… *like* to eat."

I swallow another gulp of tea, realizing this kind of discretion is important. I'm sure Sera would love information like that under her belt. She seems already on the hunt for ways to make me miserable, and it's best not to have her steal the food from my mouth while she's at it.

Grape leans back in the booth, "They'd be more than happy to see you suffer. Especially since you're not an option to tether."

"Tether?" I ask, forcing myself to work slowly on the cherry cream as my stomach ebbs in foreign bloat. I've never been this absurdly full before. I like it.

Grape nods, poking at his potatoes as his brows scrunch with contempt at my uncontrolled belch, "You know. Like your twin brothers. The famous *Davidsons.*"

I swallow at the mention of them. My relationship with my brothers still sits uneasy since the four years they've been gone. To me, they were *gods.* I wanted to be like them so badly, but the closer the auction got, the more they isolated themselves, suddenly pretending I didn't exist. But to tether?

My perplexity causes Grape to elaborate, "Well, it won't be of any use to you since you have no delta, but tethering is the ultimate goal of every player and one of the biggest perks to having a delta." He winks.

"Tethering to someone is like bonding yourself to them and their gift for all eternity. The trick is that it can only be done once, and it has to be with the right delta. Think of it like the very fabric of yourself being seeded into another person. When that happens, no matter who it is, your delta becomes, like, a *thousand* times more powerful. Both of them do, which is why Aegis won't keep a player who hasn't tethered in the end."

The information drops my jaw, and suddenly I can only think about Kole. Why did he never tell me about this? Did he mean to keep it a secret? What if he tethers to someone and forgets all about me? What if he tethers to someone… like Sera? The entire thought of it sounds so intimate.

I clear my throat, suddenly feeling way too full and fighting nausea for the rich food I've inhaled.

Merry adds, "But tethering can b-be dangerous. If y-yyou pick wrong, the process could kill b-both people."

"Or permanently remove their deltas, I've heard. My ma always told me it was the heavens' way to prevent two people from becoming too powerful." Grape points his fork at me.

"So," I ponder, "No one can be a player unless they have this weird, spiritual-bond-thing?"

Grape and Merry quickly exchange glances as the shapeshifter lowers her voice. "Correct, except for in rare instances."

My breath hitches in my throat, hoping this rare instance could be Kole. Perhaps he could be the anomaly. His delta is quite powerful, after all.

Merry leans in closer, her voice the barest whisper as she mumbles, "The c-captain."

My jaw locks, and there goes my hope again of a happy life with Kole without some bizarre magical interruption.

"Every now and then, Aegis will keep a delta that shows the most promise. A delta that's too powerful on its own, even untethered." Grape says, "I heard the captain before Jude Blackwell had cheated in the arena. Apparently, Jude sold him out and executed him to take over as captain himself." Grape adds.

My stomach threatens to unsettle at the thought of Jude. He sounds merciless. And conniving. Someone who wouldn't bat an eye at the weakest link, especially if he's too powerful to tether to anyone. What *is* his gift? Do I even want to know?

Before I can ask what type of earth-shattering delta the heavens bestowed the captain, a burly man in another Bachalorian blue uniform slides open the door to our train cabin.

"It's time for lights out as we cross the Interial Path, so I suggest you get some sleep. Lord knows y'all need it." With a clap of his thick palms, the candlelight illuminating the walls disappears, leaving skinny trails of smoke evaporating toward the ceiling.

The throbbing from the Aegis stamp sits in my pelvis now, and I can't help but grumble, shifting to ease the pain.

Grape clears his throat, addressing me with a subtle whisper, "The pain should wear off in a few hours, Blondie. Just sleep it off."

"It was just a tattoo. Why do I feel it everywhere?" I ask through a groan, thankful I'm not the only one suffering.

Grape flashes a look to Merry before sighing, "It's not just a tattoo of ownership. It's a serum to sterilize recruits." My gasp hardly meets my ears.

"As in…"

Grape nods, "We're weapons. They don't want a bunch of little knives distracting their harpoons if you know what I mean."

I take the violating information with me as I lean against the window, contemplating how I've truly been stripped of every last right. But I suppose worrying about my future children is a moot point if there's no future anyway.

I do as Grape says, slumping in the velvet booth and attempting to sleep off the pain.

My comrades across the table continue to whisper to themselves, reminiscing on their days growing up in the same town and preparing for what's to come, and I have no choice but to focus on surviving long enough to see Kole again.

I suppose the sounds of wind and far-off steel meeting brass along the tracks don't help to ease the worry sifting beneath my skin, but it makes for a soothing sound my eyelids can't stay open to. And before I know it, my temple meets the window, belly full and thirst finally quenched, sleep consuming me after a day of unprepared exhaustion.

Hopefully, when I open my eyes, this will all be a horrible nightmare I can laugh about with Kole.

CHAPTER 5: BASE

I gasp awake, white-knuckling velvet as my weight shifts involuntarily. The last time I felt my equilibrium off, I was emerging from a comatose state to find myself trapped in a dusty cart rolling through town.

My head swivels in both directions, but it's too dark to form familiar images. I rely on my hands to feel for my surroundings until I gain complete consciousness, sighing in relief that I'm not trapped in a cart—just a giant metal tin on train tracks.

The sigh of relief quickly turns into disappointment at the realization that I haven't sprung from some terrible nightmare.

This is very real.

The train comes to a complete stop, emitting a sound of metal screeching like violent nails on a chalkboard. Across from me, I make out the impressions of spiky dark hair resting on top of folded arms and a person in a white blouse slowly squinting with a yawn.

Merry nudges Grape, only for him to murmur, "Obviously, I'm awake. I can't believe any of you could sleep with all that racket."

The stationary clock hanging before the exit reads two in the morning, and before I have a chance to grumble at the hour, a horde of men in navy blue uniforms suddenly board the train in the darkness, shouting and screaming for everyone to wake up, line up, and get prepared.

If I hadn't already been knocked unconscious, paraded through town in a cage and played for my life to avoid getting obliterated today, large men screaming at me in the dark would be terrifying. But I've had my share of trauma for a lifetime in under twenty-four hours.

I slip out of the booth with Merry and Grape following on my heels, lining up behind a muscular boy with dark skin and long dreadlocks twisted into a braid. He reeks of sweat and something fermented, and I'm too tired to care how close I am to this large boy. But I should.

As we inch forward, I catch a glimpse of Sera whispering to a stout young man with a shaved head behind her, staring directly at me as she feeds poison into his ear. She reminds me of a rattlesnake hiding in the brush while her minion shoots me a sideways glance, grinning as the cabin falls silent.

Before my foot meets the ground, every last muscle locks, restricting any movement. My throat tightens in response to danger, signaling to my lungs that it's time to panic, but I'm paralyzed. What did that bald boy do to me?

"Soria, are y-you okay?" Merry whispers behind me as I stand here frozen. He must have some gift to immobilize, and he's using it on me.

Raw fear creeps its way back into my heart, as my eyes flare toward the dreadlock braid, suddenly whipping to face me full-on. I knew I shouldn't have stood so close.

The muscular man, towering a good five inches over me, strides closer with a dangerous leer, completely unpredictable. His half-ironed dress shirt hugs his shoulders tight as a breath hits my unmovable face.

In this moment, I'm more than defenseless. I'm completely vulnerable. He could rip out my throat if he wanted to, but something tells me a death that quick would be a mercy to these people. Sera and her boys mean to break me down because I don't belong here.

And they're right.

My darting eyes find the boy's, watching helplessly as he cracks his neck and then his knuckles, making a show of his preparation to strike. Before the apprehension fully presents itself, Sera's minion twists swiftly, sending a sharp elbow directly into my cheekbone, barely missing my eye that most definitely would have popped out of its socket.

The blow knocks me into Merry, startling her enough to spit a curse in my defense across the cabin, "Hey! W-w-wh…"

The boy with dreads spins back around with a disgusting laugh, "What's the matter? Cat got your f-f-*fucking* tongue?" He mocks her, as my blood boils, and I have no choice but to watch as my new enemy dismisses us with ease, cracking his neck as if nearly breaking my face was of minimal effort.

My insides scream in rage from the hit, but I still can't move. I can't even speak. I want to sob my eyes out and run far away from everyone who means me harm, but deep down, I know running is impossible. Especially now that *Aegis* is permanently tattooed on my wrist.

As Merry and Grape throw curses at Sera's nasty gang, all of my nerves suddenly come spiraling back, and I fall to the train floor in a heap, desperately resisting the urge to bawl until I'm dehydrated.

Cautious hands hoist me up as I press two gentle fingers to the raised abrasion on my upper cheek, knowing it's sure to shift colors. This is precisely the treatment Jude Blackwell was hinting at before we loaded this dreadful train. *Murder is prohibited off base, but mangling is another story.* His stupid words were intended for me, and all of these recruits are just following his orders. Was I bought to be a punching bag for his beloved players?

"Those a-a-assholes know how to play f-f-fucking dirty." Merry seethes over my shoulder, ushering me forward as more men in uniform bark their commands.

"Right now, anyone will do what they can to stand out. E*specially* if it means earning the favor of the captain." Grape grumbles, "In their eyes, Jude is the leader but still a commodity. If they impress him enough, he may choose to tether when we get to stage three… if we *survive* to stage three."

My mind feels foggy with the information as I stagger off the train and into a gaggle of recruits, coming to terms with Grape's words. These people will chew me up and spit me out because I mean nothing to anyone here. No one would risk killing a recruit on the first day if it meant they could be killing off their potential tethered. Me, on the other hand, I'm a frail sack of bones hiding amongst the hungry den of lions. No one would bat an eye if I wound up dead. I just hope it's painless, and that Merry and Grape aren't here to see it.

Another deep, gruff voice I don't recognize shouts over the group of recruits standing on the receiving platform in the dark, "Listen up and follow me! Straighten those ties and tuck those blouses because it's time to meet your makers. And *not* the ones above."

I follow the silhouettes around me as we slowly form a line. Patting my dress pocket, I ensure my incense is in place as we round the side of a tall wall, or perhaps it's the edge of a building, I can't be sure. The only light source on this warm summer night comes from the moon and stars above, gently casting a white glow on a long sidewalk leading to two giant double doors.

My heart suddenly feels heavy remembering Hera's beautiful glow. If she were here, we all would be able to see.

A pair of women wearing matching uniforms and name tags I can't make out hold the doors as we file into a hallway lit with yellow candlelight, reminding me of the eerie path to the auction stage.

Along the walls of the long corridor, trailing up to the twenty-foot ceiling, sit large frames holding paintings of different men and women. By the looks, they seem to be in their twenties, harboring stern expressions through every portrait. Their dark uniforms are all slightly similar, but they change from each picture as if going back in time the further I venture. It's only until our group of gawking recruits reach the end that I realize that's precisely what's happened. Each painting is of previous Aegis players, and by an uncomfortable process of elimination, it seems these players have died in the arena. And there are *thousands* of them.

"You see that one?" Grape whispers, pointing to one of the larger portraits near the end of the corridor, "That's the late captain Yessaro. That's the one Jude murdered to take his place."

A shiver of fear slides up my neck as I examine the portrait in passing. The captain can't be older than Jude now, and he wears the Bachalorian navy blue in his player's uniform, sporting a number across his chest I can't quite read. His hair is braided down the center in threes while the sides of his head sit shaved, reminding me of most decorated warriors in the military. Under his portrait sits a quote carved into a silver plate, reading: *No one mourns the enemy.*

It's unnerving to visualize that this mighty player who commanded a herd of human weapons ultimately met his demise by one of his own. His killer no matter how beautiful, appears to hold no regard for the weak ones.

Shivering away the bizarre feeling of strolling through a graveyard, I focus on my next steps as our group of fifty or so is escorted to a dimly lit foyer, and my eyes widen at the massive fish tank filling our view. For once today, I'm utterly impressed.

The foyer is rounded, with a domed ceiling that extends further than I can see in the dark. Several frames of Aegis artwork hang delicately along the walls, showing off the team's pride as if to commemorate it within one room.

Golden benches line the stunning glass fish tank that stands nearly fifteen feet tall, bathing the room in an ocean blue light that flutters off the walls. Within the tank sit various types of saltwater fish, ranging in vibrant colors, along with their coral and plants flowing with its filtered tide. It's beautiful. Inspiring even. I could see myself escaping here to be alone when Sera's army eventually comes for me again. Maybe when I'm of no use to this world that I've suddenly landed in.

Grape mutters next to me as we pass through the enormous foyer and into another corridor, "Supposedly, the Aegis owner is a retired hydromancer. He used to be a legend for bending water, so the tank is like an ode to him." He offers a grin, trying to expand my knowledge as if I'm going to last longer than a day here.

I nod, thinking about my poor Kole, wherever he is. He would *love* this place.

I move closer to Grape as our group reaches another set of massive double doors, eyeing my surroundings suspiciously, "Where *are* we exactly? Where's the Aegis base?"

Grape chuckles as the heavy double doors fly open to a giant courtyard lit with a thousand lanterns floating above, effortlessly illuminating the night sky.

"You haven't figured it out yet? This *is* Aegis." Grape says, and the puzzle pieces shift into place. The darkness was meant to confuse and disorient us, never to give away too many of the team's secrets before we were ready. There must be so much more to this massive training building, and for some reason, a thought in the back of my head wishes to explore further. But right now, all I really want to know is where the beds are.

We move further into the courtyard lined with pearly, cemented walls as if the builders took a page from the castle blueprints lining King Ragnar's estate.

Our group blends into the other scattered recruits. Some sit in circles among the freshly mowed grass while others form their own parties in various corners, all sporting exhausted albeit curious expressions.

Hopeful eyes scan the courtyard for that familiar head of dirty blond hair and loving grin. He *has* to be here. He has to.

"Recruits!" a shrill, feminine voice bellows through the courtyard, making me leap in my skin, "Line up player style!"

Suddenly, as if responding to danger in an attack, bodies start sprinting and shuffling all around, lining up to stand six feet apart in a perfect box. I hover, motionless and confused as recruits only exchange a single word here and there, sounding like they are reciting numbers to the people next to them. It's all so... *weird.* Nothing I've ever prepared for.

Trying to blend in after losing sight of Merry and Grape in the crowd, I fall into line like everyone else, determined to stay under the radar for as long as possible, until I see what I've been searching for. The only thing that's been keeping me going. My reason for existence.

Him.

A glimpse of messy, dirty blond hair, wide shoulders and that boyish grin I've spent countless summers adoring catches my breath. A wheezy gasp flies from my throat as I realize he made it. He's alive!

Weaving through the rows with blurry eyes, I break into a sprint, not caring about the judgmental remarks and side eyes I'm getting. I finally found him, and he's alive! That's all I care about right now.

"Kole!" I shout, making him turn around with a confused expression that quickly turns to utter bewilderment. I don't care. I fling myself into his arms, swearing to never let go as I release a sob into his shoulder. It feels like a lifetime has passed since I've seen him.

"Soria?" Kole mutters in shock, pulling me back to examine my face, probably to make sure I'm real. "What are you… how are you…"

"It was terrible. I went to your house and the next thing I know I'm in a cage and then they killed Hera and I was forced onto the stage!"

"Slow down, slow down. The *auction* stage? How did you get here?" He asks with wide eyes searching mine. Wide, beautiful eyes that I'm so happy to see. I could dive into his gaze one thousand times and never get tired of it.

"They bought me and threw me on the train. Isn't that what happened to you?" I ask, clinging to Kole as if he's my lifeline. He may as well be. He won't let Sera's group lay another finger on me so long as he lives. I'm finally safe.

Suddenly, his strong arms do something my body doesn't recognize and pull away.

"Soria," Kole's grasp tightens slightly, trying to get me to focus, "I don't know how you're here, but we're going to find a way to get you out. This must have been some mistake." His voice lowers, and suddenly, I remember that we're not alone. All around us, every last recruit has filed into their spot, forming a giant square in the courtyard center with several rows. Now they're all staring at us.

Nervously, I scan the crowd to see we're at the very front, causing a scene for the rest of the recruits to chuckle and gawk at. My eyes fly back to Kole in hopes he can save me already.

His gaze lowers to my out-of-place outfit and his face contorts ever so slightly into a light shade of pink. Is he blushing?

Kole whispers so only I can hear, "Why are you wearing that?" His cheeks flare a little brighter as he glances around at the people staring.

I offer a half smile, "I'll tell you all about it later. It's stupid, I know."

"Wow, Arnson," some pale girl with a scratchy voice chuckles behind us, "You didn't tell us you packed a whore along to Aegis."

My fingernails dig into Kole's suit jacket, knowing at any second he's about to pummel this squat girl for calling me such a name. I suppose having a powerful boyfriend has its perks.

To my surprise, only the sound of distant laughing from other recruits fills my senses. Kole stays in place, only offering an eye roll to the nasty girl. My heart sinks. He must have a good reason for staying quiet. He always has good reasons.

"Listen to me," Kole mumbles in my ear, still shifting his gaze around us, "I'll find you when we go to bed, but right now you need to move. I promise I'll figure out a way to send you home."

"I'm afraid that's not up to you, *recruit.*" That deep, terrible voice that does something to my insides sends a chill up my exposed spine. A gasp lodges in both our throats as Kole and I twist slightly to see a tall, broad figure leaning against the courtyard door frame.

Damn.

He nearly takes up all of it.

The captain stands taller than everyone present, his dark suit fitting perfectly with massive arms folded across his chest, and those sunglasses concealing who he's directly looking at. The accent in his voice makes me wonder if he hails from the eastern region of Bachaloria, but a stranger's words muddy my wandering inquiries.

"Jude Blackwell!" The voice addresses the captain in a kiss-ass manner as it had on the train platform, "Again, it's an honor, sir!"

Jude sighs in the doorframe, probably rolling his eyes behind those dark shades he has no need for. If the recruit were any smarter, he'd shut up right now if he values his life, but he doesn't. Instead, he steps out of line, walking toward Jude with a wide smile as if taking his opportunity to kiss his ass is something he's owed.

"Sir, I want to thank you for buying my delta, it really means a lot. I was hoping you…"

All of a sudden, the boy stops in his tracks, grabbing his neck as if choking on something until I recognize the fear in his eyes. That fear could only come from one thing. The struggle to breathe which I know all too well.

The recruit drops to his knees, his face turning three shades of red as he claws at his neck, wheezing and nearly losing his shit.

All of a sudden, Jude sighs, and the recruit falls to his face, gasping for air with a terrible groan in his throat.

What the fuck just happened?

The recruit gains his feet and sprints quietly back to his place, probably feeling like a total jackass for approaching the captain unauthorized.

My gaze shifts from the recruit to Jude and back again until my heart leaps in my chest, and I realize what just occurred.

The captain did that to him.

Jude was able to take the very *breath* from someone's lungs without so much as blinking. Not even the flick of his wrist and he could have ended that boy's life, all to prove a point that he is not to be spoken to without permission. I've only ever heard of this delta from history books dated hundreds of years ago. His power hasn't been revived in centuries, and probably for good reason.

My arms shiver as I cling to Kole, fear consuming my body as I stare at the aeromancer standing in the door frame.

Jude Blackwell can manipulate the air.

CHAPTER 6: INTRODUCTIONS

"Soria," Kole whispers softly, never breaking eye contact with the dangerous captain sizing us up, "I need you to go to the back of the formation. *Now.*"

Before I can process the tension in Kole's voice, a line of men and women storm through the courtyard doors, past Jude as if he gets to loom wherever he wishes. Instantly, they take the front row, eyeing our silent group of recruits with eyes more lethal than predators. A few, I recognize as the captain's entourage during the auction, so I gather this group must make up the Aegis leaders.

A thin, older man with pasty skin, a shiny scalp, and a well trimmed white beard steps forward. He wears the same navy blue uniform I've seen on others, though his are pressed with perfect pleats down the legs, and a small pin of Bachaloria's tiger-bear emblem sits on his collar. He addresses the group of recruits as I try to hide behind Kole.

"Ladies and gentlemen, or shall I say, my little *Arena Thieves*," the man grumbles the label with a knowing smile, earning several howls of appreciation from the crowd.

"It gives me great pleasure to welcome you to our esteemed training grounds, where henceforth, you shall be called Echo Company for this year's cycle. My name is President RoBjorn, and these are my team directors."

He motions with weathered but firm hands to his right, singling out a short, fit woman with chin-length black hair and a tall, strong-looking man with a firm jaw and a black beard, "Director Neera and Director Boz. They will be personally in charge of your phase one training and are single-handedly responsible for creating *legends.* Don't get ahead of yourselves. You still have a long way to go. You may think you're essential, exceptional. Special. But remember, the only thing that separates you from the Bachalorian military is that expensive name seared into your wrists."

The President's voice echoes throughout the courtyard, stiffening the spines of every last recruit in this moonlit courtyard. "You all belong to Aegis now, whether you..."

His voice faulters mid-sentence as I try to break eye contact, hoping to stay invisible for as long as possible. But that's a dream spent in vain as he approaches Kole and me with arms folded behind his back.

Kole practically *shakes* where he stands as I try to shrink to the size of a non-existent grain of rice. But it's no use.

RoBjorn lowers his voice, his gaze seeming to address Kole, "Recruit, who are you?"

Kole swallows as he says, "Kole Arnson, sir."

The President looks Kole up and down with inquisitive eyes, arms still folded behind his back, "Very good. But I was addressing the young lady behind you. Come forward."

I keep my gaze lowered, hoping he doesn't mean me, but as I slowly peek around Kole's shoulder, RoBjorn arches a white eyebrow, motioning with his chin to step closer.

Slowly, and with quivering hands, I shuffle around Kole to stand inches from the President, who reeks of power and respect—something very similar to his captain, but in an aged and mystifying manner.

The leader of Aegis looks me up and down, no doubt judging my dress before speaking in a tone meant only for me, "You *are* an Aegis recruit, are you not?" He lifts my arm with a calloused hand, staring down at my wrist. "It says so here, you are. What is your delta, young lady?"

My insides want to scream for mercy from the pain of embarrassment today. I want to run away from this courtyard and never look back before spitting out these next self-incriminating words. What if he finds me a waste of time and space? What if he has his own reaper to obliterate me for being here without a gift?

"Answer me," RoBjorn orders evenly, still holding my wrist in ransom.

I swallow, hoping my voice sounds less nauseous than I feel.

"I don't have one," I whisper, and the murmurs of recruits around me pick up.

But my answer doesn't faze the leader as he waves a hand, immediately silencing the growing murmurs around us. With the slightest arch in a furry, greyed brow, he peers back at Jude who still stands casually against the door frame, not bothered in the slightest that he's getting a silent scolding from the head man in charge.

The President drops my wrist with a nod, "And what is your name?"

"Soria Davidsdottir."

He nods once more, and it's like a new wave of understanding crosses his eyes as he measures me for what I am, but in half a second, it's gone, returning to the steely face of a leader.

"Well, then, another offspring of David to add to my collection. It seems Captain Blackwell has a few plans up his sleeve. I can't wait to see what we do with *you,* recruit." My blood turns cold at the insinuation.

Before I can ask another question I'll never get the answer to, RoBjorn dips his head, giving me an order without room for negotiation, "Now, lining up *player* style is by monetary value. So, find your appropriate place." And he turns on his heel, handing the introductions over to his frightening directors.

Obeying the President's command, I give Kole a helpless look, holding on tight to his promise of finding me later. I just need to make it through the next minute. And the one after that.

I filter through the crowd of inhospitable recruits trying to ignore disgusted scoffs. A sigh of relief escapes when I make eye contact with Grape's friendly face, who happens to be standing near Merry. Thank the Heavens.

I find my place as the very last recruit in the formation, though I don't mind. This allows me to keep to myself while the attention shifts elsewhere. If only my stomach weren't twisting and turning for some reason, I might be able to focus on forming an escape plan.

Grape offers me a friendly wink, letting me know everything will be okay as the male director addresses the crowd sternly.

"Recruits, I am Director Boz, and the pleasantries are now over." His voice makes me queasy, "From this moment on, every day will count toward your survival and making Aegis proud. As you know, we have three stages of training that will determine who among you deserves the title of *player.*"

The female director who must be Neera, speaks up, commanding the crowd even in her shorter stature, "All stages are essential, but all stages are deadly. There are five hundred and one of you standing in this courtyard. By the end of stage one, fifty percent of you will be dead. It's up to you alone to ensure you end up on the right side of that percentage."

My stomach feels like it's doing cartwheels, so I swallow the bile in my throat, remembering the mountain of rich food now settling like a rock in my stomach.

Director Boz takes back over, "And if you make it to tethering in six months, do not be surprised by your options. Your delta is either here, or it met an early grave. So you *will* give your training everything you have or die knowing you did."

Suddenly, as my palms become increasingly sweaty and my mouth begins to produce too much saliva, I notice the captain weaving his way through the formation of recruits. He inspects each face with his hands in his pockets as if he's bored already. Not a single pair of eyes dares to look directly at him.

Director Neera addresses us again, acting like Jude isn't even here, "If you *do* tether, you'll move on to your delivery with your partner, showing the cabinet you deserve to be on the team. But for now, I would focus on surviving the crucible at the end of phase one. We'll know who's alive in ninety days."

I glance toward Grape, hoping for an explanation in his expression, but his eyes seem trained on something in front of me.

My neck twists to find Jude suddenly standing before me, as close as he was on the train platform. His presence overwhelms my senses with the scent of expensive cologne.

My lips purse as the captain leans in slowly, towering above with ease as a vein in his thick neck bulges slightly. His hands leave his pockets and cross over taut arms to reveal bright, silver rings, hugging nearly every finger. He reeks of rotten wealth.

I blink, finding the breath that my traitorous body abandoned for some reason. No matter how interesting every detail appears, I need to stop examining this man.

Jude Blackwell is dangerous.

He nearly killed a boy for talking to him. He sicced his dogs on me with a casual order. And he *broke* my violin.

I retreat from Jude as director Neera's voice fades in the distance, my entire world consumed by the captain in a midnight suit. To my dismay, he steps closer immediately, closing the gap I tried creating. I huff a sigh, trying to ignore the nausea agitating in my stomach.

Jude cocks his head slightly, still looking down at me through dark lenses that match his short, clean hair.

"Irritated with my presence, Soria?" He asks, forcing me to look up at the sound of his deep voice. His lips are full against that tanned skin.

Stop looking at his lips!

"I'd think my feelings toward you are clear, considering what you've done." I grind out every word, letting pride smother the uneasiness in my stomach.

Jude's brows knit by a fraction as his hands tuck a little tighter across that enormous chest, "And what have I done?"

"You bought me."

"And I don't intend on selling. So, prove you weren't a waste of ten krona."

I feel my nostrils flare, but before I can offer a retort, his hand flies toward my face, and I flinch, almost shrieking in response to how terrified I am beneath the anger—the anger that's a mask.

But his hand doesn't strike.

Instead, his fingers hover above my jaw without making contact, motioning to the bruise branding my cheekbone. The bruise *he* ordered.

My jaw jerks out of reach, all but snarling at him as he nods in approval, "I would say don't take it personally, but you should take *everything* personal that happens to you here. This shiner is your own fault."

My brows thread together angrily, forgetting the fear entirely. How dare he. I don't deserve any of this!

Before I have a chance to spit my rage, my stomach finally gives in, threatening to heave all of the food I scarfed down on the train. I shouldn't have eaten that much.

As if knowing my body's reactions before I do, Jude takes a half step back, just out of shot as I bend at the waist, losing every last morsel without permission. I should have known my body couldn't handle all of that. It's been deprived of such rich foods for too long.

Ignoring the disgusted sounds of recruits around me, I wipe my mouth with the wrist that reads *Aegis*. My eyes find the captain watching me through those shades again, palms in his pockets as if my vomiting all over the courtyard were inevitable. Before I can blink, he's gone, turning with a shake of his head and a thousand-krona haircut.

My lips release a sigh, and I can't fight the feeling of defeat on every level. Helpless should be my new name.

Director Boz clears his throat, addressing the crowd and ignoring the scene I just created, "Now, breakfast will commence in the chow hall at zero six hundred hours. Training will commence thirty minutes later. Sleep well, recruits. If you can."

***

I follow Grape and Merry out of the courtyard, up three levels of twisting stairs until our company reaches a set of double doors on the far east wing of this horseshoe-shaped training building. The night blankets my surroundings the farther we climb, and I leave the mystery of what lies beneath the dark for another day.

Curiosity has no home in my soul.

The directors shoulder open the doors, revealing a squad bay that extends farther than I can see, hosting hundreds of metal-framed bunk beds with a singular white pillow and one cotton quilt. I suppose Aegis doesn't care about giving boys and girls their privacy, seeing how we'll all be sleeping dangerously close in the same room, and apparently, sharing the same bathing chambers.

My eyes flash to the giant bathroom at the front of the squad bay, holding nearly fifty showerheads with only a dozen sheer curtains to offer privacy. Goosebumps prickle my skin at the foreboding thought of eventually having to bathe with this target on my back. Or I could just live in my own filth forever. I'm not sure what's worse.

I follow my new companions to the end of the squad bay, noticing each bed holds three sets of uniforms with a tag labeling each recruit. By the looks of it, our bunks have been spaced out based on monetary value again, so my hopes of sleeping near Kole vanish. It won't matter, though. Knowing him, he'll guard me in my bunk no matter what rules there are.

"Here, switch me," Grape says, grabbing my uniforms from the top bunk and replacing them with his.

"Why?"

"Because if you're on the bottom, you can run away quickly." He says with a smirk, already thinking ahead.

I offer Grape a thankful smile, praying it won't come to that.

The uniforms that are supposed to last us to tethering could certainly be worse, and I know I'm only saying that because I'm overly excited to peel this dress from my body. The clothes are made of thick, beige felt in a long-sleeve fashion that cinches with countless buckles, forming to the body wearing them. I hold up the matching bottoms to find a perfect length, along with shin-length socks and black, freshly polished boots in my exact size. Each top holds the Bachalorian tiger-bear emblem on the front, and a faded, whitewashed number on the back to mark who is who.

I suppose it's fitting that mine reads zero.

Shaking my head at the insinuation that once again, I truly mean nothing, I decide to forego the bathing chambers, seeing how they're overly occupied by excited men chasing each other and a variety of girls giggling in their skimpy towels. There's no telling who will wake me tonight from the inevitable moans echoing from the stalls. That type of craving always finds a way.

I wait patiently until the candlelight fades in the squad bay, the only illumination source coming from the enormous lavatory at the other end of the room. Finally, curling beneath the quilt in my own moment of semi-privacy, I rid myself of this horrible get-up. Tugging the felt top over my torso, I slip the dress off beneath the covers and slide the pants over my hips, finding a baggy—albeit scratchy—fit.

At least I'm out of this terrible dress.

I try to keep my eyes open, knowing Kole will surely find me at any moment, but he never comes, and sleep claims me too easily. Maybe he got held up doing... *something.* But if I know him, he'll be glued to my side by the time I wake up, forever watching over me the way he always has.

For some reason, disappointment greets me in the morning to find my bed empty.

CHAPTER 7: ORIENTATION

I should have known thirty minutes wouldn't be enough time for breakfast. Or any meal, for that matter, when it's first-come, first-serve, and all five hundred recruits find it laughable that I could even be in line. As if I don't rate a meal to keep my stomach full.

Kole is nowhere to be seen this morning, though I'm sure he still has a good reason for it. Perhaps he's found a way for me to escape, and he needs to tell me at the right time. Either way, I know I just need to keep my head down for the time being.

I manage to keep the hunger at bay by scarfing down the remains of scrambled eggs the cooks had set out and shove the cracker packets everyone else ignores into my cargo pockets, tying them closed with the leather buckles. It may not be much, but at least I won't starve. I only feel bad for the recruits who slept in with not a comrade in sight to wake them. Their punishment for tardiness to our first training session is handed out without a second thought. And, of course, it's running. I *hate* running. My lungs hate running.

Our fearless directors decide to take us on an endless sprint around the *entire* Aegis training building that stretches over a mile, claiming we'll stop when the last of us laps them. Too bad the last of us fell out miles ago because she couldn't breathe.

I practically swallow my medicinal powder every chance I get in the privacy of some weeping willow trees lining the cement path, seeing how our group left me in the dust. I force myself to ignore the mocking laughter every time the horde of recruits lap me, dodging their snickers and spit. At least they don't notice the incense can nestled between dozens of cracker packets. I *have* to keep that a secret. If anyone finds out, I'm dead for sure.

After lunch, we're escorted to a large auditorium on the second floor with just enough seats for every last recruit, facing a green chalkboard and podium.

We're seated player style again, so thankfully, I end up right next to Grape and Merry, my saving graces. A few times, I think I spot Kole's shoulder-length sandy hair down in the front rows, but taller and bigger recruits make him hard to see.

Before I can ask Grape what this class is about, an older man with long, frizzy gray hair and a scruffy beard enters from the right in a rush. He stands no more than four feet tall and doesn't even spare the room of recruits a glance as he pushes up his circular spectacles and digs in boxes seated behind the podium, pulling out several stacks of thick, leather-bound books.

With what seems like a permanent scowl across the bearded man's jaundice-tinted skin, he mutters as if everyone were already supposed to be paying attention, "Echo Company, today marks day one of your orientation."

He begins to hand out the books, instructing every student to receive one.

After several minutes, he pulls a stool to the podium, clearing his throat as he glances through a book of his own, "My name is Dr. Gencavage, and during your time spent training to become a player, you will meet here on even days for knowledge."

The doctor, or more so, professor, squints through his spectacles toward the textbook pages, ignoring the disgruntled murmurs around the room. It seems no one expected schoolwork when they've trained their entire lives to play a deadly game, but I'm all too thrilled to be in a classroom setting. It means the physical torment will cease for a while.

The doctor goes on, barely raising his voice through an overly rehearsed speech, "As we move through the weeks and desks become empty, just fill in those spots. Now," he flips to another page, moving on as if he didn't just imply most of us will not make it to the end of his orientation, "You will keep your ordinance handbooks to remind you of the unwavering bylaws we hold here at Aegis. Let me remind you, though it should be evident, recruits are not allowed to murder one another within the confines of this classroom. You are here for knowledge, and that rough behavior will be handled *outside* my doors."

A sigh escapes through parted lips as I conclude the second I leave the safety of this auditorium, I'm fair game. That means I'm as good as dead the moment Sera decides she's done playing with me. Unless…

I glance around the rows of recruits, examining who sits below with a spark of an idea forming.

Protection. I *need* protection. And although Kole would lay down his life for me, I can't count on him all the time. I would never ask Grape or Merry to risk their lives to keep me safe. I need an army like Sera. But who?

My eyes flick to the pair of pasty-skinned boys who have stuck together since the train ride. They don't seem related, but perhaps their loyalty could extend farther than each other. If I remember Grape's recruit-rundown correctly, one of them can bend the night's shadows while the other holds the gift of sand manipulation. Very powerful, indeed.

My gaze shifts to a redheaded boy a few seats farther down, remembering he can do something like take a person's senses away or heighten them. That could be useful if he were to take my side. All I need is to be convincing enough in my approach.

Suddenly, my train of thought comes to a halt as the largest recruit in our group barrels through the classroom doors with labored, heaving breathing.

Dr. Gencavage cocks his head right to examine the giant recruit, standing nearly seven feet tall with thick, broad shoulders, wide bulging biceps choked by beige, felt sleeves and a long pale braid. The recruit's name escapes me as the doctor's eyes trail up and up until his neck is vertical to stare at the massive recruit.

"Ahem, The Beast—I mean, Miss Ona Viktorsdottir, I presume? Tardiness will not be tolerated from here on out."

Dr. Gencavage mumbles to the giant with fists almost the size of my head, completely unbothered she could snap his frail body with two fingers.

She stands before the class, and her name finally greets me with familiarity. Grape told me hours ago that Ona was bought for her impressive delta of super strength, but he warned me to stay far away. The giant recruit doesn't seem to speak much, but she's a killer and possibly the inventor of aggravated assault from what Grape has gathered. I wouldn't dare risk my life asking her for protection, considering she seems to be the smash first, ask questions later type of gal.

Ona doesn't answer the teacher, only gives him a curt nod and filters through the rows of seats to find hers, which she barely fits in. Even better, her seat is directly in front of mine.

I silently pray she doesn't already belong to Sera.

I don't kid myself. Sera's delta is deadly and certainly a power I'm afraid of. I hated that feeling of being blinded and having a cloud fog my mind. But Ona? Her entire presence scares the ever-loving shit out of me. From the sideways glances and nervous muttering around the room, I can tell she scares everyone else too. I wonder who her tethered will be.

Dr. Gencavage takes back over didactically, "Furthermore, it should go without saying that no recruit may slay, harm, or show intent to harm an established player, director or member in the line of Aegis duty. The act is punishable by death."

Grape flashes me an eyeroll while muttering, "Like I'd try to gut a player."

"But good luck if you come across those in dress blues roaming these halls. They have been instructed not to interact with you until you pass the crucible, but they do not take kindly to an untethered delta standing in their way."

The professor dips his head, squinting through his spectacles toward his audience of recruits.

The image of my twin brothers wandering the Aegis training building enters my mind, and I can't help but wonder if they know I'm here already.

Though I wouldn't expect them to care. They've never really cared about me the way I did them, especially when they found out simultaneously they were born with gifts. That was the worst birthday of my life.

Dr. Gencavage goes on to tell us there are over one hundred tethered pairs and one captain remaining on the team. He lets us know the maximum of tethered pairs President RoBjorn is willing to accept this year is twelve, which, according to our teacher, is quite generous, seeing as how by the end of the Diamond Games there's no telling how many players will fall to their deaths before the crowd.

My stomach feels uneasy at the insinuation of so much death. So much *wasted* death, all for the slim chance to be named a champion and receive the glory. That's the end goal, anyhow. Dr. Gencavage instructs the recruits that becoming a player and thriving in the ring is the greatest life achievement one with a gift could hope for. To die for Bachaloria at such a young age is deemed a high honor, but that remains to be understood in my mind.

"Does anyone know why our Enemy In The North despises us so? Anyone have a clue why these games are oh-so imperative? Why must we spend millions on people, supplies, uniforms and courtship of our country?" Dr. Gencavage surveys the room with a finger, but no one speaks up, "Thought so. Those history books teach you that our nemesis, Seyka, is the boogie man, hmm? The Bloodletters who wish to steal our women and children, our land and all our riches?"

Several murmurs spread across the auditorium like a wave of approval, but the professor's head shake tells me we've been taught wrong.

"History applauds the ones who author it, so let me disclose some facts to make you all understand just how dangerous the enemy is, for they are not the boogie man your mother told you so you would eat your greens or practice your delta outdoors. They are *far* worse."

"My ma calls them the devil. She said the heavens blessed me by pulling me out of their lands," Grape whispers, and a shiver crawls up my spine just imagining how ruthless and vile these people could really be. I've never seen the prison camps for the Seykans that weasel through our barricade, but I can't imagine they're any place to raise a child.

After what feels like several hours, the clock signals our orientation class is nearly over for the day, so our teacher speaks up to the crowd, finally letting his gaze fall on every recruit. If I didn't know any better I'd think he's trying to avoid memorizing any face for too long in case he never sees it again.

"Recruits, let me impart to you with invaluable knowledge, if I may." Dr. Gencavage clears his throat, "If you desire to meet our enemy in the exquisite city of Ol'Reyka in the new year, you will heed my words in becoming a player. Besides the imperative task of staying alive, it is not only important, but *necessary* that you make it to the tethering trials. And if you are one of the lucky few to reach that day, everything will *then* be out of your hands."

The teacher lifts a furrowed brow, and for a second, the expression almost seems pinned in my direction.

He goes on in a tone so serious that every recruit leans in, hanging on his words. Including me. "It is common knowledge that those recruits who make it to phase three, tethered or not, will be granted the dollar amount they were bought for and sent home if not chosen as a player. The President of Aegis is of ruthless descent, but not wasteful."

I suppress a gasp, my eyes widening at the thought that gives me hope for the better. If for some reason, against all odds, I manage to get to phase three, I could be sent home. My heart flutters as a bubble of possibility and warmth rises in my chest.

The teacher nods once to end his lecture, stepping off his podium as he mutters, "Now, good day and be knowledgeable. We will meet on Friday to discuss acolytes, and in four weeks every recruit shall receive their baby owl."

"Baby owls?" I ask Merry curiously as we descend the rows and make our way toward the chow hall. She curls a brown strand around her finger before stuffing it back into her messy bun, nodding at my question.

"You've n-n-never heard of acolytes?"

I shake my head as we round the corner.

"They're like companions we can transfer a piece of our delta to."

My brow puckers, wondering how I've never heard of this before. *Transferring* a delta? That sounds impossible.

"Supposedly h-hundreds of years ago, someone r-r-really old loved his pet c-cat or something. He lived alone in th-the woods without any t-type of protection from the mythical creatures we now k-k-keep in prisons," Merry says.

Grape spins on his heel, facing us while walking backward as he loves to do, "It wasn't a forest. I heard it was the desert." He winks at Merry, taking over the story, "And the old man *did* love the cat, but he knew the monsters were coming and he couldn't defend himself alone. So, he figured out a way to transfer a small piece of his delta to the cat, and then that cat created a force field with the man's gift, hiding his home from the monsters forever."

Grape shrugs as my jaw drops.

Merry pokes me in the side as we take our place in the dinner line, "A true acolyte is v-very rare anyway, b-b-but they're important to history, so Aegis m-makes their recruits try out the bond with s-some type of bird every year. My sister told me all of this, anyway—before sh-sh-she got to phase three and... well. She chose wrong for tethering." Merry's gaze drops, as we move forward in line, and I reach for her hand, squeezing tight to let her know I understand the feeling.

"I'm sorry," I whisper, trying my best not to let others see her in a moment of sadness, or something the ruthless recruits might mistake for weakness.

The shapeshifter's eyes gloss for a heartbeat before she blinks away the threatening tears, forcing a nod.

Grape plucks an apple from the platter, tossing it to me with a grin, "But Soria, if someone hasn't told you already, there are a few acolytes spread across base who became attached to a delta. They can be dangerous, according to Merry's sister. Especially Fenrir. So, if you see a giant wolf lurking around. Girl, you better run the other direction."

For the second time within minutes, my jaw drops, wondering how in the world the President of Aegis would allow a wolf to roam the training halls. This beast sounds like something to be locked away with the other creatures. But at the end of the day, it's just another name to add to my growing list of those who would cause me harm.

As I finish eating dinner and successfully collect more cracker packets, I spot the two pasty-skinned boys heading toward the diminishing line for seconds. The boys that could possibly offer me protection. Nightfall is on its way, and I don't trust that Sera and her comrades will let me sleep peacefully for long. I just need to be convincing. Heaven help me.

I slip back in line, right behind the boy who can move sand, preparing my plea.

Nervously, I clear my throat to get their attention, and the Shadow Bender peeks over his shoulder at me with a raised brow. I lunge at my opportunity.

"Hi there. My name is Soria. Davidsdottir. Like the twins." My insides want to shrivel for using my brothers as leverage, but I have to use everything at my disposal, or I won't see another day.

The sand mover rolls his eyes as if I'm nothing more than a piffling concern, waving a hand to dismiss me, but I have to try.

Trying my best not to stutter, I purse my lips, moving closer as they pluck rolls from a large dish, dismissing me completely.

"Wait, wait. Please, hear me out." I whisper, earning both of their attention for a single moment, and I pray to the heavens to give me an ounce of mercy.

After a deep breath, I say, "I may not know your names, but you know who I am. And I don't belong here. I don't *want* to be here. But if I have any chance of getting home, I need to stay alive until phase three. So, my question is…"

"You want us to save you from those who mean to kill you."

The shadow bender raises a brow, looking down at me with deep brown eyes.

I swallow and force a small, tight nod. Here goes nothing.

"I'll do whatever you want. I'll make a deal or give you half of my food or…" I search for something, *anything* in my arsenal of favors to grant, but I have nothing to give. I should have thought this through better.

With pleading eyes, I sigh, "I don't have much, but I would find a way to repay you for your help. Please."

I feel my heart sink because I know these two boys owe me nothing. No one here owes me a drop of loyalty, but I'm out of options if I want to survive. I have to do *something.*

The shadow bender glances at his friend, who seems entirely displeased with the conversation in general. But before I can beg for their help again, I watch a small smile tug on the corner of the shadow bender's lip as his eyes skim my body quickly. He nudges his friend with a look that gives nothing away.

After a few heart-pounding seconds, the sand mover sighs, facing me with another eyeroll, "We will consider it. But
there will be payment on your behalf." My heart leaps with
hope. *Yes!*

Schooling my overexcitement, I nod again, forcing the smile to take a hike because for once, I finally have something to look forward to. If these boys can keep me alive until phase three, I'm home free. Things are looking up.

As I try not to skip back to my seat near Grape, that ancient, deep voice greets me again, leaving me with another word as it so cryptically loves to do.

"Unwise."

***

I wait until I know that every recruit has fallen asleep before attempting to retrieve a long-overdue shower. I smell like fermented mud soaking in the sun, and it's certainly been too long since I've seen my own reflection.

Carefully and quietly, I sneak in the darkness with a fresh uniform toward the massive open bathing chambers, that illuminate the front of the squad bay all hours of the night.

Trying to keep my footsteps light, I stop near a bunk bed, crouching low toward the handsome sleeping face I've adored for years.

Gently, I tap his shoulder several times until those tired eyes slowly blink open.

"Soria?" Kole whispers, glancing around while scrubbing a hand over tired eyes. His back reveals the number *seventy-five* as he rolls to face me. Quite the distance from zero.

I ignore his confusion. I ignore the forty-eight hours that have passed between him promising to find me because we're finally together. I've endured my journey kicking and screaming all because of Kole, and I'll be damned if this was for nothing.

"Sor," my name is a breath on his tongue, wrapped in a silent apology, "I would have found you last night, but I was up for hours thinking of a way out. I just need to find building schematics."

I lean in closer, my palm resting on his arm as I shake my head, a smile breaching my lips just because I'm happy to see him. To feel him. He's here, and he's alive.

"It's okay," I whisper as Kole's gaze becomes more serious, and he pulls me closer, lowering his voice.

"I found a way. It's not surefire, but it could definitely work." He mutters, and I have a feeling he's about to tell me what I've already discovered. Stay alive until phase three. But Kole doesn't say that. "Apparently after sixty days, the President grants the recruits permission off base for a single night. We could leave, find a train headed back home, and put you on it."

My smile spreads at the possibility of avoiding the months of peril ahead of me, and every crisis fades to a nebulous concern as I realize hope isn't lost.

I knew Kole was working out a plan. He always has a plan.

He always takes care of me.

"We would both run away? Like we wanted to?" My grin grows, and I sink my teeth in my lower lip to contain the giddiness.

Kole's gaze falls before leaning closer, sparing another glance around the snoring recruits near us.

"Well, *I* wouldn't." My heart sinks deep in my chest. "They would find me easily, Sor. I can't leave, but *you* can. No one would even notice, and by the time they did, you'd be long gone, sitting safely at home until I return."

My smile fades, but I try to put on a brave face for him. Sitting at home? Waiting for him to return, hopefully alive? I felt so much better seconds ago when I knew he would be by my side. When I knew I wasn't returning to the life I ran away from. But at least I'll be alive… I guess.

"Hey, are you okay?" Kole's palm finds mine, and he tugs me closer, pulling me in for a hug, which I certainly needed. I nod, forcing a smile to show how appreciative I am of him. Of everything he's done already. Kole's sleepy eyes drift to my mouth as he pulls me in tight, brushing his lips against mine for reassurance that he still cares—that he loves me and would do anything for me. And so would I.

I smile into his kiss, pulling away once I realize I probably smell atrocious, and I'm not about to leap into bed with him while I reek like a garbage can. But perhaps *after* my shower.

Kole's eyes fight to stay open as he runs a finger along my wrist, where the word *Aegis* sits, "I hate to ask this of you, and it won't be forever, but I need you to do something."

"Anything." I run a thumb along his hand.

"We need to distance ourselves. Just for a little while." His eyes find mine with a smile, trying to sound encouraging as I try not to pull away. But for some reason, my heart nearly splits in two at the request.

"Why?" My voice breaks.

"Because it's safer for you that way. Trust me, keeping to yourself is the only way these dickheads are going to leave you alone. I'm going to work my magic in the background to keep them away for as long as I can until we get you on that train. So lay low, and don't talk to anyone."

A wave of depression hits my heart like a boulder, harder this time than the splinter that had wedged its way through. The one thing I had to look forward to was being close to the one I love. And now Aegis has taken that away from me.

I entertain the idea of telling Kole my plan to gather people for protection, but I decide against it. He would probably tell me I couldn't trust anyone, and to stay as hidden as possible.

But I have to try something. I can't hide forever.

Nodding in agreement, I watch Kole's eyes flutter closed as he turns on his back, a tired smile spreading across his lips as he tells me goodnight.

I plant another soft kiss on his cheek, wishing him the best of dreams, before sneaking into the giant bathroom.

I take the farthest stall with a curtain, sighing in relief to see every amenity I might need to shower, and twist the handle for hot, steaming water. I almost melt into the warmth smoothing my bare skin, appreciating every blissful second, as the water washes away the filth. I've always loved a hot shower, considering the only temperature of water in my family's cobblestone cottage is freezing. This certainly helps heal the growing pain my heart has been carrying.

I stay beneath the water for twice as long as I should, scrubbing until I feel squeaky clean.

Running my fingers through sopping wet blond locks, I wrap the cream-colored towel around myself and push the curtain aside, ready to get five good hours of sleep before another ruthless day of physical training greets me.

"Hello, Soria Davidsdottir. Or should I say, Zero?"

Before I have a chance to scream for help, that terrible, paralyzing feeling settles over my body, locking my muscles and forcing me to stand right where I am. And where I am, is in the farthest shower stall, dripping wet with only a towel between me and ten of Sera's minions.

Fuck.

CHAPTER 8: MIDNIGHT TRIALS

My insides spin in a terrified frenzy as every cell in my body begs to flee, but all I can do is move my eyes. And it isn't enough. I *have* to move!

Sera stands before me, surrounded by snarling recruits as she holds my felt uniform top between two fingers as if it could infect her. I start praying to the heavens she doesn't rifle through my pockets.

Sera *tsks,* nodding to someone out of view until they step into the light, fueling a fire of anger in my chest. It's the shadow bender and sand mover. They betrayed me. Although I don't know how I didn't see that coming.

Kole warned me.

She takes a step toward me, tossing my clothes into the puddle of water at our feet. Her arms fold across her chest as her dark, silky braid falls over her shoulder. She stares me down as if I'm useless. Hardly worth the time of day. That's exactly what I am to her. To everyone here.

"We're going to have so much fun together, you and I." Sera stands so close I can feel her breath against my cheek, and I want to vomit. What does she plan to do with me now?

"I say, blind her."

The tall, muscular boy with the braided dreadlocks chuckles behind Sera, but she smiles wider.

"No." She runs a long, pointed nail down my temple, her dark eyes filling with malice. "I have a better idea for night two of your punishment. Do you want to know *why* you're getting punished, *Zero?*" Sera's face flickers, knowing I can't answer her, and her voice lowers to a deadly tone, freezing the blood in my body, "Because you're an abomination. Students *died* trying to get where you are, and you don't even have a gift to show for it. You're a mistake, plucked off the streets and put into one of these bunks. But I'll make you a promise," she licks her lips, stepping back out of the stall, "I won't let you forget so long as I *let* you live. This will be waiting for you every night."

Before I can blink, Sera nods to a shorter boy with red hair I recognize, giving him the command to enhance my sense of touch. Good thing I didn't beg *him* for protection. I should have known Sera would sniff out my plan like a rabid dog.

All of a sudden, my vision fades, just as it had at the auction. A fog clouds my brain, and though my eyes are open, it's like someone has turned out the lights, blinding me completely.

Shit.

Suddenly, the air that once felt slightly cool now enrages my skin, sending ferocious goosebumps along my bare arms and legs not concealed by the security of the towel. A droplet of water races down my neck and I can feel the sensation so intensely I would think the droplet weighs ten pounds.

It feels like my nerves are on overdrive, not knowing what to expect until the worst happens. Something hard and rocklike slams into my stomach, and my world stops spinning as the capillaries in my eyes burst from the blow.

Agony washes over me instantly as the blood in my body rises to a dangerous temperature like a fever meeting its boiling point. Internally, my nerves scream out of sheer pain as the waves of nausea push me over the edge, all contained within a body that cannot react. Cannot move a muscle. Whatever that redhead did to my senses is terrifying as I stand here clutching my towel, feeling like any moment death will claim me as my blood pressure drops from too much torment taken within second.

My body was never meant to experience such pain.

A few deep voices chuckle in the distance as I stand here motionless, until too much time has passed, and my muscles finally respond, collapsing in on themselves without permission. My knees slam to the slippery ground as my vision comes back immediately. The pain lingers, but the heightened sense of touch has dissolved, leaving me with a dull ache in my lower abdomen. It hurts terribly, but it's more manageable than it was seconds ago under that disgusting spell.

Sera and her minions have abandoned me on the shower floor, leaving me to writhe in the pain that will not stop after tonight. She promised me it wouldn't.

Gingerly, I drag the sopping-wet felt over my torso, slipping my pants on and trying desperately not to let my sobs echo. I have to get out of here. Out of this bathing chamber, out of this squad bay, out of this building.

For a moment, I debate sprinting to Kole's bedside and demanding he end Sera on the spot, but I can't ask that of him. I can't let him see me like this. What if

Sera's boys retaliate against him? I'm afraid all the water in the world wouldn't protect him against those deadly deltas combined.

Suffering in silence it is.

My hair sticks to my neck as I slip through the squad bay doors, climbing the nearest flight of stairs in the darkness, higher and higher until I finally reach a set of steel doors. Without thinking, I fling them open and a rush of cool, crisp air greets burning cheeks, slightly calming the fire in my chest.

I glance around to find solidarity for once, and on the roof. Powder meets my nostrils instantly. Once, twice, three times to calm the growing anxiety building within my stomach.

I approach the edge of the massive training building, peering over the shadowed canyons that dominate the eastern side of the base, while to the west lies a thick forest within this bowl-shaped terrain. Ahead stands the hundred-foot cement wall that keeps all of Aegis sheltered from the world beyond, and to my back sits the sea that sleeps beneath the moon's glow.

I wonder what the view must look like in the light of day.

For the first time in forever, I miss my family. Or what we used to be. I miss the idea of waking up in my cot and doing the mundane things in life that I've always loathed. But even then, I had something to look forward to. I had Kole, and occasionally his mother's leftovers and the possibility of leading a life worth living. But that's all gone now.

I'll never make it through endless nights of torment. I'm not strong enough.

Before I fall into a pit of self-loathing, a terrible breeze sends a shiver up my spine, forcing me to stand straight up. A deadly, eerie feeling burrows its way into the marrow of my bones as I turn my neck slightly, squinting in the darkness as the silence stretches for too long.

Bright orange eyes flash in the shadows, and it feels like my heart stops.

Have I not had enough torment for one night?

Slowly, steadily, the giant, round eyes step forward on black, burly paws with claws sharper than knives. The rest of it stays concealed in the night, but its massive head tells me this has to be the ferocious creature Merry warned me about. The acolyte that seems keen to lurk the base as it pleases.

The huge, pitch-black wolf head opens its maw a few inches to reveal teeth like daggers. A low, guttural noise rumbles in its throat as its predatory gaze locks with mine, and I want to die. Surely this is the end for me. I hope it's painless.

I squint my eyes closed as my mouth turns tacky, fully facing the large wolf as I whisper goodbye to Kole, Merry and Grape. The only people who would notice I had been eaten alive. The only ones who wish me well.

Too many heartbeats pass before I find the courage to peek, finding the wolf only a foot away, but laying down.

Lying. Down.

He begins licking at a paw, seemingly bored as if I'm no longer here.

What the fuck is going on?

"It looks like Fenrir has decided you get to live tonight."

I whirl on my heel to find the captain leaning against the door to the roof, amused with the sight of me staring down a dangerous animal, as if he has no reason to be afraid himself.

He's abandoned his sunglasses for the evening, as well as his typical dark suit jacket, dressed a little more casually in a white button-up and sleek pants. His collar is undone, revealing the peak of tanned pectoral muscles glinting in the moonlight.

I blink, fixing my gaze back on the large dog who seems preoccupied with his own paw, hoping he doesn't change his mind and decide I'm better suited as dinner.

With a gulp, I call out to Jude while keeping my eyes locked on the wolf, "Are you always found leaning against dark doorways?"

Anything to take my mind off the apex predator inches from my ankles.

Jude snickers, and from the corner of my eye, I see his head tilt slightly as if he's curious.

"It depends on who wants to find me. Were you trying to find me, Soria?"

The way he says my name sends a bout of heat to my neck, probably out of anger. He doesn't deserve to say my name. If my life hangs in the balance already, I'm done pleading to stay alive.

With a scoff, I retort, "I would never go out of my way to look for a monster like you. Just leave me alone."

Jude releases a noise similar to disbelief, and begins stalking toward me, though I won't let myself move a muscle, just in case the wolf has forgotten I'm within mauling distance. Clearly Jude isn't scared of the creature, seeing how easily he takes his strides.

The captain approaches me from behind, his voice carrying a few feet away.

"Face me," he orders. His cologne drifts to fill my senses with that same tinge of desire.

No. I do *not* like the way he smells. His scent means nothing to me.

I swallow, calling over my shoulder, "Absolutely not. I'm not turning my back on a *wolf.* Are you mad?"

Jude makes a noise behind me that sounds similar to annoyance, and by the sounds of his polished boots against the crumbs of roof gravel, he's moved even closer to my back, still leaning casually against the edge.

"Fine. We'll play this dialogue your way. What are you doing on the roof, Recruit? Hoping to survive by running away? Or thinking of ending it early? The weak always die first on this base."

Anger prickles my skin, and for once, I have no desire to reach for my incense to calm me down. I wish to unleash my frustrations on someone. But the dangerous wolf keeps me from exploding.

"I had to get away from the squad bay."

"Because you're an embarrassment to everyone here?"

"Does it matter?" I almost find the courage to face Jude, but instead, I resort to the only thing I know. I close my eyes shut, hoping this entire evening has been an awful night terror and that I'll wake up really soon.

"Not really. I don't expect you to last long, anyway." Jude's deep, silky voice is even closer now, tickling the back of my neck in a way that feels like smooth strokes of warm air.

It's dangerous.

Sensual.

It's something that will push me over the edge if I let it.

The captain sighs, and that warm breeze curls around my neck gently, trailing up my cheek and lacing my arms as if memorizing every cell. It's a feeling unlike any other and I begin to wonder what kind of trance I've fallen into with this night's breeze as my anger slowly dissipates. It's mesmerizing.

"I suppose the reason you're here is your own fault, anyhow."

My eyes flash open, dismissing the warm ribbons of air in a heartbeat as my fists ball.

"How dare you," I growl, refusing to acknowledge how close Jude feels to my back, "*None* of what's happened to me is my fault. I didn't ask to be thrown onto that auction stage! I didn't ask you to buy me and then paint a giant public target on my back! Every bit of pain I've endured has not been my fault. It's *yours*."

Invisible strings of wind slam my lips closed and wrap around my jaw, threatening to tighten at the slightest movement.

I inhale through flared nostrils, realizing I've unleashed my anger onto the one person with the ability to end my life without moving a muscle. It would be too easy for him to steal the air from my lungs as he had with the recruit in the courtyard. What's even worse, is I would collapse ten times quicker than any other.

The easiest kill under his belt.

Jude whispers behind me with calculating emotion underlying careful words, "You would be wise to remember who you're speaking to."

I'm forced to swallow my temper in defeat, wondering if the deadly captain will now take his anger out on me the way I did him.

"Please," my voice cracks with mercy as the warm tendrils of air circle my lips, allowing me to speak, "Please don't kill me."

Jude chuckles as his presence consumes my peripheral. That wispy air slides down my neck, threatening a chokehold until I notice he's even closer now. I don't move a single muscle as the captain speaks with dangerous authority.

"Because Fenrir decided you mean less than nothing, I'll forgive your disrespect. But let's get one thing straight," Jude's tone lowers, and I fear he's about to lay me out, "Nothing here happens by accident. *You* are not here by accident. Everything that passes between now and the inevitable day that you die will be a result of your own choices—your own actions, recruit."

Nodding in petrified obedience, I silently toss away his nonsense advice, steeling myself back into the hope of surviving long enough to run away on the train Kole told me about.

Kole. My boyfriend. Who loves me. And who I… love.

I sigh, folding my arms as the night's wind tosses damp blond strands behind me, surely throwing the hair into Jude's chest. "I won't last a week whether it's my choice or not."

"Self-pity is not flattering on you."

I force another swallow to keep my temper in check, throwing away the feelings that beg to surface. But I push them down, settling with a grumble.

"Would you like advice? Or are you too stubborn to get out of your own way?" Jude whispers, and for some reason, I feel him closer now than ever. Why is he standing so close to my back? Is strangulation one of his favorite tactics?

I contemplate a sarcastic remark, but the tendrils of air circling my neck remind me of the power the captain possesses.

Watching the black wolf switch to his other paw as he licks in boredom, I say, "Of course, Captain." A faint *tsk* of his tongue fills my ear.

"Do exactly what you would do, minus the fear."

My lips part as I trail into my thoughts, wondering how on earth *that* could be advice. Do exactly what I do? Minus the fear? How is that helpful in the slightest?

Without thinking, I grit my teeth, finding the courage to finally face the captain on this rooftop in the middle of the night. Dr. Gencavage warned us to steer clear of players, but I've had all I can take in this moment.

If Jude Blackwell wanted to kill me tonight, he would have already. I don't care if he's toying with his new trinket. I'm tired of being played with.

My neck cranes to find Jude pinning me with that lethal, incredible gaze, and I'm nearly breathless by the perfection in his face. Swirling blue eyes hold my stare, clashing against tanned skin and that dark, chopped hair that looks conditioned and soft against a rough exterior. A freckle I haven't noticed before sits on that smooth patch of skin between his right eyelid and shaped eyebrow. The muscles that line his neck down to the divot in his…

No. I am *not* examining Jude's body. I hate him. He broke my violin.

I try not to flinch as his warm tendrils of air twists a piece of my damp hair, folding it over my shoulder as if this action is a courtesy. What kind of nightmare is this?

"If you don't heed that advice," Jude mutters, and I watch his eyes examine every detail on my face as if memorizing my features, "You'll be dead by morning. And I'll finally be rid of the weakest link."

Dread and anger flush my cheeks as I retreat from the captain, missing my boring life in the cottage fields more than anything in this moment. No one made me feel worthless there.

I force myself to remember the strict instructions from the one I know loves me. And his advice is the sheer opposite. A complete contradiction from what Jude is telling me, in fact. I need to be lying low, not seeking out a fight I'll never win. At least, that's what my insides are pushing me to do. My heart flutters with the idea of fighting back, but the fear of pain within the bathing chambers, standing helpless without any rescuing keeps me grounded. Fear keeps me safe.

"Someone's told me to do the opposite. And I trust him."

I tell the captain, watching his jaw tick a second before an amused smirk tugs on the scar that cuts through his bottom lip.

He folds his arms behind his back and leans down, lower and lower, ever so slowly until his lips feel like they're only millimeters from the shell of my ear.

"And where is he now, hmm?" Quickly, his swirling blue eyes find mine, just before turning toward the rooftop exit, shaking his head.

Before the nerve leaves my body completely, I shout after him, "Why did you buy me, anyway? As some toy?"

Jude's grin is wicked as he sighs, "A toy? No. I don't like to play with my food." And he vanishes through the door.

I snag the breath I didn't know I had been holding, remembering the enormous wolf I left lying at my back and spin quickly, only to realize the deadly acolyte has vanished as well.

***

After hours of self-loathing and examining every word passed between the captain and me, I decide to finally return to my bunk to retrieve at least an hour of sleep before the horn for breakfast wakes the squad bay.

Tucking myself beneath the blanket, I doze off, my eyes heavy and laden with grief for the physical torment that awaits me indefinitely. But for now, at least I get to rest before the pain calls my name.

The abyss pulls me, my jaw going slack as muscles twitch to the relief of sleep. But as visions begin to filter through my subconscious, so too does a pair of bodiless voices—strangers arguing within the depths of my dreams.

"You must be careful. I fear she will go over the edge."

"That's the plan."

"Not in the way you intend. Delicacy is key should we become successful."

"Time will tell."

CHAPTER 9: ACOLYTES

As I suspected, another evening of torture awaits me within the bathroom. I had managed to go all day without earning the gaze of Sera or her comrades, hoping maybe they forgot about my presence, or the promise of pain. But as I trailed to the bathroom in the middle of the night, I was caught again, paralyzed while Sera took liberties by lashing into my spine with a wooden bat only the heavens must know where she got it from. She had told me this specific punishment was to prove I should never think my back is safe while sleeping here. She was correct.

The next evening, I stayed in my bunk the entire night, hoping maybe Grape could sense if footsteps were approaching, but I should have anticipated the redheaded boy, Gerjack, stealing his enhanced hearing, along with everyone else's within a fifty-foot radius of my bunk.

Sera let her newest addition inflict the punishment that night—a muscular boy named Depitrio with purple curls whose fingers turn into ropes. He had practiced lacing those ropes around my neck, cutting off my air supply over and over with a shit-eating grin and black, soulless eyes. Each time felt worse than the last as he gave me seconds to come back to consciousness before strangling me again, leaving bruised lines for all to see. Kole must not have seen my neck, though. He would have been enraged if he had.

Night after night, whether I run or hide, Sera eventually finds me and displays harsher punishment the more I resist. So, exhausted muscles and ruptured vessels after endless nights of torture. I give in. Maybe life will be easier this way.

Grape and Merry have tried intervening, but to no true avail. The directors encourage deadly behavior to eliminate the weak before the crucible, so I can't count on help in the leadership department.

One evening after Sera nearly knocked me unconscious on the shower floor, my guttural sob gave me away. Grape and Merry came rushing to my defense in the bathing chambers, but they were promptly stopped by a large boy named Asaf who had induced seizures where they stood. For once, I was terrified for their lives as I watched my friends convulse on the ground, and I never want to feel that way again.

Sera assured me my friends would join in on my punishment if I didn't leave them out of it. So, every night, I decide my fate is best served alone, and I create an excuse to keep my friends from becoming suspicious of the bruises.

Routinely, I meet my captors at the back of the bathroom once everyone has fallen asleep and someone places a sound shield within the walls. I've fallen into my own personal hell as Sera lets a new recruit try out their delta on me every night, but at least they haven't found my incense yet.

I'm glad Kole hasn't found out about my nightly torture. I know he would end it or probably get himself hurt in the process. I wouldn't want him to see me this way. He needs to focus on how he plans to get me on the train. I need to focus on not succumbing to the pain. The pain I now live with every evening.

"All bleeding stops eventually," I mumble to myself after falling face-first onto the gravel during the morning obstacle course.

Other recruits sprint past me as I groan on the ground, pretending I'm not even here.

The morning sun beats onto my sore back as I crawl to my forearms, glancing down into a puddle from the night's rain. A trickle of blood, covered with specks of black tar gravel seeps from my nose. A sliver of a scab from last week that Heath gifted me with a sharp dagger sits beside my right temple. My chin sports a greenish bruise that the dreadlocked boy named Brody gave me last night, as well as cuts up and down my arms. At least the worst of the marks sit beneath my uniform. I already have too many people staring at the visible ones, and it doesn't help when my only goal is to lie low.

Suppressing the painful groans, I make it to my feet and push forward through the obstacle course that's apparently designed to mimic the challenges we'll face during the crucible.

Grape told me the directors change up the terrain every year so the crucible is never the same, but supposedly only the strong survive. That's why fifty percent of recruits meet an early death within the phase one walls, so I've been told.

After climbing a flight of stairs that nearly leaves my battered thighs shaking, I follow behind Merry into the massive auditorium to find my seat. Only this time, we shift over desks because Aegis has claimed its first recruit.

Surprisingly, it wasn't me.

A scrawny boy named Geoff had slipped on the twenty-foot rock wall of the obstacle course a few days ago, landing directly on his neck and sending himself into a permanent sleep. The boy had only been two recruits behind me, and I know I'll never forget the sound his bones made beneath the weight of his body. At least it was over for him in seconds and not drawn out. The directors make it obvious that death during the crucible will not be so kind.

"No need for your books today, recruits." Dr. Gencavage waves a hand over the group to gather our attention, "Today is what we call Acolyte Day, so I will be handing over the floor to Mrs. Furien, who will be here any moment.

"I'm s-s-so excited for today." Merry mutters across from Grape, smiling wider than I've ever seen, "My sister told me not to get too excited for some reason, but I can't help it!" I grin as I watch her practically bounce in her chair.

"Wait," Grape throws a hand out, interrupting as he loves to do when he hears something no one else does, "Is that you?" his eyes drift to my torso, "Is that your stomach making those horrendous noises?"

"What?" I blurt.

"Wait, no. It's not." Grape sinks a little in his chair, grimacing as if he's found the culprit. His eyes drift forward to the giant recruit with a long pale braid shifting in her chair uncomfortably. Suddenly, as the crowd grows a little quieter, I can hear it too.

A loud, gurgling noise erupts from Ona's stomach, signaling the only other feeling from being out of breath that I know best. Hunger.

Other recruits twist in their seats as Ona clutches her stomach, and their judgmental gazes say they're smart enough not to prod her, but not above smirking at the thought of her being hungry. Ruthless bastards.

I remember Ona being one of the recruits who sleeps continuously through the morning breakfast horn, never getting enough to eat until dinner. Judging by the size of her gigantic frame, she can't afford to comfortably miss any meals. It must take thousands of calories just to keep her going.

"Do exactly what you would do, minus the fear." The captain's advice sinks in, and for once, it sort of makes sense. If Ona were anyone else, I would offer to help in some way because I'm no stranger to the pain of an empty stomach. But what if she tries biting the hand that feeds her? Or worse, snapping the neck that bothers her.

Clearing my throat, my hands move without thinking, digging into my cargo pockets to retrieve all twenty cracker packets I've been storing like a squirrel for winter. Ona will need much more than this, but hopefully these crackers can get her through to dinner.

Swallowing, I slip out of my chair carefully, making my way down to Ona's row as my heart lurches in my throat. *Do exactly what you would do*, I repeat to myself.

"Soria! What are you doing?" Grape snaps, but I'm too far into this quest.

Gently, I creep around the side of Ona's desk, giving her a wide enough berth that I could duck from her fists should they come flying.

Before I lose my courage, I clear my throat, meeting her gaze evenly as I stand here, and she stays seated. Ona's dangerous stare fixes on me, and before she has a chance to strangle me where I stand, I toss the pile of crackers onto her desk and leap backward out of range.

"I know it's not much, but it's all I have." My voice comes out in a pathetic rasp as I swallow the fear, analyzing her every move.

For too many heartbeats, Ona holds my gaze, seeming like she's contemplating what to do to me. All around, the room goes silent, and I realize every eye is on us.

Fuck. I hope I didn't just offend the most dangerous person in the room.

But in an instant, Ona makes a chuffing noise and breaks her gaze, tearing open cracker packets and inhaling them without giving me so much as another glance.

A sigh of relief escapes my throat as I climb back up to my seat, ignoring whatever look Grape is giving me right now. I don't have to see it, I know it's a bewildered one.

Suddenly, the attention of the room drifts in a singular direction as the door creaks open, and several crates covered by white sheets roll in, pushed by people in pearly robes I don't recognize. They leave the carts in front of the podium and a tall, lanky woman with black lipstick and apricot-colored hair curled into perfect chin-length ringlets strolls into the auditorium. Her nine-inch heels slam against the marble floor as she stares up at all of us, her black lips curving into a wicked smile.

"Well, hello all," she bows in her sweeping robe that kisses her ankles, and for the first time I notice the massive, ten foot python hugging her body as if she's its perch.

The snake's diamond-shaped head sits pointed in the direction of the closest recruit, the length of its muscled body coiled around the woman's neck, arms and torso. I shiver at the thought of it becoming irritated and squeezing too tightly.

The woman grins, outstretched bony arms with long, sparkling nails as she continues to address us, "I am the Aegis Animal Handler. You will call me Mrs. Furien, and I will call you boys and girls. *This*," she gestures to the lime green python curled against her trachea, "Is Lier. He is *my* acolyte, my *everything.* I trust you have done your reading on our history, so you already know the importance of these creatures." Her proper accent reels me in as I listen intently to every word.

Mrs. Furien's cat-like gaze sweeps the room, up every row and onto every recruit. Dr. Gencavage had given several lessons already on how acolytes are born as normal creatures until finding a delta their spirit calls to. Then, and only then, may a person try transferring a piece of their delta to that creature. If the acolyte accepts the gift, the power may be transferred in a small dose to help assist the person harboring the delta. Although acolytes are not permitted within the games, once they pick a human they will never pick again, so I've learned.

Mrs. Furien moves toward the podium, unfurling scrolls tucked within one of the shelves and pinning them to the chalkboard one by one to reveal images of creatures we've been learning about over the past month.

"Boys and girls, will someone tell me what acolyte this is?"

The animal handler motions to the first painting, earning a response from a young girl in the first row, despite Merry's eager hand shooting in the air.

"The alicorn. There are only a handful left and they reside in the plethoric ruins."

Mrs. Furien nods, her black lips spreading slightly as she moves down the row of pictured creatures.

"And this one?" She points at the scaly sea serpent that has to be larger than this entire base combined.

"The hilodraxius. It hasn't been spotted in decades, though, and there's only one alive. It lives in the Bloodletter sea."

An eager boy calls from the top of the auditorium with enthusiasm, earning a gentle nod from the animal handler who encourages him to keep reciting information about each creature.

"The antlered tiger-bear!" He shouts as Mrs. Furien gestures to the image of the enormous creature adorning snow-bleached fur and grayed stripes "There is one male left in Bachaloria, but he camouflages into his surroundings, making him impossible to find. He represents our country and brandishes our flag!"

The room pulsates with hundreds of fists striking their tables in tandem as every voice bellows with pride at the mention of our tiger-bear. I forgot what it was like to be in a Bachalorian classroom setting. The pride runs deep in our veins.

Merry grumbles next to me, "I c-could have told her th-that."

"Why don't you?"

"B-b-because th-they don't want to listen to me t-talk."

I roll my eyes at the shapeshifter, but Grape beats me to it as he leans across me, "Merry, who gives a rat's ass? Let them know!"

The animal handler points to the red-flared fowl taking up the entire scroll. Flames of feathers lie outstretched in its aged painting, and I elbow the shape shifter in the ribs before she loses her nerve.

"That's the ph-phoenix!" Merry shouts, earning every head to spin in her direction, "A m-mythological creature bb-but an important one. We-we draw all acolyte knowledge f-from the phoenix folklore." She says confidently, shooting me a wink as she embraces her moment to show off in front of every recruit. The girl knows her creatures.

"And what about this one?" Mrs. Furien smiles as she strolls to the last painting, and my blood runs cold momentarily at the sight of the massive, black wolf head.

"Fenrir."

"And where does he reside?"

"Here, Ma'am. He's c-claimed Captain Blackwell."

Instinctively, I keep my gaze trained on those dangerous orange eyes, feeling my heart race like the wolf could jump out of the painting and snap my head clean off. But he hadn't done that when I faced him last time. Probably to instill fear where it rightfully belongs. I can't imagine how powerful that beast is now that it's permanently tied to untapped aeromancy power.

Mrs. Furien's proper accent reels me back in as she says, "It is important to know the pillars of all acolytes. Before man got too haughty with their deltas, these creatures were always here, ready to assist and give their lives for a gift worthy of their souls. It is a great honor to be claimed by an acolyte, not a weakness."

The animal handler runs bony fingers along the sheet covering the farthest crate as she says, "Each of you will receive a creature that I have spent my life breeding to perfection." She pulls off the first sheet, then the second and third, revealing a couple hundred pairs of yellow-rimmed black saucers staring up at the crowd, utterly paralyzed with fear.

I purse my lips to keep from swooning over the adorable baby owls, huddled into feathered bundles as if this is the last place they want to be. And I'm sure it is.

"Can anyone tell me *why* we will be practicing with infant owlets?" Mrs. Furien arches a slender brow, pointing out someone in the front row.

"Um…" the recruit stutters a moment, "Because they're smart?"

Mrs. Furien shrugs, "That is mostly the point. Baby owls are smart, indeed, but quite impressionable. They cling to the one who cares for it and offer loyalty, making them an easy practicing point to transfer a piece of your delta to. Now," she claps her palms together, making most of the room jump, "Line up and come receive your bird. Practice begins now."

After several minutes of waiting in line, it's finally my row's turn. Grape approaches the remaining cage that Mrs. Furien stands in front of, and I can't help but notice the stiffness in his posture as he tries to lean away from the python that curiously stares him down.

The animal handler cups a fluffy baby owl between her palms, turning to Grape and ordering him to hold out his hands. I try not to chuckle as he holds the bird stiff-armed away from his body as if the tiny one could hurt him. But in an instant, the little owl fixes its giant round eyes on Grape, tilting its head in a ninety-degree angle, making Grape smile down at the small ball of fluff.

"Do we get to name it?" He asks Mrs. Furien.

She snorts, "Boy, these birds are nothing but a project to introduce you to acolytes. A *true* acolyte will give you the name its mother gave it in the womb." Her brow arches as Grape stays where he is, waiting for words he wants to hear. The woman sighs, "If you must, boy." And she waves him off.

I watched as Merry lit up seeing her little owl, tucking it against her cheek as I knew she would. A shapeshifter would never turn away any type of creature. There's no doubt in my mind Merry will bond with this little bird like no other.

Finally, as the last one in line, I step up to the cage, trying my best to ignore the massive snake fixing its deadly gaze on me. For some reason, after facing a wolf in the middle of the night and surviving, this acolyte doesn't frighten me as much.

"And you," the teacher turns to me, her hands moving to grab me one of the several owls that are left. But suddenly, the snake around her neck swings its head to her ear, hissing a terrible noise, and for a moment it seems like the animal is speaking to her. He turns his diamond-shaped head back toward me as Mrs. Furien nods.

"Ah. I see. You, girl," she stands up to her full height in those heels, towering above me with squinted eyes, "You do not possess a delta. So, this project is null for you."

I sigh, my gaze dropping to the ground in defeat. Why would I think she would give me an owl? Just another point to add to my resume, reminding everyone I am beneath them.

That damned snake told on me.

I nod, turning on my heel to head back up to my seat where I belong. But Mrs. Furien mutters, "Wait." I halt my tracks.

I watch her black lips twist into a purse as if she's thinking, just before bending over to rifle through the dozens of baby owls still huddled in the cage. Her hands sift gently through the peeping feathers until she makes a noise that tells me she has found what she's looking for.

Mrs. Furien clears her throat, holding out her cupped palms toward me with something sitting between. *Something,* indeed.

Between those bony fingers, sitting smaller than any owlet is a puny, sick-looking baby black bird. It's certainly no owl, maybe a raven or a deformed robin? It's missing half of its feathers and crust lines one of its golden eyes. Its neck cranes slightly to stare up at me, a gentle wheeze coming from its beak, clearly riddled with some type of disease. I feel terrible for the poor bird.

Mrs. Furien instructs me to take it, so I hold out my palms as she gently dumps the sickly infant into them.

"This little one didn't quite turn out like the rest during hatching, for some reason. I suspect the wrong chromosomes got crossed. But he will do okay for the purposes he will serve. Maybe."

I lift a brow at the little bird, grimacing at the snot leaking from its beak. Surely, he won't last the night.

Trying to be appreciative that she lets me feel included, I look up at the animal handler and say, "Thank you. I'll take care of him."

Mrs. Furien's expression softens for a moment before she ushers me back to my seat, facing the crowd as she runs a pointed nail across her python's chin.

Once the muttering dies down, she goes on into explaining how we will now be responsible for our birds until the crucible.

"You will feed them, watch them, train them, and most importantly, you will prepare them to assist you in the beginning portion of the crucible, for it is impossible to enter the doors without your acolyte." The teacher says, earning a collection of mutters between the recruits.

She goes on, "Though an acolyte will not be permitted during the games if you are selected as a player, it is necessary that we never forget the importance of such valuable creatures. And in any case, though you may not become as attached to this owl as it will to you, it is better that way."

Merry shoots me a worried look, her little bird nestled in the crook of her neck, seeming at home already. Oh no. *This* is why her sister had warned her not to get too excited.

Mrs. Furien lowers her gaze, and her next words do not seem to come easily, "I'm afraid the crucible is not kind to baby owlets, so that day will be their last. It is better to warn you of this now so you will not be grief-stricken when you pass the crucible and your acolyte doesn't."

A saddened hush falls over the auditorium, and I can tell no one is fond of this news. No matter how ruthless a recruit may think they are, no one wants to raise a pet only to say goodbye soon. This is devastating.

I stare down at the sick baby bird sleeping in my palm, already feeling sad for him. If nature is kind, he will go before something terrible happens during the crucible. If we even *make* it to the crucible.

***

After dinner, I forgo my shower, saving it for whatever blood I'll need to inevitably wash from my body after Sera is done with me. I hope she leaves my face alone tonight, considering my eye is finally healed from last week's sharp elbow.

I place my little baby bird into one of my boots, creating a tiny bed for him out of a sock. I had tried feeding him during dinner, but he turned his skimpy little beak away from the noodles, rye bread and even the sunflower seeds from my salad. He's a picky little thing. Or maybe he's just that sick.

Running a pinkie finger over his crusty little head, I watch his eyes drift closed as I slide the boot beneath my bunk, keeping him concealed and safe from anyone else.

The very thought of Sera or her comrades laying a finger on this poor bird infuriates me to no end, so I try to think of something, *anything* else to keep me from going ballistic.

Dammit. I've gotten attached to the acolyte already. And I don't even know if he'll survive the night with his obvious diseases.

After several hours into the night, I sit up in bed, hoping tonight's pain ends quickly.

Routinely, I head toward the bathrooms, ignoring the gentle snores of those who sleep peacefully in nearby bunks while I head to my nightly torment. I wonder if Sera will beat me herself this evening, or if she found someone new to try out their power against my flesh. Either way, it's better this happens out of sight from everyone else.

My back muscles ache in response to not having enough time to heal from previous lashings. My ribs hurt the most, seeing how that's Brody's favorite spot to land a punch. I hope it's not him tonight. His fists hurt the most.

I make my way to the back stall, looking forward to the hot shower I'll gift myself when this is all over. If I can even stand.

After an hour, heavy footsteps make their way across the bathroom tiles, rounding the corner to reveal Sera in her dark braid, Lincoln, who uses his delta to paralyze me, and of course, Brody. His black dreadlocks sit twisted in a braid behind his back, and he cracks his knuckles as Lincoln yawns, a giant grin spreading across his freckled face.

That same eerie feeling greets me again, telling me tonight will be no different than the rest, and I submit to the torture.

My heart hurts from feeling so helpless.

Sera's nasty smile makes me want to curl up and die as she hisses, "It's a full moon tonight. Do you know what that means, Zero?"

I swallow as my back meets the tiled wall, and Brody rolls his shoulders, preparing to throw his weight with practiced, precise strikes.

"It means tonight is a special occasion. This marks thirty days of punishment so far, and special occasions call for the best of treatment."

Sera's sniveling grin grows with every intent to watch me writhe. She nods her command to Brody, and my muscles prepare to lock, but nothing happens. Lincoln just stares at me with a heinous gaze—a look he's given me countless times over the past month.

Brody moves with flexed arms until he's inches away, and I have nowhere to run. I couldn't even if I wanted to. This is my life now. And I've given up.

In an instant, Brody's fist comes colliding with my side, and I fall to the ground, a terrible groan echoing off the walls, but I know not a soul can hear me. Sera has Gerjack soundproof the bathroom every night.

Rough palms grip me beneath my armpits, hauling me to my staggering feet just before another fist comes flying into the same spot against my already bruised ribs, feeling like the bones have definitely snapped in two by now.

Tears stream down my cheeks as I fight to breathe through the pain, collapsing on the wet, nasty floor again.

Those same, strong palms hoist me up again even though my body cries for mercy. But there will be none tonight.

There will never be mercy again.

Instead of slamming into my side, Brody's fist locks around my throat, shoving me into the wall as he pins me, squeezing tighter and tighter until I know I'm deep shades of purple by now.

I can't breathe. I can hardly think. My vision starts to blur, and I worry this may be the end because I have no fight left in me. I'm not like them. I'm not special, and I never will be, and I'm okay with that.

The harder Brody squeezes my throat, the closer I am to forever bliss. At least the torment will finally be over.

Suddenly, the fist collapsing my windpipe releases, and a rush of air fills my lungs as my knees slam to the ground. Brody must be done with me, saving my bag of bones for future practice sessions.

At least that didn't last too long.

As I squint through clouded vision, I make out Brody towering above, but he's not facing me. His back is turned and upon further glance, so is Lincoln's and Sera's.

What are they looking at?

My gaze drifts upward to find a recruit who stands taller than the others. *Much* taller. Their body nearly blocks the entire entrance of the bathroom, and their fists are balled, vibrating in the distance.

My eyes trail up to see the giant recruit's face, finding the only one that would strike reasonable fear amongst the other three. It's Ona. And by the twitching in her features, she is *mad.*

Sera's voice raises an octave as she takes a step forward toward the massive recruit, trying to sound peaceful with raised hands.

"Sorry, but we'll be done in a few minutes. We don't mean to get in your way." Sera says sweetly as I wheeze on the floor, watching Brody slowly move into a fighter's stance.

Ona's nostrils flare, obviously not pleased with the command she's been given. *No one* commands a recruit like Ona.

I try scrambling to my feet, but Brody turns and bares his teeth, warning me to stay down. I ignore him, using the wall as leverage to get my legs beneath me.

Quickly and painfully, Brody snatches my throat again, pinning me to the wall as his fist closes, and panic ensues.

But far off, in a low, dangerous voice, I hear Ona growl, "Drop. Zero."

Brody's neck snaps behind him, his grip loosening enough for my airways to squeeze a shaky breath through. I begin clawing at his hand, desperate for more air, but it's no use.

Sera's shrill voice echoes through the bathing chambers, "I'm sorry, but we can't do that. Now, I suggest you crawl back into your bed and mind your own business before you join her on the wall." Her tone is mocking as she phrases things for an imbecile, but Ona doesn't back down. I watch Sera's gaze flick to Lincoln who moves to flank Ona's right side.

Oh no. Sera's going to hurt her just like she hurts me.

"Run." I squeak, but I can barely hear myself as Brody's grip stiffens again.

Suddenly, Lincoln lifts his arm, angled toward Ona and the worst happens. Her body immediately freezes, except her wide eyes as they dart back and forth between Sera and Lincoln.

I can almost *see* the rage boiling beneath her skin. *No one* messes with Ona. And tonight, within the confines of this slime-ridden bathroom, she proves why.

As Sera takes a malicious step toward her enormous prey, she halts in her tracks seeing Ona's head pivot, straining against the compulsion of Lincoln's power. Her anger flares brighter, and she moves a leg with all her strength, fighting past the force that keeps her standing, until she bursts through and all hell breaks loose.

Ona charges toward Lincoln like a bull who's been royally pissed off. Her roar blasts against the walls, raising the hairs on the back of my neck as she flings toward the scrawny boy with murderous intent.

Lincoln looks terrified—no, not terrified. That word wouldn't do his expression justice. Lincoln looks like he's about to pass out from the gut-wrenching fear that drains his face of all color. He tries throwing out both arms in a sorry attempt to paralyze the freight train heading for him, but fear consumes his delta the closer Ona gets.

Brody drops me again, rushing forward to help his friend, but he's too late.

Without asking any questions, or waiting for any reply, Ona palms Lincoln's face with a giant, meaty hand, raking his face forward as he backs into a wall. In one swift move, Ona slams Lincoln's head into the tiled bathroom wall, crushing his skull beneath her palm until blood splatters gruesomely across white tiles. And in an instant, it's all over.

My hand flies to my mouth as Sera slips out of the bathroom, Brody trailing right behind in hopes of fleeing quietly. The sound of Brody puking his guts up outside the bathroom makes me feel a little better, though my ribs still ache terribly.

For a second, I fear Ona may chase them down, but she doesn't. She simply wipes her hand on her shirt, and then faces me, her enraged expression returning to her normal gruff frown.

Fear nearly takes all the way over as her giant boots make thundering noises crossing the bathroom floor to where I lie. Enormous, calloused hands help me to my feet, and my head swings upward to see the massive recruit standing over me. I gulp.

Ona grumbles, brushing off water droplets from my shoulder as I flinch in the process, "Thank you."

I blink, the wheezing finally catching up to me as my lips part and I don't know what to say. *She's* thanking *me?*

"For what?" I ask.

Ona chuffs, "For cracker." And she steps back, giving herself a wide berth before turning and marching out of the bathroom, back to bed as if she didn't just smash a kid's skull in.

My heart races as my hand finds my incense, taking a deep breath once I'm completely alone.

Alone, but alive. No one messes with Ona. And now, after that display, no one messes with me.

That ancient voice revisits me for the first time in weeks as I continue to blink away the shock. It echoes deep in my mind, sounding oddly satisfied.

"Wise."

"You should always be terrified of someone

who has nothing to lose."

-Dr. Gencavage in *Rights Of The Recruit*

CHAPTER 10: INFIRMARY

"Are you sure th-this is a good idea?"

"What if she wakes up and snaps our necks?"

"Shut up!" I whisper yell at Merry and Grape, exhaling before I lose my courage.

I'm standing ten feet from Ona's bunk, staring at her massive sleeping body as it heaves in slumber, lying spreadeagle beneath a blanket that doesn't cover even half of her. It's amazing how the wooden bunk legs are still standing.

Every morning, Ona repeatedly misses breakfast because she sleeps through the horn. No one dares to ever wake her, making her late for just about everything. I fear the directors are going to run out of patience for the strong recruit, no matter if they're scared of her or not.

Gripping the staff I fashioned out of copper poles stuffed in a closet in the back of the squad bay, I swallow my nerves, hoping for the best.

"Well, hurry up! She might have saved your scrawny ass last week but who's to say she doesn't change her mind today?" Grape exclaims, his eyes fixed tightly on Ona's chest rising and falling.

"What's the matter with you?" I snap at him, momentarily displacing my anger, but he's been cross with me all morning. And to my surprise, he retaliates quicker than I expect.

"What's the matter with *me*? I thought we were friends, Soria." Grape sneers behind Merry who tries diffusing the tension with nervous laughter.

"We are." I snarl.

"Are we?"

"What are you—"

"A friend would tell me she was still getting tortured every night!" Grape throws a hand in the direction of the bathing chambers, his voice finding a bass that's foreign to me, "You let Gerjack put a *sound shield* over you every night? What was the plan? To become a martyr? We could have saved you!"

"And you would have died." I grit my teeth, but I can't help the rise of emotion easing the tension in my shoulders, "It took Ona smashing Lincoln's skull into the wall for them to back off. I didn't want to risk your lives."

Merry steps closer to put a hand on my shoulder, sighing with pursed lips, "We know...Grape knows." She shoots a look over her shoulder, beckoning him to join us, "But w-we stick together. All three of u-us."

Grape shuffles over with his arms crossed, and a weight feels lifted off my chest for having true friends by my side as the hyperacusian places his hand on my other shoulder.

"Well, us three is about to become us *four.*" Grape tilts his head toward the snoring beast behind me.

Carefully, I find the tiny ounce of courage still wandering through my veins and hold on tight for dear life, extending the makeshift poking device. It finds her ribs, and I tap lightly, but she doesn't move. Swallowing, I poke again, this time a bit harder until her eyes pop open, bloodshot and irate.

Instantly, I jump back, along with Merry and Grape as we give Ona even more space, hiding behind another set of bunks. I watch Ona fumble out of bed, scrub a meaty palm over her face and then make eye contact with us, seeming like she's deciding whether we get to live or die.

"Why wake?" Ona demands an answer, her gaze narrowing. Maybe Grape was right. Maybe she was just repaying a favor last week by killing Lincoln and now views me as beneath her. I mean, she effectively ended my nightly abuse that I had suffered through for thirty days straight, and all I did was give her crackers. Maybe she expects me to keep my distance now.

Trying my best not to stammer, I say, "You're going to be late for breakfast." I decide against elaboration because Ona doesn't need it. Nor has she ever given the inkling that she wants it. A woman of very few words.

A couple of heartbeats linger before Ona's gaze drops and she sighs tiredly, rolling to the side of her bed and stretching her cannons for arms.

Before I can release the breath I've been holding, Ona mumbles, "You wait." And she proceeds to get dressed while tightening her braid. I give her a nod, but Merry and Grape don't dare to move a muscle. I guess we have company for breakfast.

***

Five hours of a brutal ruck run through the mud has me spent. Every muscle in my back fights against locking up, my thighs scream for mercy, and my lungs threaten to cave in on themselves with every painful step.

I, of course, fell out of the formation miles ago, succumbing to the heaviness in my chest that had begged to be relieved. But I told myself I would finish. For once, I actually didn't return to the training building last.

A squat girl named Jyn ended up dislocating her knee to the near point of breaking, causing her to crawl her way back. The directors had not cared in the slightest, and I knew they wouldn't.

I had tried lending Jyn a hand, but one look at who was coming to her aid she decided she didn't need help. She turned foolishly stoic, claiming she would never take the hand of an abomination. I suppose Sera's been working extra hard in the background, considering that's her very own nickname for me. I left Jyn in the mud.

My biggest concern, however exhausted my body may feel, is the diminishing dust left at the bottom of my incense can, signaling the end is near. I try to keep myself calm, forcing slow, deep breaths as I formulate a plan.

When we get back to the squad bay for an hour of down time before lunch, I seize my opportunity, remembering the red cross painted on glass doors on the far west wing of the training building. If that doesn't signal medicine, I don't know what else would. There's no way the Aegis President wouldn't have some type of miracle doctor staff on standby for his precious players. They cost too much not to tend to even a splinter.

Before I start my venture in hopes of retrieving a fresh can in secret, I check on my little baby bird to make sure he's still alive. Merry's owl has been thriving under her care, soaring through the squad bay day and night and was one of the first ones to fly. Grape's owlet just learned to fly in short, brief distances last night, but it's a step in the right direction. Almost every other infant owl has shown great improvement in how they'll assist their recruit during the crucible… except for mine.

My nameless, sickly bird has hardly eaten a thing in the past week, and even those small bits of vegetation I got him to eat had to be force-fed, as well as water. Every day it seems he loses more feathers and his breathing grows shallower, signaling the end is coming for the poor guy. It's the worst thing I've had to witness, and I've watched Ona smash a kid's skull like a tomato.

"Have you tried worms?" Merry asks over my shoulder as I stare down at my baby bird sleeping inside my pillowcase. He seems to enjoy resting out of sight, and I don't blame him.

I give her a defeated nod, "I've tried everything you said. Worms, ants, seeds and nothing works. He just seems to be getting worse." My heart feels heavy for the defenseless creature. Never mind the fact that he'll never be able to fly and help me during the crucible—he doesn't deserve to live like this. It's too depressing to watch.

Merry places a hand on my shoulder, trying her best to be comforting as she strokes her owlet's head with a single finger, "Well, all I know is, if I were sick, I wouldn't want to be alone."

I give her a nod, understanding that any second could be this little guy's last, and for some reason, I know the word *grief* will feel like an understatement the moment that happens.

I've grown too fond of this diseased bird.

I decide my grief would be easier to manage if I'm with him in his last moments rather than coming back to the squad bay and seeing he's passed all alone. So, I rip my pillowcase using my teeth and fashion a cross-body sling for him. There's nothing in the handbook about our acolytes leaving the squad bay, so I decide if today is his last, I prefer we spend it together.

Very carefully, I place my baby bird inside the dark sling, which he seems to blend into, covering his body just so his tiny beak peeks out for fresh air against my chest. He nestles in, his little chest heaving ever so slightly to show he's as comfortable as he will get, and I slip through the squad bay doors, unnoticed.

Ten minutes of wandering through the massive corridors roll by as I try to remember which set of staircases lead where. Finally, I reach those familiar glass doors with the red crosses. The word *Infirmary* sits boldly across the front, confirming my suspicions of what lies beyond. I swallow my fear, pushing past the doors gently in hopes of not being spotted by one of Sera's minions.

The high ceilings are supported by polished, cream walls and more artwork of past Aegis players. I cross the quiet checkered tile toward a front desk manned by a woman with a pinched nose and several stacks of manila folders before her.

Clearing my throat, I catch her gaze and spill my request before I lose the nerve.

"Hello there," I try to sound pleasant, "I was wondering if I could be seen by a doctor? Or maybe even a pharmacist?" My voice comes out shaky as the woman peers over her pile of paperwork, looking me up and down with a disgusted frown.

She sighs, "The Aegis Physician does not attend to *recruits*—nor will he ever. Come back after tethering." She dismisses me with a perfectly manicured wave, and that bubble of hope in my chest deflates faster than it arrived. If I don't get more powder soon, I'm as good as dead by the next training session. My lungs will never hold up against the excessive usage.

Before I give up, my eyes wander to the doors behind her, and perhaps the medication that may lie within closed cabinets. Thievery may be punishable by death here, but if I don't try something, I'll face the same fate soon enough. I just need a distraction.

It's as if the heavens have finally decided to show me mercy, because just as my mind begins to clamber for an idea to lure the woman away from her post, another woman dressed in a Bachalorian blue nurse's attire comes flying through the double doors behind us. She tells the receptionist to clear a path in the infirmary, claiming a level two orthopedic trauma is heading in, whatever that means. In an instant, it's like they've both forgotten my presence completely as they fumble to move carts and gather supplies.

I seize my opportunity while it lasts.

Careful not to jostle the sleeping baby bird against my chest, I slip through the doors to the infirmary to find a squad bay more massive and more illustrious than the one I sleep in every night. There must be over one hundred white-sheeted cots lined in two rows for the injured and sick—as if there would ever be enough players to fill them. Massive, glorious skylights brighten the clean room with the afternoon sun, warming the space with a golden-tinted glow.

I dart down the aisle toward the unmarked door that I'm hoping holds shelves of medications. I know what I'm looking for. I just need to find it.

Quietly, I close the door behind me just as the two women from the front burst through on the opposite end of the bay to prepare a cot for whoever is about to come in. I turn around fully expecting to see vials of medication but I'm promptly disappointed to find myself stuck in a janitor's closet. Mops and brooms line the walls, along with several other cleaning tools, and frustration rises.

But before I have the chance to come up with a new plan, the closet door opens behind me and an older man with salt and pepper hair and sun-kissed weathered skin strolls in carrying a toolbox. His gaze stays focused on the floor as he sets his box down and moves closer to grab a stack of clean linen sitting on the shelf.

Holding my breath, I back up farther, my ankles suddenly hitting a metal bucket behind me, making the man's neck snap upward in fright. His dull, blue eyes find mine, a wrinkled hand flying to his chest as he catches his breath.

"Young lady!" He scolds, cocking his head as he continues to take deep breaths to calm a racing heart, "What on the heaven's green patch of land do you think you're doing?" His eyes finally adjust behind rounded spectacles that remind me of Dr. Gencavage's, and he looks me up and down, his gaze shifting to something that reminds me of understanding. He wears a gray utility jumpsuit, soaked with various stains that must be the result of years of hard work. A little cursive name tag on his chest labels him *Ivar.*

Defensively, and without thinking, one of my hands crawls over the sleeping baby bird against my chest as I try to think of a good reason for being here that won't result in my immediate death. Recruits aren't allowed to freely roam the training building, and they're certainly not allowed to break into the infirmary on a whim.

"I... I was just..." My mind goes blank, but the old man sighs, his hand grasping the doorknob behind him and he closes us in, concealing me from whoever may pass by.

"I know what you were doing, recruit. Sit down." He gestures to the flipped metal bucket behind me, not giving me an option. I take a seat, watching carefully as he digs through a hole-patched chest pocket to pull out a roll of white gauze and a tube of antiseptic ointment.

He crosses the shadowed space between us, kneeling with a grunt. I stay completely silent, my right hand still pressed against the sling to hide my bird.

"Give it here," the man says motioning to my left hand. I drop it as he pulls on my wrist, flipping my arm to reveal a six-inch laceration that's slightly scabbed. I hadn't even realized I'd been cut, but the memory of tripping along the muddy path this morning greets me. I must have gotten hurt then.

The man cleans my wound with shaky hands, revealing yellow pus that lies beneath the scab, signaling infection is on its way.

"I'm sorry if this hurts." He mumbles, his smile slightly twitching, reminding me of my brother Jon every time he would tend to his twin's bashes and bruises. Kiersik was always the wilder one of the two.

Finally finding the words, I respond, "It doesn't hurt. I didn't even know it was there." And that's the truth. I suppose I have Sera to thank for thirty days of physical abuse for a cut not to bother me in the slightest. My body's pain threshold must have spiked in order to keep me sane.

The man instructs me to hold the gauze to my arm as he leans back on his knee to stare me in the eyes. He could certainly be my father's age, and the way he tends to me with care almost forces a sense of parental trust. If only that ancient voice my subconscious created would visit me now to tell me if I should trust him or not, that would make things a lot easier.

"It's such a shame they refuse to treat recruits. Just leave you to suffer until eventually you die from infection or some other terrible reason. You're people too." The janitor's eyes wander my face, drifting to my makeshift sling until his lips purse and he nods, a small smile curving his lips as if he's come to a revelation of his own.

"Ah. I see now. I was wondering when we would meet. You're the one everybody keeps talking about." He says with a nod. Confusion furrows my brow as he goes on, "You are the one without a delta. The one who earned the favor of Ona The Beast, a shapeshifter and a dying acolyte."

"How do you know that?" I ask, pushing a blond strand away from my face. It's probably not good news that my name has traveled around base already.

The man scoffs, "It's easy to know everything that goes on around here when you're the janitor." He taps against his name tag, "Name's Ivar, and I assume they call you Soria Davidsdottir?"

"Mostly they call me zero." I try not to sound so defeated but it's nearly impossible when every force of nature is rooting against me here.

Ivar *tsks,* his eyes finding mine, "Don't you know only the best of players go by their number? True, there has never been a player who holds that number zero, considering some have said it's a cursed one, but perhaps it isn't cursed. Perhaps it was too sacred to give to anyone but the right player." His thick brows raise, accompanied by a thoughtful smile, and for the first time in a while, I smile back. That act of decency is all I need. Trust it is.

Taking a leap of faith, I slowly pull out the incense can that's been through hell and back already, flipping it over in my palm for the janitor to see. He peeks through his glasses until he presents another understanding nod.

"You're almost out. Have you shown anyone this?" He asks, and I shake my head. "Good. Keep it that way for as long as you can." Ivar's gaze unforces as if rummaging through his mind for an answer. There's something so familiar in those eyes I can't place.

"Do they have any here?" I ask, shoving the can back in my pocket. I have no doubt he already knows how dire my situation is. Weak lungs aren't becoming of a player, no matter if I'll never hold the title.

The janitor sighs, "I'm not sure. But if they do, I'll find it." He assures me, examining the laceration on my arm again and taking away the gauze. He digs in his chest pocket and hands me several antiseptic wipe packets, "Keep these hidden too. You'll need to keep that cut clean for a week but if anyone finds out they'll get you for stealing. I don't agree with it, but recruits aren't allowed any medical treatment until they've tethered."

I nod at his instructions, shoving the wipes deep in my cargo pockets against my can and cracker packets, all of my little secrets I keep on my person.

"Thank you. For everything." I mutter, offering him the same genuine smile he's gifted me, and he tips an imaginary hat, his kind eyes telling me thanks is not necessary.

"I used to be in the medical game decades ago, but I'm afraid hand tremors are not kind for surgery anymore." Ivar raises a palm level with the ground to show me his shaky hand before gripping his pockets and standing up with a grunt, "But anyhow, keep those packs hidden and I'll find you if I get my hands on a refill. And use that powder sparingly. Only in the most dire of times, you understand?"

I nod, thanking him again for his kindness when it's not something I've come across easily, and follow him quietly and quickly out of the utility room. We take a left down a dark hallway that leads to another exit to avoid whatever ruckus is about to unfold within the infirmary.

Ivar mutters as he holds the door open to the corridor leading away from the medical wing. "Get to lunch before your absence is noticed." He mutters, and a bubble of hope swells in my chest. Not only have I made a new friend, but a friend who has helped me out of the kindness of his heart.

The door closes behind me before I can thank him again, and I set off for the chow hall, hardly noticing the disaster sweeping toward me.

My eyes fling upward to see a redheaded woman lying limply between strong arms, her face twisted in pain as she groans while being bridal carried. The tall man carrying her wears polished shoes, perfectly pleated dark slacks and an ivory buttoned-up dress shirt with golden lapels. Once my gaze finds his face, it all makes sense. That dark, short hair compliments the stubble against his tanned skin, along with beautiful, swirling blue eyes with brows that are creased in concern toward the woman lying between his arms. Why is he so concerned for her? Why does he look at her that way?

Jude doesn't detect me as he rushes by, laying the redheaded woman on a cot that has suddenly emerged through the glass doors, accompanied by several nurses ready to go.

"Get the physician. Her femur is broken in three places." The captain orders the nurses who nod attentively, nearly bowing in his presence.

My neck cranes as my steps slow to watch Jude's hand find the woman's, stroking her wrist gently with a mumbled promise that she'll be okay.

She's gorgeous in a fascinating way. Something about her features is so beautiful, it's enthralling. Her lips are full, and her hair is shiny and clean, complementing emerald eyes and no doubt a toned body beneath players' dress blues that hug every curve perfectly.

And now the uniform makes sense.

Of course she's a player. Only players have that rough, ethereal beauty that causes the masses to swoon by their very presence. Kole told me it's something about being tethered that enhances a person's physical attributes to relay their power. I never believed him before, claiming it all sounded very ostentatious, but seeing a pair of players now in the flesh, it makes sense. Even Bachaloria's most acclaimed model couldn't compare to the beauty of a tethered player— though I can't begin to imagine how the untethered captain could look more ethereal than he already does. I wonder if he would ever claim a partner.

Gritting my teeth and trying to ignore the way Jude looks at her, I brush off this weird feeling that tries to scatter my brain. But before I have the sense to keep walking, Jude turns on his heel, his gaze finding mine and he halts in his tracks, his mouth slightly parted as he stares at me several yards away.

I swallow, a protective hand flying to my sleeping baby bird as I take another step backward, hoping he doesn't tell on me for wandering the halls when I'm supposed to be in the chow hall. Or worse, handle me himself.

Jude's gaze searches my body and he takes a step forward, but I retreat first, turning swiftly down the hall and slipping past another set of doors.

I scoff to myself, realizing I've actually *run* away from the captain of this entire base. Why do I do these things to myself?

CHAPTER 11: NAMES

I'm able to eat lunch easily enough without Grape and Merry questioning me. Minus my baby bird, we have a new companion who joins us for meals, sitting beside me instead of her usual seat in solitude on the far end of the chow hall. Ona's presence keeps the dangerous recruits away, but it certainly doesn't hinder their stares, whether they're judgmental of her or flat-out frightened. I enjoy her company either way.

Another long orientation class drags on, taking up the entire afternoon with the subject of crucible beasts and terrain. Supposedly last year was one for the record books in casualties, seeing how the directors decided the crucible should be held atop a mountain while they unleashed a fifty-ton dragon upon the poor recruits. My chances would already be slim within those walls, but anything sounds like a higher probability of survival than a fire-breathing monster with wings.

After dinner, the cooks set out leftovers from the previous week which no one ever touches. I, on the other hand, take delight in stuffing my pockets with bagged remains of yesterday's breakfast, looking forward to my midnight snack already. We aren't allowed to harbor food outside the chow hall for fear of pests or whatever dumb reason the directors find to strip our humanity, but I need all the extra food I can get. With Sera finally off my back, I have a chance to gain some real weight and cure these malnourished limbs of mine. I just hope no one demands I empty my pockets because if they do, I'm so fucked.

Slipping off my boots for the evening, I gently take my sickly baby bird out of his sling, which I do reluctantly. He looks so peaceful it's hard to move him, but I create a soft bed for him out of my sock inside my pillowcase, which he nestles into gratefully, giving me a tiny wheeze, as if showing his appreciation.

Just as I'm about to follow Grape into the bathing chambers to brush my teeth, a tall figure marches over to stand above me, arms crossed and body stiff. I lean out of my bunk to tell Ona I'm coming. But my jaw nearly drops to the floor to see the only other person on this entire base I could confuse Ona's size with. Jude Blackwell.

The *captain.* Who is standing above me. In the recruit squad bay.

I'm either about to die or I'm dead already. I pray to the heavens he doesn't ask what's in my pockets.

Raw, unsolicited terror lances through my body like wildfire as the entire bay falls silent to a recruit's voice yelling, *Attention on deck!*

I should be standing, giving the captain my full respect, but fear keeps me hiding beneath him in my bunk as if this fortress could offer me some sort of protection.

The endless possibilities play on a loop as I wait for my sentence. Though the notion is a leap, Jude Blackwell has already given me advice on how to survive, and if he wanted to kill me, I'm sure he would have done it already. Or maybe he's mad no one else has succeeded in that endeavor yet.

I swallow, registering the harsh look in his eyes and find the courage to speak. "How can I help you?" I regret the snide words as soon as they leave my mouth. A few gasps strike around the squad bay, signaling my response is certainly not how someone addresses the captain before me, but his expression doesn't waver.

"Don't ever run from me again." He says coldly. A warning.

The memory of slipping away after watching him handle the redheaded woman in the hallway arises. The unreadable look on his face when I had turned and fled. I definitely ran, but why? Probably because I'm scared of him. I was scared he would ask why I wasn't in the chow hall. That's why. I think.

I swallow. "I didn't run."

Jude's brow arches, his arms shifting tighter against his chest as he stares me down. He's traded his white button-up for an indigo one this evening.

"Yes, you did. You…" he pauses, as if realizing he's about to enter into an argument with someone as insignificant as a recruit. Even worse, a deltaless recruit.

Jude's arms shift as his voice carries across the squad bay, addressing the entire room with one deep command, "At ease." And the rest of the room carries on, but not as careless as before. Their attention is still on the scene he's creating.

The captain shakes his head, backing up toward the exit with his perfect posture, but not before giving me a command of his own.

With two simple fingers, he waves them at me in a come-hither motion, beckoning me to follow out of the squad bay.

I don't dare run from him this time.

Grape's eyes flash to me, giving me a wild look that asks a million questions but all I can offer him is a shrug. I don't even know how I keep finding myself alone with the captain. Now that he's personally singled me out again before every discerning eye, I know the target on my back has just grown bigger.

I slip out of the doors to find Jude standing at the bottom of the stairwell that eventually leads to the roof. Obeying his silent order, I walk past him and climb higher and higher as he trails behind me. Maybe he means to lead me to the roof so he can kill me in private. But wouldn't he have done that the last time?

I just hope there's no wolf waiting for me this time.

My mind reels with questions as I walk toward the lip that overlooks the sea, the summer breeze tossing my hair and sending goosebumps along my arms. A very faint orange hue still illuminates the sky, allowing me to make out valleys and dips within the base I hadn't been able to see under the cover of night all those weeks ago. It's beautiful from up here. So beautiful I almost forget the looming captain behind me.

Whirling around, I level Jude with an equal stare, keeping a smart distance this time. I want to ask him what he wants with me, but I won't be the first to speak.

His hands casually find his pockets as he leans against the ledge several feet away. I note how he offers me space this time. "What were you doing at the infirmary?"

I quickly find an excuse, remembering the cut across my arm and present it a little too flippantly, "I got hurt."

The laceration doesn't faze Jude. He doesn't even glance at my arm as he shakes his head, "You've endured worse. It wasn't for a slice in your forearm, so don't lie to me, recruit."

My brows shoot to the sky as my hands find my hips, fixing him with an indignant glare.

I want to tell him of course I've endured worse, because of *him!* Every last recruit wants to impress the captain in hopes of sharing his power or becoming his shadow or whatever. So I will always be the one who suffers in the background because of *him!*

But of course I don't say this. I've learned Jude is the enemy, not an ally. And releasing my anger on him won't get me home any sooner.

I shake my head, sticking to my story, "I'm not lying. My arm was infected."

"You expect me to believe," Jude sighs, moving a step closer as if he can't help himself from showing dominance. "After enduring strangulation, fractured ribs, muscle tears, and swelling, that you snuck into the infirmary for a cut on your arm?"

"Yes." I back up a step, expanding the space he's slowly closing, narrowing my glare.

A needle-like knife slices into a piece of my heart as I come to the conclusion that he's been aware of my nightly tortures all along. And he didn't do anything to stop it. But why would he? He wanted that. He encouraged that behavior. I hate him all the more for it.

I watch his jaw tick, and those lips of his purse at my blatant lie, but I'll never give up my secret. Not when he would slip that information to Sera without a second thought. That knowledge in her hands would be deadly for me.

"Fine, don't tell me. I'll find out one way or another. But the crucible is in fifty days." Jude's chest heaves with a deep breath and my expression changes into disbelief. *Obviously* the crucible is in fifty days. It's not like it's the only thing keeping me awake at night, marking the day I most likely take my last breath.

"*And?*" I throw my hands up, indignation taking over rational thought for who I'm speaking to. But I can't help it.

He doesn't deserve one nice word.

"*And* you're nowhere near ready. You fall out of every hike and can't carry your own weight. You'll be alone on that field. No one will be there to save you from whatever creature they toss in there."

I grit my teeth at his lecture because I know I'm weak, and it doesn't help that he's rubbing it in. Even though I've been able to get more rest out of the hands of Sera, I'm still not comparable to even the slowest recruit. My lungs give out too easily and my limbs don't have enough muscle. I haven't exactly been training my entire life for this, unlike every other person thriving on the training mats. But I haven't given up yet. The fear of dying a horrible, painful death won't let me give up.

"Well lucky for you and everyone else, I don't need saving."

I expect Jude to snarl and lash out. I expect him to throw another insult at my face because it wouldn't be the first time since the day he bought me that I've felt less than desirable.

I brace myself for a painful blow in response to such disrespectful behavior, but what he does next alters my brain chemistry, flipping my world and nearly throwing me off balance.

He *smiles.*

No teeth, and not mocking. A real, genuine smile that makes my knees weak for all of the wrong reasons. Why is he smiling at me like that?

The captain sighs, his hands hanging loose in his pockets while the dwindling sunset warms the left side of his face, and the smile disappears quicker than it arrived.

"No, Soria. You don't need saving. And you should always tell yourself that."

I back up a step, my body retreating as it's grown accustomed to doing for some reason in his presence. "I should get back… to my bird." Is all I can say because I don't know what else to say. I wonder if he's ever smiled at that redheaded girl that way.

Jude nods, his gaze studying me as per usual, "In two weeks, President RoBjorn is going to grant every recruit permission off base for the evening."

"I know." I say, wondering what cryptic point he's trying to make now.

"Don't leave those walls." He orders, or at least, I *think* he orders. I'm not sure if he's allowed to take that privilege away from me. The privilege I certainly earned. But before I can protest, he follows up with, "It should be common knowledge that over half of the recruits here want you dead. Out there you'll only tempt their behavior more once the tavern is involved. Don't think you can hide behind The Beast. Her privilege has been taken away by the directors for being late to every formation."

My heart sinks once I realize he's talking about Ona. If I'm being honest with myself, I was looking forward to my time alone with Kole, off base and away from all of this. Who is Jude to tell me what I can and can't do? When have I ever been one to follow the rules? Adaptation has become my middle name.

The captain searches my face, probably realizing I'm not giving into his advice, and his eyes narrow. "I mean it,
Soria."

"Don't say my name like that." I blurt, crossing my arms defensively and finding something to release this pent-up anger on. Lately, it's been Jude.

"Like what?" His head tilts like a dog.

"Like you care. We both know this is a numbers game for you. A probability of matches that could win you the game. So do me a favor and keep my name off your lips."

His grin is devious. Bloodthirsty.

"Why are we talking about my lips?" Those eyes cloud over, raking down my face with a purpose I can't figure out. The likelier option is to mess with my head or taunt me in some way because Jude Blackwell holds only disdain for me and my very existence. He's made that clear.

I avert my gaze and do the only thing I know when my temperature rises this high around him.

I retreat.

Straight for the staircase without saying another word. My palms feel so sweaty as they grip the steel rail.

Jude's voice echoes down the stairwell as I skip steps to get away from him.

"And for fuck's sake, name your bird already!"

***

"Hey Grape?" I whisper quieter than even I can hear, knowing those ears of his will pick up every word clear as day.

Spiky black hair flings over the mattress above my bunk, "Yeah, blondie?"

I smirk, my voice hardly audible as the other recruits snore in the distance, "What did you name your owl?" My hand sits within my pillowcase, my index finger resting against my baby bird's chest just to feel the barest movement for proof of life.

Jude's words have been ricocheting around my mind all night, and I can't escape the clear advice he's laid out. If he were anyone else, I'd laugh at the thought of dismissing the plans I've been looking forward to. But for some reason, it feels wrong to ignore his words. Like something deeper in my mind is pulling me toward his directions and to stray would cause more harm than good.

Grape chuckles, "I named him Apple. It compliments Grape, I suppose."

I snort at his ridiculousness, digging in my pockets to retrieve my midnight snacks and carefully unwrapping the breakfast.

"You know, you never told me how you got your nickname, *Ty Yang.*" I giggle, pulling out a stack of day-old pancakes smushed into crumbs. I lie on my stomach and enjoy every bite.

"You never told me why you brought a viola to an auction."

"A *violin.*" I mutter, though the smile still reaches my mouth. I think about telling Grape the entire story every day. How I was going to run away with Kole and leave behind the depressing life that never offered me anything. How I was knocked unconscious, made a new friend and then watched her die seconds later on the auction stage. I contemplate telling him about my incense, and how long Sera tortured me and the weird feelings between words with Jude that make me forget I have someone here I love. Or someone I think I love. I decide against all of it to spare my friend the sob story. As my late friend Hera had said, there are those who go through worse I suppose.

Before I can respond to Grape, shaggy, blond hair crouches by my face, startling the crap out of me. I almost choke on a piece of pancake until I realize it's Kole staring back at me, and utter joy washes over me in an instant.

"Kole!" I fling my arms around his neck, pulling him in tight. I've barely seen him the past few weeks, and for a moment there, I felt myself drifting away from him, afraid he was forgetting about me. But seeing those beautiful eyes and those boyish dimples brings me right back. He's always cared about me.

"I don't have a lot of time, but I have to ask you something." Kole whispers against my ear, and I sigh into his familiar scent. I've missed him so much.

"Anything." I mutter, never wanting to let go, but Kole leans back to look me in the eyes. "What did Captain Blackwell want?" I swear I hear Grape snort above us.

My lips part in disbelief, and for the first time in my entire life, *I* pull away from Kole. He hasn't spoken a word to me for reasons he thinks are keeping me safe, and the first time he has the opportunity it's to retrieve information about the *captain* of this base?

"What?" Kole asks, his eyes wandering my face.

"That's what you want to know?" My voice quivers.

"Obviously I want to know how you're holding up, but we don't have much time." I fight the threatening tears in my eyes, "Sunday night I'm getting you out of here. I spoke with a girl who knows her way around the outlying city, and she can get you on the train. So, tell me, Sor, what did Captain Blackwell say? Did it have anything to do with our leave? Or me?"

I can almost taste the desperation oozing off Kole. Desperation for something other than me—and I don't know how I hadn't seen it before, but every sign was right in front of me. The locked front door to his house. The bags that were never packed. The *fucking blazer* he wore the night I leaped into his arms after the auction. His uninterrupted nights of sleep while I got tormented twenty feet away. He never planned on running away with me. Becoming a player was always his dream. In an attempt to formulate a sufficient response, I force the smile I always present him with, squeezing his hands and blinking away the mist.

"All he said was he's very impressed with you." The lie hurts my soul as I grit out every word, but it doesn't hurt nearly as bad as Kole's enormous smile, confirming every last suspicion I have.

"Sor, this is amazing!" He whisper-yells, pulling my face toward his to brush a kiss to my lips. A kiss I now loathe.

"Think about it," his eyes shimmer, darting around as he thinks out loud, "My friend has the routes to all the trains, so by Sunday I'll get you on the fastest one, safe and sound. Then after I make it to tethering, the captain *has* to choose me. There's no way he wouldn't, especially if he's been impressed with me. This is so great!" Not a word about how he'll visit me after or create a life with me in the foreground. Perhaps that's what I've always been to him. Something to pass the time until the fame and glory arrived. I'm such an idiot, and yet, I suppose this was always a terrible truth I kept tucked away.

He pulls me in again for another kiss, this time long and hard, his hand roving up my thigh but I don't want it anymore. The boy I knew, the boy I *loved* disappeared before I met him on the grassy hilltop. But I don't have it in me to fight with him tonight. Or any other night.

Pulling away from the first kiss he's initiated in months, I force another smile, choosing to plan now and act later. I just have one burning question I need answered to seal Kole's fate before I continue with the charade.

"I can't wait for Sunday," I grin through the fib, "But I just have one question. What's your friend's name who knows about the trains?"

Kole runs a hand through his sandy, shoulder-length hair, offering a genuine smile as he says, "Oh, her name's Sera. She's really nice and I think you two would actually get along, you know… if you were staying." His smile falters, and I nod.

Every last puzzle piece has fallen directly into place.

I hang on tighter to my own words, engraving them into my brain as if to highlight my life's mantra from here on out.

I don't need saving.

I give Kole a tight nod, trying to look as grateful as possible as he brushes his lips to my cheek, telling me good night. Just like that, every last ounce of love I've harbored for the past decade for this single man vanishes as if it never existed. A massive space sits empty in my heart with nothing to fill that void in sight.

A single tear burns down a hot cheek as I fall deeper and deeper into a dangerous pit with nothing in sight to pull me out.

But just before I fall over the edge, that ancient voice warms my skin with a single sentence that helps me breathe easier. *"You are stronger now."* And I think I believe it.

Sighing, I brush away the tears and set aside my dying feelings for Kole. I'm going to need as much rest as possible if my new plan for survival is going to work, because running away is no longer an option. *Especially* if Sera already has her hand in it.

Lying prone beneath my covers, I peel back a corner of my pillowcase to see my baby bird's head resting peacefully, his diminishing dark feathers blending in with the shadows surrounding us.

I offer him a tiny piece of sausage, but he turns his beak away, clearly not impressed. I shake my head, nudging the only other food item I have, a chunk of maple pancake, fully expecting this little sassy fowl to scoff at my offer.

My jaw drops when I watch his head twist to stare directly at the bread, his beak opening quickly and tearing off a piece for himself. My heart almost stops to see him go back for another bite. And another.

"Grape!" I try not to squeal, and his head flings over the side. "He's eating! He's eating the pancake!" I can already feel Grape's eye roll from four feet above, but I don't care. We're a step in the right direction.

I run a finger over his tiny, crusty head, offering him a capful of water that he decides to gulp down to my surprise.

A smile tugs on my mouth as I chuckle at him. A smile I had no idea I would still be able to manage. "I guess you're Pancake."

CHAPTER 12: GOLDEN PASS

The morning sun beats down on the courtyard, warming the grass that crunches beneath my feet as I roll my shoulders, soaking up the rays and grateful for a break.

Today has everyone giddy because we've all received our passes to leave base for the evening. Well, everyone except for Ona. She took the news rather well, though. Only two sets of bunks suffered her wrath when she was delivered the message. I had made a mental note to myself that I wouldn't let her be late again, and even though I've decided to stay on base as part of my long-bulleted plan for survival, I don't think the directors would allow her to take my pass even if I tried.

I stand in my usual place in the back of the formation next to Grape, except I have a tiny shadow with me.

Pancake wheezes against my chest, snuggled into his sling because I can't stand the thought of leaving him alone all day, no matter whether he's made an improvement in eating or not. He still sleeps too much and is losing too many feathers for my liking.

A creaking noise pulls my attention, causing me to squint in the distance as the tall double doors open to the rounded courtyard lined by pearly pillars. One by one, the directors, followed by a myriad of important Aegis officials, pass through the doors sporting haughty gleams in their eyes. They know something we don't.

The team of officials take center stage on a cement platform, looking down on us with arms folded behind their backs.

Intimidating silence stretches for a few heartbeats until the older gentleman I know as the President enters. He is followed closely by a muscular man I don't recognize, the beautiful redheaded woman I remember from the infirmary, and… Jude. There he is in his typical three-piece suit and dark sunglasses acting like this formation is beneath him, which it most certainly is.

The massive, muscular man I have never seen before flanks the President's left side as they take the center of the platform. Besides his face, it appears his entire body is covered in dark tattoos symbolizing vague shapes that become more confusing the more I concentrate. A wicked scar sits carved into his forehead, bright against his dark skin and black, slicked-back hair that tucks behind his ears and loops into a single braid. He folds his arms against his chest, and for the first time, I believe I've found someone bigger than Jude. Hell, bigger than Ona. Where do they make these men?

The tall redhead next to him is just as beautiful as I remember. Her sharp features remind me of something animalistic with the way she switches her ever-shifting gaze across the courtyard. Besides several jagged scars along her neck, her porcelain skin is spotless and glowing, complementing shoulder-length, fiery red hair that shines in the sunlight.

Both of these strangers wear variations of Bachalorian blue and dark cargo pants, signaling they're always ready for battle, but not Jude.

The captain stands tall in a charcoal suit with golden cufflinks and polished shoes made of some reptile hide. Every dark-chocolate strand of hair is styled to perfection, complimenting a hidden, glacial gaze while the gleam of those silver rings blinds any eye that focuses too heavily on his hands.

The warriors standing next to the captain radiate beauty and sheer danger, no doubt, but they are nothing compared to the presence on the President's right-hand side. Jude's entire persona illuminates the very image no one would ever argue, since the day he presented himself to the world.

Power.

The leader of Aegis rubs dry hands together as he addresses the entire courtyard, straightening a single silver pin in a long row along his chest, "Recruits, good morning. I trust you are enjoying your time away from the training fields?"

Several voices joyously lift to the sky in unison, showing the President that his gift of respite is more than appreciated. This brings the barest hint of a smile to the leader's face.

"Very good, but let me remind you," he pulls a black card from his breast pocket that is identical to the passes we all received to get off base tonight, "This pass is effective from zero twenty to zero eight, starting tonight. You will be present for tomorrow morning's formation, or you will be found and executed for treason." RoBjorn's expectant gaze sweeps across the courtyard, and a shiver runs up my spine. So much for that ridiculous plan of escaping on a train, even if I dismissed the idea days ago.

Dr. Gencavage had warned us in a previous class that Aegis officials take one bylaw more seriously above all others in the ordinance, and that would be exposure to the team's secrets. Everything we learn in class, down to the way we brush our teeth, is forbidden to be shared, repeated, or displayed outside our base walls. The act is punishable by death— which is why failure to return to base on time is taken so seriously. Aegis only shares what they want the public to know during tours before the King's circuit.

President RoBjorn slides the black card back into his pocket, retrieving another, but in the shade of gold.

"However, because I always have an interest in rewarding the best, I will offer everyone the opportunity to secure an additional eight hours of freedom." He flips the golden pass between his fingers while several spines straighten, listening intently to the competition ahead. "Only one may receive this pass, but everyone will try."

I shoot Grape a raised brow, but he shrugs back, showing he's just as blindsided as I am. This is the last thing anyone would expect.

President RoBjorn clears his throat, "As a majority, you will choose one person within this courtyard to hold the golden pass. All you must do is take it from them. Should you be successful, you may leave immediately and skip the six-mile hike that will take place following this formation."

My stomach drops. The easiest choice for anyone is obvious. I have no way to hold my own against a single person here, marking me once again as a simple target for display.

I watch the recruits ahead of me give sideways glances to those around them, some whispering to others and passing along their thoughts until it seems the group has reached a collective decision without involving the back row in the slightest.

"Oh no," Grape mutters beside me as I fully face him, panic setting in behind my eyes.

I'm not prepared to be publicly humiliated, let alone possibly beaten before the entire courtyard. Would everyone have to take their turn on me? I can only imagine the look on Sera's face when she throws a right hook, grinning before her audience.

"Grape," I squeeze his elbow, watching his gaze dart around the recruits ahead of us as he listens to their whispers, "Is it me?" I swallow.

His breath falters as he shakes his head, and a sigh of relief soothes the anxiety threatening to make my breakfast reappear. It's not me.

"Who is it, then?" I ask, but before he answers, a short boy from the front row steps forward to address the President on our behalf.

"Who have you chosen, recruit Isakson?"

The boy answers loud enough for the entire courtyard to hear, swinging a finger to the player standing off to the side with his hands casually in his pockets, "We pick Captain Blackwell, sir."

My palm finds my forehead. This is so much worse.

CHAPTER 13: CHALLENGES

"Why would they pick him?" My voice is softer than a breeze, but I know who can hear me.

"Well, there goes my chance at all-day freedom."

"Grape!" I mutter.

He sighs dramatically, forever put out by having to explain what I don't know. "Isn't it obvious? They aren't thinking of the prize. They're thinking bigger."

"What could be bigger than twenty-four hours of doing whatever you want?"

It's not like anyone in the company has free will anymore, and some of us are surviving by a thread in our socks. A moment of peace might be nice, even if it wouldn't be smart for me to take it.

I watch Jude's smirk take up a small portion of his face while the President hands him the golden pass. A deeper level of amusement drifts between them in the simple exchange as the captain merely shakes his head, placing the pass in his back pocket.

"You don't know anything." Grape snorts as he crosses his arms, "Obviously they picked the captain in hopes of impressing him. But even more, this will count as a challenge for his title." I feel my face contort into confusion, but Grape goes on, "Do you think RoBjorn picks who wears what badge? No. You have to earn it. And the only way to earn the sole title of captain is to take it from the previous one during a challenge. It can happen anytime, anywhere as long as it's before the President and both parties agree. And no one's taken it from Blackwell in four years."

I shake my head, feeling immensely small all of a sudden. There isn't a soul on this base that could measure to Jude's power, but it seems we're about to watch people try. This is going to be one hell of a show.

I watch the captain slip off his suit jacket and hand it to the redheaded player, who takes it with a wide grin. She backs up next to the tattooed man as the officials step off the raised platform to watch their entertainment for the morning.

I try to find something else to focus on other than Jude's muscular, veiny forearms as he uncuffs his sleeves and rolls them to his elbows. I decide to pick on Grape as I wipe the stupid drool from my mouth. Traitorous body.

"You're awfully crabby this morning," I mumble, watching Grape sigh as he crosses his arms.

"He's just p-p-pissed he doesn't have a chance against th-the captain." Merry leans her head over with a grin.

I almost chuckle as Grape retorts with a snide remark, but I swallow my laughter as the first recruit takes the platform to face the captain. My heart skips a beat seeing a hand rake nervously through that shaggy blond hair.

Jude's dark gaze moves a centimeter to take in all of Kole, which, now that I'm truly seeing them side by side, isn't much.

I curse my feeble, lustful brain for weighing them both, but if I'm being honest with myself, and I allow my mind to open the forbidden box of feelings I will never repeat out loud, Kole has nothing on Jude. Their size, strength, and just *beauty* in general aren't comparable.

My teeth sink into my bottom lip as I drag myself back to reality, thanking the heavens these distasteful thoughts can only be accessed by me.

"And me."

I greet the ancient voice with an eye roll, though I can't ignore how it put an emphasis on its own sense of annoyance. I wonder if it can even feel emotions?

I shake my head, drawing the conclusion that I've been on this secluded base for too long and my mind enjoys tormenting me with outlandish voices to give narration.

These are thoughts for later dissection.

Jude's arms cross over his chest as he gives his opponent a tight nod to try his best. I can hardly breathe as I watch Kole unscrew the lid to his canteen and set it on the ground, preparing to throw everything he has at the captain he so worships. The very thought of Kole winning makes me sick with irritation. And three days ago I would have felt the complete opposite.

Now, as I stare at the shaggy-haired recruit who I would have followed to the ends of the earth, I can't help but feel sorry for the absolute ass-beating he's about to receive from the player before him.

Gritting his teeth, Kole makes his first move without warning, waving a palm swiftly to the sky and pulling a stream of water from the canteen at his feet. He spins fast as lightning, his arms following in a trained pattern as the water flows through the air, snapping behind him.

Kole slices toward Jude with a loud grunt and I gasp, knowing how sharp he can make the edges of that flowing spring. Once, I watched him slice into leaves and tree bark, splitting them in half, proving his water had every lethal capability as a knife. But my gasp is wasted when I catch the boredom painted clearly across Jude's face.

Faster than humanly possible, Jude tilts his head, just barely avoiding the blade of water gunning for his neck, and he takes a half-step forward—his hands loosely folded behind his back.

Kole pulls his water back and strikes again, this time with more ferocity and tension. Probably because he knows everyone is watching. Wouldn't want to play the fool before his peers.

Jude walks casually across the stage with his perfect posture, easily dismissing every strike Kole throws at his back, and I swear that covered gaze pins mine with a smirk before turning back toward his unworthy opponent.

My nostrils flare, almost wishing for the pleasure of knocking Kole on his ass myself. I wouldn't be in this mess if it weren't for him, and now I spend every waking moment plotting my intricate plan for survival all because of a selfish boy. I don't have any talents to work with, so outsmarting everyone is my only option. I have to think ahead.

The sound of Kole's groan reels me back in, and my eyes snap upward to watch him rub the back of his head, now completely drenched as he lies on the ground beneath Jude.

"Next." Is all the captain mutters. And just like that, a small piece of satisfaction lifts my chin to see Kole in such a state.

"What a joke." Grape snorts, and the tiniest smile tugs at the corner of my mouth. Grape gets it.

More and more recruits shoot their shot against Jude, using everything at their disposal in hopes of snatching that golden pass from his back pocket, but not a soul comes close.

Depitrio—the boy with purple curls who choked me with his ropes for fingers. He takes the worst beating so far, and I imagine it's because he vexed Jude with a cocky attitude as soon as he stepped foot on the platform. His ropes didn't reach three inches before the captain had him wheezing for air on his knees.

I don't know the captain, but I swear he's enjoying this game as he takes his time to defeat each individual recruit in an intimate and personal way. If he wanted to, he could make anyone cease before they stepped out of formation, but he doesn't. It's as if he already knows every last recruit and each flaw within themselves. All five hundred of us. He's smarter than they expect.

Brody, Sera's favorite henchman for example, is not given the time of day by Jude.

Tying his long, dark dreadlocks behind his back, the recruit bares teeth at the captain, earning a single arched brow at the affront. Brody moves to express his delta, which appears to be earth-quaking, but before he can flex a calf muscle, Jude flicks a hand with a yawn, sending him flying off the stage in seconds with the air he wields.

However, with another recruit named Phia, Jude doesn't dismiss as easily, though it's obvious he could. I watch the small girl try her best against the captain, tossing blades of grass at him as deadly as daggers, which he avoids easily. She struggles to pull roots from the ground but doesn't meet as harsh a fate as some others. In fact, Jude actually gives her *advice* on how to position her arms, adjusting her palms with precision. I hate that he's proving not to be a monster all the way through. It's spoiling my plan.

When it's Sera's turn, I can't help the grin that slips across my lips, hoping Jude gives her his worst.

Her wicked, fake smile flashes toward the captain as she flips her braid over her shoulder, trying her best to be seductive as she does with every male who dares to meet her dripping gaze. I don't even want to know what she's making Jude see right now, and the endless possibilities make my blood boil. Is it darkness? A nightmare? Her naked?

Sera giggles, spinning circles around Jude with light footsteps, "Don't take it easy on me, now, Captain. You should know I like it rough."

My mouth falls open.

Sera's licentious laugh vibrates through my skull as she follows up with, "A rough *opponent,* I mean. Forgive me." She sidesteps Jude as he turns. I shake my head, ready to watch her back hit the ground with a swift flick, but it doesn't happen.

The Captain shrugs, moving around while keeping tabs on her every move, no matter what she's doing to his vision, "There's nothing to forgive. Give me your worst, Sera." The way he says her name sends a red-hot flame down my spine.

"Just toss her off the stage already." I grumble as Grape chuckles next to me.

"Girl, you got it bad."

I throw a middle finger at my friend without looking his way. If there was one thing my brother's taught me, it was that incredibly useful gesture.

Grape tosses both hands up defensively, "Hate me all you want, but I'm not the one pining over the captain."

"Shut up." I swat at him.

Sera snakes around Jude, weaving past him as he turns away from her hand, probably blinded at this point. Perhaps overwhelmed by pornographic images with the way she's lacing every word with lust. I'm not sure what she's capable of.

I note how quiet Sera's trying to be as she comes up behind Jude, looking to fish for the golden pass in his back pocket, but he already knows she's there.

On his heel, the captain spins out of his opponent's grasp, crossing his arms and smirking at Sera.

He's fucking *smirking* at her. This truly is a game to him.

All thoughts of decency for the captain evaporate as my cheeks flare unreasonably. Sera Jonsdottir deserves a lifetime of pain for what she's put me through, and what's worse is Jude knows exactly what she's done to me. I was right. His advice and distant mentoring was a hoax. An elaborate scheme for selfish reasons that will never come to fruition. He doesn't care for anyone but the potential tethered pairs he can create.

For some reason I find myself on the verge of roaring when I watch Sera bow to my captain, accepting she's lost with grace. The palm he places on her lower back to guide her off the platform makes me bite my cheek to keep from fuming.

I become consumed with anger and it's everything I can do not to scream, so I ball my fists and try to focus on something else. *Anything* else.

Ninety more challenges sweep by as I keep my gaze shifting to stare at different backs of people's heads, but the distraction is no use. It isn't until I realize Merry has been knocked to her side, shifting back into herself from the previous lop rabbit form she took, that I look up.

Grape nudges me as he walks by, "Wish me luck."

I shake my head. He might as well give up and bow out now. Hell, *I* might as well give up…

The idea tastes too sweet to spare myself the mockery, but also to not give the captain satisfaction. I won't let him remind everyone how weak I am. I'm done being humiliated.

Grape's turn is over in seconds with a swift blow of air to his chest, but Jude manages to give him an admirable nod, which has my friend utterly giddy on his way back.

Rolling my eyes, I slip my sling off and march toward Merry who nurses a bruised rib with a grimace.

"Hold Pancake." I mutter, and loop his sling over her shoulder, making a beeline down the middle of the formation toward the platform.

Sera and several others snicker at me, along with despicable comments, but I grit my teeth and keep my strides even. I can't wait for this to be over. One night of peace is something to look forward to.

I march up the steps to stand on the opposite end of Jude. His smirk fuels my fire. How dare he look at me that way.

Gently, I return a sarcastic smile, moving my foot back and lean into a bow to show I've forfeited, but something's wrong. An unrecognizable gravity pushes against my torso, keeping me from completing the movement.

Confusion creases my brow as I take a breath and try again, but to no avail. What the hell is going on?

I try once more, but only to find it impossible. It's only until a wisp of my hair blows behind me that I realize this is all Jude's doing. He's concentrating his winds to keep me from giving up.

He doesn't want a draw. He wants a fight.

I shoot the captain a glare across the platform, but I'm met with another indignant smirk. He removes his hands from his pockets to fold the dark shades between the V of his creamy dress shirt as if my presence will take more concentration. As the captain gives me that same come-hither motion with two fingers, I can feel my cheeks flare fuchsia. He's forcing me to challenge him.

My arms fly up, "Why?"

I ignore the unsubtle gasps amongst the company in the distance. Even several Aegis officials shift their weight uneasily at my blatant lack of respect for the captain, but Jude doesn't miss a beat.

"Because you can't get better if you give up."

"More advice?"

"Just for you."

I brace myself for whatever trick he has up his sleeve, storming back, "I don't have power like you, *Sir.* Why make me fight you? Your ego wasn't stroked enough by beating the entire company?"

A wave of gasps ricochets across the courtyard, but I couldn't care less. I hate the captain's advice. I hate his deep voice, the way he smells and that fake, caring attitude.

"Oh, Soria," Jude's smirk disappears for a moment and a rush of air hits me in the stomach like a gut punch, "Because I *fucking* said so."

With a venomous glare, through the stomach pain, I move to step in rage, but wind catches my ankle, tossing me to the ground with a *thud.*

I fix the captain with a stare so hateful it falters his expression for a heartbeat before I'm on my feet to charge again, only to be knocked sideways by the air he wields.

Shaky fists meet the cement platform, drawing blood across white knuckles until I run at Jude again.

And again.

And again, never getting within a yard of the captain.

I ignore Jude's repetitive encouragement to keep going, finding myself dangerously angry every time his wind throws me to the ground. Before I melt from the heat rising up my neck, I force myself to take a deep breath, remembering I can't use my incense anytime soon. I need to force myself to get it together because there's no way Jude will let me off this platform until I try everything I can. I need to outsmart him.

But how do you outsmart the best there is?

As I'm knocked to the ground for the fiftieth time, I tune out Jude's stupid direction on how to move and attack from a different angle, scanning the other challenges from memory to find anything I've missed. Any recurring weaknesses.

Dr. Gencavage told our company a long time ago that no singular delta has the power to be omnipotent—that there is always a balance, always a center to outweigh the heavy, as the heavens and nature require. So, what am I missing?

With other recruits Jude found unworthy of instruction, he simply blew them off the platform in seconds with no warning, no guidance on how to be better. With Phia, he positioned her hands to move plants at a faster rate. With a lanky boy named Tym, he kicked at his boots to help his stance. Even with Sera and Grape there was some type of teaching that had to do with briefly fixing their forms. But he won't let me get within a yard. And come to think of it, he's never…

A light turns on in my brain, my neck snapping up suddenly as I toss around a new plan of attack. A crazy plan. A plan that will most likely earn more than bruised knees and ripped knuckles. But I have to try or else I'll be up here forever, held captive for not trying hard enough.

I jump to my feet once more, ignoring the ache in my ankle as if it's nothing more than a paper cut. I've gone through much worse for a rolled ankle to bother me. Perhaps I should tell Sera thanks for that.

"Ready for more?" Jude rolls his neck as if facing hundreds of challenges this morning has only been a slight inconvenience. I wonder if he's more exhausted than he lets on.

Swallowing, I raise both palms defensively, stalking forward as the captain watches me with a leery eye.

"Just give me a fighting chance." I plead, circling him with the impression of giving a wide berth, but really I'm getting inches closer, slowly closing the gap between us. I keep my palms up, remembering where that golden pass sits in his back right pocket.

"What's your plan here? I'd love to know the thought process *out loud.*" Jude crosses his arms, his back facing me as I circle him. I'd never attack from behind. The way his air moves, it can probably feel me coming miles away, especially with his senses so heightened. I need to face him.

Trying my best to slow these ragged breaths and trust in the plan I've contrived, careful steps inch to stare at Jude's profile. His beautiful, perfectly sculpted profile that would make the angels above cry.

I blink, reigning in my concentration.

"Any day now." Jude's tone is playful, but I can feel the tension. The overwhelming curiosity for what kind of dance I'm leading into.

I seize my opportunity while it lasts.

Doing the opposite of what my muscle memory tells me, I leap with my dominant foot but throw my weight into my left at the last second. Jude's air hasn't anticipated such a tight switch up, and it helps that I've creeped so close—a near foot away as I bound for him with every hope that my hands land on target.

Without overthinking, Jude's arms move to protect the golden pass on his backside, but that's not my goal. I have a theory, as well as a hypothesis to test and I'll be damned if I ever get another opportunity. It has to be now.

Faster than I thought my body could ever be capable of moving, I leap, and time seems to drive in slow motion. I hook my right arm around Jude's neck, my left palm rising to meet its target as the captain moves with the motion, completely caught off guard and almost off balance.

My palm meets his cheek softly as his arm instinctively wraps around my waist to catch my body that's just been thrown into his. My touch throws him off completely, rendering him speechless and startled as I suspected.

Since the day I met the captain, he's treated me differently. He's taunted me and tormented my emotions from afar but follows up with advice that's meant to be lifesaving. He gives instructions with half-threats, but the one thing he hasn't done is touch me. Not a single caress. Not an accidental brush and certainly not to fix my form as he has with everyone else.

I watch Jude's eyes widen slightly, his breath hitching as his face lingers only inches from mine, breathing the very air I exhale.

In this exceptionally brief moment that I finally have Jude caught off guard, a free hand swings downward as I retain eye contact, my fingers brushing the edge of the golden pass sitting in his back pocket. Before I get any further, the captain pulls himself from the trance, snatching my wrist behind his back and thrusting me to an arm's-length distance.

Damn, I almost got him.

The heavy rising and falling of Jude's chest matches my own as he stares at me with an unreadable expression. His eyes dart around my face for mere heartbeats before he releases my wrist, swallowing and returning to that unfazed, deadly facade he's mastered. But now I know the truth. Jude Blackwell may have broken my violin, painted a target on my back, left me to suffer in the bathroom stalls and sided with my enemy, but he loses focus if our skin meets. Not so almighty now, are we?

"Do not be pompous."

I shrug off the voice in my head, facing Jude and finally dipping into my well-earned bow, smiling the entire way down. He barely acknowledges the gesture, flipping those dark shades back over his eyes within seconds, concealing his gaze to the crowd.

I purse my lips to keep the grin at bay, silently giving myself a pat on the back as I retrieve Pancake and take my place in the back of the formation.

Grape whispers with wild eyes, "Um, what the hell was that?"

"*That,*" my arms fold over the sleeping bird, "was me winning."

President RoBjorn takes the center stage once more, facing Echo Company as the other Aegis officials line up behind him.

I guess no one gets the golden pass today.

"Recruits, a very valiant effort from you all. And because I am a man of fairness, and I do believe this afternoon deserves *some* kind of victor, I will give captain Blackwell the opportunity to present this golden pass to the one he believes shows the most promise." The President backs up, allowing Jude all the space he needs.

I can practically *feel* the excitement vibrating off the people around me.

"That's weird," Grape mutters. I give him an arched brow in question, his eyes shifting around while he listens. "The captain's heartbeat. He's nervous?"

My brow furrows at his obvious mistake. Jude looks more calm and collected than I've ever seen. Frankly, I'm half convinced there isn't anything in the *world* that could make a man like that nervous.

Jude speaks up, his baritone voice spreading across the courtyard for everyone to hear, "Today was very insightful. Some of you have shown great improvement, but most of you still have a lot of work to do." The captain flicks the golden pass from his pocket, holding it between two fingers as he scans the crowd, "This belongs to someone who I believe will make a fine player one day. Someone who I believe can make it all the way."

Jude shifts to his right, and my breath startles for a moment, because in this single second before he spills the name worthy of such praise, I have the smallest sliver of hope. I have just the tiniest inkling that maybe, just *maybe* he might say my name. Delta or not.

"So without further ado, this belongs to Kole Arnson."

"What?" My arms drop from my chest, but my blurt is drowned out by the cheers and claps from the other recruits. Kole's dumbass smile exudes delight as he hurdles onto the platform, gingerly taking the pass and all but kissing Jude's hands in the process.

Of all people, the captain of Aegis thinks *Kole* really shows the most promise? I'd rather see Sera earn the pass because for some reason, this one feels personal.

I refuse to believe what I'm seeing right now. What I'm seeing is Jude removing his shades to stare directly at me through the masses.

I pin him with a glare only he's able to get me to conjure, offering him a single nod across the courtyard.

Game on, I guess.

CHAPTER 14: BOOK OF MONSTERS

After a well-deserved shower that leaves my body soaking up every ache from the six-mile hike, I slip through the squad bay doors unseen, leaving Pancake to rest in my pillowcase in peace. Thankfully, every recruit's priority this evening is to get off base for as long as possible, so part one of my survival plan can finally commence.

I hide on the roof for a few hours, watching the trains far off in the night pass through the one-hundred-foot Aegis walls, carrying recruits to heavens-knows-where.

Earlier, I had wished Grape and Merry a good night, claiming I didn't feel good enough to leave. They had protested, of course, asking if I wanted company, but I insisted they enjoy their freedom and to make sure they come back alive.

According to Dr. Gencavage, the first night off base for recruits is statistically the deadliest, considering these fresh talents are strapped with ten-ton egos, prone to showing off for the wrong crowd. I'm thankful I decided to stay on base.

When I'm confident the last train has successfully hauled off the remaining recruits past the one-hundred-foot walls, I stalk down the stairs.

Quietly, I round the corner to the auditorium, carefully moving past the double doors to find the empty room lit by scattered gas lamps along the chalkboard wall.

At this moment, I'm still in the clear. If anyone finds me roaming around in the auditorium, I can make a simple excuse saying I'm bored and just exploring. But that's not what I'm doing at all.

Gingerly, I begin rummaging through several stacks of leather-bound books and aged scrolls that lie stuffed beneath Dr. Gencavage's podium. I know what I'm looking for. I just have to find the right piece of knowledge.

I remember the professor telling us something about a limited number of monsters still held within the Madden Penitentiary walls on the secluded isles of Jh'door. Some are forbidden for training use, but others have not been cycled through in decades for any Bachalorian purpose, making the options scarce.

I thumb through more and more scrolls, shaking my head at all of the options. *Auction Bylaws.* Nope. *Recruit Orientation Guide.* No. *Timeless Acolytes.* No. *Petitions Against the Diamond Games.* What?

I flip the scroll over to reveal a golden official Aegis seal, holding together several pieces of parchment inside. Curiosity tickles my brain, daring me to see why, or more importantly, *who* has written a petition against the games. I thought the entire world was obsessed with the sport, but a silver-covered spine with the Bachalorian symbol for *Monster Prison* catches my eye on the very bottom, and I dismiss the nosy inquisition altogether.

I peel the book from beneath the pile of rolled parchment, careful not to disturb the placement, and sigh in relief. I found it.

Bending to my knees, I splay the large book out on its spine, hunching over to allow the gas lamp to reveal the words.

Right now, if I were caught, I wouldn't have any excuse. Maybe I could say I wandered into the wrong room, or that this book fell open and I'm merely retrieving it. That sounds completely believable.

Shaking my head, I decide to cross that bridge if I get there, and flip through the pages to find the section of monsters still up for debate on crucible use. Of course, the monster has already been chosen, it's just up to me and my survival to deduce which one it is.

The dragon was used last year, so I skip past that frightening portrait and description. By process of elimination, the Stallion Minotaur was slain a few years ago, and they wouldn't use the Cockatrice considering they thrive in the mountains, and that terrain was just cycled through.

I twist my lips into a purse, as I flip through more portraits of beasts along with their descriptions, feeling relieved each time I cross a deadly monster off the list. On a good day, I wouldn't want to face even the smallest monster that lies within this book. And so far, the smallest seems to be over three thousand pounds. I'm doomed.

An unrecognizable noise makes me jump, and I peek up from the book, scanning the auditorium slowly. Carefully. But it's silent besides my ragged breathing and my own heartbeat.

I return to the pages, skimming past the sea creatures because according to Dr. Gencavage, the ocean was already used six years ago, and apparently it was the quickest crucible anyone had ever witnessed.

That same noise creaks, sounding farther away this time. I crane my neck quickly, scanning the room to find it still empty and curse my brain for continuing to make up noises in my head.

Sighing, I look back down at the pages, but suddenly, a soft, hot gust of air caresses my cheek, and my blood runs cold.

I turn slightly to see a mouth full of razor-sharp teeth, bright orange eyes and fur dark as night staring me down as if I'm its meal. My heart leaps in my throat as my mouth goes dry.

The giant wolf stands taller than me as I kneel over the book, open-mouthed breathing inches from my face. Perhaps it had been full that night on the roof and didn't have an appetite for young recruits sneaking around where they don't belong. And perhaps now it's starving and perfectly enraptured with the idea of swallowing me for dinner.

Slowly, and pathetically, I try scooting away, keeping my eyes trained on the bright orange pair staring me down. I shouldn't have left the squad bay. I hope Merry takes care of Pancake when she realizes I've been gutted like a fish.

I swallow my nerves, wondering what I would do in this moment if I were not afraid. To do what I would normally do, minus the fear of course.

"Minus the fear." I whisper, squeezing my eyes closed as I repeat the captain's words that have burned themselves into my subconscious. What would I do to a terrifying wolf twice my size if I were not quite literally shaking where I kneel?

I wouldn't take an animal's life just because it looked frightening. I wouldn't run, because I would not be afraid.

I've always been fond of the world's creatures. Not fond in the way Merry obsesses over each shade of gray that pigeons come in, but enough that I appreciate and respect an animal when I see one.

With my eyes squeezed shut beneath the towering wolf, I throw a Hail Mary in hopes my idea works. And if it doesn't, at least I tried something. At least I didn't give up. I just hope I don't offend the maw with blades for teeth.

Tucking my head to my chest, I raise a shaky hand out. I can feel my palm vibrating through the air between the creature and me. Never have I prayed so hard for the heavens to grant me another day. I'm sure they're tired of accepting my pleas, seeing how I've managed to survive against all odds to make it to this point, but I've come so far. I deserve a fighting chance, I believe.

A low, guttural snarl reverberates from the throat of the wolf, but I don't dare look up. I try to control my breathing as my hand shakes unsteadily in the air. I keep my palm where it is, knowing at any second it will be ripped from my body, but the terrible pain doesn't happen.

The sensation of soft, fuzz-like hair brushes against my fingertips, along with something wet, and I gasp at the feeling.

My head snaps up to see the wolf has vanished, and has been replaced with a small, black puppy with tall, hairy ears that don't fit its face. It sits expectantly, wagging a long, bushy tail while continuing to lick my fingers as I scan the room with a wide, unbelieving gaze.

"Where did you come from?" I ask the puppy, scratching behind its ears as I continue to swivel around the auditorium, "And where did the big bad wolf go?"

"He's right in front of you." Jude answers from the doorway, casually leaning against the frame with his arms crossed.

I roll my eyes at him, wondering why I'm not surprised to see the captain pop up out of the blue again. It's as if he always knows where I am. And suddenly, something clicks.

My gaze plummets to the black puppy whose tongue hangs sideways out of his mouth, feeling like more and more puzzle pieces have begun to shift into place.

My head shudders with disbelief, "That can't be."

"But it can." Jude smiles, "This is one of Fenrir's favorite forms. It seems he's taken favor in you."

"But...but..." I stutter, staring down at the harmless puppy that could never turn into something so ferocious. So
frightening and deadly. "It's not possible."

I blink, and all of a sudden, the puppy has disappeared, replaced by the massive, dark wolf dripping drool from its maw. My blood runs cold again with a shriek, throwing myself against the podium and squeezing my eyes shut. But after several silent heartbeats, I squint to find the puppy back, and the wolf nowhere to be seen.

I shake my head, leaping to my feet and trying to ignore Jude's amused laughter.

"What… what is he?" I ask, trying to school my shaky hands by shoving them into my pockets.

"Fenrir is one of the oldest acolytes, with many talents, but I wouldn't ask any more questions. He doesn't take kindly to prodders."

I glance down at the puppy who now finds interest in licking a paw lazily, realizing I should be grateful for being able to keep my head tonight. I find it within myself to give the captain an appreciative nod, though I still don't trust him.

"So, this is how you keep finding me." I mutter to Jude, then glance at Fenrir sprawled along the auditorium floor, "*You* keep telling him."

I remember the way the snake hissed in the animal handler's ear. It was as if he was speaking to her in a language only she could understand. And the night on the roof, the wolf had found me first, shortly followed by Jude. These two are linked, and somehow able to communicate. Fenrir is Jude's spy around the base.

"I'm glad you finally figured that out," Jude sighs, stepping into the auditorium and taking a seat on the front row. He shifts slightly, sliding into the desk with ease, although his wide frame takes up more than the chair. His dark shades are nowhere to be seen, and his hair looks just slightly damp, giving away the idea that he's fresh out of the shower. That rich cologne fills my senses from several feet away, and I swallow to keep myself in check. But *damn,* I can't deny the fact that he looks good.

Deceivingly good.

The captain pulls a small black book from his pocket, glancing through the first few pages as if he has all the time in the world. And the way those brows dip in concentration toward whatever he's reading has me wishing to be the pages in his book.

I clear my throat to collect myself, giving up on trying to hide the reason why I've come here in the first place. It seems Jude Blackwell knows what I'm doing before I do it myself, and it would be a fool's errand to try and hide from his wolf on this base.

Shamelessly, I scoop up the book of monsters, placing it beneath the gas lamp on the professor's podium, and continue skimming through the pages. I can feel Jude watching me as his acolyte shifts to another paw, licking as if he has nothing better to do in the body of a puppy. But I won't let his presence throw me off. I will figure out which beast I'm facing so I can prepare as best I can. I'm already at every disadvantage.

We sit for several minutes in silence, the only noise echoing through the domed ceilings being the flip of a page, but I've almost narrowed the monsters down to the last ten.

Eventually, Jude slaps his little book closed with a question, his voice deep and inquisitive, ruining my train of thought, "You're bad at running. Why?"

I snort at the pages, skimming through the passage on the chimera and wondering how the captain could be so blunt. *Maybe because I can't breathe,* I wish to say, but I think better of it.

Without looking up, I snip, "I thought you knew everything. You tell me."

"I *do* know everything, but some things remain a mystery—like why it took you this long to come looking for the prison records of creatures. Or why you went to the infirmary. Or why you continue to fall out of every training event, including a simple run around the base." The captain's tone stays inquisitive, his arms crossed and his head slightly cocked. He's fishing for the answers his spy can't give him.

"I haven't exactly been training for this like everyone else."

"That's an excuse. There's another reason you aren't telling me."

Jude's eyes darken as if he's trying to see through me.

I clench my jaw shut in response. He doesn't deserve to know I can't breathe. It would be more ammunition in his arsenal.

"You can trust him."

That ancient voice rattles my brain, and I purse my lips, knowing it has to be wrong. There would never be a world in which I trust Jude Blackwell. Never a time or a place. I continue to remind myself of each and every grievance he's given me, and there are too many to justify spilling my biggest secret that I hold carefully within my cargo pocket.

Though it feels oddly wrong, I ignore the voice in my head, stepping around the podium and further testing my theory from earlier this morning. I need answers of my own, and I'll do anything right now to steer clear of the topic of my incense powder.

I step closer to Jude, and a hint of amusement warms my nerves as his neck stiffens, his body fighting against retreating. I raise a brow, stopping in my tracks to lean against the front of the podium. This action causes Jude's shoulders to relax by a fraction. Interesting.

Taking his tactical lines of questioning, I probe him for answers, "You have a problem with me touching you. Why is that?" I try to keep the grin at bay as the captain's jaw ticks, his expression fighting to stay neutral, but I can see through the charade. I've figured out his secret.

Jude's sigh sounds more like a grumble as he says, "Because I have boundaries."

His answer doesn't satisfy me in the slightest, considering I've watched him handle other recruits without a care in the world, but one touch from my skin sets him off balance.

"I guess there's something you're not telling *me.*" I take one step closer, pushing off the podium as he shifts slightly in his chair. I seize my opportunity and stalk closer, demanding answers of my own. Am I diseased? Am I truly the abomination everyone says I am? To touch me is to feel stained?

"Like I said." Jude's gaze narrows on me as I approach. He steeples his fingertips, "I have *boundaries* when it comes to you."

With a flick of his wrist, I'm sent flying back into the chalkboard, his wind pinning me to the wall. I groan a frustrated noise, my blood sizzling within my veins. I hate him.

"That's funny," I spit, moving behind the podium to finish what I came here for, "Because I remember having boundaries once. And somehow, I found myself on the auction stage. And then, *somehow,* miraculously I've ended up here. So don't give me a sob story about boundaries when you're the one who has single-handedly ruined my life." I flip angrily through the pages, not sparing Jude so much as another glance.

I've long given up on biting my tongue around the captain, dangerous or not. If he wanted me dead, my body would be six feet under by now. And I'm still here.

My nostrils flare as Jude's voice carries calmly across the room, and I realize he's walking toward me.

"You seem to hold a lot of animosity toward me, Soria. Very hostile. Why is that?"

Rage and fury climb my spine as I fix Jude with a glare at the use of my name instead of *recruit,* but it doesn't stop his slow strides toward me.

I shake my head. "No. You answer one of my questions then I answer one of yours. That's how it works."

Jude chuckles in placation, now standing to face me with the oak podium between us, folding his arms over the lip to show off those silver rings decorating nearly every finger.

Apparently, the captain finds no problem with being close to me if it's on his terms. It's as if he doesn't trust the unpredictability of me reaching to touch him. And I imagine now he's anticipating the move from my hands more than ever with the little show I created this morning. But I have no desire to touch the captain anymore. I just want to be left alone to suffer in silence.

Jude sighs, and a warm wind surrounds us, caressing my neck thoughtfully, but I dismiss the feeling.

"Very well," he says, "You may ask a question first."

"Oh, *may* I?"

"You may. See, now you've asked a question and I've responded. So, it's my turn." He flashes a white smile, and anger heats my cheeks. Of course his smile is bright white with perfectly straight teeth. He probably grew up being fed with a silver spoon and golden chalice, forever too rich and powerful to be put into check.

I spit a curse low in my throat, flipping furiously to another page. "Oh, fuck me."

Jude's stupid chuckle only fuels my irritation, "Not tonight, Love, but thank you."

My nails dig into the wood as I fix the captain with another nostril-flaring glare that has the vein in my forehead thumping. His eyes rake to my lips before I realize I'm doing the same. What the *fuck* is wrong with him?

I force my question out before I do something so vile even *I* wouldn't recognize myself. The question that has a piece of my heart aching for some stupid reason. The question that I need answered more than anything.

"Why did you give Kole the golden pass?" I whisper, watching Jude's smile fade slightly. "Do you really believe he shows the most promise?" I can hear the hurt in my own words. Never mind what kind of pride I felt being the only one to even graze the pass in his back pocket; I would think someone strong like Ona showed the most promise. Or someone cunning like Grape or talented like Merry. But *Kole?*

His eyes search mine for a long time—too long, before he finally says, "Maybe I sent him away so I could have you to myself for the night."

I shake my head at his response because I know it's not the truth. Though I can't shake the spinning feeling that just shuddered through my body. My traitorous body.

Jude clears his throat, a warm tendril of a breeze pushing a strand of hair from my face, "Don't compare yourself to anyone here. Each delta cannot possibly be held to the same standard, and therefore, neither can you. You need to focus on preparing yourself."

I force myself to list the things I hate about the captain to keep me from dwelling on the things I… *don't hate.*

I hate his proper sentences that reek of wealth, as well as his suit jackets and polished shoes. I hate that his deep voice collides against every cell of my skin and does something to my stomach. I hate that he gives me advice that seems lifesaving, only to turn around and commit an act so contradictory it makes me question everything all over again.

And I *hate* that he broke my violin.

My gazes follows Jude as he backs from the podium, taking all of the tension that lingers between us with him. Thank the heavens.

I can't shake the feeling of defeat as the captain strolls toward the exit, leaving me alone with the book to figure out my fate for myself. It irritates me, for some reason, and for a moment I wonder if I really *do* hold all of this animosity for the captain. And as I watch him walk away, I realize I don't necessarily want him to leave.

Without thinking, I blurt before he can pass through the doors, "You're wasting your time on me, you know. I'll never be anything special. I just have to make it to tethering and then I can go home." I curse myself for sounding so desperate. Why can't I just let him walk through the doors?

Jude stops where he stands, Fenrir following slowly behind in his puppy form. The captain's head turns so his profile is visible against the gas lamps, his voice low and husky, "You believe you will go home after tethering?"

His question takes me back. He didn't ask if I believed I would *make* it to tethering… that I would go home… after…

I blink, remembering the strict laws Dr. Gencavage had laid out before our class—that no man or woman will be wasted and will be granted permission to return home with the amount they were bought for at the auction.

"Of course. I can't tether to anyone." I say confidently.

"So, you want to return to the cottage in the woods? The life that offered you nothing."

A gentle gasp gets lodged in my throat as I whisper back, "How do you know that?"

I watch the corner of Jude's lip tug into a smirk as he calls over his shoulder, "You forget, two of my best players are Davidsons. I have eyes everywhere—especially on you." And he slips past the exit, his wolf suddenly in his massive size, trailing his heels.

A breath of relief escapes as the captain leaves me more confused than the first day I arrived. Obviously, the only goal for survival is to make it to tethering alive, and then catch the first train home, but now that I think about it, what kind of life *would* I be returning to? A lonely existence nursing my deteriorating mother against her will? Maybe I'll get a job in the mines as Hera had, considering they're always looking for labor workers, no matter the age, gender, or qualifications. It would be a poor quality of life, but at least I would be *alive.* Just not living.

I shove those thoughts away for another time, because right now, with only a few hours of freedom from the other recruits remaining, I need to study these pages for as long as I can.

It isn't easy, but I force myself to set aside all thoughts of Jude, Kole, my brothers, my impending doom and any other distractions that fight to hurt me, and pour every ounce of concentration into these pages.

A mental checklist forms of each monster as I check off the basilisk, remembering Mrs. Furien referring to it as a female, claiming she will be hibernating for the year to prepare for her offspring.

I've finally narrowed down the options to the only two monsters that could possibly be chosen this year, and I would be lying to myself if I said I don't feel helpless toward my options.

I flip back and forth between pictures of the twenty-foot tall, deadly arachne or the enormous three-headed hydra. It has to be one of these, so I study each page listing their flaws and strengths.

According to the text, the arachne is able to use every leg to feel vibrations within the earth, so it can easily track its prey to every corner where they may try to hide, suffocating its meal to death with the webs it weaves. Though it doesn't have a mouth large enough to bite, it's wicked fast and able to shoot a web with one hundred percent accuracy as soon as its prey is detected. And from this horrifying painting of its likeness, the prey the arachne prefers shall be no smaller than a deer. Wonderful.

With hope for the best, I move on to the hydra's description, only to sigh at my ever-lowering odds of seeing my next birthday.

The hydra, spawned with three, serpent-like heads that stand taller than its tree-towering body, is seemingly unkillable. According to its description, once a single head is sliced off, two more will take its place, creating the ultimate weapon for destruction.

I swallow, reading the text out loud to make sure I'm seeing the right words, "Though it can be oversensitive to noise, the hydra has extra sets of eyes, making it impossible for the prey to hide for long. Along with its four paws that sprout talons and razor-sharp teeth in each mouth, the hydra's tail sports an orb of spikes that will swing on impact to destroy buildings and small structures. Do not approach."

I slap the book closed, huffing at my choices and feeling utterly useless. My options for survival are between a giant, man-eating spider or a three-headed monster that can never die.

Stuffing the book back onto the shelf, I head to the squad bay to retrieve hopefully a few good hours of sleep, feeling more than defeated—though I don't know what I was expecting to find. It's not like the President would hand out lightning bugs to attack. I really *do* need to prepare.

I have one month until the Crucible, and now more than ever, my odds have never been stacked so low. Even those with deltas don't have good chances against either beast, marking the mortality rate possibly the highest it's ever been. I lie down on my bunk, careful not to disturb Pancake as I wrestle with my options, but I have no answer. It could be either one and I'm out of luck.

My eyes begin to feel heavy as Ona's snores reverberate through the squad bay from several yards away. The idea of asking the almighty, know-it-all voice comes to mind, and I decide it might be my only option. I can't exactly ask the directors or the President.

Quietly in the dark, just before sleep claims me for the evening, I whisper into the void, "Hey, um, ancient voice, thing?" I pause for several seconds, giggling as

I realize I *must* be talking to myself, though I've never directly *spoken* to the voice. This isn't real. None of it.

And yet, I suppose it's worth a shot.

"Could you send me a sign or…anything to tell me if it's the hydra or the spider? I would really appreciate it… Sir. Your… Majesty? Amen." I sigh to myself after several minutes of silence, knowing it was all in my head.

I turn on my side, letting the abyss take me deeper and chalking up my idea to a question that will never be answered.

As my eyes get heavier, my hand brushes something beneath my pillow.

Gingerly, I grasp the small object beneath my pillow and pull it out to reveal a brand new incense tin with a small piece of parchment attached with a string.

"I've always been a fan of an underdog——-The Janitor."

The biggest smile creases my mouth as I press the can to my lips, kissing it with new hope for the better. Breathing is one thing I can cross off my growing list of worries.

I will not die today. I will not die tomorrow. Probably during the crucible, but not anytime soon.

A sigh of relief releases a bundle of apprehension I didn't know I'd been harboring as I send a silent thank you to my new friend Ivar, the janitor. I only hope this didn't cost him his job or safety.

Just before I slip away completely, there is no mistaking the answer I finally receive from the ancient voice—and an answer that I loathe because it means the directors have picked the worst beast to ever exist, just for me and my year's unfortunate recruits.

"Atenalod, the arachne, is out of commission."

CHAPTER 15: FIRESIDE

I would trade the physical pain Sera had put me through for days on end over the mind-numbing torture of waiting for my own funeral. At least, that's what this slow-paced, load-heavy hike feels like. In less than twenty-four hours, I'll be thrown into a terrain that I've deduced is either a jungle or a richly seeded forest. I can't shake the feeling that today will certainly be my last if my plan fails.

The morning lineup after every recruit used their pass to get off base proved to be exactly what Dr. Gencavage had claimed. It was a statistically deadly night.

Our recruit numbers dropped by ninety-three, making a total of eighty percent of students bought from the auction that would actually see phase one. Grape gabbed about the entire evening, concluding the main consensus was that such a horrifying number of dead recruits had been chalked up to ego, mixed with alcohol. Exactly what our professor had warned. I was glad I stayed in, though my absence had certainly been noticed by one very drunk Kole Arnson.

I remember being shaken awake just minutes before the horn blew for breakfast, the moment the passes expired, and standing above me was a hiccupping, tired-eyed boy with sandy hair pulled into a bun at the nape of his neck. I'd seen this look before and I knew his drunk intentions before he had a chance to speak.

In so many words, I tried dismissing Kole, but he followed up with too many questions about where I had been and why I didn't meet him off base. Thankfully, I had thought quickly on my feet, claiming my ankle hurt from the previous challenges. I sprinkled in some other sweet lies about love and lust to get him off my back. I had already come to the conclusion that if my survival plan is to work, Kole will have to be kept in the dark just as he had with me. This time, there's not a sliver of guilt behind my actions. Survival mode can be brutal.

Now, as I stare down at a sleeping, nearly featherless Pancake who continues to breathe against all odds, I can't help but think he represents a version of myself. We may not look good doing it, but we are still living. We are living, and plenty of recruits who held deltas and a perfectly strong set of lungs are not alive. Right now, tomorrow marks the most important day to keep that fact true.

My eyes drift past Pancake resting in the sling against my chest and toward the clay that claims every crevice within my boots. I've fallen to the back of the squad, but the pace is manageable because we have about one-hundred extra bodies leading the front.

Apparently, every Aegis figure who holds some type of leadership position has decided to take up a pack and hike the fifteen miles to witness this year's crop face the crucible. I don't blame them, I suppose. Albeit sadistic, I can understand the curiosity of seeing who comes out alive. Their goal is to figure out who will hold a fighting chance to tether and then ultimately claim the title of player.

When night falls along our ever-bending trail, our company finally sets up camp as the directors instruct the field of recruits to feed our owls so they're prepared in the morning. No one knows exactly where the crucible will take place, but by the burning in my calves and the feeling of my lungs disintegrating within my chest, I can tell we're close. But even fifteen miles of hell sounds more appealing than the torture my mind is unfurling.

"Whatcha thinking about?" Grape pokes me with a stick, pulling me back to reality. The log I'm perched on is warm against the fire Merry created, and it offers my feet perfect elevation after being on them all day.

Running a finger over Pancake's bald head, I mutter, "Oh, nothing—just the color of my casket."

Merry rolls her eyes at my dark comment while Grape cackles, "Who are you kidding, Blondie? You think these saps care enough to buy you a casket?"

I can't help but laugh as I usually do when Grape speaks. He has a likable charisma that draws you in until you realize the dripping sass sits on top of a thin surface that cares too much. He would never admit that, but I see it.

I pick at the dehydrated jerky that had been passed around the field for dinner, taking comfort in our little cozy spot elevated near the trees. The crackle of the bright fire between my two friends and me would be more beautiful if only I could stop thinking of my own death.

Several yards away in the grassy field sit too many campfires to count, all surrounded by people who seem to be having a much better time than me. And they should. They have a fighting chance.

"Enough self-deprecation. It is taxing."

I sigh, shaking off the ancient voice's advice it so loves to throw out at the oddest times.

Before I have a chance to lighten the mood for my own sake, the log I sit on suddenly tosses me with a jolt, sending me crashing to the ground with a *thwump.*

Groaning, I swivel to find the culprit is none other than Ona, settling down uninvited on the opposite side of my log, denting the bark with her weight. Her eyes are apologetic, though her face still holds the stern, no-nonsense demeanor. In her cupped palms sits an owlet that looks microscopic between her sausage fingers.

Grape and Merry shoot me nervous glances as I pull myself back onto the log, twisting to face Ona.

"You okay?" I ask, watching the massive recruit shift on the log that begs for mercy.

Ona makes a grunting noise, glancing down at the baby owl peeking between her hands, "Bird broke," she mumbles.

Before I can ask, Merry is already on it, moving around the fire to stand at Ona's side, asking her several questions from a respectful distance, careful not to anger Ona in the slightest.

"He looks p-p-perfectly h-healthy to me," Merry smiles, nodding firmly as her giant frizzy bun bounces in the night, "Do y-you mean he can't fly, or you haven't b-b-been able to transfer a-a piece of your delta to him?"

Ona grunts at the second option, forever a woman of very few words.

Merry offers another smile to show her she means no harm, reaching a hand toward Ona's owl but immediately regretting it.

With a protective grumble, Ona pulls her owl to her chest, baring teeth toward the shapeshifter in the process.

Nervously, Merry raises her hands, giving Ona space, "Sorry, s-s-sorry! How about this," she shoots a high-pitched whistle in the air, calling her own owl from the wooded brush alongside the field, "Transferring p-power is fairly simple once you've bo-bonded." Merry explains, running a finger over her owl's head as it lands on her shoulder gracefully, "For starters, I gave m-m-my owl a name. She's K-Kiteya, and she knows it. How about you try?"

Ona's stern face is unmovable as she grunts, "Has name. Bird."

Merry's brows knit and I pin Grape with a glare to keep him from laughing.

"Oh, good. Yes, ver-very good. Now, all you n-n-need to do is focus on… *Bird,* and visualize your delta as s-something tangible. Like a ball or a p-p-pie."

"Pie." Ona grumbles in repetition.

"Yeah pie! And imagine taking a s-s-slice of it and g-giving it to Bird. It's simple. As long a-a-as Bird accepts."

I feel myself leaning forward slightly, all too intrigued to see if this works, because Ona's survival depends on this moment. It speaks volumes that she's mustered up enough courage to ask for help in the first place.

I watch as Ona shifts uncomfortably on the log, staring at Bird as he twitches his rounded head in her palms. She closes her eyes, breathing deeply as concentration consumes her, and I can tell she's trying to imagine that pie.

Several minutes of unwavering silence floats by before Ona sighs heavily, her eyes popping open and her expression turning to irritation.

"Can't." She grumbles, and I watch her shoulders drop in defeat. My heart sinks for her. Ona needs this acolyte to enter the crucible gates. We all do.

"Just keep practicing," Merry encourages Ona, then takes a seat on the grassy floor adjacent, going over the instructions again.

Grape slides next to me, whispering as the other two find themselves wrapped in a one-way conversation about what *pie* is supposed to look like. "So, what are *you* going to do tomorrow?"

I purse my lips, knowing this question would come eventually.

"I have an idea." Which is the truth. An idea. A *single* idea that all of my hope rests on to get Pancake and me through those gates to the crucible tomorrow.

"As long as it works. He needs to be able to fly. Can he fly?" Grape asks, concern creasing his brows as he peers down at the sleeping black bird in his sling.

I swallow, forcing another lie that I loathe just to keep Grape from worrying too much, "Yeah, a little bit. He's nothing like your Apple, but he manages." I offer my friend a shrug to alleviate the tension, but it hardly works.

"You know I can hear your heart beating faster when you lie, right?" Grape's eyebrow shoots up, waiting for an explanation I don't want to give. He deserves to know every last secret, but I just don't want to burden him with my problems.

I shake my head, hoping to drop the conversation. It's better this way.

"It'll be fine." I offer a grin, but I can tell it doesn't settle him.

Before Grape can argue with me, a cornucopia horn bellows across the field, silencing the hundreds of people settling in for the night around their campfires. Several yards away, in the center of the field, stands the President surrounded by directors and strangers who, based on their ethereal beauty, must be a handful of players.

"Recruits and esteemed Aegis leadership, I welcome you on the eve of our beloved crucible!" Hundreds of cheers and boisterous chants fill the sky in approval as RoBjorn continues, "It is my honor to congratulate every recruit for making it this far, and to remind you that tomorrow will be the first test of many to prove your worth to this sacred team. Many of you will pass, and many of you will perish, but your fate is in your own hands."

I watch from our slightly elevated hilltop as our fearless leader massages weathered hands together, gesturing to the players around him, "Look at these fine examples who stand before you. None of them got here by chance. They took what was theirs and *claimed* their victory!"

Another eruption of cheers echoes through the starry night, and my breath yields in my throat at the sight of two familiar white-blond heads that swivel to show off profiles I've known my entire life. Profiles I never thought I would see again.

My brothers stand at the President's left side wearing the same players' dress blues as the others and looking unbothered in their stature. Besides their typical haircuts, they've chosen to keep them identifiable since childhood, they look... *different.* Rough and firm like a stone that's been tossed against every last wave and molded into people who define the title of player. And... are they *taller?*

A desperate pang of homesickness hits my heart, and I can't shake the tear sliding its way down my cheek. They've known about my presence on this base for several months, and yet not a single night have they bothered to see me—to visit, offer encouragement or even send a note saying, *hang in there!*

I thought I recognized my brothers, but I'm mistaken. I don't know those boys anymore.

The redheaded woman with the perfect face catches my attention as she moves next to my brothers, lighting a match in my soul for some unknown reason. I don't even know her. I don't even like my brothers. Why does that simple movement bother me?

And just before I thought the irritation couldn't get any stronger, I prove myself wrong when my eyes follow a muscular arm that wraps around the redhead's shoulder. It is an arm that would refuse to ever touch my shoulder in such a way.

I bite a hole in my cheek to reel myself back in.

I don't care. I don't care. I don't care.

"It seems as though you do."

"Shut up." I mutter to the voice, earning a weird look from Grape as he realizes I've just talked to myself. And I most certainly did. Am I going crazy?

My eyes flit back to Jude as the President goes on with his motivational speech. I tune out the empty words that are meant to inspire while focusing on my plan for survival tomorrow.

I watch from my silent perch on the hilltop, examining the captain's every move. His head turns slowly as darting eyes skim the spread-out company as if looking for someone.

Jude hadn't spoken a single word to me since the night in the auditorium. In fact, besides a couple of times in passing through the courtyard, this is the first time I've seen him in weeks.

"So anyway, back to what I was saying," Grape mutters as I huff at Jude's arm draped over the player. "I don't know what you have planned tomorrow, but I hope it's something good. It better be."

I offer Grape a nod while watching Jude laugh at something the girl says. What's so funny?

"And I know a lot of things. Like a *lot.*" My friend mumbles, but I'm too focused on the captain's eyes crossing the field, seeming to examine every face with intensity. Who the hell is he looking for? I bet it's another gorgeous redhead. One for each arm.

"Like I know what sits in some people's pockets, for example. I know if certain people aren't careful, the information about those contents could fall into the wrong hands."

I snap my neck toward Grape. "What do you know?" I interrogate him for answers as the President's speech elicits another explosion of cheers into the night.

"Ah, *now* I have your attention," Grape grins, "Riddle me this, Soria. If I'm able to hear the heartbeat in your chest, do you think I'd never hear the sound of medicinal powder being snorted?"

I shake my head, realizing I should have trusted Grape all along. He's one of my only friends, and he could have sold me out months ago. But he didn't. He's kept my secret for me, and probably others.

"I'm sorry." I mutter, "I should have told you. I just…"

"Didn't know who to trust." Grape smiles, nudging my shoulder, "I get it, girl. But I hope you know now that you have someone. More than just someone."

He gestures to Merry and Ona on the other end of the log bickering, "You have *people.* We're your people, and we don't care if you have a delta or an acolyte or were traded for a

turtle's ass. You can trust us."

"A turtle's ass." My laugh sounds sweet in my ears, because it's the first time I've laughed like this in a while. And I miss it.

My heart expands an ounce to make room for my friends, and it would have never been possible had Grape not told me what I've been missing. I've never had friends like this before.

"I have people." I whisper.

Grape giggles, squeezing my hand as he turns his attention back toward the speech that has recruits leaping to their feet in approval.

"Now, if I can address another secret you've been hiding," Grape mumbles in my ear, "How could you keep such *hot* brothers a mystery to us? I mean I knew they were good looking from their portraits, but not *mouth-watering.*"

"Amen to th-that." Merry swoons, and I want to throw up.

My gaze flicks back to the captain as if magnets pull me in, and in seconds, that swirling blue stare finds mine from the center of the field.

"There goes that heart rate again. I'm sensing a trend." Grape snickers.

I throw an elbow at his side, "Oh, fuck off."

Grape hardly schools his laughter, throwing knowing eyebrows toward Merry before sighing dramatically, "I'm not talking about *your* heart rate, Soria." And he gestures to the captain in the center of the field.

CHAPTER 16: THE GATES

"Echo Company! We will start player style, so be ready to get on the chopping block once you're up."

Director Boz orders. As we linger in the dark, staring down an intimidating set of rusty doors carved into a canyon wall.

It must be nearly three in the morning considering we resumed our hike over an hour ago, to begin the crucible on time. The pack of leaders had shuffled us down the ravine for a few miles, following a hollow cavern until finally reaching an enormous rock wall standing over one-hundred-foot tall, kissing the stars above.

The slate gray stone is abrasive against my palm as I press against the side, wondering what lies beyond. Of course, no recruit is permitted to observe to keep things fair, as Dr. Gencavage had instructed during orientation. But every discerning eye that came for the show will be perched high above, watching from the safety of the sky.

From what I understand in our ordinance handbooks, the crucible is a deadly arena with only one way out, and I'm not sure if I can scrape by with my talent of 'outlasting' the others anymore.

"You'll have unlimited time to conquer the crucible, so be wise, but be fast." Neera instructs, arms crossed, "Whatever sits beyond these walls was made to destroy you, and the monster hasn't been fed since the auction, so he's hungry for the ones who…*fall out*." Her dead gaze finds mine with a scoff.

"Well this is different from the President's motivational speech." Grape mutters by my side, "Good thing you had the brains to figure out it was a hydra."

I offer him a nod, remembering the evening I pulled Grape, Merry and Ona together to let them know what I had found. I owed them that much, and I would give anything to prepare my friends for the fight of their lives.

The director instructs the company that there will be a key to enter the gates, and another key to leave through the opposite end. Simple. Brutal.

"Anyone bearing a delta cannot pass through these gates without the entrance key. This is what you've trained for. So, good luck to you all, and we hope to see you on the other side."

The directors part, peeling off toward the staircase etched into the jagged wall to take their seats out of view. I wish I had one of those seats.

Every eye rests on the shaggy-haired recruit who takes his spot at the front of the gates, his taupe-colored owl sitting nervously on his shoulder.

I swallow my complicated feelings for Kole, feeling a surge of guilt for not telling him goodbye when the next few minutes could certainly be his last. That guilt is quickly overtaken by anger for his betrayal and sheer ignorance toward everything I've gone through since setting foot on this blasted base. And yet, I hope he doesn't succumb to a horrifying death. I wonder if he feels the same for me.

Though I'm several yards away in the crowd, lost against the side of the wall, my hand reaches out for him in silent hope he survives. Kole doesn't turn his head away from the gates.

"He'll be fine. He's the *chosen* one, right?" Grape grumbles next to me, no doubt watching my emotions unravel without my permission.

As every pair of eyes studies the first recruit to enter the chasm of death, silence befalls the group as a familiar redheaded woman flicks her wrist, revealing a copper key on a ring. And so her delta is revealed at last. A stunning, lethal metalist.

With another wrist movement, the player sends the key flying to the top of the wall above the gate. Every neck cranes upward as the key gets lost in the dark, hooking itself to a protruded nail.

The beautiful player turns to Kole with a grin, instructing him to fetch the key to begin his Crucible. Now we know where the owls come in.

Short of biting my nails like a fidgeting schoolgirl, my heart races to think this may be the last time I lay eyes on my first love.

I watch as Kole gives his owl a nod, motioning up the wall toward the key, and after several heartbeats of twitching without movement, his owl finally shoots into the dark sky. Every head cranes as his owl is swallowed by the night, until gentle wing beats are the only sound, soon followed by the soft clanging of metal keys. Success.

Our company cheers on Kole ferociously, probably further inflating his ego as he proves himself to be the first recruit to victoriously slip the key into the lock and open the massive rusty gates. I send him a silent prayer of good luck as he steps into the darkness that conceals what lies ahead. He never turns to look for me.

***

Sometimes, I loathe the fact I was bought for ten measly krona because it means I'm the least valuable. The least likely to survive. And today certainly marks the worst day to be as valuable as a pair of buttons.

"It's like waiting to die. Why do they make everyone go player style?" I mumble to Grape and Merry, watching as Ona sits crisscrossed with her bird, trying in the final minutes to transfer her delta, but she seems defeated.

"Don't think like th-that," Merry nudges me against the wall, "Look at it this way. Now y-y-you have more time to p-prepare."

I shrug at her positivity, trying desperately not to slip into brain-numbing agony again. It only pulls my concentration and makes me rethink my thought-out plan.

The hours tick by into mid-morning, and each time the redheaded player descends those stairs, my stomach twists to realize I'm another person away from agony. My heart races every time she gives the recruit their instructions before sending the key back to the top.

The average recruit seems to last about ten minutes before the next one is sending their owl to retrieve the key. Any longer and they're most likely dead. Any shorter and they're *definitely* dead.

The numbers dwindle throughout the day, leaving the remaining bodies spread out through the chasm as we wait our turns. As Ona finally takes her place before the gates, I pray with everything I have that she makes it through, whether or not her bird is able to assist. Maybe she could smash her fist into the wall and send the key down that way.

A hungry sigh of relief greets me when her owl finally launches toward the sky and returns with the key. Ona shoots me a look over her shoulder that others might mistake for a glare, but I know it as *thank you.*

I nod to Ona, smiling widely as I mouth, *you've got this!* I know she'll make it to the other side. That monster has nothing on her strength. If anything, the President will be lucky if there's a monster left after Ona's done with it.

Soon, it's down to me, Grape and Merry. My stomach sits in knots as I pull them both in for a hug, squeezing as if it might be the last time I see them. I know that it most certainly could. This is the most dangerous and wild thing I have ever done in my life, and yet the sliver of hope that lives within my chest keeps me standing.

I watch as Merry's owl soars up the wall with ease, higher and higher until she snatches the key, diving headfirst toward Merry in a great show. The shapeshifter's bright smile gives me confidence in her skills, and I know she's going to do amazing. I repeat the words in my head over and over until I believe them without a shadow of a doubt.

After about half an hour, it's Grape's turn. I try to tell myself that's just enough time for Merry to make it out alive, but I don't let myself dive down that road.

The player makes her way down the stairs to collect Grape, and she has brought another with her this time. They're locked in conversation about whatever they just witnessed Merry do. That's a good sign, I think.

Desperately, I grab Grape by the shoulders, wanting to force every bit of luck in the world into his veins. I want to give him *anything I can* to help at all. He's on his own in there, and I don't have the right words to help him.

"You're going to do great." I promise him, fighting stinging tears.

Grape grabs my shoulders back, forcing me into a tight hug as he plants a kiss on my cheek, "I know," he whispers, making me giggle through the mist, "And so will you. Whatever you have planned, I know it'll be amazing. I'm just mad I won't get to see it."

I shake my head against his, swallowing the sob that tries to force its way out.

Against his ear, I murmur in the slightest whisper that I can manage, "Grape?"

"Yeah?"

"What I'm going to do in there… if everything goes to plan, it's going to look… *different.* Unorthodox. But I don't have another choice."

I grip onto him tighter as the players nearly reach the floor, never wanting to let go.

Grape pulls away from me, brushing aside a stray tear to look me in the eyes. The corner of his mouth quirks up as he steps away, his owl meeting his shoulder.

"My ma always told me that you can't be doing it wrong if no one knows what you're doing. I'll see you on the other side." With a wink, he turns on his heel to receive his final speech, sends his owl to the sky, and walks through the gates with all the confidence he can pack in such a small frame.

I begin counting the seconds to keep track of how long Grape has been behind the wall, but my mind ruins the numbers with obsessive worrying. I wait until I'm completely alone and out of view from anyone spying above to use my incense, breathing deeply to calm the nerves begging to spiral out of control.

Before I know it, I'm facing the tall, rusty gates, taking in every detail because I can't afford to focus on anything else. I won't allow myself to, even though the thoughts of death are never-ending.

Old splatters of cerulean paint along the river-bear emblem catch my attention, my gaze studying years of corrosion from exposure to the elements.

What if there are dead bodies piled up inside?

I shake my head, my eyes finding a patch of moss thriving along the bars, and I wonder how old these gates might be.

Will I throw up at the sight of my dead friends?

My jaw clenches at the thought, focusing on the intricate details of worn algae.

Will my brothers shed a tear if I die before their eyes? Will they step in to save me? Would Jude?

"You ready?"

A gasp escapes my throat as I jump at the question, balling my fists to keep from shaking violently.

The beautiful player with bright red hair stands tall above me, even taller than I thought. Her voice is like honey. Am I falling into a trance? How can a person be so gorgeous? I see why Jude is so smitten.

"She's ready."

My head snaps to my left, my heart picking up faster than before to see those swirling blue eyes smile down at me. His arms are crossed casually, and I wonder why I'm not surprised to see him in an expensive dress shirt perfectly ironed even though we've been hiking for two days. It seems he'd never be caught dead in something as meager as scratchy felt or even the thick leather blues his players don.

The captain sure is a mystery.

"I don't know if you've been introduced, but this is one of my players, Marble. Marble, this is Soria Davidsdottir."

Jude smiles between the supermodel and me, and suddenly I want to shrink into a ball and roll very far away.

I have to be a foot shorter than Marble, my greasy blond hair lying limp behind my back as I wear nothing impressive but my smelly felt with the giant number zero plastered to the back. And she stands tall with authority, radiating power as if it's always been hers. She scares me.

"It's wonderful to finally meet you, Soria."

She gives me a small smile. Fuck, she's nice. Now I really want to die.

"You too." I mutter meekly, my hand instinctively creeping toward Pancake against my chest.

"So, here's your instructions," Marble says crossing her arms, her voice soothing but serious, "You will get the key to get through the gates. Inside you'll need to find the key to get out, and get out fast. And..."

The player's eyes drift to the sickly bird in my sling, "Whenever you're ready, go ahead."

She seems like she wants to say something else, glancing between my bird and Jude until she finally gives in, "Your... *owl*... it can fly, right?"

"No." I answer, watching the reaction I knew was coming. But before Marble can address the captain about how to proceed, I follow up with, "But every person obtaining a delta needs a key to get through, right?"

Marble's perfect brows knit in confusion as she nods slowly, and I let my train of thought carry me further.

"Since I don't have one," I swallow, finally testing my own theory I'd come up with weeks ago to solve Pancake's flying issue, and rest my palm on the gate handle, "I should be able to just..." and with a satisfying *click,* the handle obeys my turn, opening into the darkness with ease. For once, being mediocre has its upside.

Among the book of monsters, there was an interesting passage in the prologue about the original arena creators being human with no special gifts or power. They were necessary to create the gates that confine magic or else nothing would get built. That knowledge made me realize there has to be a way in for someone like me. Someone without power.

Marble crosses her arms, her chin tilting in approval. My eyes find Jude's, and the vein in my neck quickens because I'm not sure how to read his knitted-brow expression. Is he impressed? Annoyed? I can't tell, but I certainly don't have time to decipher what this look means.

"Good luck in there!" Marble says, "And if I can offer one bit of advice from girl to girl," she leans in slightly to block Jude's gaze, lowering her voice as she gestures to her face with an open palm, "Do something to keep hair out of your face. Thank me later."

I force a nod, grateful for any tips even though my hair is the last of my worries.

Jude steps closer as his player marches up the stairs, not looking back. His scent drives me crazy and I curse my feeble mind for thinking about such ridiculous things before my death that awaits eagerly behind rock walls. Perhaps it's only normal to crave the things that make us human before we take our last breath.

I feel myself inching closer, wanting to give in to the tension that has my mind and body in a spiral, but I keep my sweaty palm on the door like a lifeline to reel me back in.

Jude's eyes rake over my face, down my cheek, toward my lips, to my neck, and finally fix back on my gaze. I'm surprised to see him standing so close.

"Remember," he says, his voice low and thick, "No one cares if you make it out. Not a soul."

My grip tightens on the doorknob. He's wrong. Grape. Merry. Ona. Ivar.

I have people.

Before my snarl reaches my lip, Jude says, "Do you feel that anger? *Use it,* because no one cares more about your life than you. Do whatever you can to survive."

I clear my throat, nodding through the pitiful advice, even though I want to run away. I want to run far from here and never look back. I can't. Running isn't my fate anymore. Fighting is. I'm going to put up one hell of a fight if it's the last thing I do.

Just before I walk through the doorway, I throw out one last question to the captain, mostly because it might be my last chance to find out the real answer. Away from any listening ears, any prying eyes and certainly in the heat of a life and death moment, I need to know.

"Jude?" His name on my lips feels so odd as I recognize this is the first time I've spoken it.

Jude's jaw ticks, his eyes finding mine in response.

"No one cares if I make it out. I know that, but," my voice descends to a whisper, pushing aside every reason I have for hating him and untying the bottle of cravings I've kept under lock and key, "Do you?"

Those eyes fall, and for some reason, this hurts more than the words that follow.

The captain faces me with a cold stare, squaring those broad shoulders as his tone finds an octave so intense I wish I had never asked.

"I think you've mistaken my presence for something other than it is. I care about strong deltas and smart matches for the Diamond Games, recruit."

"Got it." I purse my lips, mentally slamming that glass bottle of superficial cravings against a brick wall and cursing myself for opening my mouth in the first place.

"You were never supposed to survive the train ride. Think about that." Jude says as a last jab, studying my face carefully. Funny. His words don't match the haunting expression on his face right now.

"And yet, here I am." I spit, turning toward the entrance and feeling a new torrent of anger I've never known fill my stomach, but an uneasy despair douses the rage. I guess I thought he would say something else. Stupid me.

CHAPTER 17: THE CRUCIBLE

The door slams closed behind me, and I'm left cloaked in never-ending darkness accompanied by shuddering breaths. I don't have time to think of rejection, or whatever the fuck kind of mind game the captain has been playing. I have my own game to play right now, and the only way to win is to survive.

I bring the powder to my nostril, inhaling deeply as my legs take reluctant steps until the motion triggers ten gas lanterns. They flicker on straight ahead, illuminating a long, cedar table full of weapons.

I inch closer to read the sign that sits on the table in old Bachalorian:

You have thirty seconds to choose a weapon.

Searching the table frantically, I know I have seconds to make the right choice, but none of these options would be useful in the slightest, especially if I have no idea how to wield them.

The table holds everything from double-edged swords and curved daggers to staves with spears and wrought-iron chains. This would be a dream for someone skilled facing a lion or even the arachne, but a hydra? It's pointless. And I'm almost out of time.

Before the seconds tick away, my gaze lands on something shiny at the far end of the display. It's something so out of place that it only makes sense to choose it. It wouldn't be here by mistake.

Sweaty hands lunge for the handle of the sleigh bells just before the table disappears altogether, and a slab of rock before me crumbles away and light floods my vision.

Shielding my face, I step forward in the bright afternoon sun to take in the terrain. The exact one that I guessed it would be. Ahead of me lies a deep jungle forest, thick with bright green foliage and all sorts of bugs whirring around. Fifty-foot trees scrape the sky, towering above the smaller ones with ease. They absorb the sun shamelessly, but are not taller than the rock walls that surround the jungle in a bowl shape, keeping the monster and I trapped together.

"Okay, Pancake," I mutter to the bird peeking out from the sling, "It's just you and me now."

I find a shaded spot to assess what I have to work with, and lay out everything before me. The sleigh bells will be the most practical tool because the hydra is oversensitive to sounds. That's what I learned from the book of monsters. I have three cracker packets remaining to keep my stomach semi-full, and one sick baby bird who can hardly move a wing. What wonderful odds.

First things first, I rip my felt sleeves off by pulling at the loose stitching in the shoulders, and wrap the sleigh bells tightly inside to keep them from making noise at the wrong moment.

Through chapped lips, I can't help but mutter one last Hail Mary prayer to the heavens. I slip Pancake back in his sling offering him a piece of cracker as I inhale the rest. I have to keep our energy up no matter what.

Following Marble's advice, grimy fingers braid the sides of my hair out of my face, tying them behind my head as I take a deep breath, ready to do the impossible.

"Now where's that key?"

***

Several minutes of creeping through the jungle brush drifts by until the only indication of how long I've been in here comes from the auburn sun above. Soon it'll be nightfall, so if I want to face a hydra with daylight on my side, I need to hurry.

I can't see anything above the walls, but I know people are watching.

I can feel the condemnation with every step while anxiety slides down my spine through each noise that comes from the jungle.

My boot sloshes in a puddle, my sweaty arms flinching with every slither of leaf birthed of the swampy greenery until a slice of hope presents itself. I've finally reached the other side of the terrain where another pair of opaque gates etched into the rock wall greets me.

Out of curiosity, my palm rests on the handle, turning slowly, but it doesn't budge. I throw my weight into the gates, but the gates don't give. The empty keyhole stares up at me tauntingly, along with dark bloodstains that I don't let my mind ruminate on. I guess I have no choice but to find the key, otherwise I'll be trapped in here until the hydra finds me. But where is it?

Suddenly an idea clicks in my head. It needs to find *me.* In that case I need higher ground.

"Hold on Pancake," I mumble, stuffing the felt-covered bells tightly between my belt and begin to climb. I reach the top of a tree, only to nearly slip and fall once I lay eyes on it. My heart springs in my throat to see the monster finally in the flesh.

Far off in the distance, not three, not four, but *five* hydra heads swivel in every direction above the tree lines, searching for its prey. Its prey that is most certainly… *me.*

I was prepared for three heads as the book said. I was prepared for something the size of an elephant whale. This is the size of a *dragon.* I suppose I have my ten measly krona to thank for that. There's no doubt a few other recruits took off a head hoping to end the monster, but I can't imagine the look on their faces to see more growing back after the destruction of one.

I unleash a curse, feeling defeated already, but immediately regret the swear once all five heads snap in my direction.

Quick as a fly, I fling out of view, pinning myself to the other side of the tree and forcing my ragged breathing to halt. The hydra's over-sensitivity to noise can either be my saving grace or my own destruction. The problem is, I didn't plan for five heads. Five sets of supersonic ears.

My lips pin shut to minimize hyperventilation as the sound of heavy steps sends goosebumps up my arms. The cracking of trees jump-starts my heart as the monster weaves its way through the jungle on a mission.

No, not a mission. A *hunt.*

A low, guttural growl vibrates through the greenery, sending chills up my back as the tyrant of the jungle searches for its food.

It's the most terrifying noise I've ever heard. That is until it ceases. All sounds evaporate, not even a frog gurgling from the jungle floor. I swear the hydra must be able to hear my heart racing through my chest. I beg my breaths to come out softer.

Slowly, a set of huffing nostrils creeps into my peripheral vision, lowering between branches, inhaling to scope out the fresh body for dinner.

Shaking where I stand, I pray to the heavens that Pancake stays silent, and turn to take in the scaly head only a couple feet from my face. Its eyes are pinstriped and glossy with a pair of bloody horns protruding between two scaly ears that swivel at every noise of the jungle.

The ears. Those are its biggest weapons. My plan could still work. I just need absolutely and utterly *perfect* timing.

Eventually, the head rises to the sky to join the others as its body departs through the trees, and I do everything I can to stay as silent as possible. To make my movements blend in with the ones already existing within the jungle.

As the massive, scaly body passes, something coppery and shiny catches my eye, and everything makes sense now. The reason why only the best and most powerful deltas survive. The explanation of necessity to transfer power to an acolyte for assistance. Someone without the right skills could never make it out alive. Not when the key to the gates sits draped around one of the hydra's necks.

I resist sighing in defeat, trying to think quickly before the orange tint of the sun grows any more burnt orange hues.

Carefully and quietly, I ease down the branches with little to no noise. The crumbling sound below my feet with every step sends me into panic mode.

Despite my fear, I force myself to keep moving as fast as possible.

Taking a new assessment of my surroundings, I try to find something, *anything* that will help create a diversion, but I can't think properly. If only I was facing the arachne, I might have a fighting chance against something just a tad smaller.
At least with its webs I could…

I suppress the gasp at my own idea. A *brilliant* idea that I've had to improvise ever since seeing the hydra in person.

I find the sharpest rock possible and take it back to the low-hanging trees, cutting into the six-inch-thick vines that choke the trunks like a snake. One by one, they drop to the jungle floor, but not conspicuous enough to catch the monster's attention on the other side of this jungle prison.

Hot sweat drips into my eyes as I move onto another tree, sawing into the vines and using every ounce of energy to collect as many as possible. I'm going to need hundreds of them if this is about to work. The strength in those limbs can push through *trees* with ease, so this trap needs to be stronger than its prey. And that's exactly what I'm turning the hydra into. *My prey.*

I'm not sure how much time has passed at this point, but I've certainly been in here long enough for the sun to set. Hours maybe? I can't tell. My light is going to run out soon if I don't pick up the pace.

Pancake's crusty, bald head peeks from the sling as I tie together the last vine against a tree trunk, wiping the sweat from my face for the thousandth time and hoping dehydration doesn't claim me. I decide to rip up the rest of my top and fashion a wrap around my breasts to keep me cool. The humidity in this terrain alone could take me out before the monster has the chance to.

I chose my trap spot for a specific reason, although it cost me a lot of daylight to move every last vine to a different patch of trees. This area is imperative to make it a successful snare.

With every second that passes, it becomes increasingly difficult to ignore the agony in my legs and back, as well as the invisible eyes from above. I keep repeating Grape's mantra to myself. *You can't be doing it wrong if no one knows what you're doing,* and I guarantee the watchers in the sky have *no* idea what I'm doing.

"They will know soon enough. Focus."

I sigh at the voice in my head, brushing it off as I step through the vines, careful to avoid the pools of tree sap that lie beneath. I eyeball the distance from the beetle-hive above, hoping the heavens give me the right aim and the right timing.

Slowly and steadily, I round the rock wall, listening for heavy footsteps to make themselves known, and from what I can hear, the monster still sounds far off on the other end of the jungle.

With a deep breath, I tuck Pancake as far down into his sling as he can go, and gently unravel the bells from the felt, careful not to jostle a single one until it's time.

The sleeves drop to the ground as I peek over my shoulder, mapping the path back one last time before sealing my own fate.

I gently pat the baby bird on my chest for encouragement, promising him I will do what I can to keep him alive, and commit to my plan with every last fiber of my soul.

My steady, sore arm raises gingerly above my head, my palm squeezing the sleigh-bell handle with the grip of death. One last breath. One last goodbye to my friends. My family.

The ones I care about. To my country, and my captain.

I shake the bells violently, screaming along with them.

A loud, thunderous noise booms through the jungle, followed quickly by heavy footsteps that scatter the fowl in the treetops and shake the brush beneath. I turn on my heel and sprint faster than I ever have before, bobbing and weaving through the marked trail and toward the trap I've laid for the monster.

Hanging thorn branches swipe at my bare skin as I rush past, ignoring the slices to my arms and ribs because I'm about to face a hell of a lot worse if I don't keep trucking through. Nothing else matters but getting past those vines. *Nothing* else. Not the pain in my lungs. Not the blood seeping down my abdomen from thorns. Not the blurriness in my vision from lack of water. *Nothing.*

I hurdle a fallen log as the earth quakes behind me, and another spine-snapping screech fills the sky, louder than anything I've ever heard. It's deafening. I wonder how I hadn't heard that terrible noise from the other side of the wall. Perhaps there was a sound shield. Or perhaps no one has pissed off the hydra like I have.

From memory, I slide past the giant trunk I recognize, feeling the hot breath of angry heads gaining on my path. I'm almost there. I'm so close! I can see the trap ahead. I just need to…

Suddenly, a shadow envelops me for a split second, momentarily confusing me before I realize the worst has happened.

The hydra comes crashing down in front of me after leaping over me, mere feet from the webs I've arranged. It stares me down, now facing the opposite direction than I need it to go.

Every head swivels to pin me with a ravenous glare while five mouths snap open to reveal hundreds of razor-sharp teeth, just waiting to claim my bones for a snack. I am so fucked.

CHAPTER 18: ENEMY'S FUR

Gut-wrenching, terrible fear threatens to crash my blood sugar and surrender my body to destruction as I stare down five treacherous heads that inch closer and closer. I can't move a muscle.

Every last vein freezes with paralyzing fear as the images of a painful, gruesome death flash before my eyes.

The five pairs of knife-like horns are stained with clotted blood, probably from half of the company. Their maws must be seven feet tall when open, and hot, horrendous breath surrounds me like a fog. The reddish-brown scales lining its massive body remind me of a poisonous snake by the way they roll and move as each muscle contracts on all four paws with talons longer than my arm.

I'm out of ideas. I'm out of Hail Mary's. I have nothing left and no one will ever remember the silly little girl who thought she could outsmart a monster. What was I thinking?

"*There's no time for resignation. Focus.*"

I grit my teeth as the ancient voice rattles through my mind, bringing me back to reality. What would I do if I weren't afraid? What would I do! All I have is a handle of bells.

"*Run!*"

Narrowly escaping snapping teeth that lunge for me, I leap to the side, finding shelter behind a thick tree trunk, but not for long.

The hydra screeches its rage as a massive, spiked tail comes crashing into the tree I seek protection behind. Just barely avoiding being flattened into the earth, I roll to the side and find my feet, sprinting even faster than before.

As Pancake chirps from my chest, I mutter, "Not now. Food later."

I duck to avoid another falling tree, searching for the path I created. My trap is the only thing that will work. My only hope. Even if I had a knife or a sword or the world's biggest crossbow, nothing man-made is going to take down this beast. So, I need bigger. And I need it *soon.*

Bounding over another log that comes tumbling into my vision, I try telling myself everything will be fine to ease the heaviness in my lungs, but a stump clips my leg and that hope tries to melt as I come crashing onto the jungle floor— the floor that is nearly cleared by the hydra's rampage— everywhere except my trap. Hopefully it's none the wiser.

I force my body to twist mid-fall in order to protect Pancake, though a small squeak comes from his throat as my knee takes the first impact, and a stabbing pain shoots up my leg.

My side scrapes the ground with rocks and thorns carving into my flesh, earning a sharp yowl of pain. There's no doubt I'm a bloody mess, but I have to keep moving if this is to be the worst of my injuries.

Ignoring the throbbing pain in my knee, I try to remind myself that I've gone through worse. I have been through *much* worse with Sera and her army of demons. I limp forward, running as fast as I can with the hydra hot on my heels, hoping I've given it a wide enough berth to land perfectly.

Every muscle in my body screams for mercy and rest, but I ignore it. I need my body to give me every last ounce of strength. My life depends on it. My future depends on it. Maybe, just maybe, the look on my friends' faces seeing me alive and victorious will be worth it in the end.

I'm doing this to survive. I'm doing this for myself. This time, no one can save me. But that's okay. I don't need saving.

Pitching a loud grunt as I brace myself for the monster's impact, I jump with everything I have. I leap straight into the carefully knotted vines woven between the trees. Through a half-stumble, I find my balance and push forward. I follow the intricate rows as the monster's heavy steps shake the ground behind me.

Just a little closer.

Battered legs carry me faster through the vines, leaping over the lofty ones and ducking beneath the low-hanging in a zigzag pattern that I've memorized by heart now. The thundering steps get even closer as I finally reach the edge and roll out of the way, peering back to watch the chaos unfold.

The hydra comes in fast—too fast for its own good. It snaps the first several yards of vines until a good thick set catches its front leg, causing the top-heavy creature to fall. It tries to correct itself in the air, but another set of vines tangle its back leg, causing the hydra to come slamming to the ground in a messy heap.

It roars in almighty rage, the octave of anger reaching an unparalleled pitch, forcing me to slam my hands over my ears to keep from going deaf.

The hydra struggles helplessly as it tries in vain to gain its footing. It is stuck in tangled vines and sticky tree sap that pools beneath its scaly stomach. The sap coats its necks and massive chest, further enraging the monster as every attempt to stand proves to be harder than the last.

I seize my opportunity while it lasts, knowing at any moment it's going to get angry enough to continue its death march for the one who tricked it.

Heads snap at every angle, and it seems like they're talking to each other. Or rather, *screaming* at each other.

With my bells in hand, I limp around the safety of the tree, shaking them furiously toward the hydra. I emit a war cry so brutal I swear the blood boils in my own veins.

I will not succumb to the death this monster demands.

I am the anger in my blood.

I am timeless.

Above all, I am ruler of this jungle, and this hydra will bow to the death I deliver.

Each head twists in agony against the high-pitched noise I create. My lungs draw in the most air they can manage. I bellow my fury toward the monster who has claimed too many lives today. Determined that mine will not be one of them.

Time seems to slow as I deliver the final blow. Heavens, don't turn on me now.

I aim quickly as the milliseconds depend on it, and launch the heavy sleigh bells into the sky, right toward the beetle hive that sits above the hydra's head, nestled secretly between tree branches.

For a split second, the monster regains its senses and moves a head to lunge for me with target-locked precision, but it's too late. It was always going to be too late.

The instrument meets its mark, bursting open the hive of beetles, or should I say, *bell* beetles, exclusively native to the jungle and my very own saving grace.

On impact, the beetles shoot from their destroyed hive, aiming downward in self-defense to ward off any predator. Their buzzing creates a terrible bell-rattling symphony that frazzles the hydra, earning another mad roar that has me wincing from the pain in my eardrums.

Instantly, the thousands of beetles find their target as they fall to the forest floor, sticking along every inch of sap that covers the hydra's chest. The heads snap furiously as the shrieking bell noises grow infinitely louder, causing the hydra to experience a severe degree of distress.

Every ear swivels and pivots on the hydra's body until it can't focus on anything in particular, driving it more than mad. Driving it *insane*.

With no other defense but to kill whatever causes the monster pain, a single head comes flying towards the most noise, meeting its chest with sharp teeth. The other heads respond in unison, oblivious with rage until it's ultimately the product of its own destruction. Long necks swoop downward in a frantic rush, swiping madly toward their own chest, ripping, biting and clawing at the beetles until nothing is left but blood and teeth and heads.

The hydra sends up one last deafening cry to the sky as its tail swings forward, knocking over lines of trees in the process. Trees that are coming for me.

I spin on a heel and haul ass in the opposite direction, trying to out-sprint the trees that rush for the ground. I leap to my back as everything goes dark.

***

I cough myself back to consciousness, feeling the mother of all headaches weighing down against my temples. My back aches and my skin feels shredded to hell, not to mention the throbbing in my knee that elicits a terrible groan from my throat. My throat that's parched for water and raspy from screaming.

But suddenly every bodily concern ceases as I realize something.

My hand flies to my chest to find an empty sling. I shoot upward in a panic as my forehead slams into a thick tree branch. I rub my eyes quickly, taking in my surroundings as the orange glow of the sunset has almost faded completely, nearly absorbing every speck of light within its wake.

Several branches lie on top of my body, but I've just barely escaped being crushed by the thickest part of the fallen trunk.

Rolling out of the brush, I pull myself to my feet, feeling my heart race faster than ever because I can't find my bird. I *can't* find my bird. Where is he? Is he okay?

Panic consumes me as I scream, "Pancake! Pancake!" Vibrating palms cup my mouth to carry the shriek across the dark jungle.

I will never forgive myself. He was just a baby. He deserved to live as much as me.

My painful torso twists madly, searching for any sign or sound that my little bird is okay as a desperate gaze rakes the ground.

He doesn't belong crushed beneath trees.

He doesn't deserve to be trapped in this jungle, fighting to survive.

Pancake was the most pure and precious creature, and the world chose to throw him away!

He can't be dead. He can't be.

Bloodied legs carry me in a blind rage, my screams echoing his name through a chasm of grief. I lunge for something small falling from a tree above, but as my hands snatch it up, a cry rips through me—it's just a leaf.

A stupid *fucking leaf!*

"Pancake!" I shriek into the air, tears streaming my cheeks as I scan the jungle floor for him, "Pancake, where are you?" A sob cuts through my cry as despair begs to cut me at the knees.

"I am here, human."

Every hair on the back of my neck rises to the response. A gasp escapes my throat.

No. It can't be.

It can't.

"It can and it is."

I turn toward the warmth that pulls my attention. The warmth that attaches itself to the deep, ancient voice that's been sitting in my mind for months, weighing in, giving advice and calmly keeping me on track when I almost lost myself.

My neck cranes as tear-stained cheeks lift to see *not* a half-pound, flightless, sick baby bird staring me down— but a large, *beautiful* bird flapping its wings of flame above, peering down at me with those same golden eyes.

I've seen this magical and enchanting creature only in storybooks before. One of the oldest and rarest creatures that was always proven to be a myth. Even Mrs. Furien said this creature—this *being*—is only known to be a beautiful and magical figurehead that all acolyte lore derives from.

The phoenix.

Its wings flutter gently and slowly, as if it takes minimal effort to keep afloat in the sky as it descends like a beautiful nightmare, dangerous and marvelous.

"Wh… what?" I stutter, trying to catch my breath and understand what's going on, "What do you… who are you?"

The bird lands on a low-hanging branch, still several yards above in the air, illuminating the night with its fiery glow.

"I believe you know me as Pancake, or some other farcical breakfast item."

My jaw plunges to the ground. This can't be. Its beak doesn't move, but that voice fills my head, assuring me it belongs to the mesmerizing creature above. They are one and the same.

"You mean… you mean *you're* Pancake? That voice in my head… It was you all along? *Pancake?"*

My eyes are unbelieving. I can't get a grasp on any of this.

"*My given name is Sicar, but I suppose you may nominate an alternative."*

I can't believe what I'm hearing. Hell, I can't believe what I'm *seeing.* The phoenix has only ever been a myth. A creature so obsolete the world tossed it up to make-believe. Yet, it's not. He's here in front of me. Perched on a branch right above my head, claiming it's been the voice in my mind this entire time. Not a figment of my imagination. Not my subconscious thoughts. A voice from a phoenix.

A thousand questions rattle my mind as I amble closer, weighing precautions.

"Why are you here? Why have you been talking to me?" I hold my breath as I wait for an answer I'm used to. Because you're weak. Because you need help. Because you're the abomination to steer clear of and I need to warn others.

"*Because I have chosen you. And we are not done yet."*

I blink at the phoenix, or Pancake or… Sicar? Whoever he or… *it* is. The power that radiates off of him is overwhelming. As he turns to take off, I try to stop him from making a mistake.

"I think you chose wrong. I don't have a delta… I'm not like the others."

I release a sigh that's been pent up for too long, succumbing to my own words that must be true. I had deserved a flightless, helpless bird but not a magical, rare creature. He doesn't know who I am.

"*As your acolyte, I do know you. We will discuss this later. But now we must go."*

There's no room for argument in his tone as the voice warms my skull, and I follow the phoenix as he lights the way in the dark, leading me toward the mess of blood and vines I had left behind.

His flames illuminate the attack scene and the stench of blood fills my senses when my gaze falls over what I caused. What I… *achieved.* The hydra lies dead in a pile of flickering bell beetles, sap, blood and vines. I won. I killed it.

"*We should advance with haste before they deem that you've fallen to Halkiya The Terror.*"

I swallow the bile in my throat, not wanting to put a name to the monster I've murdered. The monster who still holds the key to my freedom, and the key that keeps me from knowing if my friends survived.

I dig through the sap and blood, holding my breath as my hand plunges into the chest cavity to retrieve the copper key that only fits one lock.

My eyes graze the sharp teeth that told me I would die. The horns that promised I'm not strong enough. The scales that deemed my skin easily breakable, but it was wrong. This beast lies dead at my feet while I still stand. I survived.

"*Wear the fur of your enemies.*"

Several minutes of grotesque carving later, I haul my trophies with me, along with the key as the bright, fiery phoenix lights the way above.

My knee aches terribly and I can't help but grip my bleeding side as I hobble along the path, finally reaching the gates that lead to freedom.

I lift the key, but hesitate.

My voice trembles, "What if all of my friends are dead?" I don't want to ask, because I'm sure Sicar already knows, but I *have* to know. I'd rather sob in the privacy of the jungle than in front of the recruits who've kicked me down.

"*We shall have to see.*"

Without thanking the mystical bird, I sigh, pressing the key into the lock and slipping past the gates that held me hostage for half a day.

CHAPTER 19: TENT INVADER

The gates sit empty in the night, but I follow the voices and chattering up the chasm walls to find a grassy meadow lying below. Several campfires sit in groups scattered across the field with joyful laughter and musical celebration. Drinks and food are strewn about as every person embraces the fact that they have completed an incredible feat. They survived phase one.

Our company has shrunk noticeably, and I can't imagine how many recruits have died today, but I am not one of them.

"*Head high, now. We are about to make our entrance.*"

"What?"

And before I can ask another question to the cryptic phoenix, he soars overhead in the darkness, shooting fire into the sky with ease, dropping my jaw at the glorious sight. His wings spread wider and wider until he's enormous, forcing every head to turn his direction as the chattering and shouting ceases and all eyes land on me at the lip of the hill. All eyes falling on what lies in my hands, and what sits draped around my neck.

Swallowing, I throw away every coiled thought of nervousness, because honestly, I'm *tired.* I'm exhausted, and I'm over this day. I'm thirsty and starving and I need space to decompress. There is little hope of that by the looks on every face.

The crowd grows silent as they part for me, allowing me to pass with room as I limp along. Every eye stares at the hydra horn in my palm and the scales leaking crimson from my neck like a scarf because I've earned them. They may have run from the Hydra, but I conquered it.

As I trudge along, the murmurs pick up, which I can't make out until slow smiles appear, and I wish I could ask Sicar what they're saying. Or thinking? I have no idea what he's capable of, and I make a mental note to ask him about his limitations later.

Instantly, a slow clap begins, followed by more and more hands until cheers lift to the sky. All of a sudden I'm surrounded by shrieks of joy and cheers. What's happening? What is this?

"They respect the hydra-slayer."

"Soria?" Grape shouts across the field, and instant tears fall down my cheeks to see he's alive, "Soria!"

More tears follow suit when both Merry and Ona trail after him, wrapping me up in a desperate hug as the rest of the crowd tosses their praise in our tight circle.

This moment is surreal. It's make-believe. It's something out of dreams because I'm not special enough to earn this type of reward or attention. And yet, it is happening to me.

Me.

"You bastard! We all thought you died hours ago!" Grape wipes misty eyes, pulling me tighter as Ona slaps a calloused hand on my back in approval, "And look at you!" Grape slides a finger over the scales, waggling his brows, "A real badass! I knew you could do it."

"How did th-th-*that* happen?" Merry asks with a giant smile, pointing to the flaming bird flying off into the night, "A phoenix? Soria, h-*how?* I mean… they a-a-aren't even real! Or I thought they weren't."

All I can do is offer her a shrug and an I'm-not-sure because that's certainly the truth. My heart sinks for a moment to see Merry's little owl is nowhere to be seen. In fact, the field is sparse of any owls.

Before I can console Merry about her loss, rough hands grip my shoulders and spin me around. They land me right in front of charming eyes and shaggy blond hair.

"Soria! I can't believe you did it!" Kole's smile is wider than I've ever seen.

Of course he can't believe I'm alive. He would call any bluff that said I would actually manage to kill the hydra. For now, keeping Kole in the dark works better for me in the long run. I have to keep this charade up however tired of his presence I am.

I throw a tired smile back as his jealous gaze rakes over the scales and down my bleeding body.

"You have to tell me everything. Who helped you kill it? And the bird? Did that firebird kill it?" Kole's questions nearly make me laugh at my own stupidity for being so blind. I keep smiling, promising him stories for another time, but claiming I need rest more than anything right now.

Kole nods, his lustful gaze finding my lips, "We both could use the rest. I'll join your tent tonight, Sor. I've missed you more than you know."

Disgust falls over me as Kole spills his empty words that no longer have an effect on me. Through the fake smiles, my eyes catch tall, dark silhouettes of recognizable players in the distance that move toward a canopy that holds the Aegis higher-ups. I notice the beautiful Marble holding hands with that giant, tattooed player, following him into the crowded canopy and out of sight. The last player stops at the entrance, locking eyes with me in the distance. Those swirling blue eyes are the ones that told me he only cares about strong deltas and perfect matches.

Unfortunately for the captain, I'm *still* here. And deltaless. Whatever game he's been trying to play with me, I'm winning.

Keeping my eyes on the swirling blue pair, I give in to the animosity begging to make a move, and lace my fingers around Kole's sweaty neck, bringing his lips to mine.

Kole makes a hungry noise in his throat, his palm finding the small of my back as it always does and I lean in harder to his kiss.

The recruits that circle us shout cheers and toss '*oooo'* noises like we're in grade school, but something doesn't feel right. Though I've kissed Kole more times in my life than I can count, this time feels… *wrong.* It feels like a stranger's lips and it makes me want to bolt out of his embrace.

I peel away from Kole slowly, though his ragged breath signals he wants more.

The plot of my revenge thickens for this sandy-haired boy who couldn't care less about me until I do something worth talking about. I suppose he's not embarrassed of me now, considering several of his new friends slap knowing hands on his shoulder in approval.

"We all can't believe you're alive," Kole grins, searching my face, "Isn't that right, Sera?" He turns to the snake slithering behind him, her evil smile spreading across full lips, but I'm not afraid of her anymore.

I've faced worse. I have my trophies to prove it.

"Good job, Zero!" Sera sneers, her hand snaking through Kole's arm, "We've all been so worried you wouldn't make it, but I'm glad Arnson has his little girl back."

I resist the urge to slap that smirk off her face. The insinuation. The disgust. Everything threatens to fuel the rage boiling in my chest, but frankly, I don't have the energy to attack any other monsters today. So, I suppose leaving my rival with a threat will have to suffice.

Mimicking Sera's sly smile, I close the space between us, clocking that fresh gash along her chin and the way she discreetly holds the right side of her rib cage.

Keeping up the charade of best friends in front of oblivious Kole, I hook my arm around Sera's neck and pull her in for a hug, whispering against a messy dark braid so only she can hear, "Thanks for the abuse, you little bitch. It only made me stronger. But next time, I'm coming for you." Once I let her go, I spin back to my friends quickly, sending a sharp elbow into Sera's battered ribs without anyone noticing.

The look on Sera's enraged face and the painful grunt she tries stifling is just enough to send a real smile to my lips, because I won't be pushed around by her anymore. I will never be her plaything again so long as I live.

***

My gaze instinctively wanders toward the last place I saw the captain looming, but he's gone.

My friends clear a path toward a tent they'd set up, saying they'll stand guard while I clean up and rest. Ona brings me a plate of food while I drain three canteens of water, pouring the rest of the fourth canteen over my shoulders and finally welcoming sleep like an old friend.

As I pull myself into a cotton sleeping roll, fighting the pain that shoots up every inch of my body, a breeze furls the back flap of the tent.

Oh, please no. Not Kole.

"I'm too tired tonight." I grunt, but he doesn't respond.

Sitting up gingerly, I peer into the darkness with a frown until the breeze pushes open the flaps completely, and in slides the captain with a canteen in his hand.

My heart skips to see his stunning face in my tent. Alone. Is he here to kill me? No, he wouldn't. Is he here for something else? No, he despises my touch. And yet, the way he's looking at me doesn't make any sense.

"I thought you were someone else." I mutter, falling back on my elbows and wincing at the movement.

Jude grunts, his voice soft and deep, "Oh, your little hydromancer? Don't worry. When I'm done here, I'll wake him back up."

My brow arches in response, "What did you do to him?" I fill my tone with fake worry because I couldn't care less what happens to Kole, but my concern for him seems to tighten the captain's jaw. Which is a fascinating sight.

"Nothing I can't reverse. Your boyfriend's easy to poison."

Jude watches me intensely as he takes a seat on the other side of the tent, his gaze sliding over what my bedroll doesn't conceal.

I don't bother covering up.

"Are you saying you poisoned my boyfriend?" I play into his underlying game, holding my own cards close.

Jude folds his hands, "I'm saying you're not allowed to have a boyfriend."

"Is that rule anywhere in the ordinance?" I challenge.

"Section Bravo, sub-paragraph fifty-three, *established recruits shall not be married or bound deeply to another before tethering.*"

I offer Jude a tight nod, my voice dripping with insolence, "I guess that sucks for me and my hydromancer."

I watch the captain hold my gaze that floats across his presence. His hair is a little messy, as if hands had scoured the strands. There's a slight smear of dirt on his shirt collar and his top three buttons are undone, his white sleeves rolled haphazardly up his elbows. I realize for once, in this lighting, the captain doesn't look as put together as he usually does.

"Rough day?" I ask sarcastically to change the conversation, but Jude ignores my question. "Where are your other injuries?"

The question takes me back as he studies my arms, neck and chest that's covered by a ratty strip of felt. Why does he care?

"Everywhere." I manage to mutter, though I'm still suspicious of his inquiry. It's not like the doctors would attend to even the worst off recruits. I saw a few lying on the grass as I had made my way into camp, barely conscious and bleeding from their stomachs or legs. I have no doubt they had escaped in time from the hydra, but bearing wounds that very likely won't heal without treatment in the process. We have all the supplies necessary to treat them, but a person doesn't matter until they make it to tethering.

Ivar was right. It's wrong to act like we aren't people.

The captain moves closer, kneeling above me as he sets his canteen aside, digging in his pockets to retrieve a bag with some sort of damp cloth inside.

"Let me see." He orders. And for a moment, I contemplate arguing. I think about telling him to fuck off and let sleep consume me as I endure the pain of the day. But simply put, I'm just too damn tired to fight.

Sighing heavily, I peel the bed roll from my body and sit up gingerly, wincing from the soreness that's caught up with me now that the adrenaline has worn off.

"I'm only obeying because I'm too exhausted to be hostile toward you tonight." I grumble.

The captain makes a noise that sounds awfully similar to a chuckle, "I prefer it that way."

"What? That I obey you?"

A heavy breath hits me in the face, and I force myself to focus on something other than the ache I've just created between my legs.

Traitorous body.

Ignoring my leading question, Jude's jaw tightens as he scans the dried blood along my ribs, arms and probably face. His strong scent fills my nostrils and I swallow, realizing how close we are. Yet he would recoil from my hands should they come near him. He said so himself that he doesn't care. He never has. Maybe I'm not winning this game after all.

"Let me see your back." Jude orders with an edge in his tone, and I listen, wincing as I pivot to face the tent wall.

The barest hint of a growl echoes from the captain's throat, making me wonder what he's looking at. I had tried to take every fall to my back in order to keep little Pancake safe. I can only imagine the bruises and cuts that line my skin.

"How bad is it?" I ask over my shoulder, but Jude's eyes don't break from my spine as he scans every square inch carefully.

"Infection is setting in." He mumbles while raising the cloth, "If you don't get this clean, you'll be dead in a few days."

Eyeing the cloth in his palm, I sigh, "And I suppose that's what you're going to do? Dress my wounds like you care?" I feel the bitterness rise, and I can't help my anger, "Are you visiting every tent tonight to tend to the wounded? Or am I just so lucky?"

Jude sighs over my shoulder, and those warm tendrils of air caress my back, running up my shoulders and encompassing my body like a blanket.

"Just the ones who look shredded to ribbons."

"You're healing other recruits? Isn't that against the rules?"

"You sound surprised," Jude pauses when I don't respond, "I've never been a fan of watching people suffer if there are means to end it. But tell me, Soria," the cloth presses gently to my shoulder blade and I purse my lips against the sudden sting, "Why are you the only recruit to come out of the jungle dripping in blood? Should we change your nickname to Slaughter?"

I bare my teeth as the cloth moves to another sore spot along my back, grumbling through the pain, "You told me to do whatever I can to survive."

"I did."

"So, I *killed* the damn thing."

"You did." Maybe I'm dreaming, but I swear I hear a tinge of pride in his voice, "That move kept you alive, but it cost you." I turn quickly to face him, disbelief scouring my mind as he continues, "The directors are pressing RoBjorn to have you executed for murdering the hydra. To them, it wasn't your choice to make."

"But what choice *did* I have?" My stomach flutters, adrenaline threatening to take back over to keep me in survival mode.

"Everything you did was justified, and there's no bylaw against killing the monster to escape the crucible. It's certainly been done before. The directors are just mad that it was *you* who did it. A recruit without a delta who falls out of every training exercise slew the monster that others couldn't. It doesn't exactly make them look like they're doing their jobs."

I sigh heavily, feeling defeated all over again even though I should be triumphant.

"So, what's going to happen?" My voice tries not to break as I face the tent wall again, letting Jude tend to my back once more, "Are they going to feed me to another beast?"

"I'm not going to let anything happen to you. Even if I weren't here, the President is too intrigued by what you're going to do next to take your life. It makes for such good publicity for Aegis. Not to mention we have your new phoenix to worry about."

Those words. That promise he just made. It sinks deeper into my skin than any wound could, wrapping around my body in a protective spell that I can't help but hold onto. He's not going to let anything happen to me. But when did things change?

I want to ask him a thousand questions. I want to force Jude to spill every last secret that I'm kept in the dark from, and I want to know what exactly is going on here. What's happening to me? What does he know about the phoenix? *My* phoenix? Why am I here? But I don't know where to begin.

Jude sighs again, that warm air encompassing me and soothing my rattling concerns.

"I want to…" he falters for a moment before clearing his throat, his voice hardly a whisper, "I… need to try something."

I feel one of my brows raise in question, but I keep my back to the captain as the cloth slowly falls away. And so does the warm air.

"Just…" Jude mutters, his voice sounding a hint timid, "Just don't move."

After several heartbeats pass in the silence, suddenly I feel the barest touch along my shoulder blade. Rough fingers gently graze my skin before I realize it's Jude's hand and my breathing doesn't come so easily anymore.

His thumb pad sweeps ever so slowly across my shoulder, and I swear it's so silent he has stopped breathing. The air within our tent stiffens, and for a single moment, nothing else exists outside of these fabric walls. There is only him and me who linger in this space where our bodies finally meet, if only connected by a single digit.

My heart vibrates in my chest at the warmth of his fingers just barely skimming my shoulder, and I close my eyes. This feeling has me wishing for more. I want to feel his palm trace strokes along the parts that crave touch. Only *his* touch. I want him closer, so much closer, but before I know it, it's over.

Disappointment greets me like a train wreck.

"You need to drink this." Jude places his canteen by my side, pulling his hand away and moving toward the back tent flap, "It has properties to heal the infection and take away the swelling."

The captain will forever remain a mystery to me.

I whip around to see his gaze finding anything but mine and I'm confused. More than confused, because I deserve answers. I deserve to know what that was and what's really going on, but I know I won't be getting explanations anytime soon. I guess the next part of my plan will include seeking information.

I swallow, not knowing what words to offer and certainly steering clear from any subject that involves him touching me. Probably because I want him to do it again.

"Um, thank you." I whisper as Jude makes to leave.

He finally meets my eyes, scanning my face with those wavering expressions before he shakes his head, "No. Thank *you.*" And he's gone.

I decide to down the entire canteen he left, and I'm more than surprised to find it tastes nothing like medicine or anything that could contain healing properties. Instead, it tastes like rich chocolate, sweet and divine. The more I drink the heavier my eyes grow until I'm lying on my side, stomach full, and my body slowly shutting out every ounce of pain.

Damn, I need more of whatever that was.

I can't help the endless questions that plague my mind as the abyss pulls me away. I want to know more about the phoenix. I want to know what the President plans to do. I want to know why Jude continues to visit me and how I'm going to make it through phase two, but that familiar voice that I can finally attach to a physical form sails through my mind, ceasing all concerns for the evening.

"Rest, now, Percipient One. Tomorrow will have its challenges, but you are victorious today."

CHAPTER 20: RETURNING

Except for a withering headache that I nurse with water, my body feels amazing as our dwindled group of recruits round the Aegis training walls, falling into our typical formation in the sunny courtyard.

It feels like we've been gone for months since we left for the Crucible, but it's only been one week. Since then, so many have died in those short seven days.

To keep my mind off of so much death, I had kept quiet on our trek back, listening to the stories of my friends fighting their way through the Crucible heroically. Grape had used his super hearing to *out-listen* the hydra, always one step ahead of it until he swiped the key with ease, but not before earning a nasty cut across his torso from a swinging claw.

Merry had created a diversion by flying from tree to tree, outsmarting the hydra until it didn't know which way to look. And from what I gathered of Ona's one-word answers, *she* was the one who took off a hydra head by launching a spear clean through its neck. By the look Ona had given me, it's safe to assume she regretted that decision the minute two more giant heads sprouted.

Though each one of my friends had told their stories with gusto and triumph, I couldn't help but realize they all left out the parts about their owls, so I kept my details about Pancake to a minimum, especially after seeing the pain in Merry's eyes. Shapeshifters form attachments to animals deeper than people.

I drop my pack next to Grape's on the crunchy grass that's beginning to yellow for fall. According to the hour-long lectures we had received on our hike back to base, October is the month every recruit should look forward to because the changing of the leaves signals the physical torment has met its end, and mental endurance takes its place. Of course I have no idea what that means.

"Does anyone know why Aegis players receive the nickname, *Arena Thieves?*" Director Boz had asked our group yesterday, ignoring our labored breaths and sore muscles as we ventured up the ravine, "Anyone at all?"

"Because… they are… like the reaper." Answered Phia, the plant mover through heavy breaths. Her dark, pixie hair sat plastered to her forehead lined with sweat as she stumbled along our hiking trail.

"Close. Elaborate, recruit." Boz ordered.

Phia had swallowed to catch her breath, "On the auction stage… the reaper takes lives…" she wheezed, "And in the arena… the players…take souls. The thieves of the arena."

"Very good." Boz had nodded as we followed his steps up the canyon side, "That nickname was given to our players by our Enemy in the North, and what name did we give them?"

"Blood… Letters… Sir." Kole said through panting, "The enemy comes… to siphon… what isn't theirs."

Boz slapped a rough hand along Kole's shoulder with a grin, "Yes! You're all doing so well in your knowledge. Another question: why did we exchange nicknames with our enemy over one hundred years ago?"

"Because they fear us." Sera sneered.

"No," Boz shook his head, "Because they hate us. And we hate them."

Yesterday's memory fades as I drop to my knees next to my pack, letting go of an exhausted breath as the rest of the company stretches their limbs, sprawling out across the courtyard.

"Grape?"

"Mmm." He groans through the grass, his arms covering greasy, spiky hair.

"Why do we hate the Enemy in the North? I mean I know they're *bad* or whatever, but what's the reason?"

Grape makes an annoyed noise, which he does every time I seem to ask a dumb question.

"I feel like you never paid attention in school." He mumbles, flipping to his back as we await instruction in the courtyard. We're all hoping the President grants us the rest of the day to relax. Though, I wouldn't put it past him to sentence us to more classes or excruciating exercise for the sake of training.

"Just tell me." I swat at him with a slow arm, falling to my back against the cool ground.

"The Enemy in the North used to be part of Bachaloria and there used to be one king," Grape grumbles in his arms, "Until hundreds of years ago the king's mother got angry that she wasn't respected or something. She threw a big ol' bitch fit saying she wanted to be queen again and that it was never fair she had to step down from the throne just because her husband died."

"She kind of had a p-p-point." Merry mutters through closed eyes across from us, throwing an arm over her face, or should I say, *wing.* A giant, black-feathered wing lies draped over her face, creating perfect shade for the shapeshifter.

"I guess so," Grape yawns, "You know women weren't treated exactly the same back in the day, but what she did next changed the course of history. The mad queen had loyalists across Bachaloria, but mostly in the North. She rallied them on her side and waged war against her own son for the throne."

"I'm guessing he slew her." I mumble through closed eyes. "No," Grape says, "*She* killed *him.*"

My eyes pop open, "The mad queen killed her own son?" I know I should have paid more attention in class, but it's hard to focus on Bachalorian folklore when your nights are spent driving fence posts into the ground for a local farmer. My teachers were lucky if I showed up to class once a week.

Grape nods with a tired sigh, "Yeah, she murdered his ass, claiming she'd bring hell on earth to every last person who was against her. The king's wife, who was an Earth Mover, was filled with so much rage and despair at the sight of her dead husband that she split the ground, pushing the queen and her army away. That one move kept Bachaloria safe."

I let loose a sigh, "That sounds impossible."

"Not if you're tethered." Grape shoots me a look.

Before I can ask any more questions, someone shouts, *Attention on deck!* I follow the action of every other recruit, leaping to my feet to stand at attention and ignoring the protest of tired muscles.

My stomach settles immediately to see it's only the President accompanied by some officials in their matching uniforms. But his captain is nowhere to be seen.

"At ease," RoBjorn waves a hand and every recruit relaxes into a casual stance. None of us have seen the President since he gave his motivational speech right before the Crucible. I have no doubt he caught some personal train or cart back to the training building, considering someone of his rank and stature would find such a grueling hike laughable.

"You've all done marvelously. You should pat yourselves on the back for such a momentous feat of making it here."

I scan the company that looks diminished to roughly half of what we had after the auction. My heart aches for my peers who will never again see the light of day.

Even though they mocked me and wouldn't blink twice if I fell dead before them, I still feel unmitigated sorrow for the mothers and fathers who lost their children to the auction. No matter how you look at it, the second Aegis claimed a delta, they put a clock on each student's life. My clock just hasn't run out yet for some reason.

The President clears his throat and folds his arms behind his back, "Now, as you all know, only one more phase stands between you and tethering. Pass this test, and everything will change."

The general consensus across the courtyard is exhaustion as several recruits sway and bob their heads where they're standing, hoping these words meet an end very soon.

As if RoBjorn can read our minds, he chuckles, "But that will come in due time, recruits. For now, head to your bunks and take the weekend to rest. You've earned it."

A roar of appreciation echoes across the courtyard as everyone stretches grateful smiles across tired yawns.

I sigh in relief for much-needed respite. I should have known I'd let my guard down too soon.

Just before the President leaves his podium, he adds one last order, his powerful voice carrying across the grassy space, "Oh, everyone except for recruit Davidsdottir." My heart falls into my stomach. "See me in my office."

CHAPTER 21: SEALED FATES

My nail beds are particularly fascinating this evening as nervous hands fiddle in my lap, resenting the ghostly silence.

I sit alone on a granite bench in an empty corridor outside the President's esteemed office, waiting to receive my sentence for taking the hydra's life. Even through felt cargo pants, the granite is freezing on my rear, and I shift uncomfortably, swallowing my nerves and hoping for the best.

Four nights ago, Jude Blackwell had promised he wouldn't let anything happen to me. He assured me the President wanted to see more of whatever I could possibly produce, but was it all a lie? I haven't so much as spoken a word to the captain since that night he visited my tent and gave me a life-saving elixir. He had avoided me at all costs along the hike back, keeping out of sight with ease. Is he still someone I can trust?

I would give anything for some answers right now, but a familiar warmth wraps itself around my mind, settling in and reassuring me. I've deduced this must be my new mind mate, Sicar—or Pancake or whatever the ancient mythical creature wants to go by.

"To you, Human, I have no preference."

"Well, you could call *me* something other than *Human,* you know." I whisper back, and the warmth in my mind meets the edges of my vision in a slight red hue. Interesting.

"Your true name is not for my use, but if a worthy title is of your preference, then I shall accommodate, Hydra-Slayer."

I roll my eyes at the voice in my head, realizing I'll never understand every acolyte's custom. And this new mind sharing will definitely take time to get used to.

Before I can pester Sicar with questions he's particularly good at avoiding, the massive double doors to my left open, revealing Director Neera. She marches out with a scowl, motioning with a single finger to follow her, and I obey.

"Do not be nervous. Elicit confidence."

"Gee, thanks," I mutter to Sicar, wherever he may be. I hadn't said it quietly enough. Neera snaps her head back at me, running those sharp eyes over my face quickly before motioning me to have a seat in the center of the grand office.

The ceilings must be over thirty feet tall, rounded at the top in a dome shape, with cream walls holding various Aegis artwork and motivational sculptures to accent the room. Several feet from my singular wooden chair sits a marvelous copper desk with President RoBjorn seated at the mast, flanked by Director Boz and now Neera.

My heart sinks when I realize who's been behind these doors, deliberating on my behalf. Not a single friendly face who holds my best interest in sight. Then again, those are very few and far between on this blasted base.

President RoBjorn folds his arms, leaning slightly back in his seat to take in my presence. His presence consumes the room like no other.

The monarch of Aegis levels me with a challenging stare that would make any recruit shrink in their seats. Fifty shiny, silver pins decorate the right side of his chest for service to his country while the left side harbors a blue rope with notches, commemorating his hydromancy delta and strength of position. His freshly pleated, Bachalorian blue suit maintains perfection as discerning eyes regard me with an emotion I can't comprehend.

"Miss Soria Davidsdottir, do you know why you're here right now?"

I swallow, snapping myself out of a trance and forcing my hands to sit still in my lap. What a loaded question. Here, on this base? Here in this room? Because I couldn't answer any of those daunting inquiries if my life depended on it. And yet, I can't shake the terrible pressure in my lungs as if it does.

"Because I killed the hydra." I take an unsteady breath, relieved my response didn't sound as shaky as I feel.

The corner of the President's lip slants, looking out of place on his light, leathery skin, but still terrifying to say the least.

"No, Miss Davidsdottir. Though that *is* a reason for my attention toward a recruit with no delta, but not the reason you're sitting here before me."

I force another wheezy breath, keeping my eyes on RoBjorn as he delivers my verdict. There's no way I didn't offend the fuming directors with my actions. I just hope the punishment is quick and painless.

The President waves his hands in a general gesture, "Why do you think we put recruits through such dangerous events?" I keep my lips pinned for fear of answering wrong, but he goes on rhetorically, "For a game? For a spectacle? Perhaps for the money at the end of the day? Anyone who has a brain can understand the basic rule that players are highly compensated for their efforts on the field."

He raises a brow in my direction, looking for some type of answer, but all I can manage is a slow head shake. It's probably true that the vast majority involved in the Diamond Games are tied to the funds, but according to stories from Kole, the yearly tradition is about keeping the peace with our Enemy in the North.

RoBjorn sighs as he continues, "We put recruits through such dangerous events because it is *necessary* in order to find true tethered pairs. Only those gifted deltas can compete to keep our team strong and, ultimately, our nation. Our neighbors in the North hold a precarious position in their lands. They train their players just as hard, if not in even more dangerous climates. So, we must be prepared on all fronts."

I manage a careful nod, staying silent and wondering where this conversation is leading.

RoBjorn steeples his fingers, leaning forward to rest sharp elbows on his desk as he stares me down, "Seeing how the end goal of every recruit that stays on this base is to become a tethered pair and compete for my team, the question remains," gray eyes narrow as he asks slowly, "Why are you here?"

My eyes flick to Neera and Boz, noting their unimpressed scowls that await my slip-up, but I have no idea how to answer that question. I've been wondering the same thing myself for months without any answers.

"Confidence."

Swallowing, I force the words I don't believe because it might be what the powerful leader before me wants to hear, "To become a champion… Sir. For Aegis."

The President's brow arches slightly, and I know I've given a better answer than *I don't know.*

Several heartbeats pass before President RoBjorn sighs deeply, crossing his arms as if his mind has been made up, "Very well. Though your existence on my base has created quite the conversation on all corners of the world, my patience for time-wasting is quite thin, so you will prove
you are not here to waste my time, agreed?"

"Yes, Sir." My mind begins to unravel with a thousand questions I know I can't ask.

"Captain Blackwell had his reasons for bidding on a young girl with no delta from the cottage fields, and I am willing to give you more time on his behalf, but my generosity has limits. Despite King Ragnar himself sending me telegrams every fortnight on the matter, my say will be final."

I suddenly crave my sweet, medicated powder as I hang on the edge of my seat for the President's next words.

As casually as ordering a morning meal, he seals my fate faster than the captain did with his bid.

"In order to prove your quest to become one of my champions, I will take away temptations to keep you on track. I trust you know that recruits not chosen are typically granted freedom back to their original home should they desire. You will be offered *no* such luxury."

That familiar warmth settles in my mind, and for a split second, the edges of my vision flash a burnt orange hue, and despair floods my veins.

"You will either succeed and tether, or you will fail and become an interesting anecdote for the next decade. The choice is yours, but I will not tolerate skirting around my bylaws or cheating in any way."

My mouth goes dry, as it drops open in protest, "But… Sir, I…" Neera's gaze darkens, threatening me to say one wrong word, but I can't help myself, "I don't have a delta. I can't tether."

"Then, consider your days limited and my time no longer wasted."

He steeples his fingers with a shrug, "I am in the interest of weaponizing athletes, so I suggest you produce a gift or succumb to the trials of phase two."

RoBjorn's steely gaze shifts into boredom as I realize his tone is final. Jude had made it clear the President was intrigued with me and my performance, but it seems even the entertainment grows dull after a while. Even Kole had warned me a long time ago that phase two is nothing more than mental warfare, designed to break down a recruit and test their emotions. I may have killed the hydra, but my luck has officially run out.

Just before the leader of Aegis dismisses me with my new devastating fate, his gaze drifts past me as if looking for something else in the room.

"As for the matter of your acolyte…" his brows arch slightly in a question I don't understand. Thankfully, Neera has no problem answering for me.

"He's already linked to her, Sir. I witnessed her speaking to him." Her smile reminds me of Sera's. She looks like a snake ready to devour their wide-eyed prey.

"Very well," President RoBjorn exhales as if he expected the answer already, "A rare pairing everyone believed to be extinct, but all the more reason to keep you on track. Your phoenix will not be permitted to assist you until you've tethered. If you disobey these bylaws, consider your time on this base… *terminated.*"

With that, before I know it, I'm escorted out of the President's office and alone once again in the long corridor with shaky hands and a new terrible fear settling in my gut.

When I faced the hydra, I was afraid, but I had hope of survival. Enduring Sera's pain was horrifying, but I escaped each night with my life at least. Even the moment a price was put on my head I still held an ounce of hope for going home one day, but that hope is officially burnt out.

"This is it, then," I mutter to myself, and possibly Sicar, wherever he may be. I'm not even sure if he heard everything or what he knows, but I should have guessed my luck would run out eventually.

"Worry not, Daughter of David."

"You heard them," I whisper, trailing down the dark, empty hall, throwing my incense towards my lips in hopes of easing the upcoming hyperventilation, "It's simple. Tether or die. I was never enough, Sicar! They just wanted a show."

The warmth settles deeper in the caverns of my mind, and a strange sensation slides down my spine as if to comfort me. For a moment, the worry subsides enough to make a path for the phoenix's ancient voice, clearer than ever.

"You are enough."

Sniffing, I push past a set of doors, finding my way toward the spiral staircase that leads to the rooftop's nightly fresh air. I just hope I remain alone for the hysteria rising in my chest. I don't have it in me to deal with the captain's cryptic questions if he comes looking. Not that I want him to.

I rush to the rooftop ledge and lean over, suddenly heaving up the dinner I didn't know was threatening to reappear.

My lungs hurt. My head feels heavy and my eyes sting as my blurry gaze finds the tumbling sea in the distance.

I never had a chance, and now that my days are numbered, what's the point in any of this? If I can't produce a power I was never born with, the directors will have my head in a matter of days.

The Elijahn Sea below pulls my attention and the tears cease their flow. My fingers grip the smooth concrete of the ledge as my mind ponders the saddest thought of all. Perhaps I should give up if I already know where this journey is leading.

"Abandon that idea immediately."

I shake my head, ready to argue, but a bright auburn light fills my peripheral vision, forcing me to spin in its direction.

To my right floats the magical, impossibly beautiful phoenix. His feathers drip red-hot flames in the night, and those golden eyes fix me with an inquisitive stare. Black talons gently scrape the ledge to find purchase with ease as the mythical bird folds his wings in and faces me dead on. This is only the second time I've seen Sicar in this breathtaking form, and he's even more mesmerizing than I remember.

Finding my thoughts again, I shake my head, leaning over the ledge once more to contemplate my very short future.

"I don't understand. I did what they wanted! I passed the crucible and killed the monster when several other recruits died, and they had a delta to protect them. I had *nothing!*"

Sicar's head tilts slightly in an animalistic way as if he's listening to my complaints and that warmth surrounds my mind once more.

The tears return with a vengeance as I struggle to breathe deeply, "Here you are, listening to me cry, when you don't even know me. Why would you pick such a pathetic person if you're so rare and powerful? I hear the others whisper. Everyone wants to know."

My voice trails off at the last few words, probably because this might be an answer I dread.

I hate the way my voice sounds as if I'm begging for pity, but Sicar doesn't show any pause. With a simple blink of those dangerous golden eyes, his voice fills my head again.

"I have been asleep for one hundred years and awoke at the sound of your birth, My Pride. Do not believe an acolyte chooses on a whim, for such a match has always been sewn into the fabric of the heavens."

I stifle my gasp, "But *why* me?" I turn to face the beautifully lethal creature who glows in the darkness, "*Why* am I here? You don't want me to give up, but I can't become something I'm not. In two weeks they're sending us to heavens-knows-where to survive phase two, and I'm going in blind!"

I should realize the absurdity in arguing with a powerful mythical creature who's probably older than the earth, but I'm so frantic for any shred of hope that I don't care how irrational I sound.

Sicar's calm, ancient voice fills my mind again, settling in as if he's always been there.

"Some questions may not have answers, but I will reassure you of one thing. Your presence here is not by mistake. Trust in the ones who've proven their loyalty and know you will not be abandoned."

I sigh, feeling a pang of anger rise to more cryptic proverbs without any actual answers, but Sicar snaps his dark beak to demand my attention.

"You will not *be abandoned. Do you understand your native words I am relaying? You do speak Bachalorian, do you not?"*

I nod, rolling my eyes at his promise that doesn't help me in the slightest, and watch as Sicar makes a motion with his neck that looks familiar to a curt nod. After which he gracefully takes to the sky once more.

"Now, collect your rest. You shall require it."

I contemplate arguing with the phoenix, but something tells me that conversation wouldn't end in my favor. Whatever he has up his ancient bird sleeve, if *anything,* I hope he uses it soon, because I'm quickly running out of time.

CHAPTER 22: SENSES

"Oh, things have *definitely* changed around here," Grape murmurs as I follow him up the seventh row in the auditorium, instead of climbing all the way to the twentieth row.

Ignore the death. Fill in the empty spots.

My chair squeaks as we await our professor, and I can't help but notice the lingering exhaustion in every recruit's face. I'm just thankful this week my butt will be habitually planted in a classroom seat, giving me time to fully heal for whatever mental torment awaits. The elixir the captain had given me several nights ago worked wonders in quickly closing the gashes and siphoning the infection from my body, but the muscle aches still linger. As I shift uncomfortably, watching our professor unravel an extended map along the chalk wall, I can't stop thinking about all of the lives that didn't make it back to their classroom seats.

"You have earned your seat. Do not forget that."

I sigh, nodding to Sicar's warm voice that flashes colors along the rims of my vision, wishing to speak back to him, but I don't want to draw attention to myself. A young girl without a power who managed to take the life of a beast that was thought to be invincible certainly doesn't need any more prying eyes. My mother used to tell me that one will always find what they go looking for, and she quickly learned her lesson after discovering my father's distasteful secrets.

"You can converse with me as I do you, Blonde One." Sicar's words fill my mind as Dr. Gencavage passes out textbooks.

I shake my head at the phoenix in my brain, dismissing the thought altogether. I don't have a delta, and I certainly don't possess whatever power is needed to mind-speak. I'm not special like that.

"What did I tell you about self-deprecation?"

My eye roll is so dramatic that the edges of my vision flash a burnt yellow color, which I have deduced is annoyance from Sicar. I'm not even talking. How does he do that?

"I've claimed you as my own and therefore, bear rights to you. Now, speak back to me."

I can't help the sigh that escapes, feeling overwhelmed by the ancient voice commanding me to do something impossible.

"Turn to page eighteen to observe mental fortitude," Dr. Gencavage instructs the room, and I shake my head, snapping myself out of the distraction that is the magical bird in my brain. I still can't believe any of this is real.

The professor takes his stool before his podium while announcing, "In the past, phase two has proved to be even more deadly than phase one, where a large majority of recruits succumb to mind torture, inevitably taking their own lives in one way or another to relieve themselves."

Oh, wonderful.

"If you do not try, I will have to resign my current task and visit your room of knowledge."

"No!" I blurt out loud to Sicar, earning dozens of eyes snapping in my direction. Our professor lowers his chin, lifts a bushy brow and stares me down.

My cheeks heat and I want to sink so far down into my chair that I disappear, but all I can do is keep quiet as my eyes dart to the book pages.

Grape leans in close as our professor carries on with the lecture. "Are you okay?"

I nod to him, offering half a smile that wouldn't convince anyone.

"I am waiting."

"For fuck's sake."

"Soria, what?" Grape shoots me a worried look, demanding to know what I'm not telling him, and Dr. Gencavage also pins me with another skeptical glare. I wish I could ask Sicar if this is something I'm allowed to speak about or if it's some sacred-bond-thing only between an acolyte and their human. I should have paid more attention during those classes, but I was too concerned with surviving.

"My patience is up. I am en route."

"Stop!"

My own voice fills my mind, loud, feminine and assertive.

My jaw drops, firing a gasp for something that feels so impossible, and yet, so right. The nerves in my body subside and the edges of my vision flash a bright white, and it's like a puzzle piece locks into place. Suddenly, my vision is not my own as everything in the room fades and the image of a crimson-colored string floats down until it is straight and strong.

"Was that so difficult?" The red string vibrates slightly and glows as Sicar speaks, and my eyesight returns.

I scrub a hand over my face as a grin stretches across giddy lips, *"Yes, actually. Where are you? What are you doing?"*

I respond excitedly in my mind. Now that I have twenty-four-seven access to him. I have so many questions I need answered.

Sicar makes a noise that I confirm is routine annoyance with the flash of yellow, *"We have plenty of time for inquiries, but your professor's knowledge takes precedence."*

I want to argue with him, but I know he's right. If I have even the longest shot in the dark of moving forward, I need to make it past phase two. And then… we improvise, I suppose.

My smile calms every last anxious thought as I realize there is a *we.* I'm not alone anymore.

"And you never were. I have been here all along."

"When can I see you again?" I ask.

"When the time is right. I am across the Elijahn Sea at present. Now, concentrate on this knowledge."

I feel my shoulders drop with disappointment, and something in my chest suddenly hurts knowing he is so far away, but that's not information I'm about to let anyone know. I'm sure the other recruits have kept their distance because they fear my fire-breathing acolyte will burn them alive, so the whereabouts of his location needs to stay a secret.

"Precisely."

"Recruit Davidsdottir, are we in imagination land, or is my life-saving knowledge not to your standards?"

Dr. Gencavage drums impatient fingertips on his podium, and my cheeks flare once again. I need to get better at acting present when Sicar talks to me.

"Sorry…sir." I mumble, slouching further into my seat.

"Right then," the professor strokes his beard, peering down at his pages, "On to discuss the importance of the five senses."

Someone snickers a few seats down from me, "Aww, Zero gets her bird to kill one monster and now she thinks she's one of us." I'm not surprised to find the insult comes from Depitrio as he fixes me with a nasty leer, blowing a kiss my way.

"Can you kill my enemies?"

"Concentrate."

I grumble at Sicar's answer, flipping to the next page until Grape's expression catches my attention. His eyes are telling me he better get an answer or I'll never hear the end of it.

I hold up a finger to Grape, *"Okay, I'm going to focus now, but I have one last question then I'll shut up. Can I tell Grape?"*

Sicar is silent for a long moment as if he's pondering, and he finally answers, *"Yes."*

"Thanks. Love you, bye. Or, fly safe. Be careful."

Sicar makes a noise that sounds like a chuff, or maybe a snort? He goes silent, stealing the warmth that his presence brings my mind. I don't like the feeling, but I know he's shutting me out so I can focus on the professor's lesson.

"Sense of sight is the doorway to the mind, but sense of touch instills the fear. Pain is a warning to the body, and things can go awry without that warning."

Dr. Gencavage goes on, calling on a recruit to read the next passage.

Grape coughs expectantly with wide eyes that wait for an answer, which I reply by drawing invisible letters on my desk. My finger spells out the word *phoenix,* earning a disbelieving look from my friend.

I whisper softer than my own ears can hear, knowing which ones can, "I'll tell you about it later."

Grape nods, a knowing smirk meeting his mouth as we turn the next page.

***

"I think I c-c-could tether with Marta. Or m-maybe even Svein. It's too bad Ojer d-died. I think my delta could have paired with wood-we-we-wielding." Merry says as she crunches down on a green apple, limbs hanging off the top bunk adjacent to mine and Grapes. Below her sits Ona, weighing down the bowing mattress that begs for mercy.

"In what world does *wood wielding* complement a shapeshifter? Please explain. Don't say it's because you liked Ojer's rack." Grape scoffs from above.

"Oh, and y-y-you aren't thinking of t-tethering with Tomas for similar re-reasons?"

Both of them have been arguing this same topic for the past few days, each contemplating someone new to tether while the other always offers a reason why that wouldn't work.

"Their mental fortitude is to be tested tomorrow and this is the theme of discussion they wish to dissect." Sicar's ancient voice fills my mind with a judgmental edge.

"It's a good distraction." I say back. Though we've been studying the ins and outs of mental endurance this past week, all anyone can talk about is tethering.

"It is foolish to assume phase two does not warrant as much effort as phase one. It is deadlier by far."

I let Sicar's warning sink in, repeating those words several times until I tune out the back-and-forth debate above me and dive into the study book we're permitted.

Flipping open the worn leather to the textbook entitled *Phase 2 Critical,* I scan through the first section we'd gone over days ago, refreshing myself on grounding. According to our professor, grounding is the basic technique that keeps you level with the earth and reins you back in when the most frightening parts of the mind try to take over.

I crunch into one of the apples Merry snagged from dinner, skipping to the next section to reread mental shielding, blocks and walls, but so much of this is foreign to me. Apparently being able to withstand mental torture is a necessity for being a player, considering mental games are a specialty for the Enemy In The North. Players have gone mad in the arena from rare deltas able to attack the mind without moving a muscle. It frighteningly reminds me of Sera's bitch-ass.

With a tired sigh, I land on the section Dr. Gencavage had briefly recited about the importance of the five senses and read through each description carefully.

"Grape, apparently hearing is the most important sense." I tell him, knowing that stupid haughty grin of his is already carved into his face.

Grape swings his head over the side of the bunk bed, his spiky black hair nearly brushing my forehead, "Don't you ever forget it, girlie. Why do you think Aegis bought a hyperacusian in the first place?"

I roll my eyes, focusing on the text until something piques a curiosity that's been sitting with me for too long.

Beneath the passage of touch, I read, *According to any natural human law, should one be robbed of sound, smell, taste and then sight, touch would be the most mentally gruesome to obtain in solitude.*

My fingertips grip the leather-bound book tighter as I read on, *Although withstanding time and space, should every sense be obtained besides touch, one could be mentally omnipotent. For touch, dreaded students, relays fear to the mind, and fear safeguards the body.*

"Holy shit." My palm flies to my mouth as I reread the passage over and over again until it all makes sense.

"Hydra-Slayer, do not repeat what you know." Sicar warns me, his voice vibrating the shell of my skull. I swallow the words I want to spew, tucking my newfound information away. It all makes sense now but I want to be sure.

"Zero. Problem?" Ona huffs in her deep voice across from me. Her eyes are bloodshot from a long day of staring at written words on parchment, and I bite my lip to keep from spilling what I've discovered.

"Nothing, Ona." I mutter, my head finding my pillow as I scan the intricate metal loops that hold up the other mattress, contemplating every single day since I've been on this blasted base and how I couldn't have noticed sooner.

Hell, how could *no one* have noticed?

"It will do you no good to dwell on this." The phoenix declares in a matter-of-fact tone.

"This is all I can think about now."

Sicar makes a noise I can't quite place and says, *"I can see that. This information is unfurling into an obsession that is a never-ending stream."*

"That's dramatic." I chuckle out loud, earning Grape's swinging head in my face again.

"Are you talking to the phoenix?"

Merry's eyes light up as she flips to face me, almost rolling off her mattress.

"Can you tell 'em we said hi? And ask how the weather is. Wherever he is. Where is he, anyway, blondie? I thought acolytes were supposed to stay with their person." Grape rambles, taking too big a bite out of his apple.

Before I have a chance to speak, Sicar's voice thunders in my mind, *"Tell the hyperacusian I do not answer to humans, and I have ripped apart beings for far less."* I swallow, the edges of my vision flashing a bright red hue, *"Tell him now."*

"He says he doesn't answer to humans, and he's ripped people apart for less." I purse my lips, watching my friends shrivel backward at the words of the powerful phoenix.

"They're my friends. They mean well." I tell Sicar in my mind, and the red pigment ceases as he speaks back.

"My only concern is you. Now, you should rest, for tomorrow will be the first long day of many."

I nod to his voice, tucking my arms beneath my pillow as I listen to Merry and Grape go in circles again about the technicalities of who would be good to tether.

"If any of you tether to Kole or Sera, you'll be wishing phase two took you out first." I mumble with closed eyes, feeling the uncertainty of tomorrow dissipate the further I fall into sleep.

Ona's deep voice carries across the space between us before sleep greets me, "Goodnight, Zero. You did good."

CHAPTER 23: FOR THE MIND

The morning sun peeks through soft pine trees, reminding me that today is *not* just another day.

Dr. Gencavage taught our dwindled class everything we would need to know about mental warfare, but each point had boiled down to one simple instruction: expect the unexpected.

"Remember, none of it is real, though that fact may become difficult to keep in the forefront of your mind," Dr. Gencavage had warned, "During the Diamond Games, you will face players with far deadlier talents, so your mind must be sharp enough to withstand all that the directors throw its way."

Sharp. Keep my mind sharp.

I repeat those words to myself, engraving them deeper into every crevice of my brain, flushing out every last distraction.

I decided a long time ago I'm not giving up. Even if the President of Aegis sees my life as a coin toss, I'll do what I can until I can no longer.

I have no choice.

This hike is different from our two-day journey to face the hydra. We have no packs, no supplies, no weapons of any sort.

In fact, before we left the squad bay, each recruit had to be patted down to ensure that all we possessed were the clothes on our backs not even giving us an option for breakfast. I'm just glad I started hiding my incense in my boot, courtesy of a tip from Sicar. I suppose sharing my mind with a powerful and magical creature could have its benefits.

Jude is still nowhere to be seen, though I don't know why I bother looking for him. He hasn't bothered to show his face in weeks and I've already decided I won't be spending a second of my precious time thinking of him.

Keep my mind sharp.

Only our two fierce directors lead our brief trip instead of an audience like last time, and our hike has only lasted about ten minutes, taking us to a clearing in the forest that holds a very bizarre sight.

Sitting silently in the middle of the green clearing is a long wooden structure with no windows or openings, concealing what it may hold inside. It's simple in its build, standing as one never-ending rectangle until I notice distinct lines carved in the thick, dark oak signaling compartments attached from within.

"Are you thinking what I'm thinking?" Grape mutters next to me, and I'm positive we *all* are.

Merry answers for me, her voice skeptical as she tucks a frizzy brown strand back into her bun, "Yeah. What the f-f-*fuck* is that?"

"Line up along the building! *Now!* Director Neera screeches, nodding to her companion, Boz, as we're herded forward like beasts to the chop-house.

Following orders, I find a spot along the wooden structure, exhaling deeply to remain calm.

Phase two could have started weeks ago for all anyone knows, and a sense of peace is precisely what I need to keep in mind. Expect the unexpected. But something menacing catches my eye for a split second before disappearing behind another set of trees in the distance. Something enormous with dangerous eyes and a color-shifting hide. With another blink, the creature is gone.

My sense of peace begins to unravel.

Shaking my head, I toss away the idea of something watching me because there's no time to worry about creatures in the shadows. I gather my thoughts as the wooden wall welcomes me, shooting a look of good luck to my friends down the row and even catching Ona's eye several recruits down. She gives me a slow thumbs-up that doesn't match her permanent scowl, and I can't help but smile. The Beast is my friend.

Once every recruit takes their place along the building that stands no taller than eight feet, Neera's shrill voice echoes through the clearing with severe instruction, "Today marks the day you decide your future. Should you pass phase two, you will no longer be labeled as recruits. You will become *prospects* in order to tether."

Director Boz speaks up, his cold demeanor trying to frazzle every nerve around him, "To pass phase two is simple," Boz says, and with a swift motion from both his palms, the wood before us shoots upward, revealing what I thought might be inside, "Escape your room and you will make it to tethering." I should have known his wood-wielding had something to do with this odd structure.

My jaw locks to keep a disappointed sigh internal, but defeat settles faster than I knew possible.

This long structure is precisely similar to a storage case, offering every recruit their own enclosure, completely isolated from anyone else. The inside holds a single dusty mattress with various stains and one small glass of what appears to be water.

Suddenly my throat feels parched at the thought of going without water. Surely, they wouldn't let us die from dehydration.

"I hope you all ate dinner last night because you won't see another bite of food until you make it out," Boz bellows down the line.

"*If* you make it out," Neera snickers behind me before addressing the long line of recruits in the dewy morning sunlight, "You are permitted to use your delta, your surroundings, your imagination, *anything* to get you out, but the faster you do it, the better. The mind is a very fragile thing, after all."

I shoot a last glance to my friends. Ona should have no problem punching an Ona-sized hole through the wood. If Merry has been practicing, she could transform into an animal small enough or big enough to escape. Even stupid Kole could use the water from his single glass to slice through the wood, but by the look on Grape's face, his delta seems to be weighing heavy on him.

I whisper softly enough for only his ears to pick up, "Don't worry. You'll find a way."

Grape nods from several feet away, swallowing the lump in his throat as he forces his humorous mask back on.

I have no idea where Sicar is, though he seems to enjoy disappearing when I need him most. I'm not sure if he's allowed to help me or what he's capable of yet, but I wouldn't call on him even if I wanted to. I got myself here; I can get myself out. Hopefully.

"*Simply request help if you desire it. Do not be stubborn.*"

"And what? Bend the rules again? I'm sure the President won't mind me cheating." I mutter back, realizing I can't keep my mind sharp with Sicar invading every other second to offer his two cents.

"Recruits, step forward, and good luck." Director Boz announces, officially commencing phase two.

Adrenaline floods my veins as I exhale, stepping into my wooden cell just before the oak slams back down, sealing me in with no way out.

I have no idea how to measure time in this ridiculous wooden room I've been locked in, but thankfully, a few cracks in the ceiling allow three single rays of sunlight to illuminate a portion of my surroundings. By the hue of the rays, I estimate we've gone long past noon.

Shifting for the hundredth time on the stained mattress, I stretch my legs with a sigh, wondering how people have gone mad enough to take their own lives during this phase. The act feels so foreign that I can't imagine a mind being weak enough to give in.

"Remember my guidance." Sicar's voice warms my mind, and I'm thankful I'm not truly alone. He's still hundreds of miles away, doing whatever ancient phoenixes do, but he's still with me.

"I know. Stay calm and breathe." I brush my boot that holds my can of limited incense. I should have found Ivar to get more before phase two, but I underestimated how much powder I had left. I hope I don't run out.

No, only happy thoughts.

As long as I stay calm, I'm sure I can find a way out. If I don't run out of water first. How quickly does one die of thirst?

"This is the opposite of calm."

My mouth goes even drier at the thought of water, and my stomach rolls with hunger. Damn my body for getting used to three decent meals a day. It's certainly helped fill out the anorexic portions along my body from a life of malnutrition, but that doesn't help me now.

Thankfully, I know I can last without food. I've once gone eleven days without a single bite when my mother went missing for two weeks, leaving me behind during a scarce winter to fend for myself. The high snow made traveling impossible to find food or beg from neighbors. I was trapped in that cottage, alone and slowly starving to death, but at least I had water for days.

I eye the glass of water sitting a foot away, licking my lips at the thought of downing its entirety, but I have to make it last.

Deciding on the smallest of sips, I lift the glass to my lips, feeling immediate relief in the form of soft, cold water to cleanse my palate. Using the willpower I have left, I set the nearly full glass back down. If I'm going to escape, I need to give myself as much time as possible. That cup will be my new measure of time.

Another hour or so passes as my mind churns for ideas on escaping, but I keep coming up empty. I've already tried everything from kicking with all of my might at the wooden walls, inspecting for any corners that might give way easily, and even searching for a hidden button, *anything* to give me back my freedom, but to no avail. It's useless.

But I can't give up.

Sooner or later, there has to be a way out. There just has to be.

By the time the sun rays signal nightfall approaching, I hear the first noise that rattles my bones. Up until now, the four walls trapping me in this dark room have silenced any outside sound, but I should have known I wouldn't be so fortunate.

A terrible, deafening shriek echoes through the wooden walls, startling every last nerve in my body.

Do I know that person? It sounds like a young girl's scream, and I can only pray that it doesn't belong to Merry.

"Sicar? Who was that?" I ask into the night, waiting for his warmth to fill my mind, but it never comes. He must be busy.

I sigh, trying to keep positive and forcing myself to focus on something other than my single glass of water until the shriek echoes through my room again, rattling my insides and making me frantic to help or see what the problem is. Suddenly, I miss the silence as the screaming picks up an octave and becomes relentless. Painful.

With every breath, the blood-curdling shrieks fill my eardrums, nearly sending me into panic mode before the noise settles into my mind and becomes more of a terrible irritation than anything.

I slam my hands over my ears and squint my eyes closed, hoping whoever is screaming will soon find their way out. New fears emerge as I ball myself into the fetal position after what seems like hours have passed without peace. What if it *is* Merry? What if she's going through the worst type of torment without anyone to save her?

I leap to the wall and start shouting, "Merry! Merry, are you okay? Can you hear me?" But no one answers. Only the terrible shrieks respond and even louder than every cry before.

"Merry!"

"Soria, calm down!"

"Grape?"

Suddenly the screams cease as my friend's wonderfully familiar voice echoes through the walls.

"Yeah, it's Grape. You have to calm down. Remember, none of this is real. What you're hearing isn't real!"

His voice sounds so calm, so nurturing and I exhale in relief to hear he's okay.

"So, that's no one? The screaming? Can you hear it too?"

"What screaming?" Grape's voice is more muffled now, and my eyes widen, realizing I have no idea how to decipher what's real and what's not. Grape goes on, though his voice sounds so far now, as if he's several compartments away instead of a few feet, "Just take a seat, relax, and drink some water. You've got this, Soria."

I nod, catching my breath, and I feel around for my mattress in the dark, gently pulling my knees to my chest and driving a small bit of incense to my nostril.

I shouldn't drink any more water. I should make it last, but perhaps I deserve a sip after who knows how long I've listened to screaming in my mind.

Reaching for the glass in the darkness, my fingers hit the cold surface too aggressively, knocking it over. My heart sinks at the sound of my only water spilling onto the wooden floor.

I scramble in a panic to the floor, clawing at the ground and trying to force the liquid back into the glass, but it's useless. I bring my fingers to my lips in hopes of soaking up a morsel of water but immediately start gagging on whatever I've just inhaled.

Throwing myself back onto the mattress in terrible shock, a shaky hand slowly rises toward the single ray of moonlight cascading through the ceiling, inspecting the sticky black substance staining my fingers.

Dread fills my stomach as blurred eyes focus, realizing it was never water in the glass. It was a trick. Something for me to consume to mess with my mind.

"Grape! Grape! Don't drink the water!" I scream, throwing myself to the wall, "Can you hear me? Grape!"

Suddenly, his voice carries through the other side, but it's not in response to me. It's a cold, mocking laugh. And it's his. He's laughing at me. My only friend is finding amusement in my mistake. How could he?

Grape's laughter fills my head as I throw more incense to my nose, desperate to find some sense of peace when I'm on the verge of flipping the fuck out. But what's real? Is Grape's voice even real? He was the one who told me to drink the water, and perhaps it was all in my mind.

"Sicar!" I shriek, pulling my knees to my chest, but I can't feel him at all. What if that black tar did something to shut him out?

Suddenly the shrieking is back, and it sounds terribly close to Merry's voice, along with Grape's incessant laughter shaking my skull like a fierce breeze tossing needles of the pines.

With no other option, I hide beneath the nasty mattress, wrap my arms around my head, and hum to myself in hopes of drowning out the voices that won't relent.

"It's not Merry. It's not Grape. It's not real. It's not Merry. It's not Grape. It's not real. None of this is real." I repeat the same three sentences because it's the only thing I know how to do, until I go numb and those words are the only ones I know.

***

Hours must have passed before the voices finally ceased, and I'm left shivering in the corner from the cool night's temperatures, hungry and sleep deprived.

I can't help but wonder if any of this is real, but that begins to become a very dangerous game to play. I can't assume everything is real or I'll go mad. I can't begin to pick apart every atom of the room or that will drive me crazy as well.

All I'm left with are my thoughts.

If only Sicar were here. Perhaps he could end this torment for me already.

No. I can't let him help. The President would know. They would have my head for skirting around the rules again. What's the point, though? I only have a future if I produce a delta and that's impossible. I may have brothers who possess powerful gifts, but I was never the special one. I'm nothing.

"You're right. You're useless."

My eyes shoot from my arms to find a feminine figure seated on a stool in the opposite corner of the room.

I squint in the darkness until the familiar woman's face becomes clear, and I suck in a breath, wishing to be alone with a dangerous serpent rather than this conniving bitch.

Sera Jonsdottir's evil smile sends a chill up my spine as she inspects her nail beds, seeming altogether bored with my presence.

I swallow, shifting further into my own corner to create as much distance as possible. How did she get in here? This can't be real, either.

"You wanna know something interesting, Zero?" Sera purrs, slowly unfurling a concealed dagger from behind her, playing with it like a toy in front of me, "That might be the only truthful thing you've admitted to in your entire life. You're *nothing.*"

Slowly, I pull my knees beneath me in case I have to dodge this dagger.

"I mean, let's be honest. You thought you were in *love* with beautiful blond Kole, but he was always just a ticket to a better life, right?" Sera's words grow colder, freezing the room with a layer of ice I can't see but feel deep in my chest, "How can you claim to be in love with a man when all you can think about is the captain's lips on your—"

"That's enough," I warn her, or whatever she is, "You're not real. You're not here." Carefully, I make it to my feet as Sera stays sitting, watching her watch me with those dark, shifty eyes.

Her brow shoots up as she matches my tactic, slowly gaining her feet in the opposite corner of the room, "I'm as real as your fantasies of surviving until the morning, Zero. Believe that."

"You're in my head. You're not really here." I grind out the words, slamming my eyes closed to concentrate.

"Right again."

My eyes pop open at that voice, and I hurl myself back to the wall in response to the ghost smiling at me in the room.

In her short stature and stained tunic, she stands exactly as I remember, her bright smile complementing beautiful dark skin.

"Hera." I breathe her name, and watch those honey colored eyes light up to the sound of my voice. But this doesn't make sense. "I… I…" My voice quivers in the night as the words fail me over and over, "This *isn't* real. I watched you die."

Hera takes a step forward, and something in my heart feels relieved she's taken the place of Sera. But my brain feels so foggy now, open to possibilities that I know in my heart can't be real, yet I want to believe they are.

"Soria, if I wasn't real, could I do this?"

Suddenly Hera's standing a foot away, and she reaches for my hand. And… *grabs* it. Her flesh against mine is so real. So tangible.

She smiles brighter, reassuring me I'm not making this up, and I can't help but relish in the far-off idea that maybe, just *maybe* she survived the reaper somehow. Perhaps her delta of glowing had given her a gift to escape. Perhaps she *is* real.

"How are you here?" I ask her, feeling the adrenaline from fright ease in my veins. My mind calms as if a blanket has been thrown over the troubled parts, and it becomes a little easier to breathe.

I watch Hera take a seat on my grimy mattress and pat the side, motioning me to join her. I can't wait to tell Grape she's here.

Inching closer to her, I inspect her face, which appears illuminated in the night. She grins back at me, "I found a way to escape that terrible reaper. But never mind that. How have you been? You've gotten so far!"

My heart feels lighter talking to her, and I spill my guts for the next hour, unloading every small detail I've been harboring and catching her up on every memory. "A phoenix? That is so wild! You must be really special." Hera beams, her excitement spilling everywhere.

I shake my head, shifting uneasily at the insinuation that I could be anything special, "No, that's not it. I'm sure he just chose wrong."

"But he told you he didn't." Hera inches closer.

"Yeah, but…" I pause, the blanket over my mind moving slightly enough for me to create my own rational thought. I never told Hera that.

I inspect her face again. She's exactly as I remember. *Exactly.* As if she's been pulled from my memory.

The terrible feeling returns to my stomach as Hera's head cocks to the side, confused at my expression, "What's wrong, Soria?" Her voice is so convincing.

A painful sigh fills the space between us, and I grab her hand, noticing the sensation of touch is slightly off. *That's* why we studied the five senses.

"You're not real." I blink away the tears threatening to escape.

Hera chuckles, "Of course I'm real. You're touching me right now. You can see me, right?"

I shake my head and look in her soft eyes, cursing my mind for playing such a terrible trick on me, "No, you're not." I cry, pitying her poor family, her grandmother who would probably give anything for the past hour of delusion I've had with the world's sweetest soul. "And you have to leave now."

Hera's gaze becomes misty as she nods to me, "You're right," her voice is hardly a whisper filling my foggy brain, "But before I go, let me leave you with a gift." Gently, she pulls something from behind her and I recoil in confusion to see the same black dagger Sera had held.

"What…Hera, what are you doing?" I mutter as the urge to flee floods every last receptor, but my friend's gentle smile keeps me seated next to her.

"Oh, don't be afraid. It's a gift for you." She smiles, placing it on the mattress between us.

"To… to defend myself?" I spare a quick glance around the room in case of a sudden intruder.

Hera laughs in her bubbly voice while shaking her head, "No, silly! To end it before things get too bad."

My mouth goes dry. My heart falls to my stomach, and ice rushes through my veins, threatening to make me pass out from terrible shock.

I leap to my feet and Hera follows, embracing me in a hug that I don't fight.

"It's okay," She coos in my ear, sounding nurturing and soft, "The minute you stepped foot in here it was over. It's okay," she looks me in the eyes, smiling as a single tear slides down her ghostly face, "This is a *gift* for you. Accept it."

My brain feels torn in two. A piece of me wants to run away, fight the figure that clearly isn't real and find a way out. Another overwhelming piece of me is so tired of fighting.

"You'll never be able to produce a delta you never had." Hera nods, confirming the thoughts that stream unconsciously through my mind, "At least this way, *you* decide your fate. Not them."

I blink, pulling away from Hera and the dagger that now rests in her palms. I feel horrible in this moment, but for her and the life she was never allowed to lead. For me, I still have a choice.

"You're right," I whisper, dropping her hand, which begins slowly dissipating into mist. "I get to decide my fate, not them."

"Soria, don't," Hera begs, moving forward, but I've already closed my eyes and shut her out. When I open them again, she's gone, as well as the dagger and the glow she filled the room with.

I settle onto the mattress and bring my incense to my lips, and finally feel the tidal wave of tears catching up to me. I let them flow, weeping terribly into my palms and cursing the cruelty of this phase. I would rather face one hundred hydras than shuffle through the list of lost loved ones, trying to decipher what's real and what's not.

I pull my shirt to my eyes in a sad attempt to dry the streaks, but it's useless. Perhaps in sleep I'll find relief from the mind games.

Shivering and feeling the mother of all headaches approaching, I pull myself into a ball on the cot, facing the wall in hopes of drifting away quickly. Just before I do, my head quakes with a new rush of fear to see Hera's ghost hadn't taken everything with her.

Staring back at me on the mattress sits the black dagger, glinting in the single ray of moonlight as if it's always belonged here.

CHAPTER 24: DYING BREATH

I should have known finding peace in sleep would be an impossible feat. My eyes are too heavy to stay open, but every time I close them, some new disturbance sneaks its way in. It's maddening.

In my dreams, or rather, *nightmares,* all lucidity fades, leaving me with whatever wicked creations my mind throws together, courtesy of that vile liquid I had drunk. The hope of it leaving my system soon has faded as the nightmares persist. At times, I begin to believe this is all I will ever be. A prisoner of my own tortured brain.

I should have memorized every word in those textbooks.

A few sun rays peeking through the ceiling signal I've survived an entire day and night, but my stomach begins to ache in protest at being locked away in the woods. And soon, food and water will consume my thoughts until one of the deprivations takes me first.

"There's a simple answer to escape all of this, Sor."

I shake my head, feeling anger take the place of this lingering headache. I've seen everyone in this rotten wooden cell, from my parents and long-lost childhood acquaintances to enemies I've made here, but none have sparked rage as much as the boy sitting across from me. He seems to reappear too frequently.

I pull my ankles closer on the mattress, creating my space from whatever creation my mind has been cooking up. He doesn't bat an eye at my disdain for his presence.

Kole tosses shaggy blond hair out of his face, fixing those glinting eyes on mine as if that boyish grin has any residual effect on me. His jaw is strong, but his features are soft and familiar. He lacks a certain roughness.

"You're thinking about him when you look at me, aren't you?"

I resist baring my teeth at the image I know isn't Kole, but his question has me thrown completely off guard. In the past several visits, he's tried reminiscing about our life together, our joyous memories and what we could have been, but all of it was a trick. A scheme to make me yearn for the abyss in which he would present the dagger, urging me not to wait anymore.

Phase two has proven itself to be torturous indeed, but also predictable after hours of facing its tactics. My mind will create someone new to bother me, whether with flattery, fear, or immense sadness. Even though I know what they're doing, each person who appears gets harder and harder to dismiss the weaker I grow.

"Leave me alone," I mutter to Kole, shifting away to face the wall. He wouldn't leave; he's relentless.

"We both know I can't do that." Kole sighs, sounding closer to me on the mattress, "Answer my question, Sor."

I shake my head, trying to find the clarity to force this vision away, but it's too difficult.

"When you *look* at me," Kole's voice raises, forcing me to glance his way, "You're thinking of him, aren't you? I mean, let's be honest, he's everything I'm not, and yet, you know nothing about him. How could you be pining after someone so dangerous who's already wished you dead?"

"Shut up." I seethe.

"He *literally* bought you. He doesn't view you as anything more than a horse in the ring who can't perform. You're not a person to him. You're an experiment that isn't working out."

I pin Kole with a dangerous glare, feeling myself inch closer to the thought of unleashing everything I've wanted to say onto this fake version of him.

Slowly and quietly, I respond, "I don't know what you're talking about."

My answer enrages fake Kole, and he leaps to his feet, yanking the mattress from beneath me. In an instant, I'm slammed to the ground, my chin smashing into the wooden floor without warning.

Groaning in pain, I roll to my side, propping myself up on an elbow and feeling the rage boil over uncontrollably. Without any more hesitation, I release the pent-up anger onto this painful mirage of the boy I used to love.

"When I look at you," I spit coagulated saliva mixed with blood onto the floor, cursing the throbbing feeling in my lip, "All I think of is regret."

My response only makes Kole smirk as he folds his hands behind his neck, looming over me with curious eyes, "Why do you regret what we have?"

"*Had!*" I shout while wiping my mouth, "You were *everything* to me. You promised we could run away and start over, but you *left* me, Kole!" My heart suddenly aches at the distant memory of my love promising to meet me in the early morning, telling me to pack my bags and bring my violin.

Kole's face remains the same as tears I didn't know I'd been holding for him fall down my cheeks, and I whisper, "This is all your fault. I'm going to die because of you."

He bends to his knee, his eyes level with mine, though his calm expression remains.

"Oh, Soria," Kole's hand slowly reaches forward, brushing a greasy, blond strand from my face, "It's time to stop lying to yourself, hmm? You're going to die because of your own stubbornness, not me. You made it clear you don't need anyone's help, and that's what will get you killed in the end."

I swallow the tears that taste too salty, narrowing my eyes on Kole's as he runs a smooth thumb over my cheek.

I have nothing left to say to him. I want him gone more than anything.

As I suspected, Kole's mirage once again pulls the black dagger out, twisting the hilt in his palm before resting it on the ground before me.

"You know how this is going to end, so stop blaming everyone else for what you can solve by yourself." He smiles thoughtfully as familiar brows arch in question, but I slam my eyes closed, wishing him away for good.

Just before his presence leaves my mind, Kole gifts me with one last unwanted piece of advice.

"To answer your question for you, when you look at me, all you ever think of is him."

I force his image out of my mind with the last bit of clarity I can muster, and when I finally open my eyes again, I'm back on the mattress in the dim light, the pain from my mouth gone completely.

These visions are starting to get out of control the weaker I become. If I'm going to escape, it has to be now.

My feet peel me from the ground, sizing up one of the wooden walls, and roll my neck, preparing to use everything I have. After a deep breath, I charge the wall at full speed, slamming my shoulder into the wood with as much force as I can manage, but it doesn't budge. I'm left feeling sore, but that doesn't matter right now. All that matters is getting out of here. No one will do it for me.

Backing up and forcing a medicated breath, I go again. My shoulder slams into the wood even harder, rattling the ceiling enough that a mess of dust floats to the floor, and I feel a bubble of hope rise in my chest. There is hope that with enough force, I can break down these walls.

I ram into the wall, again and again, each time more and more dust from above litters the floor, telling me the integrity of the structure is nearly giving way.

My reflection stares back through the bottom of the incense can as I inhale the last of it without a second thought. I push that out of my mind. I can't think about that right now. It won't matter as soon as I tear down this wall. I'll worry about breathing later.

With a ferocious war cry and a throbbing shoulder, I kick off the opposite wall and hurl myself into the other side, shoving with every pound I have until the sun's warm light greets me and the green trees flood my vision.

I fall to my knees on top of the wooden wall, my hands scrambling for purchase as the clear forest air fills my lungs, and I inhale a satisfying breath of relief.

I did it. I escaped. And I did it by myself.

I let out a hearty, rich laugh, excited for the future because delta or not, I made it out. And no one will take that from me. Maybe I *am* special.

"That's an amusing thought." My he sinks.

In a matter of seconds, my mind fills with the fog I thought I had rid myself of, and my lungs grow heavy with despair as tired eyes flutter back open to the darkness.

I'm resting against the wall, my entire right side sore and throbbing in pain while sweat drenches my shirt from hours of slamming my body into a wall that was never going to give.

How could I have been so stupid?

Behind me, Sera's evil voice wraps itself around my mind like a python I can't shake.

"Did you really think you could do it? You weigh as much as a sack of flour, Zero. You were never going to get out."

I sink to my knees, the tears spilling over as the very real idea of dying in this wooden cell settles into my brain, becoming reality.

My sobs hardly make a noise as my worst enemy laughs above me, "That's a good idea. Lose even more water, you'll never get back."

Her words should sting, but I know now that everyone I've encountered in this horrible room has come from a deep and dark part of my mind. Every word lives deep within the caverns of my brain, and I can't escape even the deadly thoughts forever.

Weeping on the ground, I roll onto the nasty mattress, curling into a depressed ball, and let exhaustion take over.

My stomach aches with terrifying hunger pains, my lungs heave dangerously slow, and my mouth feels drier than the Tujave Desert, but at least Sera's vision disappears, leaving me alone with my deteriorating body and a shiny black dagger.

I welcome sleep this time, knowing whatever demons I'm about to face can't be as bad as the devastation of tasting freedom that was never real.

***

I've given upon wondering if I'm dreaming or awake because it truly doesn't matter anymore. Nothing seems to matter.

After navigating a thorny maze that leads nowhere, I'm suddenly transferred back home to my bathroom with peeling paint. This must be one of my nightmares because I know in the back of my mind I can't be here. I'm isolated in a wooden box in the middle of a forest, and I'm getting closer to death with every second that passes.

My reflection in the dirty, desilvering mirror shocks me.

My hair is shiny, golden, and voluminous, flowing down my back like ocean waves. My usual stained, felt uniform with the number zero plastered on the back has been replaced with a very familiar red dress, but it's less revealing. The halter top sits perfectly against my collarbones, and the fabric hugs beautiful curves I never realized I had.

I'm too weary of the pleasant view, knowing something is about to ruin it, but perhaps this is my mind leaving me with something peaceful before my body gives into the exhaustion.

Confirming my suspicions of one last enjoyable vision, the light from the bathroom window catches on a metal string, and I whirl around with joy in my heart.

Sitting propped against the wall is my prized possession I never thought I would see again. My beloved violin.

I reach for the instrument carefully, finding the dark bow in perfect condition behind it. An easy relief cascades over every nerve, settling the anxiety like the calm before the storm, and I ease the violin into the crook of my neck. If this is truly one last gift before the bleak abyss, I welcome the end with all I've ever looked forward to.

Closing my eyes, my breath falls over the auburn wood, and I slide the bow delicately across tight strings, playing a melody as familiar as the back of my hand.

I've never needed sheet music for this piece of my heart, and my hand works in muscle memory. The chords slide through the air, and my feelings soar along with it while appreciating every note as if it were my last.

And it is.

The song carries me far away without remorse, forgetting every last trouble that plagues me, even if it may be my demise.

I don't care.

All I know at this moment is I'm letting myself drift away with the melody as softly as I began.

"Beautiful."

Sicar's voice fills my mind for the first time in days, but even he can't break the pattern of bliss that slowly steals my vision, encompassing every thought. Even though I try to ignore him he persists.

"Do you wish to be left here as you are, Violinist?" There's sorrow in his tone. A longing I've never heard before.

I nod as my eyes remain closed, my hands following the flow of the song with ease. Something in Sicar's voice begs to pull my attention, and for a split second, I allow his words to take over, momentarily disrupting the ease of playing.

"If this is what you desire..." His ancient voice grows further away, and a pang of guilt hits me for some reason as he mumbles from far off, *"Then I will find you in another life. I promise."*

My hand breaks away from the strings, and I'm met with silence, staring at my reflection through blurry, brown eyes. Something terrible settles into my heart. A feeling of regret and hopelessness as my violin proved to be a beautiful distraction that would never truly save my life. *I* can't even save my life this time.

Suddenly, my lungs fill with such a heavy weight I drop to my knees on the cracked tile floor, my violin bursting in two along with me.

It's so hard to breathe. Why can't I breathe? Is this the end?

My eyes flutter open and I'm lying prone on the nasty mattress in my wooden cell, but I'm not entirely alone. A terrible, bright red fire trails up the walls, eating the wood with greed as smoke fills the ceiling and my lungs.

I try to blink away the vision that can't be real, but nothing is working. Whatever mind trick this is, is meant to kill me for good.

The side of my face suddenly feels hot, and I throw myself off the burning mattress, aggressively patting out a flame that's begun to burn a hole through my uniform.

Soot stains my hands and forearms, threatening to claim my life had I stayed asleep for one minute more, and I begin to panic. I don't want to die. Not like this!

Panic turns into desperation as I cough up everything in my lungs, clawing at the ground in a sorry attempt to escape this death trap. I'm going to burn alive if I don't think of something. I have to *do* something!

"Enough foolishness! I will send an army to retrieve you."

I wheeze, digging at my throat to find any air, "You… can't… help…" I manage to mutter back, knowing if Sicar rescues me right now, I'm as sure as dead in the President's eyes. His voice bellows through my mind louder than I've ever heard before, laced with devastation.

"Call upon me, I beg you."

My mind feels so heavy, my lungs burn as if the fire filling this room has made its way inside my body, soaking up every last feather of air I possess and drying my lungs from the inside out.

I reach a dark palm out, giving in and pleading for mercy. I don't want to die.

"Please…" That single cry for help is all I can muster before the air slithering down my throat becomes tight and hardly breathable. My head hurts so bad. My chest aches, and my body feels like it's on fire as fear pins me to the ground.

"Hold on," Sicar tells me, his voice loud and reassuring before his next word trails off, though it doesn't sound like it was meant for me, *"Fenrir!"*

I try my best to stay conscious as my seconds tick away, focusing on what little air I'm able to consume through poor and damaged lungs.

As I lie here, sprawled along the ground, I cling to the hope that Sicar's voice isn't a figment of my imagination. I've already been misled to believe I've escaped once, but that sliver of hope is all I have as I attempt to moisten cracked lips, incredibly vulnerable and fighting to stay alive.

Maybe I should have given up a long time ago. A knife certainly would have been easier than this.

"Wake up." Sicar whispers, urging me to take a smoke-filled breath as the violin music softly floats through my ears—a figment of my imagination, no doubt.

"Soria? Are you in there?"

My eyes crack open to that voice, and my ears can hardly believe it.

"Soria? Answer me!"

He can't be real. He's not real. He wouldn't be here to save me. And yet… what if he is?

I open my dry mouth to answer, but only exasperated, painful coughing takes the place of any audible words. Flames swallow the darkness and creep closer from the burning mattress. I have seconds left if I'm lucky.

"Listen to me. Move to the left wall *right now!*" His voice is so deep and severe. I can tell he's frantic on the other side of this wooden prison.

With no other option, I use the last ounce of strength I have to crawl toward the left corner, taking half a breath filled with smoke and begging the heavens to take pity on my lousy soul once more.

A few more seconds pass before the melody in my head grows louder, and time seems to move in slow motion.

My last breath is guttural and painful before half the wall that's held me captive disappears, slamming into the back corner to create an entrance into the dark forest.

A large silhouette consumes the opening, twisting to me with urgency as I feel myself pale with lack of air. Limbs create movements to put out the remaining flames, but it doesn't help me as I wheeze in the corner.

In a rush, the large body moves to mine, hovering with intensity as sturdy palms set me upright. His voice is calling my name but these deflated lungs have nothing left to give.

Instinctually, my mouth grasps for the air it can't swallow, and the deep voice above grows even more panicked, asking what's wrong and trying to keep me awake. But unless he has an extra incense can in his pocket, this is how I'll spend my last moments—fragile and blue in the face.

I grab the captain's shirt, desperate for air as the edges of my vision begin to blur. Those swirling blue eyes meet mine amongst the flames, and an understanding crosses his face in an instant.

With a flick of his wrist near my mouth, cool oxygen rushes down my throat, filling my lungs with an abundance I have never known, not even with medication. It's too delicious for my weak chest, too rich so that I bend at the waist, retching up smoke and soot while greedily sucking in the fresh air.

"Stay with me, Soria," Jude whispers as my body finally succumbs to exhaustion after receiving the air it has been dying for. Strong arms wrap me up, and I feel so frail between them as my head rests on a pounding chest.

"Wait," I wheeze, the word hardly audible as I point in the distance, "My… friends…"

Those arms tighten around me with a grumble as Jude sways his options. To my request, he sets me gingerly amongst cool grass, abandoning my heaving body for a brief moment before returning with haste.

"I pulled Yang out and the others escaped yesterday," he whispers as my forehead brushes dark stubble, and I swear I feel him quiver beneath my touch, but I can't tell if this is real or not. It can't be.

"It is real. You are safe." I can barely hear the phoenix as my fingertips grip smooth shirt lapels.

My eyes flutter open to see dark green leaves amongst treetops rustling in the night, wondering if this is yet another mind trick. Something about the roaring heartbeat against my ear confirms this is the most real thing I've felt in a long time.

"Stay with me," Jude repeats in a whisper against my neck.

CHAPTER 25: NEW ROOM

The morning light threatens a migraine as I force my eyes closed tighter, curious palms roaming to find anything familiar.

Buttery silk slides against my forearms and my head feels weightless as it floats on something plush and soft.

Besides swallowing to clear a sore throat, my body feels… *good.* Well rested. I'm not weak or sluggish as usual when I wake from my bunk, and my lungs don't feel as heavy, though they certainly crave a medicated breath.

Looking out the window, confusion hits me faster than a ton of bricks when I find I'm not staring at the springs of Grape's rusty bunk, but instead at a beautifully crafted chandelier hanging from an alabaster-painted ceiling.

Panic ensues.

"Sicar! Where am I?" I shriek through my mind. Am I dead? Is this heaven?

"You are safe." Is all he responds with, leaving me to freak out by myself.

Finding enough courage to scan my surroundings, I do a slow sweep of the room, concluding I must be nowhere near base. Everything in the room, every object, even every smell, is so foreign that I could never place it at Aegis.

To my left sits a nightstand with a pearl-diamond gas lamp and a black-leather chair ornamented with a haphazardly draped quilt, along with a small stack of books balanced on the armrest. Further off lies a beautiful kitchen sink below a massive bay window, polished cabinets that meet the ceiling and another door further back that must lead to a private bathroom. This entire room screeches *wealth,* and I toy with the idea of moving in permanently. Maybe I've reached heaven after all.

A heavy metal door swings open before me, revealing the captain in a typical midnight suit, clean-cut chocolate hair and golden cufflinks.

Forget moving in. I need to get out of here as fast as possible.

"You're awake," Jude says as a statement rather than a question, hardly making eye contact as he rounds my bedside carrying a bundle of black-parchment scrolls. The information has to be confidential if it's written on that type of paper. I remember one of our first lessons from Dr. Gencavage was that to read a single word without permission that is written on black-parchment was a treasonous offense, punishable by death. What is the captain doing with those? Why is he here?

"Where are we?" I whisper as Jude sets the scrolls next to me, moving toward the nightstand to mess with a clear bag filled with fluid attached to the wall. I follow the line connected to the bag, noticing it turn and bend until it connects to a giant needle… protruding from my arm.

Self-preservation kicks in once more as I yank the needle from my arm, hardly wincing at the sting from the tape keeping it anchored. In one quick movement, I throw the expensive silk blankets from my body, leaping away from the feathery mattress while earning an annoyed scowl from the captain across from me.

His eyes narrow as irritated hands find his hips, "What's the matter with you?"

"With *me?* How do I know that bag isn't poison? Are you trying to kill me?"

I slide my feet into a fighting stance, taking mental inventory of my surroundings should I need to defend myself. I can't trust him. I can't trust anyone.

"Damn. That room really did a number on you."

I bare my teeth in response, slowly inching toward the door. I'll get out of this wooden cell one way or another.

"Prospect, you are safe. Phase two has concluded."

An exasperated sigh leaves Jude's throat as he unbuttons his suit jacket in one swift, muscle-memory movement, taking a seat in the leather chair. He crosses a leg, cocking his head with a *go-ahead-and-say-whatever-the-hell-is-on-your-mind* look.

I want to believe Sicar. I want to believe it's really over, but I've tasted freedom already, and it was too painful to realize it was never real.

Swallowing, I repeat my question, demanding an answer, "Where are we?"

"We're at Aegis." Jude responds in a tone that says I should know better.

My head oscillates in disbelief, catching a glimpse of the Elijahn Sea that lies beyond the massive bay window.

"Is this your room?" I ask without looking at the captain, taking in the tiny details of the perfectly polished boots sitting in a line beneath the bed.

"You make a wonderful investigator," Jude rolls his eyes as my surroundings submit for inspection.

Everything is so… neat. So *clean* and organized. A massive closet sits behind me holding over a dozen suit jackets, perfectly pressed and hanging in color-coded order as the gradient lightens a minuscule amount. A row of corresponding ties hang from above the collection of suits, though I've never seen the captain wear one.

My eyes meet the bag of fluids that was connected to my arm seconds ago. "What is that? What were you doing to me?"

"You've got to be fucking joking," Jude sighs, shifting his legs, "That protein bag has been keeping you alive and hydrated for the past eight days."

"Eight days…" Shock consumes me as the memory of someone carrying me out of the fire emerges. Someone large, worried and… "You. You brought me here? How did you find me?"

"Now, that's not how we play our game, remember? Question for question. It's my turn."

My gaze shifts to an array of decorative silver-studded daggers mounted above the headboard and a back-up plan begins to form.

Jude huffs, "Why didn't you tell me you have asthma?" My breath leaves my body. How does he know that?

I school my expression, attempting to act as though I have no idea what he's talking about.

"What's that?" My lungs beg for mercy already as anxiety heats my neck. Why are my palms so sweaty?

With a flick of his wrist, a rush of air hits me in the face, tossing blond strands as a sudden burst of cool oxygen slides its way down my throat. In an instant, the air fills my lungs, forcing me to devour the breath as the memory of the captain resurfaces.

My wide eyes meet his dangerous glare, and I don't know what to say. He knows.

"Now, answer my question," Jude crosses massive arms with a no-bullshit tone, "Why didn't you tell me you have asthma?"

Outrage heats my cheeks, "Isn't it obvious? *You* were the one who put a price on my head, and I did whatever I could to survive. What do you think Sera would have done with that interesting piece of information?" I toss my empty incense can onto the silk covers as the thought of Sera's goons playing with my life sends me into a rage. I'll be damned if I become a punching bag again.

The captain's jaw ticks, "You should have told me. How have you been getting refills?"

"Does it matter?"

"Answer me."

My neck feels sticky with heat as adrenaline-filled hands stab through my hair, "None of this matters anymore. You took me out of that wooden cell. You locked me in here, gave me medicine and kept me from training. In the President's eyes, I've *more* than cheated and I'm as good as dead."

I feel so shaky with nerves it seems impossible to calm down, and my nervous legs begin pacing on my side of the room.

Another annoyed sigh leaves the captain's throat as he stands from his chair, "Calm down, Soria. No one's sentenced to death yet."

"Not funny." I spit as he takes slow strides around the bed frame. How am I going to survive this? I used to have answers, but not this time.

Jude moves as if approaching a rabid animal, his tone deliberately gentle, "You need to relax. I have everything under control."

"Grape and Merry! Ona! Where—"

"They're safe. Stop worrying about them." Jude purrs, his gaze narrowing the closer he gets, but I'm an anxious wreck. Nothing feels right.

"I'll never stop worrying about them. They've saved my life more times than I can count."

"Add me to the list then." The captain's voice is a touch playful, but it does nothing to calm the horrors unfolding within my brain. Why is it so hot in here?

I can't stop wondering if the President prefers the old fashioned hanging method or the guillotine—or maybe he'll dig up some new terrible monster to feed me to. That would make a statement.

"All you have to worry about is staying in here, reading what I bring you, and letting the rest work itself out." Jude's suddenly standing very close. *Too* close. I can smell him like never before, and it's driving me insane.

"I can't stay in here!"

Retreating from him is the only smart option as this terrible ache returns with a vengeance. I'm not sure what I'll do if he gets any closer. What's the matter with me?

"You can, and you will." Jude motions to the stack of books on the chair's armrest across the room, "Those hold everything you've missed from your classes.

You're going to read, eat, sleep, and wait. That's an order. Why do you fight everything I tell you?"

"What do you expect? That I worship the ground you walk on like your submissive army of recruits? You were the one who said you didn't care."

Rage prickles my forearms recalling his harsh words before I had entered the hydra's jungle.

A spasm of emotion flutters across the captain's face, but it's too fleeting to decipher before he says, "Do you think I'd risk my career and my principles every day to ensure your well-being if I didn't care?"

"My *well-being?*"

Disbelief hits my heart like a storm, and I decide to throw the grenade I've been keeping in my back pocket ever since I made the connection about the five senses. I need a change of topic before I go crazy with these overwhelming nerves racing up my spine—nerves of fury and lust that are becoming too difficult to separate the closer Jude steps.

"Isn't it my turn for a question?" I bite every word through flimsy breaths, withdrawing as he follows, "When did you lose your sense of touch?"

Jude stops in his tracks, and his arms that were folded behind his back slowly move over his chest defensively. Those swirling blue eyes search mine, giving nothing away, but I'm not backing down.

Finally, he whispers, "That took you longer to put together than I thought."

"That doesn't answer my question."

"Stop glancing at those daggers above my bed and I'll answer anything you want to know." Those eyes drop from mine to my mouth.

My back hits the wall in a sorry attempt to retreat, but my body has always been traitorous.

"When did you lose it?" I force myself not to look at his lips.

"The same time I almost lost my mind. During phase two." He tilts his chin, "I haven't felt anything for the past four years. And yet, for some reason, I can feel *you.*"

I have so many more questions to ask, but they evade me the closer this beautiful man gets, and the anxiety of the unknown begs to push me over the edge.

Jude's wide frame encompasses mine as he advances to stand inches away. The tension is too much. He smells too delectable and I'm not strong enough to deny what I've been craving for so long.

In the weakest whisper, I ask, "What are you doing?"

Jude's face is dangerously close to mine, those lethal eyes roaming over every detail.

He lifts a hand slowly, his gaze concentrating on my mouth in an unspoken question. I practically melt as his thumb pad sweeps delicately across my bottom lip, his other fingers holding my chin captive. The ache between my thighs grows the harder I fight it.

With a rough exhale, Jude answers, "I told myself I wouldn't touch you until you discovered my little secret, but you kept trying to die before you could figure it out."

"You have a million secrets." I whisper as Jude's lips curl into a delicious snarl, and I press closer to devour his next
words.

"Then let me disclose one," he whispers every syllable, "I'm glad you're alive, because I couldn't sleep without knowing what you taste like."

And his lips meet mine, soft and delicate as if to test my waters. The perilous heat that was threatening to send me over dissipates. The tension releases like a cool breeze washing over a searing surface as my eyes close to feel his mouth. That scar that's carved into his bottom lip. That stubble lining his upper lip.

I need more.

Not a second later my traitorous body gives in to the glorious lust it's been craving, and I press into the captain with a hunger that's been brewing for months, sliding greedy hands up the soft suit lapels to wrap around that perfectly clean-cut hair.

Damn, it's as soft as it looks. I can't believe I'm touching the captain's hair.

I can't believe I'm *kissing* the captain's lips.

Jude's fingers glide up the side of my head, tangling themselves into my hair as his other hand frames my throat, keeping me pressed gently against the wall.

"You taste better than I've been imagining," he growls against my lips, confirming that I'm not the only one who's been wondering what this would feel like. What *he* would feel like.

Jude's mouth acts utterly *starving* as it lays claim to mine, barely stifling a seductive moan as I sink my teeth into his bottom lip, pulling him closer and swallowing his tongue.

I need him. I *want* him. Right here.

As if the captain can read my thoughts, he slides ravenous palms under my thighs, barely bending at the waist to bring me eye-level, and taking two backward strides to sit on the bed. His lips worship my neck, trailing up the spot behind my ear and making me reel from the ache he's creating.

"Oh fuck," I whisper through a moan as my knees grip his waist tighter, and I grind against Jude's torso, straddling what I need between his legs, "Tell me what you want." My hands slide down his chest and the rumble in his throat tells me we're on the same page.

"I want you on a silver-fucking platter," He grips my ass, palming it with both hands, "But I want one thing…" His mouth grazes the shell of my ear, "More than anything."

"What's that?" I need him out of this damn suit.

"I want…" Jude leans back to gain eye contact and I'm ready to get on my knees, "For you to obey my command."

"Yes, sir."

He brushes a strand from my face, those eyes returning to normal, "Read. Eat. Sleep. And wait."

My heart sinks as he picks me up and places me back on the ground. Fully clothed. What a nasty trick.

I can't get away from my chest that pounds in disappointment. In… what feels like anger. Rage for the unfinished business my body demands.

"Soria," Jude straightens his suit jacket, and the anger grows exponentially as I realize he never meant to finish what he started. Jude's hand finds my chin, his lips begging to brush mine but he's keeping himself at a distance.

"Why did you stop?" I can't help the bitterness that lines my voice. I don't like how I sound.

"It's not right. Not in your condition."

"I'm perfectly fine!" I shout louder than I mean to, raking vibrating hands through my hair as I back toward the door. I know it's a lie as soon as it leaves my mouth. I don't feel like myself. Something's wrong.

"Listen to me. This afternoon all leadership is being sent to Tir'jah, three cities away for briefings. You need to rest and—"

"Don't tell me what I need!" I shout, ignoring the pit in my stomach threatening to make me heave. But not here. I won't throw up in front of the captain again.

I need to get out of here. I can't stay a prisoner in Jude's room, no matter how nice of a cell it is. I need to get back to training and pray the President takes mercy on my soul.

"Soria, stay here!" Jude reaches for my hand but I'm too fast. I'm already past his door and sprinting down the corridor of the west wing.

CHAPTER 26: GOODBYES

It doesn't take me long to find our incredibly dwindled group of recruits training in the courtyard, and *dwindled* is an understatement. Minuscule. Pathetic. There must be fewer than one hundred of us left, and they look beat to hell. Well, most of them.

Keeping my distance for fear of the President popping out of nowhere to claim my head on a spike, I watch from afar beneath the shelter of shadows and training equipment. My palms feel abhorrently sweaty as if I've dipped them in a warm paste and my entire body crawls with an unbearable itchiness. Whatever was in my cup in the wooden cell is continues to do a number on me, and I can't wait for these residual effects to vacate my pores.

"What exactly is this plan?" A flash of gray light lines my vision. A color I haven't seen before, as Sicar dances around my mind.

"I don't know... I just... I couldn't stay there." The thought of Jude's lips, his teeth, and roaming hands is too much to think about. I want more. I want every last piece of him, but something nagged at the darkest part of my brain, telling me it was too good to be true. Just another one of his games.

And yet, if he had been quicker to prevent my escape, I know I would have given in.

To keep my mind off what I can't have, I throw myself into survival mode yet again. It's all I have.

"Whatever you do, it is wise to steer clear of officials until the decision has been made."

My heart sinks further than it did the second Jude pulled away. I have no idea why I've been trying so hard. My life has never been my own.

A new plan formulates. A bitter, risky plan that results in me loading up on incense and hightailing it the fuck out of here forever. Never looking back.

"Can it be done?" I ask Sicar, knowing full well he understands my escape plan involves his help. I need to disappear like I'd planned all those months ago. My life depends on it.

The phoenix pauses in my mind, contemplating his response before replying, *"Yes. But I advise against it."*

"Then I'm leaving now." My mind is made up. I can't hang around any longer waiting for my death sentence. I was promised a way out if I made it to the finish line alive, but that deal had always been a lie. I just need to reassure myself of one thing before I go.

Scanning the group of recruits far off, a familiar head of spiky black hair catches my attention in the distance, and a sigh of relief leaves my mouth to see the shapeshifter spinning around him as they practice hand-to-hand combat.

"The Beast has survived as well."

A nervous hand flies to my chest as overwhelming relief floods my nerves, and for a moment, the emotion tosses ease over the worry that has begun to manifest into something tangible within my body. But it returns the moment I spot Sera and Kole's perfectly healthy faces among the living.

"Sicar?" His name quivers in my mind as I drop to my knees, feeling the weight of the world on my shoulders, *"What's happening to me?"*

He doesn't answer, and it makes me worried.

"Am I going to die?" My heart races faster as sweat beads form along my forehead, and I can't control the panicky feeling that threatens to rip me apart. Is this a fever?

Sicar's voice is like smooth thunder in my mind, ancient and powerful, *"This I vow to you, Daughter of David: the heavens would have to collide with the earth before I let either take you from me."* As he speaks, my nerves finally cave, and I vomit the foul contents that have been lining my stomach since phase two.

When I finally gain my feet, the itching is gone, the heat has evaporated and the uneasiness feels bearable once more.

Before I have a chance to pick apart the terrible feeling sizzling beneath my skin, a shriek pulls my attention, and my fists ball as I see a group surrounding my two friends. But they're not closing in on Merry or Grape. They're… watching.
Waiting.

Curiosity gets the better of me as I inch closer to get a better view, rounding a cement wall to peer straight into the crowd.

Time moves in slow motion as the entire courtyard falls silent, and my pair of friends face each other, arms intertwined, faces still and concentrated.

"Remember to stay calm, but strong." Director Boz instructs them from the farthest edge of the circle enclosing them, "Phase one taught you to bury yourself in strength. Phase two instilled calmness and rationality. Do not let your heart get overwhelmed. And breathe."

"Holy shit." I whisper in disbelief through my mind, *"Are they—"*

"They are."

Every worry plaguing my soul ceases for the time being as I witness an ethereal, beautiful, and *magical* moment take place before my very eyes. Something of privilege to watch.

Grape closes his eyes and Merry follows suit, releasing a pair of massive auburn wings from her back as her body relaxes. I watch as their mouths draw breaths so deep one could imagine they're inhaling the very essence of each other, and a golden glow flows from their locked forearms, snaking its way towards both their chests.

The air feels frigid and I don't dare move a muscle during this vulnerable and powerful moment they share. Whatever happens next will seal their fates forever.

Dr. Gencavage instructed us briefly on the laws of permanently attaching one soul to another. The fear of making an incorrect decision and the fear of dying is what keeps the average deltas roaming Bachaloria from performing this sacrificial act. If a gift chooses wrong, both parties will die immediately.

"In this moment, the light that creates them is consorting for power. It is determining if there is space for only one, or room to combine in permanence." Sicar's voice fills my mind, and my chest heaves with a new bundle of nerves for the unknown.

"What happens if there isn't room?" I immediately know the answer before I ask.

"Their hearts will give out in response to peril, and they will cease living. This is why remaining calm is of most importance." I barely notice the pain I'm creating as nervous nails dig into my own palms. Please, *please* let this work.

Suddenly, both of their arms drop, but their bodies stay standing. Grape's eyes flutter open to find Merry breathing heavily. Her massive wings sheathe themselves, disappearing into her shoulder blades. The slow smile across Grape's face tells me all I need to know.

In one quick movement, Merry and Grape embrace, clinging to each other as the crowd of recruits shouts their praises to the sky, cheering for the newest tethered pair.

A shapeshifter and a hyperacusian.

"They did it," I whisper out loud, unable to hide the tears in my eyes as Grape's gaze quickly finds mine from my hiding spot across the courtyard. I knew he'd hear me. His expression softens into relief as his own eyes well with overwhelming emotion.

"I'm so happy for you." I say under my breath as Grape clings to his tethered. He gives me a nod as those tears spill over, and I make him a silent promise to say goodbye before I leave. I owe them more than they know.

"I suppose my journey can wait a few hours to tell my friends I'll miss them." I sniff, drying my eyes, overcome with emotion after watching this beautiful moment unfold. A moment that I fear I will never know myself.

"As I have instructed, avoid any officials, for I am a day's trip away."

"What super-secret business are you up to, anyway? Am I allowed to know?" I prod, finally noticing my full sleeves are missing, leaving me with singed felt that meets bare elbows.

Odd.

"You will know all in time, Nosy One."

"I knew you'd say some shit like that." And the mythical phoenix creates a bird noise that sounds oddly similar to a human grunt.

***

The squad bay hasn't changed much in the night, besides painting a clear division of who the recruits believe to be the strongest and the weakest among themselves.

The middle of the bay holds hundreds of empty racks that will never again harbor the life it claimed. Closest to the bathing chambers, Sera, Kole, Brody, and the other evils I wish to avoid set up shop, settling in for the evening like a self-sufficient band of executioners.

Good. I just need them to stay on their side of the bay so I can relay my goodbyes to my friends.

Keeping as quiet as possible, I weave through the empty racks, making a mental note to visit the infirmary in hopes of finding Ivar for a medicinal refill when this is over. It doesn't help my growing anxiety that I've been out of incense ever since I was carried out of the woods. And I'll never see the captain again…

"As I have mentioned, I still advise against this plan." Sicar butts into my train of thought as he loves to do.

Brushing him off, I round the last set of bunks with feet lighter than a feather, but before I speak a word, strong, enormous, veiny arms wrap me up in a lethal embrace, nearly popping my eyes from my skull.

"Zero alive." Ona mumbles in a hot breath against my cheek, dangling me in the air just before setting me on my own two feet.

A shrill squeal escapes from Merry as she leaps from her bunk, folding me into a giant hug, her frizzy hair bouncing all over the place in excitement.

"You're alive! You're *here!*" Through teary eyes the shapeshifter grabs me by the shoulders in disbelief.

"We all thought you were dead. *Again.*" Grape mutters with a grin, wrapping himself into our hug. My heart feels so full knowing they're all okay. They survived and that's all that matters.

A fourth pair of arms joins the circle, and my head swivels to see a stranger infiltrating the group. One of the most unlikely of recruits.

"Phia?" I question the small plant-mover with the dark hair, surprised to see her amongst the living. A sheepish smile caresses those thin lips as she steps back, her eyes darting from me to Ona and back. And an unfamiliar, toothless grin creeps across Ona's face. Well, *half* grin.

"No way."

"They've tethered." Grape nods and I watch as the plant mover steps closer to her protector five times her size, easing into her presence like a long-lost soul, and I see it. The bond that's settled between them, unyielding and permanent.

It's beautiful. It's everything my friend deserves.

"Congratulations." I smile, nodding to all four of them,
"What was it like?"

"F-f-fucking surreal." Merry says, her gaze drifting as if reliving the experience all over again.

Taking a seat eagerly on the edge of my bunk, I watch her unravel with joy as she describes the feeling to the best of her ability.

"Imagine the b-best orgasm you've ever e-experienced," she says, and I blurt out an uncontrollable laugh. I'm quickly silenced by the four serious faces all nodding in agreement,

"It's like th-th-that, times one hundred, but over your entire b-body. Even over your brain. That's n-n-not even the best part—"

"Merry," Grape gives her a look and her lips clamp shut.

"What?" I ask, balancing on the very perilous cliffhanger she's just subjected me to.

"Well…" she exchanges glances with Grape that tells me she's not allowed to spill anything else.

"As my bond with you is sacred, so is theirs, My Human." I nod in understanding, though I'm dying to know.

I'm not special enough to be allowed that information. Dr. Gencavage had taught us that the act of tethering is more sacred between those two souls than any celestial event. Even though I respect it. It doesn't mean I'm happy to stay in the dark.

"So…" I roam for questions they might be able to answer, "Who else has tethered?" They know what I'm asking without any elaboration. I just need to know.

"Sera and Brody, the earth-quaker, Eula and Isak."

"Creepy twins."

"Sollace and Asaf and Kole…" Grape's grin sends a wave of relief through my body, "Well, let's just say that little kiss ass is about out of time. He's practically been begging the remaining untethered to try latching but no one will. He even approached Ona the other day."

One disgusted look from The Beast throws us all into a fit of laughter, and I've never felt such justice served for the one who ruined my life in the first place.

"Enough about those jackasses," Merry insists, sitting next to me with a wide smile, "How did you escape phase two? Where have you been?"

"Now that's a long story. One that involves a fire." I laugh, and the others begin exchanging their stories about the dangerous fire that had lit the entire wooden building we were trapped in and how they had all gotten out just in time.

"It might sound weird but… that fire saved my life." Grape mumbles, scrubbing a hand through black hair, "I was seconds from using the rope. Then suddenly I was lying on my back, staring at the trees."

"Mine w-was an axe." Merry shudders and I place a hand along her arm in reassurance, which causes Grape's protective gaze to sweep over the simple touch. Pulling back my arm quickly, I sigh, "Hey, she's all yours."

"I'm sorry, Soria." Grape laughs, and so do the others, "I just can't help it. You'll never know how it feels, but it's like I can't… live without her now. Merry is… everything." His eyes soften over the shapeshifter, and I see the physical change in them already. Their lives are forever intertwined, and the heavens could never separate them now. It's so beautiful it creates a longing within me for something I'll never have.

Leaning back on my pillow, my hands sweep beneath the familiar case to find a single slip of paper, which I pull out quickly, reading, *To my favorite number—The Janitor.*

Hope fills my heart as eager hands scour beneath the pillow to retrieve the refill I've been longing for. But I don't feel a thing. I peek under the pillow in search of the fresh can, but there's nothing. There must be some mistake, unless…

"I'm so glad you decided to drop by."

That disgusting voice elicits a gasp from my throat as Sera and her minions surround us, closing in gradually with wicked grins.

"Otherwise, I wouldn't have been able to return this," Sera flips the shiny copper incense can between her fingers.

CHAPTER 27: AT LAST

Dread fills my chest, forming a meaty cloak of fear as recruits slither out of the darkness. They circle us like a horde of vermin, closing in on their meal with dripping fangs, ready to attack at the drop of a hat.

"Isn't this what you're looking for?" A cloud falls over Sera's eyes as she inspects the can with no more interest than her nail beds. Brody appears out of nowhere, positioning himself behind her lean frame, casting a massive shadow in support of any command she's about to throw.

I stay silent, clocking the recruits who shift between the bunks in a casual yet deadly manner, trapping the five of us with no way out.

"W-w-what the fuck do you want, Sera?" Merry spits as Grape subtly places himself in front of her. He did that for me once on the train platform when Sera's minions were closing in.

"You better get your stuttering dog, Yang, or I'll have to leash her myself."

To my immediate surprise, Grape erupts in laughter, bending at the waist with real tears in his eyes as he shakes his head at her ridiculous insult. His blatant response sends a ripple of fury across Sera's face as nostrils flare at his disrespect.

Wiping tears, Grape sighs through dying giggles, "Oh, girl, just know that if no one else on this earth hates you, it means I've finally died."

"I'd hate to lose my biggest fan," Sera pouts.

Merry takes over, snarling as her fingers dig into the mattress beside me, probably seconds away from turning into claws, "N-n-nice try, you nasty b-bitch. How 'bout you fight me without all of *your* attack dogs? Are you afraid I'd r-r-rip your beady little eyes from your s-skull?"

"I'm more afraid of killing myself if I have to spend one more minute listening to you get out a sentence," Sera shrugs, "But I'm not here for you, pet. I'm here for what's mine."

Damn. She'll rot the day Merry figures out how to shapeshift into a dragon.

It's not until Brody bellows behind his tethered that I come to the very real conclusion that Sera has finally come to collect what she's owed. My life.

The threat hovers in the air as the entire squad bay falls silent, and I realize what she's doing just before it happens.

"You won't lay another finger on her," Grape collects himself with one last chuckle, shifting to stand in front of both me and Merry, his body locked in a firm fighter stance, arms dangling calmly at his sides.

Sera's smirk is filled with malice as she whispers, "Just for that, I'm going to make you all watch as I bleed. Her. Dry."

"Sicar!"

"I am not in range! Run!" And hell breaks loose.

Menacing violin music fills my mind as my worst nightmare unfolds, and my friends gain their feet to fight for my life.

Grape pulls a knife tucked behind his back, launching it toward Sera's face, but she's faster than him. She dodges the blade with ease, flicking her palms out to blind him.

Rage consumes Merry in a tangible form as she shrieks a terrible war cry, quickly transforming into a one-hundred-pound black hawk with talons like daggers. In an instant, she hurls those deadly claws at Sera, but thick, dark ropes catch her outstretched legs in a hog-tie and she plummets into a bunk with a maddening screech.

Mayhem unfolds as Depitrio, Sera's purple-curled goon who spent countless nights choking me with his ropes for fingers, laces those thick bounds across Merry's bird form, strangling her without a second thought.

Ona picks up the metal bunk with one hand and rams it into two boys lingering behind her, pinning them to the cement wall with a roar so deep it sends a shiver down my spine, rattling the walls with her might. She doesn't mean to disarm—she means to destroy.

Ona's arms vibrate with terrifying strength as she presses the metal frame harder against the pair of recruits, and before they have a chance to fight back, their mouths spew crimson foam as the metal bars meet precious organs.

Leaping to my feet against Sicar's warning, I lunge for the recruits who land swift punches into Grape's ribs, clawing and screaming for them to release my friends.

I sink one good elbow into a boy's jaw, eliciting a bitter groan before another pair of arms lock mine, rendering me immobile.

A tear falls down a hot cheek as I realize we've always been beaten. We never had a chance. Ona may be able to tear apart every last body in her way, but she's forced to surrender when a grinning recruit holds a blade to Phia's throat, demanding Ona to bend a knee or her tethered will lose her head.

They treat Grape to the same punishment, compelling him to give in as they keep Merry tangled within ropes that could crush her trachea at any point. It's over.

Brody's calloused hands rip me from the floor, tossing me over his shoulder against my will.

Sera instructs her remaining recruits to gather my friends, and they follow me kicking and screaming toward the massive, brightly lit bathing chambers.

No. *No.* Not again!

"Sicar! Help!"

A shriek of outrage and a flash of bright red light fills my vision as panic seeps into my pores because he's too far away.

He won't make it in time.

"Get Jude!" I plead through my mind as my mouth releases curses to my captor.

"All officials are on the isle of Tir'jah!" Sicar's voice offers me no reassurance as I'm hauled to the very back stall, and this time I have an audience for my torture.

I watch helplessly as my friends are all forced to a knee, blades to throats as they're made to watch my last punishment with their own eyes. This is why I took my beatings in private. I never meant to put them through this. I should have run when I had the chance.

Sera *tsks,* her boots filling the white-tiled room with a menacing thump as she circles the bathroom like a shark. I watch her laugh at Grape whose body is held captive by those nasty ropes.

"Depitrio, trade with Brody." She commands, and he obeys, switching to hover above me as those ropes for fingers unfurl.

"What? Don't want to risk your precious tethered? Afraid her phoenix will show up and rip you to shreds?" Grape seethes, his eyes flicking to me for a mere second before he spits at Sera. If only he knew Sicar can't save the day this time.

"Bluff to them! Lie right now!"

"Whatever you're about to do, I'd think twice before my acolyte gets here. He's on his way."

"Lie better." Sicar begs with desperate agitation in his tone.

Gritting my teeth, I shout with all the fabricated fear I wish to instill in my enemies, "He's going to kill you all!"

For a moment, Sera's mouth falls ajar as she takes the smallest step toward Brody, weighing her options before that nasty smirk returns and I know she's called my bluff.

"See, I think you're full of shit. You want to know why?" Sera licks those full lips, crossing her arms, "Because if that phoenix gave one flying *fuck* about you, he'd have been here the second I found your incense can. You have no one."

My heart sinks as Sera gives Depitrio a simple nod, and pain flashes at the strike of his hand across my face, sending me to the damp floor with a yelp.

Anger rises along my spine, filling my brain with malevolence and pure outrage, but it doesn't all belong to me.

"Tell them I will unleash hell on earth for this act! I will burn their bodies alive and feast on their flesh for these crimes."

Fury sizzles beneath my skin as Depitrio lands a deep kick to my ribs, and my palms shake in response.

"Sera? What's going on? What are you…"

Wheezing on my back, a shred of hope sparks in my chest to hear that idiotic, familiar voice in the bathroom doorway. A voice who owes me more than his life.

Rolling over with a groan, I pin Kole with a desperate plea, wishing for any decency in his miserable heart to save me.

Sera turns to him with crossed arms, hardly acknowledging me lying on the ground, "Kole, you were going to see this sooner or later, but this is a pest I need to end permanently. You understand, right?" She gives him a nodding smile but his expression tells me he's not convinced. His brow furrows in disbelief to see me writhing in pain on the ground.

"But…" Kole stares at me and moves closer, only to be stopped by Brody with a thick palm to the chest, "But why are you doing this? What has she done?"

Sera shakes her head, feigning miserable concern, "The question should be, what *hasn't* she done? Ever since little miss Zero got here, she's slowed us down, made us weak and created a laughing stock out of Aegis. Is that what you want to be known as for the rest of your career, Kole? A *joke* who plays on the same team as some abomination with no gift?"

Fuck. Her words cut deeper than I care to let them, and for a moment, I watch those very words settle with Kole as he contemplates his future. I would expect nothing less from the man who tossed me aside.

Nervously, he rakes a hand through shaggy, sandy hair, his wide chest heaving with uneasiness of his decision.

Finally, Kole murmurs, "You shouldn't hurt her. It's not Soria's fault she doesn't have a delta."

Sera responds quickly with Kole's kryptonite before he gets too carried away with standing up for my life, "But it *is* her fault. The heavens discovered she was worthless the day she was born and now she wants to become one of *us?* It's an insult to who we are. To who we've spent our lives training to become."

Sera snakes around Kole as her muscle man drops his arm, and they block out the pleading from Grape and Merry.

"I know you love her," Sera whispers in his ear.

"Kole! Don't do this, you motherfucker!" Grape screams at the top of his lungs, but Sera's more convincing. She's always three steps ahead.

"So, to make this easier, I'll make you a deal."

She laces her fingers through Kole's, "You know the captain declared three days ago he is not tethering this year. But I'll give you Depitrio. He's willing."

With that promise uttered in an unnerving sing-song voice, Sera has just sealed my death with a stamp more permanent than the Aegis tattoo on my wrist. She's smart. Calculated. She knows what Kole wants more than anything. What he wants more than life, love and loss. To become a player.

Kole's gaze locks with mine, and he blinks away the tears as my shoulders sink in defeat.

"Please." I beg him, reaching out a weak hand, but those tears race down his face in response, and he looks away. The boy I would have followed to the ends of the earth just gave up my life for a chance at fame. I'm the fool in the end.

"Human, do not dive into despair." Sicar says with urgency, and it sounds like he's moving faster than the wind.

"It's over." I whisper through my mind, wincing as another strong foot meets my kidney. I can't take the pain anymore.

I know I did my best.

"Do not do this!" Sicar screeches as Depitrio's ropes lace around my throat, and he drags me to my knees to face my sobbing friends.

"Tell Jude I—"

"Enough! I declared a vow, and by my ascendancy, you will not succumb to death tonight. Now, concentrate! Find the anger and let it rise."

His words don't make any sense as my air supply begins to slowly dissipate and Sera flips my incense can from afar, watching with an evil disposition through that sick grin.

Depitrio chuckles a low, mocking laugh as his ropes tighten and my remaining oxygen slowly disappears. I'm afraid I have seconds left.

"The anger! You need to locate it right now!"

A slow blink is all I can muster as memories suddenly flood my mind like they're being played on a reel without my permission. Kole forsaking me. Sera abusing me. My mother leaving me. My brothers abandoning me. Jude pulling away.

My skin sizzles with familiar resentment and I feel like I want to throw up again as Depitrio plays his game of giving me oxygen and taking it away.

"That's it. Let the anger spread out of control." Sicar instructs. His voice is stern in my mind and I do what he says, staring down my biggest enemy in the room. The man who won't even look at me as I die a miserable death on his behalf. I've been paying for his sins since the day we met, and I'll be damned if I ever do it again.

I feel it now. The rage. It's a tangible and horrible feeling in my stomach that crawls up my spine like a warm wave. It's wild. Unpredictable. I don't know what this is or how it's going to help me, but I know I need more, and I know it's been there for longer than I care to admit.

Endless memories resurface, and I know this is Sicar's doing to fuel the madness begging to spill over. And whatever he's doing is working as I relive every terrible thought I've had since stepping foot on this dreaded base, and my lungs fill with a breath I draw myself.

"What's she doing?" A nervous voice quivers from far off, but my eyes are closed and I'm too far gone for anyone to intervene now.

I am the typhoon that knows no anchor. I am the violence and obsession I was cultivated from. I will not be contained any longer. I will remain a nightmare in the making for anyone who grieves my triumph.

The rage shoots up my spine with pure, vicious intent as my palms heat and my skin feels ready to melt off. It's right there. So close.

"Hey, back up! Back up!"

"What the fuck is happening to her?"

Shrieks born of pure terror fill the bathing chambers as I resurface every last thought that tears me apart. The anger meets its peak at the base of my neck. It floods my entire body like a storm that has no commander, and I know I'm ready.

"Explode!" Sicar shouts, and so I do.

Everything in the world bows to my anger as my eyes shoot open, my jaw dropping lethally. The very element of this rage projects from my mouth and hands in the form of deadly, searing flames.

I am the wrath I wield as I unleash an inferno onto the tiles that made me bleed, the recruits who wished me dead, and the one with the ropes.

My hands think for themselves as one furious palm grabs the neck of Depitrio, the other gripping his shoulder as I blast scalding flame into what used to be a vicious boy with purple curls. My enemy sits in a pile of soot at my bare feet as the rest of the recruits scatter, and I'm left alone, staring down the hollow bathing chambers that drip with flames.

My chest heaves and singed felt falls from my body in tufts, landing along the stained tile floor that will mock me no longer.

* * *

I give myself approximately five seconds to breathe before I freak the fuck out.

"What's happened to me? What did I do?" I pant as sizzling palms try to cover my naked body. The heat had melted my uniform, so I'm more vulnerable than ever, though I suppose it's good I sent every recruit sprinting to the opposite end of base from that dangerous display.

"You are not vulnerable. You are power." Sicar reassures me, but it doesn't calm my racing heart and feverish skin. I still feel so hot. I feel so warm. I feel as if I'm going to light myself on fire again at any second.

My heart races as panic ensues once more, and my hands ignite, flames trailing up my arms to wrap around my body like a deadly cloak. It's unstoppable. Will I always be this way?

The feeling sends me into a mad spiral because I can't comprehend what I'm looking at. Am I on fire? Do I need to put myself out? I should be burnt to a crisp like Depitrio, but my skin accepts the flames with ease.

Oh fuck. Depitrio. I *killed* him. I've never killed anyone before. Am I a murderer?

"Sicar… I'm… *losing* it!" My arms begin shaking and I feel violently ill as the flames rise. I have no way of controlling my body temperature or these rolling swells of emotions. I feel out of control. Destructive. Untamed.

"You need to take a moment and find peace. Just—"

Before he can finish his phoenix-bird-wisdom, I'm already gone. I need to run away. I need… something. Anything to calm me down.

The fire floats in wild wisps and pops up my torso, arms and legs and I can't handle it. I don't want it. This was never meant to happen. I need to put out these flames!

"Human, no!"

"It's the only way!" I shriek out loud, barreling down the empty corridor to the west wing and head straight for the first exit I find, charging through the door. A trail of flames follows me as I streak through the night, screaming like a wild maniac on fire, heading to the one place that can put me out. The sea.

"You will perish! Why do you disregard my instruction?"

Ignoring Sicar, I bolt through the brief patch of trees just before my feet meet the sand and I sprint harder, gaining speed I've never known as the water calls to extinguish what I can't control.

As warm toes skim the first ripple, I squeal in pain at the sea's touch. The water splashes up my shins and I fall backward, crawling away madly as if the tide has made me rabid.

"Immerse yourself in the sand."

I gain enough consciousness to follow Sicar's advice and pile the frosty, dry sand across my bare body, feeling a sense of calm seep into my pores as the flames slowly disappear and my mind gives in to exhaustion.

My head meets a pile of soft sand, and I ease into the shore as the crackling and popping of my skin lessens.

The stars above give me a single wink before I'm off into oblivion, submitting to the shadows.

CHAPTER 28: WINTER SHORES

I'm so over these migraines.

The sun beats across my sand-covered body, my throat raspy from inhaling the chilly November air.

Winter is on its way.

A shiver renders me wide awake as I brush doughy sand from my forearms, freezing waves tickling my toes as they sheath the shore like a blanket. The training building lies somewhere far in the distance. I'm sure. Along with terrible nightmares.

"How do you feel?" Sicar asks in my mind, but the sound of feathers rustling from behind send me whirling on my side. Unbelieving eyes grow wide toward the prestigious, beautiful phoenix perched on a large branch of driftwood, hovering above a neatly folded recruit uniform—where he got that from, I have no idea.

"Are you in pain, Pyromancer?" Those golden eyes demand an answer as wings of heat drip with flame a few feet away. His nicknames get more confusing by the day.

"I thought you could feel if I was." I sigh flippantly, chalking up last night to a terrible nightmare.

"Your delta makes your physical pain difficult to decipher." "What the hell did you just say?"

A familiar warmth fills my mind as Sicar gives me a deep nod that looks strangely like a bow.

He's wrong. He didn't mean that.

"I am never wrong."

A sharp beak claps together to make his point, but I still can't believe what I'm hearing.

"So… last night. When I killed Depitrio?"

"And saved four others."

"When I *killed* Depitrio. With *fire.* That was all me? I can shoot flames from my arms… and mouth and shit?"

Panic greets me again like an old friend. This isn't me. I'm not gifted.

Sicar shifts slightly on his perch, and that very movement tells me something's off. There's more he's not disclosing.

I pin him with demanding eyes, and I know he's aware of my questions before I ask them.

Finally, Sicar says, *"As of last evening, you are a pyromancer. The delta lives within your soul, and it will never be taken away."* "Taken away?"

"As it was taken from me." His head swivels, and that voice leaves a pit of guilt in my stomach for stealing what was never mine. There's still a very prominent piece of me that believes this is a dream. This can't be real.

"I took your power?" My voice shakes, and a shiver rises up my spine, feeling like I've betrayed the one I care for most. If that's what really happened.

"No. This power was taken by you, but only because I gifted it. There was no other option. You were out of time."

"Let me get this straight," I snatch the uniform, brushing off sand as I pull the thick felt over my limbs, fiddling with the same, tiresome buckles, "Instead of letting me die, which I've been living on borrowed time anyway, you gave me a thousand- year-old delta that allowed me to set the entire squad bay on fire. Am I getting this right?"

Sicar blinks, flaring his wings with a pause, *"There is more."*

"What?"

The phoenix levels his stifling gaze, his thorax rising as he admits, *"During your phase two, certain precautions were not taken."*

Tugging on the buckles that cinch my waist tight against the number zero, I force trembling hands to keep busy as Sicar stalls his information.

"What did you do?" I whisper, thinking back to the fire that nearly took my life in that wooden cell.

"I did what was necessary, Pyromancer. You elected to give up, and I abided by your wishes. I have chosen you and I will not remain physical in a world where you are not."

"Sicar," my voice trembles remembering burnt sleeves. The flames engulfing the dirty mattress. The heat that nearly drove me mad in Jude's room.

"My decision to follow your soul required a release of power. When an acolyte releases their gift, it feeds the earth to enrich life that no longer harbors it. At the last moment, you chose to live. To fight."

My jaw trembles as I examine my hands. They're different.

They feel tingly, hot, and *sizzling.*

Sicar stretches fiery wings once more, *"Therefore, at your wish, I took back the power I had unleashed. But a considerable volume did not meet the earth. It was consumed by you, My Pride."*

"How is this possible?" The words fall out softer than I can hear as puzzle pieces fall into place.

My knees hit the sand and tingling hands consume my vision. I flip them obsessively as if to examine the underlying power I can't see.

This can't be real. I'm nobody. I'm not equipped for this.

"You are more than you know," Sicar thunders in my mind, causing me to flinch, *"You slayed the hydra of five, conquered your enemies and befriended The Beast. I will not hear of your doubts. Anchored One."*

Anxiety shoots up my neck as the mighty words fall on deaf ears, and nerves threaten to flip my stomach. I never asked for any of this. All I wanted was to survive, not harness the fire of heaven and hell combined.

"Survive and then what?" Sicar demands, and I know what he's asking. I wanted to survive more than anything, and that's what I've been doing. But it's never occurred to me that I could actually *live.* And now maybe I have a chance. Whether I've asked for it or not, these are the cards I've been dealt. And my father may have been a gambler, but this time I have no choice but to manage what I've been given—or taken.

Minus the fear.

"Very good. Now we have one last task to accomplish."

I tug the last straps of my uniform across my chest, buckling them into place as I gain my feet to face Sicar at eye level.

"You were not successful at bluffing before, but this time you must be."

With a nervous swallow, I nod, "Let's do this."

It's difficult to ignore the gawking eyes of strangers as I round the Aegis training walls, dismissing the sand that rubs me in all the wrong places.

Men and women stop in their tracks as I pass them along the corridors, making my way toward the parade deck where Sicar says everyone is gathered. I watch as jaws drop, mouths whispering in shock while disturbed expressions give their fear away. I'm guessing it has something to do with the large fiery phoenix balancing on my shoulder.

"You're too modest." Sicar chortles.

I had braided the hair that frames my face, folding it into long, free-flowing locks that whip in the gentle wind. Sicar told me we can never take back a first impression, so this one needs to make a statement. My life depends on it.

"Every official just arrived this morning. They came back immediately once word was received of last night's affairs." Sicar says as we pass through another long hall. Scalding talons sear holes through my uniform down to my bare skin, but it doesn't bother me in the slightest. I can't feel how hot he actually is, and I suppose I have this new delta to thank for that. The delta of fire.

"Is... he going to be there?" I ask, knowing Sicar's aware of who I'm referring to.

"He was the first to get off the train."

Something in his response settles a separate bundle of worries I've been carrying. Ever since I left Jude's room, I can't stop thinking about him. I had wanted to run in order to live another day, but I can't run now. I'm about to show everyone on this blasted base why.

"That train of thought is correct. Elicit confidence."

Sicar's beak snaps as we push through another set of doors, and that breeze tosses my hair once more. I'm not the same defenseless girl I was when I first stepped foot on the auction stage.

I'm angrier.

CHAPTER 29: COUNTER MOVES

The black tar parade deck falls silent as my heel meets the ground, striding with rigid fervor across the quarter-mile landscape. A false confidence, but it's necessary if we're about to convince all of Aegis that I'm not to be fucked with anymore.

"Remember, you have no control over the flames yet, but this is about a show of force. Heed my commands."

I let a steely mask of impenetrable authority fall over my features as a slow, calming breath escapes. These weak lungs ground me, reminding me that failure is very imminent with one wrong move. I'm still out of incense.

In the distance, a giant group of officials in Bachalorian blue snap their heads toward me. As I look to the right, I'm more than pleased to see my company in a gaggle.

Sera bares her teeth in silence as I get closer, and Brody places a hand along her back. Grape catches my attention with a smile prouder than I've ever seen, and Merry slaps a hand over her shocked, open mouth.

I want to run to them, but I can't. I need to focus.

Scanning the crowd, my gaze searches for that one face I need to see above anyone else's. I halt in the middle of the parade deck, scanning the crowd impatiently until I find him.

The captain stands next to the President who delivers a scowl across his pasty lips. Jude's arms are folded over his massive chest, and he leans in, mumbling something to President RoBjorn, who never takes his gaze off of me and my acolyte.

"It is time," Sicar's voice fills my head, *"Close your eyes and feel."*

I block out the possibility of failure. I throw away any thoughts of inadequacy, weakness, and fear. I use all my energy to dive deep into the only emotion that fuels the fire.

Rage.

Sicar flashes the images in my mind that drive me mad with ire, and I give in to the inferno that trails up my spine.

"Remember, we have the wind on our side for amplification, but keep the heat contained to your hands."

Right. It wouldn't be a show of force if I end up screaming and naked like last night. Though as the heat grows in my palms, all I want to do is run again. I push the fear out of my mind and keep my boots planted firmly on the black tar.

The perilous heat ignites in my hands, burning away at the material along my wrists and forearms, but I ignore the melting fabric and hone in on the flames.

"Steady now. Let it collapse and build on its own."

Sicar instructs as I keep my eyes closed, ignoring the gasps from across the deck at my display. Despite my best efforts, their discerning eyes are getting harder to ignore. What if they can see through this charade?

The flames weaken, sparking pathetically with a quiver.

"The magic in your veins fights to settle on your strongest emotion. Do not open the door to apprehension or the heat will burn no more."

Taking as deep a breath as I can manage, I toss the worry aside, and instantly the flames grow. But the wind is too strong and it blows the flames all over the place. I begin to lose my sense of peace as fire catches along my thighs, searing holes through my uniform.

"Do not muddy your mind with concern. Focus on your anger."

Sicar warns, and I try to find my way back to the rage, but I can't. I'm getting out of control. The flames are all over the place.

Until suddenly, they're not.

A warm breeze meets my neck, tossing familiar tendrils along my cheek, playing with my hair just before the wind sends the flames directly above. My eyes shoot skyward to watch the fire explode through the air, causing the large group of spectators to flinch, gasping at the fire created by the girl everyone ignored.

They're not ignoring me now.

"Did we do it?" My voice is breathless in my mind as I scan the mixed emotions of recruits and officials in the distance. A small smirk tugs at Jude's lip as the President furrows his brows, staring at me with a gaze so intense I can't tell what he's thinking.

"They are deciding if your delta is too unpredictable." Sicar chuffs against my ear, *"The world has not seen a pyromancer in hundreds of decades."*

"You could have told me that."

"The decision has been made." Sicar says, and my breath hitches in my throat.

President RoBjorn pulls director Neera to the side, muttering something for a long time. Too long for comfort. Until he finally steps away, hardly acknowledging the salutes of his cabinet members as he disappears through the crowd.

With pinned lips, Neera strides forward to face the recruits, her voice undulating as she finds the words she seems hesitant to relay.

"Deliveries will begin in one week. Recruits, pack up for an eighteen-mile hike in the canyons. You can thank your newest delta."

I finally release the breath that I have been holding on to for good news, fighting the urge to fall to my knees in relief. I may be a fraud, stealing a gift that was never mine to take, but I'm a fraud who's alive. *"You would not have been able to take it if I had not opened the doorway to give it."*

Before I can argue with Sicar, my friends surround me, and I'm reunited once more with the ones I would fight for all over again.

"You continue to be the biggest badass in the world," Grape grabs my hand, not daring to look at the massive phoenix perched on my shoulder directly in the eye.

In the next second, Sicar pushes off me with so much force it nearly knocks me over. A familiar gust of wind stands me back upright, and I know exactly where it's coming from.

Merry throws me into another hug, begging to know every detail between last night and now. I catch a glimpse of Jude on the other end of the parade deck, his dangerous eyes glinting with pride as he dips his chin ever so slightly. When I see his fingers wave in a *come hither* motion, I go to him immediately.

I'm not sure what's gotten into me, but as my feet move in purposeful strides toward the captain, all I can think about is how I want to finish what we started. And I don't care who's watching. Not Sera. Not the President. And certainly not—

"Kole! Get the fuck away from her!"

Grape's voice in the distance is a deadly warning, throwing me off guard as Jude's eyes darken from across the parade deck, and suddenly someone's hand is holding mine.

No. *Grabbing* mine. With force. Authority.

Spinning on my heel, I find the one keeping my hand captive belongs to the boy who left me for dead too many times to count.

Kole pulls me to his chest, and his shifting eyes are so desperate—unbelievably pleading as he stares down at me with a quivering lip.

"Sor," his voice is hardly a whisper, and I watch his throat bob as a pathetic sob escapes, "Please. Please, you have to understand."

Rage boils as I yank my arm free with a scoff, pushing off his chest as my friends hustle to drop kick this motherfucker back to hell where he belongs. I get to lay him out first.

I snarl, "You left me for dead!"

"Soria, *please!*"

"Shall I destroy your enemy?" Sicar asks in my mind, and I know he'll fly back in seconds if I ask him to. No. This is my fight.

"He's mine."

I level Kole with a disgusting glare, gripping his collar with hands that beg to lose control of their newfound heat, "You were never going to meet me at your house. You were never going to help me. You were going to watch me *die!"*

I shoot my friends a look that says *backoff* as they approach, and they halt in their tracks.

"Sor, I love you," Kole's voice is barely audible through those pitiful tears as he wraps his arms around mine, "And I'm so, *so* sorry. You have to believe me!"

"Sorry for *what?"* I shriek, my palms burning holes in his uniform. In his stupid number seventy-five.

Those bloodshot eyes blink through the tears as he sucks in a breath, his forearms locking mine in an immovable grip.

Something isn't right.

Kole cries, "I'm sorry for everything. And I'm sorry for this… but I have no choice."

"No!"

And suddenly, I am not myself.

Everything happens so fast. Too fast.

Time and space cease as the entire world goes quiet, dark and listless. I'm standing alone with nothing to fill my head but my own breathing, without a thought of who I am or where I'm supposed to go.

Until a bright light makes itself known before me, and I creep close to it, not knowing any better. A curious finger unfolds to grace the light that I find beautiful, and it dances, molds into a sphere of grays and greens until it's given purpose. Purpose that takes the form of something I don't want anything to do with. It's a harsh, giant wave that I want to run from, but I can't.

My feet stay planted, and my arms weigh one thousand pounds as my soul begs for mercy from the giant storm that chases me, *hunts* me, and I can't get away.

It's suffocating.

The fire in my veins tries to fight the water with everything it has, but it's powerless beneath the weight of the tide as my arms go numb and my body bleeds from the inside out. I can't get away. I can't stop it.

This is all Kole. He's going to kill me, once and for all.

Abruptly, something heavy and forceful wraps around my waist, tearing me away from the spirit of evil that demands my life, and I'm tossed to the ground with a *thud.* My lungs beg for air, and I feel like I'm coughing up water as my nails dig into the ground helplessly.

"Are you out of your *fucking mind!*"

The captain's deep voice bellows, and I gain enough consciousness to peer up between coughs to watch Jude send his heel into Kole's chest. Instantly, Kole's back meets the hard deck, and he heaves, clawing at his throat as smoke spews from his mouth. *My* smoke.

Grape and Merry rush for me, followed by Sera leaping toward Kole, but Jude isn't playing anyone's game. Not anymore.

In one quick movement, the captain sweeps his arm out, tossing every recruit back by several yards with a powerful wind, creating a stringent circle that only holds him, me and Kole. One of us isn't making it out alive. In that moment that was clear to me.

A massive fire suddenly lights the foggy sky above, and the clouds roll away to reveal the enormous, *furious* phoenix carrying flames along those outstretched wings.

As I struggle to catch my breath, I watch Sicar fill the air with a hurricane of fire, and everyone within a one-mile radius falls to their faces in mercy, shaking where they lie.

Everyone besides Jude.

The captain stands over Kole's shivering body with a heaving chest and taut fists, his body rigid as he lays out a threat, low and serious.

"You dare try to tether with someone you know isn't yours. You're pathetic. I'm going to do you a favor," Jude takes a single stride to stand directly over Kole, his teeth bared in warning, "I'm sparing your life today, but only because your life is Davidsdottir's to take. I'll make it my personal mission to keep you alive until the day she comes to collect."

Kole chokes on my residual soot in his throat as the captain turns to me, revealing a face filled with calm wrath as those eyes dart over my body in quick assessment. I'm so glad I'm not Kole right now. That look would have me hiding under the heaviest rock for all eternity.

As Jude flicks a hand to fill my asthmatic lungs with rich oxygen, Sicar rumbles in my mind, *"Are you well, Pyromancer?"*

"I'm okay." I reassure him as he soars through his cloud of flames. In a blink, he disappears in a storm of smoke, swallowing that storm with him.

If that doesn't caution my enemies to think twice, I'm not sure what will.

My friends give us a wide berth as Jude helps me to my feet with ease, and Kole continues writhing on the ground.

A large, gentle hand finds my lower back as Jude leads me away from the disaster that I'm lucky to have escaped, but Kole has one last pretty lie to leave me with.

"Sor!" Kole shouts through a wheeze.

Funny. Now he knows what it's like to struggle to breathe.

My anger flares as I shoot Kole a look of malice, but there's only feral desperation in his eyes as Brody helps him up.

"Sor, don't trust anyone. *He's* the reason you wound up here, not me!"

Kole's finger is pointed at the captain by my side, and I feel his hand tense along my back, but this is just another one of Kole Arnson's lies. Creative and destructive.

Leveling him with a deadly scowl, I seethe, "If you ever touch me again, I'll fucking kill you." And I mean it.

CHAPTER 30: DEALS

"So, now what?" I ask Jude as we walk side by side down the west wing, leaving the mess on the parade deck behind. I can't be sure if the President just watched that monstrosity unfold, but he certainly knows about it by now. The endless possibilities of what he plans to do with me rack my brain.

The captain is overly calm as we turn down another long corridor that leads to his private room, but I haven't questioned him once since I left that room the last time. Even though I should be thinking of an entirely new strategy with everything that's happened, I hold onto hope of feeling Jude's lips against mine again.

As Jude opens his door for me, he finally answers, "Now, you do what I said," his palm finds the small of my back again as he guides me through the doorway, "Read, eat, sleep, and

wait."

A sigh of annoyance leaves my throat as I throw my hands indignantly in the air, "No! I'm not going to be your little prisoner.".

Before I have a chance to argue with him further, a massive black wolf stops me dead in my tracks as it lifts its dark muzzle from Jude's bed, offering a dangerous stare.

My heart nearly stops and it's suddenly hard to breathe as fear sends perilous shivers up my neck.

Jude makes a noise that sounds like he's unimpressed, and he walks past the wolf curled up on his bed as if the giant predator isn't there.

"Fine. We'll play this your way." Jude grumbles as he digs through the back of his closet, quickly flicking out his wrist to send another refreshing breath down my throat. How does he keep doing that?

I swallow the oxygen with my gaze locked on Fenrir as he drops his jaw to yawn, tucking that enormous head back into his side.

The captain pulls out a large rucksack, identical to the ones every recruit hauls on the hikes.

Oh shit. I forgot the stupid eighteen-mile hike the President just ordered.

"We can follow your rules to the T since you haven't done a single thing my way since you got here," Jude gripes, tightening the pack straps and pulling out a neatly folded pair of player's dress blues. Something I've never seen him in before.

"Oh, thank you, dear wise one, for allowing me to have some control over my life," my voice trails off as Jude begins to undress, sliding off his dark suit jacket and unbuttoning a perfectly ironed dress shirt.

I try to keep my eyes busy by staring at Fenrir sleeping, because I'm not about to get caught leering at the captain who holds all the cards right now. He needs to know his shirtless presence does nothing to me.

"May I interject to confront a lie?"

"No, you may not!" I shriek through my mind at Sicar, digging my teeth into my bottom lip in hopes of dissolving the embarrassment. It's like sharing a brain with a parent.

"Oh, stop doing that, Soria." Jude says, and my gaze shifts to see his half-naked body tightening a black belt to his blues. His physique is exactly what it felt like. Beautifully sculpted muscles protrude from sun-kissed skin clear of any distinctive scar, cut or imperfection. His delicious pectorals flex with every movement, and my wandering eyes trail down his body to fixate on the V forming just above his waistband.

I hope I'm not drooling.

I steel myself, crossing my arms to appear defensive rather than hungry for him. "Stop doing what?"

"Stop biting your lip like that. It drives me crazy." Jude orders calmly without so much as a change in expression. Is this the game we're playing?

I watch him slide on the navy blue jacket to complete the player's ensemble, buckling the straps over his wide chest as if the movement, is second nature. I never would have imagined Jude could be so used to the intricate buckles and clasps that come with the Aegis uniforms, but I suppose I forget he was once me before he was *him.* As the captain rolls his shoulders, standing up straight in this new attire, I read the number he's been given for the first time, etched into his jacket sleeve below the Bachalorian tiger-bear emblem. And I wouldn't expect anything less.

He wears the only number befitting a dangerous leader who commands the most lethal people in the world.

Number one.

Without batting an eye, Jude crosses the room for more supplies, flicking his wrist here and there to move things back in order within his closet, and his entire routine is so mesmerizing to me. I've never seen him like this. So… *human.*

I would have never imagined the almighty captain who wears priceless, pleated suits and perfectly coiffed hair could pack his own rucksack.

Keeping a healthy distance from sleeping Fenrir, I take a seat in the bedside recliner, watching Jude as he organizes.

"Do all players get their own rooms like you?" I ask, my fingers keeping busy so they don't reach for what I want. What I want keeps pacing the room with a determined expression. Damn my feeble, lustful mind.

"Sure. But that doesn't mean they use them." Jude responds, holding his end of the bargain he created the last time I was here. He'd answer any question I wanted to know.

I just have to ask the *right* questions.

"What do you mean if they use them?" I ask.

"Tethered pairs don't often leave each other's side. Even for a night."

"Why haven't you tethered?"

That's the inquiry that does it. My curious gaze scans every inch of Jude's face as he pauses, thinking of an evading answer to give instead of the truth. I feel like I know this about him already.

Expressionless, Jude looks me in the eyes and replies,

"Because then I wouldn't be able to keep my secrets."

His answer isn't good enough. I've been kept in the dark for far too long and I deserve to know what's hidden from me. What am I becoming?

With a huff, I cross my leg, which finally earns Jude's gaze

as I grumble, "You're full of secrets. Why won't you tell me one of them?"

Maybe it's the fact that I've felt his lips against mine, or that he's saved my life too many times to count, but I'm owed explanations. I'm tired of acting like the captain is untouchable. *I've* touched him, and there's no going back.

Another eye roll from Jude locks us in our states. Neither one of us is budging. I won't give in to that mouth I crave if I don't get some real information this time.

Jude grumbles, "You want a secret? How about this: you've managed to royally piss off the most powerful leaders on Aegis, as well as send your name to the military commanders, the *king* and I bet the Enemy In The North. This isn't a game of survival for you anymore because now, *everyone's* watching."

My stomach feels queasy at those words. I never asked for any of this.

Jude shakes his head, tucking filled canteens into their respective pockets, "Your delta changes everything."

"He is right, Stubborn One." Sicar's voice floats through my mind without permission and I feel like I'm a child being ganged up on.

My arms cross tighter, following the direction of my leg in defiance for once again, feeling like I have no control as I give in, "Why's everyone watching? Is there some beauty pageant I should be training for?"

"Because the last pyromancer known to man was the Mad
Queen."

The admission renders me speechless for too many dangerous reasons until I finally find my voice, "Does that make me a target?"

The world thinks I'm one in a million, but really I'm a hoax, holding onto a deadly power without being born with it. This is my secret I'll take to the grave.

"A wise decision." Sicar whispers with intent.

"You've always been a target. And what Arnson just pulled on the parade deck is something every untethered recruit will try the closer we get to deliveries. You would know that," Jude points to the stack of books on my armrest, and a breeze flips open the top cover to a boring prologue, "If you bothered to catch up on your knowledge like I suggested."

Any smart quip escapes me as I realize the captain's right. If I had listened to him the first time and taken his offer of resting and reading, I'd be in a much different position now.

"You know, you're not as bad as they say," I mutter, picking at my fringed sleeve as familiar exhaustion settles in, setting my worries aside for a little longer. I just avoided being killed by my ex-lover. I can't handle thinking about millions of eyes waiting for my next move.

The captain makes a huffing noise as he tosses a gust of wind to the open cabinets, "Is that so?" he responds without looking at me.

"Mmm," I mumble, fighting the sudden heaviness in my eyes that reminds me I'm carrying the weight of a thousand-year-old magic, "You might have killed the previous captain to get ahead, but I think you care about people. You're not the ruthless murderer they say."

Out of the corner of my eye, I see Fenrir's ears twitch, but he stays sleeping, curled up along the expensive silk blankets as if he owns them.

Jude's gaze finds mine, and I can't tell what he's thinking before he disregards my words and goes back to adding the last of his necessities to his pack. He throws it over his shoulder in one sweep as if a ninety-pound rucksack is light work.

In three easy strides, he bends to a knee before me, those calloused hands, gripping the arms of the chair as his face becomes eye level.

In this moment, I want to lean in. I want to give in to the string that keeps pulling me toward him and swallow my desires without consequence, but his expression keeps me seated.

Jude says softly, those eyes serious, but near pleading as he slides a palm beneath my knee, uncrossing it, "I'll make you a deal. I won't make you stay here, where you're *safe*, but just do one thing for me."

I suck my teeth, lifting a brow to hear something good.

"Just take a shower here. Then the rest is up to you. Leave, don't leave, whatever you want to do."

I swallow my surprise, trying to keep my expression neutral as if, that wasn't the most unorthodox and charming thing I've ever heard.

Kole used to make me deals too, but what he wanted in return always had to do with my mouth on a different part of him. The clearer my mind becomes these days, the more I curse myself for making those deals in exchange for his mother's food.

Giving in to those swirling blue eyes, I give in with a sigh. My gaze falls to Jude's hands gripping the arm rests, caging me, and I can't help my finger as it traces his wrist in question. I know he hasn't forgotten our kiss. I hope he hasn't.

But in the next second, the captain regains his feet, standing above me in dismissal of my touch.

Got it.

My hand drops from the rest in silent response, cursing my naive self for thinking he'd want to finish what he had ended so abruptly. He's probably seen what I am now and is scared, just like the fear I had seen on my friends' faces. They didn't know what to think when I nearly threw Kole in a choke hold.

"Fenrir will eat anyone who walks through the door, so you're safe while you shower." Jude promises as he cracks his neck, heading for the door.

Leaping to my feet, I call out, "But won't they come looking for me when I'm not on the hike?"

The captain shakes his head as he pushes open his door with his air, "Not if I take your place." In an instant he's gone, locking the door behind him without moving a muscle.

My mind is a mess as I stare at the beautifully crafted walk-in shower built for royalty.

My bare toes stay planted along the marble floor, nervous fingers gripping a plush, cotton towel as the water spews before me with a warm invitation. I remember the last time I tried to touch water. The sea nearly suffocated me, and I have no idea what it's capable of. Will I never again be able to take another shower?

"What do I do?" I ask Sicar, hoping he has some mythical-bird-knowledge about bathing with a pyromancer delta that was gifted from a magical acolyte. I can't exactly look that up in any scrolls.

"Must I assist in this as well?" His ancient voice brings comforting agitation, and I can't help but laugh at the ridiculous nature of what I'm about to do.

"Please." I grip my towel tighter.

"You will be fine, Paranoid One. Just avoid thoughts of wrath."

"These nicknames are getting out of control." I snort, earning a chortle through my mind from the phoenix.

With a deep breath, I slowly drop my towel, testing the burning water that steams the entire bathing chamber with one foot to find a perfectly comfortable temperature. A sigh of relief washes over me, melting the tension in my body with ease. The steady stream drapes my scalp and shoulders like a glorious cloak, washing away the worries of now and pains of tomorrow.

Every fear ceases as I find a fresh uniform seated on the bed in place of the wolf. And on the nightstand sits a full dinner plate consisting of braised lamb, sweet greens and roasted potatoes—though I have no idea how it appeared.

Jude's blankets feel softer than I remember, and I can't help but moan as I curl under them. Cursing the captain because he knew exactly what he was doing. Get me to shower, draw me out with delicious food and a luxurious bed. He knows I'll never want to leave. He may be a sorcerer, because he is certainly playing chess instead of checkers with me.

As I dig into my dinner, an image appears in my mind, courtesy of Sicar, wherever he is. It's not something from my past that causes anger, nor something that creates pain.

It's an image of Jude leading the recruits in their night hike, taking every painful step so I don't have to. The mess in my mind unravels just a bit as my heart opens for something it's never known.

CHAPTER 31: CANYON QUARREL

Four days of reading, resting, and eating my fill have me oddly uneasy by how much relaxation I'm consuming. It doesn't feel right that I'm enduring what feels like a vacation while my friends and the rest of the company survive heavens-knows-what trials as they prepare for deliveries.

Jude hasn't come to visit me since he left for the eighteen mile hike, and besides Sicar answering my occasional questions, I've had no contact outside these four walls. So to avoid thoughts of seeking trouble, I continue to read the knowledge on tethering. It's a tedious text to decipher.

According to elders known as *The Six Exoda,* whose stamps of feather and bones brandish every scroll, parchment and book cover, they were the original tethered pairs ages ago. Every source derives from them, which makes such archaic encryptions hard to translate without Dr. Gencavage doing it for me. But I'm trusting in Jude when he says I'm safer here.

I never want to experience what Kole attempted again. The act of tethering without my consent felt so… violating. I'll be damned if another person tries to take something from me again.

Anger flashes just thinking of what Kole tried doing, and I drop the scroll in my lap, wringing warm palms so I don't destroy a copy of the priceless transcriptions I'm supposed to be learning from. I can't help but wonder why I'm learning about tethering. It has me confused on another level. It's not like I can bind myself to someone anyway. Kole's delta might have nearly killed me, but who's to say I wouldn't destroy anyone with a power that isn't mine? It's too risky.

"The power is yours." Sicar interjects in my mind.

"It's definitely yours," I correct, "And that reminds me. What was all of that mumbo jumbo on the parade deck about opening doors to the magic and fighting for an emotion?"

Sicar makes a far-off noise that sounds like he's burning something before responding, *"The magic that flows through your body has yet to anchor to an emotion you provide. But be cautious, because once you allow it to seed into a feeling, it will never be separated."*

My brow arches in confusion to the old wise owl in my head, "What the hell does that mean?"

Sicar chuffs, *"Should your delta fall into grief, it will only be possible to wield if grieving. Should it fall into despair, it will only be possible to wield if distraught. Shall I go on?"*

The sarcasm in the phoenix's voice has me chuckling, "I get it. I mean, I'm angry all the time. What if it picks anger?"

"That would not be wise, Pyromancer. Rage is a very unpredictable source to fuel a gift with."

"Okay fine. Don't get too angry. Got it. Now can you help me out with this?" I ask, shaking the parchment at my fingertips, but Sicar falls silent. As usual.

After another hour of thumbing the same five pages in silence, I begin to understand why Jude left me these books to analyze. There may be a new way out.

With a calming breath, I focus on the description of post deliveries written by Aegis' late commander from several decades ago, President Tallgai.

In the dawn of a new era, we shall forever remain triumphant under the law of man, declaring wastefulness of a powerful life unsavory. Therefore, prospects not chosen for competition by deliveries shall not be gifted a second opportunity for the title, but a second chance at life. Those not arraigned will be endowed freedom for their sacrifice and endeavors withstanding any impending unlawful discrepancies.

I unleash a nervous breath, because all I need to do is make it to deliveries alive, and I'm home free.

But to what home?

Shaking my head, I throw away the questions that beg to be answered in the deepest parts of my brain and flip to a section in one of the books written by the Six Exoda, trying to decipher what I couldn't last night.

For some reason, when I got to this particular page, the corner was folded inward, as if this section required my attention. I had tried asking Sicar, but he chose silence in response.

Crunching on a spiced carrot slice that mysteriously arrived at my door like all the other meals, I dive back into the coded message in hopes something will stick this time.

Albeit disastrous, the riddled soul mandates this.

If thou harbor a delta, thou exceeds normality.

However, should the riddled soul bind in unison,

whomst begot the gift forgoes demise alone.

I shake my head, rereading the passage over and over again for some type of clarity.

The message before makes sense, considering whatever old wise person went on a fifteen page rant about tethering being the heaven's blessing. Deltas were originally granted to the extraordinary humans to protect themselves from the dangers of the world. But this part makes less sense the more I read.

"Sicar? A little help, please?" Sighing, I wait for the typical silence, each time I ask for his help when I don't understand what I'm reading, but I'm surprised when he answers in a low tone in my mind.

"One line at a time, Studious One."

I grumble back at him, reciting the passage out loud,
"Albeit disastrous, the riddled soul mandates this."

"An unbreakable law. Continue."

Relief washes over me to find the phoenix helping decode for once, though there's an edge in his voice that tells me these words are important. But why?

I go on, "If thou harbors a delta, thou exceeds normality. Well, that part I understand." I huff, moving to the next lines that have been confusing me, "However, should the riddled soul bind in unison,"

"Should a delta tether," Sicar translates slowly without me asking, and I nod, reading the last line with confusion.

"Whomst begot the gift forgoes demise alone… meaning whoever has a delta forgoes… getting hurt?"

A flash of white illuminates the corners of my vision as Sicar tells me to try again. I guess this line is all me. No help this time.

"Whomst begot the gift, so the person with the delta.
Forgoes demise… doesn't…die?"

"No." Is all Sicar says, and I shake my head, ready to give up, but I can feel the urgency from him. He needs me to understand this on my own.

Reading the last line five more times, I finally sigh, "Whomst begot the gift… forgoes demise alone." Something suddenly sparks as the words make sense, and my mind immediately shoots to my friends. My *tethered* friends.

"You now understand." Sicar says, and the urgency is gone, because I do. Now I wish I didn't.

"So…" I read the paragraph once more with a new heaviness in my chest, "When you tether…"

"You forgo demise alone. Should one die, both die."

Sicar doesn't answer me when I ask him if my friends know this. I can't imagine the President would ever let Dr. Gencavage inform recruits that if they tether they're giving up full autonomy over their soul should their partner perish. People would be too scared to tether if they knew this. Which is why my friends deserve to know.

"Human, I advise against leaving."

"Don't I know it. But if no one's told them, they need to know. I'm not afraid of Sera or Kole."

After I tighten my boot laces, I push through Jude's bedroom door for the first time in four days, marching down the long corridor without looking back.

***

I've already checked the squad bay, chow hall and parade deck, but every area is devoid of my friends, or any recruits for that matter.

The courtyard proves to be empty as well, and I wind up going to the last place I know to get a height advantage.

Which of course is the roof.

A freezing gust of wind hits me in the face as I shoulder open the door, blinking at the chunky snowflakes littering the rooftop. Peering over the edge, the white shore is clear of any bodies besides a person or two picking up debris for maintenance.

The woods on the North side give nothing away, and I'm about to give up just before I spot a group of people in beige felt and buckles, hauling packs half their size as they trudge through the canyons in the East.

A smoke screen of heat rises from their bodies as they march forward in the glistening snow, repeating the cadences their leaders in the front call out.

Among them, I make out Ona in the back, followed by Grape holding up a limping Merry as they struggle to keep up.

Without a second thought, I fly down the stairs, cursing the President for ordering another hike in freezing temperatures.

Haven't they proven themselves by now?

Ignoring Sicar's warning and suspicious glares from strangers, I dart toward the canyons in pursuit of the dark mob of recruits.

"Grape!" I call out when I finally catch up over the first hill, straining to disregard the heaviness in my lungs from the cold air's bite.

Enormous canyon slabs cast ominous shadows along the winter path as I gain on the group trudging along. Frozen, bright red cheeks flash to me as I shuffle through the snow, followed by wide eyes as Grape turns in the back of the formation. A pang of guilt washes over me to see him so drained.

Grape's voice is a low warning as he faces me with blue lips, "What are you doing here? You need to leave, *now!*"

"What?" I ask, brushing off a shiver and wishing I had brought gloves in this treacherous weather, "I need to tell you something."

"Soria, *leave!*" Grape begs, and confusion furrows my brow, but before I can question him, Sera's voice sends a bolt of anger up my spine.

"Well, well. Look who finally decided to join us."

Suddenly, the entire company of recruits halt in their long, stretched line, and Sera pushes through the stragglers in the back, pinning me with bloodshot, vicious eyes.

Her porcelain face is just as red as Grape's, and she looks like an exhausted mess for once in her life as she sneers with rage.

"I found Zero!" Sera screams at the top of her lungs, and several recruits let out breaths that sound similar to relief, bending at the waist as they stretch their legs, groaning.

Before I can smack that devious glare off her face, someone pushes through the crowd, coming nose-to-nose with me with a disbelieving head shake.

Director Boz crosses his arms, and Neera lands by his side with the same, bright red face as the others, ready to end my life with that death-glare.

Boz hisses, "In my entire life, I've never seen a recruit go AWOL while her fellow comrades pay the price. Are we that selfish? Or do you think you're too good to finish out your training?"

Instinct sets in and I take a step back shaking my head. Neera snatches a shivering Merry from behind her, "Tell her, recruit. Tell the pyro what you've been suffering through since she decided to run off."

Merry shakes in her boots, hardly able to keep herself standing as she mumbles, "W-w-we can't to s-stop hiking… "

"Until *what?*" Neera shrieks in Merry's face, demanding she finish the sentence.

"Until… the p-p-pyromancer j-j-joins."

Forget a pang of guilt. A *storm* of shame and regret washes over me as the realization hits. While I've been living it up, eating until my belly is warm and full and sleeping fourteen hours a day, my friends, dammit, my *family* has been suffering in my absence.

Tears beg to form as I watch Merry nearly convulse with exhaustion. The look on Grape's face tells me she's close to death if she doesn't warm up soon.

"Please," I whisper, reaching for Merry before Neera yanks her away, tossing her into Grape who catches his shapeshifter, cradling her in his arms.

"Let's get one thing straight, *recruit,*" Neera lunges for me, her chin-length hair sticking to her neck as she snatches the collar of my uniform, "I don't care if your bird is powerful. I don't care if you have famous brothers. I don't give *one rat's ass* that you somehow gained a fire delta in the last seconds of your time here. Get this clear: you will *not* get special treatment just because the leaders find you interesting."

I taste her words like a sinful cocktail, spitting them out with a few of my own.

"Neera," Boz tenses, changing his tone quickly. In the distance, I see the crowd beginning to separate rapidly from something barreling through.

"I'm not special." I challenge her, feeling more than irate at the insinuation of unique treatment. I've been an experiment for everyone to watch.

"Are you sure about that? Because I'm willing to choke you with that pretty blond hair to find out." Neera vibrates as her bitterness rises to meet mine, and I can't fight the warmth in my palms as the snow begins to cloak our shoulders like a glistening shawl.

"Neera!" Boz shouts, but her rage doesn't let anything get by.

"Try me," I snap, reaching for her neck with burning hands, but in the next second, she's gone. Thrown from my range and replaced by a tall, furious man with slightly rosy cheeks and a heaving chest.

"She tried to kill me! You all saw it!" Neera screeches, pointing a finger at me with bared teeth, "I demand execution!"

Jude's suddenly standing above me, his swirling blue eyes searching my face, wishing to say one hundred things, but he can't. I know he doesn't need to. I know he's infuriated that I left the safety of his room again, but I would have never stayed if I knew my friends were being punished by my absence. By the look on Jude's face, I can tell he's received my explanation. And he accepts it.

Neera screams again, irate that she's being ignored, "That recruit attempted to lay her hands on me. It's my right to demand execution!"

The captain sighs ever so slightly, and suddenly my lungs are filled with rich air, medicated in their withered state by the gift of the aeromancer before me. He's always making sure I can breathe.

In the next second, Jude turns his back to me, facing Neera as her body pulsates with rage.

"The hike is done." Jude says calmly, and not one inch of his posture gives way for argument, but Neera doesn't care.

"No." She barks, ignoring Boz's plea for her to back off, "You've cared a little *too* much about this girl ever since you bought her, Blackwell."

"Pyromancer, it would be wise to back up." Sicar rumbles in my mind.

Oh shit.

I watch Jude's shoulders move, tensing in response to Neera's blatant disrespect. She may be a director, a trainer over the recruits, but he is her captain. If there's anything I've learned from the numerous books and scrolls I've been analyzing over the past few days, it's that no one outranks the captain.

When Jude doesn't reply right away, Neera presses again, "A lot of things have happened a little *too* conveniently for your girl, here. We all saw her getting her ass beat every night, and then suddenly she slays the hydra? Tethers to a phoenix? Tells the world she's a late bloomer and now is a
front runner? I don't think so."

"Wait. Did you tether to me?" I ask Sicar as I analyze Neera's every move, watching her push off of Boz and close the distance between us.

"You would know if I had. The teacher knows not what she speaks of."

Neera's small, lean frame undulates with anger as she growls at the silent captain, "And you want to know what I think? I think you bought her as a toy, had her, and now you're through. Just like—"

"Enough." Jude orders, and suddenly, Neera's mouth clamps closed, as if by force. Her entire body goes still, her hands locked at her sides as the captain circles her slowly like a predator.

Jude's natural poised mannerisms return, even through dirty, dark blues and sweat-filled hair. The entire company surrounds the three of us, observing quietly as their leader folds gloved hands behind his back, cracking his neck.

Jude addresses the wide-eyed crowd, "It seems some of you have forgotten who I am. Well, let me remind you."

Without moving a single limb or digit, he sends Neera to her knees in the crunching snow with a strong gust of wind, still keeping her mouth shut to prevent any further humiliation.

I'm *so* glad I'm not her.

"For some of you, I've already expressed my interest in securing your place as a player. For others, you're not making the cut. But let me be *crystal* clear," Jude snarls toward Neera on her knees, "Every single one of you, dead or alive, were bought because we saw the potential to become one of the greats. The elite. And if eighty-five years of undefeated competition doesn't prove that, I don't know what will. This is the only explanation I will ever give."

Something warm unfurls in my chest as Jude says his piece. It's almost as if he's speaking to me.

"With that being said," Jude releases the grip of his winds on Neera, and she plummets face-first in the snow, trembling in rage, "The next time someone on this fucking base so much as *looks* at me without permission, I'll rip their eyes from the sockets."

Several gazes drop as the captain moves with a single stride
to stand above his director, waiting patiently for her to gain her feet.

When she eventually does, gasping and grumbling the entire time, she pins Jude with a nasty glare, "Say whatever you want, but the truth will come out, *sir.*" And she flicks out a dagger from her thigh pocket, tossing it on the ground a few feet from where I stand in one last act of defiance.

Jude holds her stare, and suddenly I pick apart Neera's expression for what it truly is, and it's not anger. It's... jealousy.

A sigh of relief escapes as I watch Neera turn on her heel and march past Boz, accepting her defeat. But as soon as the sigh leaves my lips, it's replaced by a cry for what the director does next.

Neera glances back at me, rubbing shoulders with Grape, who still tends to his tethered, and in one quick move, the director sends a sharp, painful elbow into Merry's face.

Fury ignites in my chest faster than a lit match, and suddenly my palms of flame are gripping the dagger thrown at my feet. Before I lasso any rational thought, the blade leaves my fist as my arm follows through. And the weapon is aimed straight for Neera's head.

CHAPTER 32: FRUITION

Once again, to my rescue, a swift current of wind tosses the dagger upward before it meets its mark. But even though I missed, it's too late.

Neera spins to face me with an evil sneer, raising both arms to address the company of recruits, "We all saw that? Everyone here is now a witness to the attempt on *my* life. I demand my captain to execute the recruit for such a heinous act!"

The fire dies in my hands as Merry shivers, regaining her feet, and Grape shoots the director a homicidal look.

Neera crosses her arms, stepping back into the circle that contains Jude and me, "Let me remind you, *sir,*" she chides with that same terrible smirk, "Per the bylaws in our ordinance, any untethered recruit who attempts to maim, harm or slay an established member of the base is subjected to execution by the closest, highest-ranked official."

"Should I be worried?" I shoot my question to Sicar. When he doesn't answer, apprehension tangles itself like a knot in my stomach because Neera may be onto something.

I throw Jude a desperate glance, hoping to hear some trite remark to her insane allegations, but when he holds her stare and says nothing, I know she's got him in a figurative hold.

"Face it," Neera steps closer, darting devious eyes between us, "There are too many eyes to deny what's just happened. If you don't kill her right here, right now, I'll just have President RoBjorn do it. The bylaws demand satisfaction, and your little pyro has broken too many."

"Sicar!" I shout in my mind, praying to hear an answer to get me out of this mess. That rat used my anger against me.

"I'm afraid there is only one way to survive." The phoenix finally answers me as the snowy canyons fall silent, and my gaze meets Jude's.

The captain steps away from me, deep in thought as he ponders Neera's demand. He can either kill me himself right here where I stand, or deliver me to the

President's doorstep. Either way, Neera will see to it that I don't survive another day. I'm done for.

"What do I have to do?" I whisper to Sicar as Jude takes a deep breath, coming to his own conclusion.

"What you're meant to do."

Quivering where I stand, I follow Jude's every movement as he gives Neera the slightest nod, finally turning to me.

"Help." I beg Sicar, remembering his promise to obliterate my enemies who wish me harm, and tears form in my eyes because I know I can't fight off Jude. Nor do I want to. My heart aches terribly for him to make this decision, but I would rather he be the one to do it.

Several gasps echo around us as the company separates, and a massive black wolf takes a seat on the edge, tilting his head to watch us with bright, dangerous eyes. It makes sense Fenrir would appear to observe my death, especially if Jude called for him.

"Soria," Jude mutters, taking another step, and despair crosses his face as tears stream down my cheeks.

"It's okay," I whisper, swallowing the sob in my throat as I offer him a hopeful smile, "It's okay. You can do this."

I watch Jude suck in a deep breath as he blinks quickly, now only inches away.

Neera's venomous voice calls out from the outskirts of the crowd, "Come on, now. One recruit's life is not worth a director's. Kill her."

She sounds too much like Sera, who watches from a distance with crossed arms and a devious grin. Even Kole's plea for mercy fall on deaf ears because not a soul can save me this time.

"It's okay," I whisper to Jude again, and he slips his gloves off, keeping those misty blue eyes on mine until my ears are filled with a familiar flapping sound. The company releases even more gasps, followed by numerous murmurs to the noise reverberating above.

I blink through the tears to see the beautiful, magical phoenix with wings of flame soaring high, reaching a nearby canyon ledge to peer down on us where we stand.

Sicar's massive, sharp talons grip the rock shelf with permanence as those red-hot wings fold in, and I swear not a single fleck of snow touches him where he sits.

Hope dies in my chest to realize Sicar doesn't move a muscle to my defense, no matter how much I plead for help.

I don't want to die like this. Not like this.

To be slain in the cold by someone I care for, someone I love.

"Why are you here?"

I ask Sicar in my mind with a trembling voice as Jude takes a deep breath, preparing to steal mine forever.

"My Pride, I would not miss this for the world."

It feels like a sword just pierced my heart with his response, and the tears spill faster as I ask, *"Miss what?"*

"As I said before, what you are meant to do. Now focus on your captain and remain calm."

If I weren't so terrified to die, I might want to pick apart Sicar's advice. Or his warning? Whatever he's trying to relay doesn't sink in as I stare down Jude, planting my feet to take what I've been running from for months.

"Soria," Jude repeats my name, and for the first time, I notice he's holding out his hands, bare palms up, "Did you read?"

"Did I… did I what?" My voice is barely audible through tired sobs, and I can hardly hear the cries of mercy from my friends on the edges of the crowd. But one terrible howl from Fenrir keeps them in their place.

"Did you read what I left you?" Jude asks, his voice so quiet I can hardly hear above the chaos of my labored breaths and crying friends.

I shake my head, wishing for the agony to be over with already, "I read everything."

"And you understand?"

"I—" A whistle of a gasp leaves my throat as I realize what the captain before me is asking, as he holds his palms patiently in question.

"Do you understand, Soria?" Jude's eyes are pleading as he waits for me to take his arms, and the company falls completely silent, the only noise coming from my thumping heart.

He's asking me if I read and correctly deciphered the passage about the tethered pairs. If one dies, they both die. He's asking me for my own sake, so I can decide for myself if our lives are worth gambling so long as we both live.

Because in this moment, Jude means to save my life, one last time. And every fiber of my being knows Sicar is right.

This is what I'm meant to do.

With a slow nod, the tears cease, and all clarity surfaces as I raise my hands to take his, locking my arms and ignoring the distant cries of objection from my enemies in the crowd.

"I understand." I tell Jude, and the entire world fades away as the violin music plays beautifully in my head, and I'm greeted with pure, unmistakable bliss.

I do not know who I am, where I belong or what binds me to the earth. Everything is so dark and unrecognizable, until I'm met with a beautiful spark of light. It floats before me with a glow so radiant that I can't help but reach for it, admiring the stunning gleam as it shifts and molds into hues of blue and silver.

A warmth along my spine reminds me I'm human, and not immune to the dangers that my soul steers from. Yet, I know this is where I need to be. *Exactly* where I need to be.

When the gorgeous ball of light takes its final form, I feel overjoyed to find something I didn't know I've been looking for my entire life. It's all for me.

The form folds into a magnificent, royal blue sheer, drifting into the abyss before it floats toward me, playing with my hair and sliding across my body with intent to save. Protect and serve. I give it a precious piece of me without asking because I know what it needs to survive.

My breath falls easily as my heart slows to a calm speed, releasing a golden sheer to float toward the blue one, and their dance is mesmerizing. Unearthly.

The two sheers finally meet, curling and bowing to each other in respect until they twist with the wind and flames, growing bigger and bolder as if they were meant to find each other in any life.

My beautiful music spreads a cloak of peace across the darkness as the sheers bind together, and that same bright light melds them for all eternity.

Without my approval, every thought I've ever had, every taste, sensation, emotion shoots across the void. Circling around the blue sheer as it absorbs the information with ease. Though I'm not prepared for releasing such intimate parts of myself, the sheer demands it, so I give in, and relive my entire existence in a matter of seconds to ensure the bond is saturated in trust. The bond that Jude is creating.

My first birthday, pale ribbons line the door frame as my father polishes the silverware. My first broken bone, my leg screams in pain as the teacher blames me for falling, though I was pushed. My mother's plea for my father to stay. My brothers leaving me for the auction without saying goodbye. The goosebumps along my arms as I feel Kole's lips for the first time. My calloused hands from scrubbing the chaplain's oxen cart to earn half a krona. My throbbing face when Kole's mother caught me stealing her rice wafers. The fear melded into my heart on the auction stage. The grief to watch Hera die. The lust every time the captain's tendrils of air let me know he's close by. The pride of being chosen by Sicar. The worry to keep my friends alive and cared for. The love for Jude when I look at him.

Just like that, the blue sheer swallows my memories with appreciation, and I reach to request the same from him.

Hesitantly, memories trickle their way in, and then too quickly. I'm prepared to see a handsome man adorned by jewels and women, but that's not the case for this sheer. Not even close.

A young boy's first birthday, spent ignored and forgotten in a moldy room. A trip into town, holding an older boy's hand who looks after him intently. They don't own shoes, and their mother earns her keep by selling her body. The older brother has a name, but he goes by Baron. He is the most powerful, though it's a secret to everyone. At night the father, who remains faceless, tucks them into the same tattered cot, and the smell of rum fills the room. He's cruel, but he's lost as he takes his anger out on his children with hands that will never work properly again. Every morning the older brother is forced to fight the younger, and his gift is horrendous. Electrocution is outlawed, but Baron remains a secret. He has to. The sparks of death nearly hit the younger brother every time, instilling fear in his heart until one day the bolt meets his chest, and agony rises. Air shoots from the younger brother's hands, slamming the older into a tree stump, and he no longer moves. A bloody cut oozes from his temple.

The memories suddenly cease without warning, and I'm cut off from the knowledge I need. Jude has decided against sharing what I want to know. Memories or not, the bond has been formed.

A warm rush shoots across my body, surging every nerve with a feeling so precious and powerful that I want to cry out in exhilaration. It's an emotion I've never known as I eventually come down to earth, and I finally feel Jude's bare arms on mine once more, my feet planted in melted snow while every knee is bowed.

Jude's breath hits my forehead as his arms grip mine tighter, and a myriad of emotions cross his face to realize what we've just done. What *he's* just done. To save my life. No one would dare touch me now. Not when they know I've just tethered to their captain. *My* captain.

"Welcome, Pyromancer." A voice I don't recognize, but I know with every fiber of my being belongs to the massive, perilous wolf behind us.

"We are all connected now." Sicar thunders in my mind, but I can't take my eyes off of Jude as his tendrils of air curl around the small flames that keep our hands locked.

What did we just do?

"The enemy studies what it desires to break,
but those who have championed a true mate are
not so easily destroyed."

-Dr. Gencavage in *The Player's Handbook*

CHAPTER 33: TRUST

Snowflakes leave a trail of scattered water droplets as I follow Jude's massive frame down the bends of the corridors toward the only place that offers sanctuary. I need to be away from watching eyes right now to collect myself, and from the deep rise and fall of Jude's shoulders, I can tell he does too.

The captain's bedroom door slams shut behind us as the memory of tethering replays over and over in my mind. I can't get enough.

When our arms had finally broken apart and the flames died, every wide eye begged to lunge for the newest tethered pair. Jude swept me away before the crowd could close in, blasting a hole through the company with a strong wind.

I can still hear Kole's plea to undo what we'd done. As if that's possible.

Vibrating hands run through my damp hair, eyeing Jude as he takes a seat in his leather chair near the bedside, busying his hands as he unties soaked boots.

There are hundreds of things I want to ask, but I don't know where to start, so I settle for the easiest thing to say. "You saved my life again."

The vein in Jude's neck tenses as he slips his boots off, and he doesn't respond. Fair enough. He's taking this remarkably well.

Fishing for something better to ease the awkwardness hanging in the air, I mutter, "Was that… your brother? In the memories?"

Jude inhales deeply, still not answering me or even looking my way as he gains his feet, striding toward the kitchen sink to grip the counters.

Why would I ask that? I shouldn't bring up an obviously painful memory that he chose to close me off from. Stupid.

I follow him into the kitchen with arms crossed over my chest, shivering from my snow-drenched uniform.

Suddenly, the captain turns to face me, those eyes darting over my body in quick assessment as they've done many times before, and I'm thankful to see him acknowledge me for once.

"You're freezing. You need to change," Jude says expressionless, moving past me toward his closet in search of dry clothes.

"I'm fine." I purse my lips, following him again with helpless steps, "I'm... *more* than fine. Are you? Fine?" I hate the way my voice sounds.

"I love the way your voice sounds." Jude mutters, tugging a black dress shirt from its hanger before making his way toward me.

I swallow the shock, wondering if I've just said that out loud, and I know a bright shade of pink paints my face in embarrassment.

"I... I just..." I'm utterly speechless. I have no idea how to speak to him now as he takes my hand, guiding me toward the bed and motioning for me to have a seat.

Jude bends to one knee, untying my boots one by one in silence, working with efficiency as he slips my soaking socks off next, replacing them with a fresh, warm pair while I sit here in awe, my trembling hands folded on my lap. When his fingertips gently trace the bend of my foot, I realize I'm going to go mad if I have to sit in this perilous silence much longer.

"Why are you doing this?" My voice is hardly a whisper, waiting for something, *anything* from the captain.

His fingers lace around my ankles, realizing there's no more work to keep busy as he mutters, "I don't know. But I
know that you're freezing and I have to fix it."

I shake my head, finding the courage to reach for Jude. I tilt his chin to look him in the eyes, "Why do you have to fix it?"

He blinks, and those beautiful eyes seem to see me for the first time as he says, "Because I have to. Don't you feel it?"

Of course I feel it. I know exactly what he's talking about.
There's a shimmering string wrapped around both of us, tying us together and I never want to leave his side again. There's a tangible *need* between us that begs to be explored. I'm tired of pretending I don't want to.

Before my fingertips have a chance to outline the strong curve of his jaw, Jude bows his head, deep in thought.

"There are too many things you don't know," he says.

"Then tell me what I need to know."

He swallows before responding hesitantly, "It's not that simple. Everything has changed now. I wish we had all the time in the world, but we need to focus on surviving."

"Surviving?" Puzzlement consumes my expression as I watch Jude shake his head, trying to find the right words. I'm so sick of hearing that word. *Survive another day* has been the living, breathing mantra that sees me to the morning, but I'm tired of simply surviving. I want to feel again.

Jude levels me with a serious stare as he says slowly, "When you took my arms, you made your choice. I lead the company of players, and it's my sole purpose to win. So now that you're mine, you're in the games, Soria."

That label on his lips has my mind foggy, because I can't think of anything else other than his mouth on mine. The bond between us sends chills up my spine, and I know Jude can feel it too.

He stands and starts pacing the room while my chest tightens from withered lungs.

Instantly, Jude flicks his hand out, sending a rich, deep breath of oxygen down my throat as he says, "We can't."

My emotions feel so tossed as I question him, "We can't?"

"We shouldn't." His lustful gaze drags across my body, "We need trust."

"Trust?"

The captain crosses his arms over his massive chest, and I realize I've never seen him so distraught as he shakes his messy, dark hair, "You can't even lock me out of your mind yet. We need trust if we're going to outlast The North and bending you over this bed is the last thing you need."

My jaw drops at the realization that Jude's in my mind right now. He's consuming every one of my thoughts as I mentally undress him and fight the ache between my legs. The ache that the bond demands.

Frustration greets me as I snap, "Don't tell me what I need. I trust you enough." I stand, keeping eye contact as I unbuckle my uniform jacket to reveal a snow-soaked undershirt accenting every curve that craves his touch. And thankfully, after months of finally eating real portions, curves that don't mock the meaning of the word.

Jude's ravenous eyes scan my body as he mutters, "You need to trust me completely." I wish I could read his thoughts as he does mine, but that expression gives everything away, though his words are the opposite.

"Completely." I repeat.

"Love…" That nickname on his lips has me reaching to undo my belt, but in the next second, a gust of invisible wind tosses my hands from my hips, halting me from undressing myself.

The tension is too much to stay here any longer, and a terrible thought crosses my mind that I can't let go of. Jude doesn't want me. He must not if I'm begging for him to take me and he's refused more than once now.

"Don't ever think that." he growls, but I've already sunk too far into my own thoughts of rejection.

The floodgates of anger and embarrassment beg to spill as I school my disappointment and head for the door, "Trust it is. Have it your way, but I can't stay here. Not anymore."

"That's not trust. And we *need* it to survive. Do you think everything's going to be easy from here on out? You could die in the Diamond Games—*we* could die if you don't give yourself to me completely." Jude argues, following me across the room as I reach for the door handle.

I spin around madly, inches from his steaming face, "I want to give you *everything!* But it seems like you're the one who has the problem with trust. You shut off your memories from me!"

"Because there's too many things you don't know!"

"Here we go again, full fucking circle." I toss an indignant arm in the air, "You want me to trust you so much, then start telling me what I need to know, or else we're both dying at the end of this."

Jude's mouth clamps closed as if to keep the words from pouring out, and anger heats my palms, driving me mad with too many emotions I can't control.

To avoid sending his room into flames, I grumble, "I'm not staying here anymore. Not until you open up."

Jude's head dips to pin me with a glare so fierce it almost strikes fear into my heart as he fumes, "Then leave, Soria. Like you always do. You ran from your life in the cottage
fields, so this is nothing new."

A shriek of fury leaves my throat in response as I slam the door behind me, bolting down the corridor with flames trailing up my bare arms. I have *got* to get a handle on these emotions before they eat me alive.

Through my furious strides, I curse the captain in my mind, knowing if he wants to, he has full access to every nasty thought of him. Good. I hope he hears them.

I round the farthest north wing, but before my hands reach the squad bay doors, a rush of wind pulls me back, and I'm slammed against a hard, thick chest.

"We're not finished." Jude declares as he grabs my wrists in one hand, bending at the waist to toss me over his shoulder.

My stubbornness fights him every step of the way, calling him every sinful name in the book, but Jude doesn't say a word as he marches me back toward his room on the opposite end of the training building, ignoring the sideways glances from wandering eyes in the corridors.

Oh, nothing to see. Just the captain and his new tethered recruit having a screaming match.

His door swings open and slams shut. He locks us inside to continue our fight.

"I don't understand why you keep trying to run away. You've had one foot out the door since you've been here." Jude gripes as I leap from his shoulder to land on my feet.

More than appalled, I seethe, "Maybe that's because *you bought me!* I never wanted to be here in the first place!"

"Do you still want to be here?" Jude's tone matches mine as he stands in front of the door, not giving me the option to flee. And his question takes me back as my mouth parts to argue, but not a single word forms.

I don't. Yet, leaving isn't an option. Not now.

As I stare down the captain across the room, I come to the steady, *dangerous* realization that maybe leaving was never an option. Sicar had told me before that tethered pairs are sewn into the stars, predestined by the heavens to reward the special ones. But… I can't help but wonder if he knows…

"You want trust?" I ask, flipping open my belt that he stopped me from undoing the first time, "I have asthma. When I was born, the midwife said I wouldn't survive the night because she had to keep breathing for me."

Jude's eyes darken as they follow my hands tugging at the wet buckles around my waist.

I go on, "I've only ever been with one person. You know who that is. Great guy. He traded my life for a chance at a title. Sometimes I'm disgusted that I ever knew him." My pants fall to my knees.

"I hate mushrooms, not for the taste, but because I had to survive on them for months at a time."

I kick off the pants completely, reaching for my skintight undershirt, and Jude's jaw tenses with every minuscule movement as he watches me with eyes like a predator.

"I thought I would never get over killing Depitrio, but I know if I had to do it all over again, I'd kill him one hundred times to save my friends."

I fling the undershirt to the floor, dropping my arms at my sides as I stand with a heaving chest in only my bare undergarments and shin-high socks.

"And I don't have a delta." Heat rises along my neck as I force out the next sentence, "Sicar gave me his power to save my life. The most important secret. I wish everyone would stop sacrificing so much to make sure I stay alive."

The last admission feels like a terrible weight has been lifted off my chest as Jude's gaze trails down my body slowly. Madly. He inspects every detail with wicked curiosity as those eyes tell me he's tired of fighting what he wants. Is that drool at the corner of his mouth?

He chuffs, stifling a laugh at my thoughts that flow freely before his hungry gaze finally lands on mine.

"Trust it is." Jude narrows his focus as his hands begin unclasping the buckles across his chest, "I don't have any physical ailments, minus my little secret you've already discovered."

My mouth salivates as he rips open his jacket, exposing a beautifully sculpted bare chest.

Jude continues, "I've never met a woman who could make me weak, but when I met you, I decided you're who I want to
worship."

My heart skips a beat as I keep my feet planted, and Jude tugs off his jacket, sending it to the ground in a heap of discarded afterthoughts.

His chin tilts as he says, "I've killed thousands of people, and I don't feel a thing."

Rough hands undo the metallic buttons on his pants.

"I already knew about your delta coming from Sicar."

Jude tosses an arm out, sending a rush of air into his bed, pushing the entire frame against the wall to create a giant, open space in the middle of the room. With another hand gesture, the expensive silks and plush blankets lining the mattress land on the floor between us, inviting two bodies to get wrapped up between them.

"I have more I want to tell you. *Show* you." His feet finally move toward me, those pants undone at the waist, waiting for me to rip them off myself, "But I've never done this before." "You've never done this before?" I mutter, in disbelief.

Jude blinks, and a flicker of playful annoyance crosses his face as he elaborates, "I've never done the relationship thing. The sharing of power. It might not sound fair," Jude halts a few feet away, his brows dipping to show he's serious, "But I need you to abandon who you used to be and trust me beyond the shadow of a doubt because our lives depend on it. In
return, I'll try to do the same."

The mysteries that create this gorgeous specimen perplex me to no end as we stand, half-naked, waiting for the other to make the first move, until I realize Jude's waiting to hear an acceptance on my part. But I need something more. Something truly real if I'm going to follow this man blindly as I wait for him to hand over everything the way I have.

Jude sighs, clearly feeling the effects of the sexual frustration before he speaks into my mind, low, purposeful, *"And I've been waiting too long for you, Soria. Is that real enough?"*

CHAPTER 34: THE CAPTAIN

The mother of all gasps flies from my throat as I clamp my hands over my mouth in disbelief, "How did you do that?"

A dangerous smirk finds the corner of Jude's mouth as he moves slightly, and his wind thrusts me into his chest with a *thump.* Firm hands brace my hips, sending a shiver of excitement up my back as I feel Jude shudder beneath my touch.

"Like I said, there's more I need to show you." Jude's deep, sensual voice echoes through my mind as his mouth falls to my collarbone. His tongue sweeps up my neck to quiver every bone in my body as I stand here, folded in his arms.

"Teach me," I sigh into the crook of his neck, delicate fingertips brushing his forearms, trailing up taut biceps,

"Teach me how to talk to you in your mind."

Jude's breath sends a streak of heat up my neck as he nips at my ear, *"I will. If you promise me something."*

"Anything." I give in, hardly holding back a tremble of pleasure as his hands play with the delicate strap of my half-corset bra, sending it to the floor with a single tug at the right string. If I'm being honest with myself, and this may be to my own lustful demise, but the captain could ask anything of me at this moment and I would agree without a second thought.

If it meant I would get to feel him closer than ever.

"Promise I'll be your only *teacher."*

I know exactly what Jude means. It is something he never needed to ask.

"I promise." The words are barely out of my mouth before Jude plunges to his knees on the blankets before me, his hands wrapping around the back of my thighs in silent order to stay standing.

"Now, try to focus. My lessons aren't free." The captain rumbles in my mind as fiery palms grip his shoulders, though not a single flame singes him—courtesy of a pyro bound to an aero, I suppose.

A ripple of a deep, hearty chuckle caresses my mind as Jude sighs, *"I forgot how short you are. Stay still for me."*

I watch with a gaping mouth as Jude's teeth scrape the skin beneath my navel, biting into the lining of my underwear before dragging them down with a growl.

"Mmm," he hums hungrily, revealing my flesh inches from his watering mouth, and I tremble in his grasp.

"Forget the lesson," I gasp at his touch, feeling an unquenchable thirst for whatever spell his fingers are conducting against my hips. I couldn't focus on a stupid lesson if I tried.

Jude ignores my plea with a grin, *"Do you remember the starry night mural across the auction ceiling?"*

My brows pucker, "Yeah?"

Jude releases another groan into my flesh as his silky voice caresses the barest parts of my mind, *"I've spent a lot of time memorizing that mural, and now I'm about to paint it on you."*

A warm breath hits me right where I need it, and my fingertips dig into Jude's shoulders to curb the carnal behavior boiling beneath the surface of thousand-year-old magic. I know if I'm not careful I could send this entire base up in flames by the way he's driving his tongue across me.

"That's not focusing." Jude's deep voice is a delicious distraction as those hands on the back of my thighs pull my legs apart, and his mouth dives between with raw hunger and precision.

I can't wrap my mind around the insatiable pleasure as a moan slips and my nails embed themselves on their perch. Jude's voice in my mind doesn't relent as he feasts on me with expertise.

"First thing's first. Search for me in the crevices of your mind. It shouldn't be too difficult since you've already done it with your acolyte."

I try to throw away his lesson as I sink into the pleasure he's creating, but Jude corrects me.

"Try and focus. Look for me."

His tongue slides up and down, and the pressure between my legs already begs to unfurl, but I rein myself in enough to follow instructions.

"You taste so fucking good." He groans, sending a vicious shiver up my spine, *"So good that I want you for every meal."* Look for him. Look for him?

I quake beneath Jude's jaw as those hands slide up to grip my ass, pinning me to his mouth.

My brain is more than foggy as I press into him with weak knees, but I gain enough consciousness to remember the bright red string that symbolizes Sicar at the forefront of my mind. There has to be another one somewhere.

Jude snarls against my flesh in encouragement to keep searching until I find an entire collection of strings. There must be over one hundred variously colored strings floating without purpose in the abyss. What are all of these? Which one is Jude?

"Holy shit," I falter as my knees buckle, but he keeps me standing.

Grinding my teeth against another tremble caused by the captain's famished mouth, I search harder, until only one stands out in a glowing shade of royal blue. The same pigment as the sheer that binds my soul to his.

"You found me." The string lights up as Jude speaks into my mind, and suddenly my feet lift off the ground as he picks me up with ease.

Our mouths clash desperately as I swallow his tongue, tangling my fingers in messy hair as the pressure between my legs begs to feel more of him.

"You're so beautiful. I can't believe you're mine."

I shudder in delight at his praise, and I can't help but think the same thing.

Wrapping my legs around Jude's thick waist until both ankles are locked, I lace greedy fingers behind his neck, devouring his kiss like the best meal I've ever had.

"You're the best meal I've ever had," Jude rasps as he bends to his knees while holding me, calloused hands roaming upward as I'm placed on my back with urgency. The rich, creamy silks meet my bare skin as I keep the captain close, praying for more.

"Try speaking back, Darling." Jude tells me as I press into him, but fear of failure keeps me hesitant. What if it doesn't work?

"It'll work. Just try. I need to hear your voice." Jude sounds determined, and yet reassuring as I reach to free him of his pants, but the massive man above me has other plans.

In one quick move, his hand snatches both of my wrists, pinning them above my head as his other hand finds the small of my back, his lips grazing the peaks of my breasts.

Jude's flicking tongue sends a thrill through every tangled nerve as I squirm beneath him, wanting so much more.

"Please," I whine, arching into his pelvis, unashamed, "I need you inside me, Jude."

"I love when you say my name." He purrs, *"But I need you to tell me that in your mind. Focus."*

I force myself to find the captain's string again as my eyes close to feel him, and delicately, I caress the glowing string. A familiar tendril of warm air brushes my cheek, tossing a strand of hair from my face.

"Thank you for being my air." My own voice vibrates against the string, and the immediate grin that meets the captain's lips tells me it worked. He hears me.

"Oh, this is going to be fun." Jude says as his hands release my wrists, but I'm one step ahead of him.

Digging my toes into his undone waistband, I shove his pants down, earning an amused noise from the captain as I hold his bottom lip captive between my teeth.

"What are you waiting for, Sweetheart?" I tease, wanting to give him everything as the pressure between my legs demands the waiting to end. Enough games.

"Are you sure this is what you want?" Jude asks, dragging his teeth across my chest until he pulls back enough to stare me in the eyes, awaiting my response. Though he has access to my free-flowing thoughts, I can tell he wants my answer out loud.

My thumb pad traces his cheekbone with a whisper, "Yes.
Don't make me wait any longer, please."

"As long as you're saying please."

A flash of a smirk crosses those lips before Jude presses two fingers to my mouth, requesting entry until I open wide. I coat his fingers in saliva, wanting to be absolutely, utterly *amazing* for him as his gaze darkens to see my mouth work.

Jude replaces his fingers with lips in gratitude for my help. Eager eyes dart all over my face as he mutters, *"You're
terrifying, you know that?"*

"I learned from my teacher," I wink, purposely biting into my lip just to watch that jaw tick with raw lust.

In the next second, those wet fingers slide between my legs, circling me and drawing out a terrible moan from my throat before he presses his tip to the very edge.

I can't help the buck of my hips as every inch of Jude stretches me, cramming deeper and deeper until a glorious, profound moan reverberates from his throat. My teeth scrape his ear to feel him pull back slowly, just to drive deeper with the next thrust.

"Holy shit." Jude gasps in my mind, his voice breathless.

Our mouths collide as we swallow each other's pleasure, and I roll into him, my shouts of praise rattling the walls as goosebumps line every inch of the captain's skin.

It finally hits me. He hasn't felt something like this in... *years*. The touch of a woman. The feel of an earth-shattering orgasm. The breath of someone pleading for more against his lips. I'm giving that to him. A gift. He chose me.

"I can't help it." I tell him as my breathing demands a rush of air that Jude immediately provides. I know how my next words are going to sound. I know I fall quickly and carelessly, but I've had too many close encounters with death to bite my tongue another second. I don't care what his answer is... as long as he knows.

"Can't help what?" His voice is shaky in my mind as rough hands lace tightly around mine—our bodies collide in repetition while the pressure begs to burst, and I run desperate lips up his neck.

"I can't help that I love you."

Jude trembles above me as the words I can't deny any longer wrap around his brain, sinking in with nowhere else to hide. The pressure reaches its peak in my body as a shriek of satisfaction fills the air.

Jude thrusts into me harder, faster with every intent to send my wave of bliss as far as it will go, until he reaches the same high seconds later, roaring into my neck as the feeling overtakes him.

"Oh, fuck." He growls, and if I were not on the other end of his lust, I'd be terrified of the noise that just erupted from Jude.

His shoulders vibrate just before a furious wind blasts out of nowhere and everywhere, shaking the walls of his large room as decor and items mounted fall to the ground in a loud tumble.

The delicious scent of Jude's sweaty chest pressed against mine almost demands a second round, but every nerve in my body knows more would light this room with a fire that can't be contained.

And we do it anyway.

***

After I inhale enough oxygen to steady the shakiness in my lungs, Jude rolls gently to the side, sending quick winds to wrap me up in the silks below us before he tugs me close, scanning my face and heaving chest in quick assessment.

"Why do you do that all the time?" I ask through pants.

"Do what?" He mutters, bringing a filled canteen to my side with a single flick of his wrist—from where he snatched it. I have no idea.

"Why do you look at me like you're checking for wounds?" I answer, taking a few gulps to quench the thirst he created. I still can't believe I just had sex with the captain of Aegis.

Four times.

Jude shrugs, "I guess I've gotten used to it. But now I can do something about it."

His words take me back a moment as I swallow the last of the canteen, contemplating the man I thought him to be. The man who broke my violin. Who put a target on my back.

Who bought me.

Jude's hand runs up my back as he holds me close, his gaze landing on my mouth as he whispers, "I can still hear those thoughts, Soria. And… you need to know."

"I know. You're not that person anymore." I cut him off, hoping for a beautiful elaboration that explains every terrible thing he's put me through. But that doesn't happen.

"No," he says, still unable to meet my gaze as his arms tighten ever so slightly—perhaps to keep me from running again, "You need to know that I'm the bad guy. Everything that's happened to you… it's all my fault. But I'm going to make you a vow," Jude's voice has a hint of a quiver as his eyes find mine, "So long as I live, I will *never*... let anyone hurt you again."

"You can't make that vow," I sigh, shifting uneasily in his grasp as the memory of those disgusting blood-soaked bathroom tiles resurfaces, "I'm the enigma in all of this. The anomaly that no one wants. So they're going to keep coming for me every second I'm not by your side."

"Then you'll never leave my side," Jude growls, his tone heavy and solemn.

I stifle a chuckle as my hands tangle themselves in beautiful, dark hair, "That's not an option. But I'll make *you* avow," I cock my head, offering my tethered a smile as I whisper, "I will never die, because if I do, that means you die."

Half a smile lines the captain's lips as he says, "What did I do right in my miserable existence to deserve you?"

A pang of grief strikes my heart to remember the terrible memories Jude had hesitantly shared when our souls merged in the snowy canyons. A miserable existence. Is that what his life has felt like? I certainly know the feeling.

A nervous finger traces the stubble along Jude's jawline as I mumble, "When I first saw you, I was convinced you came from money. Like, *old* money. I thought with your fancy suits, rings and perfect hair, that you were born from royalty." I admit, pursing my lips, "But I was wrong. You've earned everything you have, and you deserve the title more than anyone."

Jude's chest heaves quickly with a chuff, shaking his head, "Oh, Soria."

"What?"

His gaze darts between my eyes as he pauses, thinking for a moment before nodding once, "I'm going to show you something. Close your eyes."

A nervous laugh escapes as I roll my eyes, wondering what his winds are about to bring me now.

But Jude doesn't give me anything physical. He gives me an intimate piece from his mind at an understandable distance, *willingly.*

It's the same boy with longer, dark hair and swirling blue eyes from the memory, now older. Rougher. He stares at his stern reflection in a still pond, lit by the summer's afternoon sun, sweating in a long-sleeve wool coat and gloves cuffed to his wrists.

Hesitantly, he brings a sharp knife into view, raising it higher and higher as I begin to think the worst, but in one swift movement, the knife slices into his long hair. He saws in repetition until he's left cropped, and seemingly unrecognizable.

The young man digs into his pack, his head on a swivel along the pond bank as he drinks the last of his water, clearing sweat along his forehead. He opens a letter written to his father, telling him he will never forgive his cruelty and that he would die a thousand painful deaths rather than succumb to his wishes. In his words, he tells his father he's done being his personal punching bag—but he couldn't leave the note.

And suddenly, the young man is not alone.

Along the pasture's horizon, several men dressed in King's Guard clothing charge on horseback in the distance, ordering the young man to stop with threats of death.

He's quicker than them, gaining his feet and slinging his pack cross-body as he takes off in a sprint.

He runs for an hour before finally stopping, but the guards have a seeker with them, and he was never going to get away on his own.

The young man flings his arms out, tripping several of the horses that carry the guards, but he's too exhausted to take them all out. One guard lunges for him on foot, but the boy anticipates the attack, slamming a huge gust of wind into his chest before the guard's body tumbles into his own comrade, his stomach pierced by a friendly blade.

He doesn't have time to think about what he's done before he does it again, whipping out winds of fury that send every skull smashing into something, placing their souls in a permanent sleep. But more guards stampede over the horizon—there's too many.

They've been looking for him, and they're victorious. All the air in the world won't save him now.

The young wind wielder wakes with a terrible migraine in shackles alongside a dozen others his age. They're dirty and starving, forced to perp-walk to the Black Top Cathedral, made into spectacles before the ton who spit in their faces.

The young man watches the other runners take the auction stage one by one, and the horrid reaper obliterates them where they stand as the bidders laugh at each pitiful attempt to beg for their lives.

When he finally takes the stage, he stares down death before inhaling deeply, flinging both arms out in a last attempt to save his own life. Powerful winds send shrieks of fear in the air as hats, ribbons and bidding signs fly across the room in a threatening storm.

The bidders aren't laughing now.

I gasp as my eyes shoot open and the memory ends abruptly.

"You…" I swallow, searching Jude's face as he nods, "You were a runner?"

"I was. And they caught me." Jude's arm around my back pulls me in tightly as he rests his chin on my head, and I feel the thumping of his heart slow beneath my palm, "But I spent my life running from who I was supposed to be. And when I landed on that stage, I decided I was tired of running. So, I trained the hardest. The longest. And I proved to them that…" His voice trails off, and I breathe against his chest patiently, knowing the words that are too difficult to say.

"You proved to them that you're not a joke." I speak into his mind, firmly. Reassuringly.

Jude's eyes soften as he dips his head, brushing lips to my forehead, "Something like that."

CHAPTER 35: DELIVERIES

The joints in my knees ache this morning as I stretch beneath expensive silks, sighing against a warm pillowcase.

Before I gain complete consciousness beneath the sun's early rise, a gentle kiss flutters against my cheeks as my tethered whispers into my hair, "I'm being summoned to an emergency meeting, but I'll be back before breakfast."

As soon as the door closes, my eyes shoot open, rubbing stiff ankles and sore wrists. Even the knuckles of my fingers throb for some reason. What the hell did I do last night?

The memory of lying on the ground, wrapped in Jude's arms as he listened to my stories consumes my thoughts. His mouth on mine. His hands bracing my hips. I couldn't get enough, and now I look for him in everything.

Propping myself up on my elbows against the plush mattress, I find the room has been put back together. It is now organized and meticulously clean. Minus one large, mysterious black box wrapped in a stunning glittery bow that stares me down from the foot of the bed.

I can't help but smile as I reach for the gift, removing the lid with curious hands, reading the note written in chicken-scratch writing.

A little something to make sure your clothes don t

melt off again,

unless I bring my own match—J

My cheeks heat as I delicately remove the tissue paper enclosing a uniform that's certainly not like the others.

Recruits typically wear the tired, beige felt consisting of jackets, undershirts and fitted pants that harbor several buckles to keep the material in place. But this uniform couldn't be more opposite. What I hold between two gentle fingers is the epitome of every second spent suffering in the shoes of a recruit.

This is a *player's* uniform.

Instead of the usual Bachalorian Navy Blue with midnight stitching like every other outfit, this one is pitch black, and made of a soft yet immovable material I've never felt before.

The midnight sleeves of this single-piece bodysuit stretch easily, darkening in gradient the closer they reach the thin shoulder pads, complimenting a neckline that would meet the beholder's jaw. The center cinches in a corset-style, and the pant legs that hold multiple sheath pockets go on for miles. Much too long for my legs.

"Do you like it?" Jude asks in my mind, and I jump to the sound of his voice, clutching the uniform to my chest.

"I love it." I respond. I am still getting used to sharing my mind with the captain, *"But I think you got the legs wrong. I'm not this tall."*

Jude pauses for a moment in my mind as if he's busy, then finally responds, *"I had my tailor add a few inches for tethering growth. Let me know if the fabric is uncomfortable."*

I'm already slipping on the suit, mesmerized to find that a perfect fit, though the pant legs are just a hair longer instead of six inches as I had assumed.

The cloth on the inside feels buttery soft and breathable, but the exterior appears to be the opposite to the naked eye. Rough, rigid lines give the uniform a metallic, yet *rock-like* appearance. Something I couldn't have imagined or created in my wildest dreams.

"It's beautiful. What's it made of?" I ask, turning in the full-length bathroom mirror to catch the number *0* etched on the back in white-washed lettering. Although, this time, there's a slash through the number in secret meaning.

Several silent minutes pass before Jude eventually responds, *"Black diamond and fiberglass."* Interesting.

The more I think about the material as I turn to adore my reflection, the more it makes sense. It's no secret that the north holds several lethal metalists, so adorning any kind would be a death trap. My delta incinerates any fabric that meets my skin.

I am *literally* wearing diamonds.

"I bet you look ravishing."

I sigh at the compliment before my gaze catches something peculiar in the mirror.

Carefully, I cock my head, examining my roots with delicate fingers. The strands that used to be blond are now faded to an unrecognizable bright white, bleeding into my natural hair from my scalp as if grown overnight.

Bewildered eyes flick to find my once dull brown irises have… changed color? Bright, golden eyes stare down a foreign gaze as I realize my entire face seems different. Sharper. Smoother, as if every crevice has been molded over and polished. Is my neck longer?

And now I'm thinking about my sore and aching joints, realizing I feel… taller?

"There's no way." I mutter, glancing down at my legs that *do* feel… longer. What did Jude say? Something about tethering growth?

"Um... Sicar? Is this normal?" I ask him in my mind, thrumming against the bright red string I know belongs to him alone.

"You truly do not retain tethering knowledge that well." That *is* all Sicar says as I continue to stare wide-eyed at the body I don't know.

Before I have a chance to sass the magical phoenix, a heavy fist pounds repeatedly on the bedroom door, making me jump in my skin.

Fear crawls up my spine, rattling me as I contemplate answering the door or hiding, but another set of heavy slams tells me if I don't open it, they're coming in on the next knock.

Swallowing the nerves, I fling the door open, and I'm more than surprised to see Ona staring down at me with a giant, raised fist, mid-knock.

"Zero." She grunts, and I can't help but notice she looks different than I do. Ona's always been the tallest person on this base, towering over the others by a landslide, but the creases in her face have gained an intense edge. Her eyes are brighter and her hair appears thicker as it sits in its typical gelled braid, trailing down her muscled back.

"What are you doing here, Ona?" I ask as our gazes collide.

Ona huffs, motioning to nothing behind her, "Delivery now. We go."

Confusion creases my brow as I argue, "No, that can't be right. Deliveries are on Sunday. They said—"

"No. Now." Ona growls, turning her back to march down the corridor without another word.

Rolling my eyes at her familiar no-bullshit attitude, I have no choice but to follow her, but just to make sure, I reach out to Jude.

"Deliveries are happening now?"

"Apparently." His tone is filled with malice for whatever situation he's facing right now, and I shrug off the continuous curveballs the President tries throwing

my way. The games may not be for another month, but they're starting now. Whether I can see them or not.

I catch up with Ona, following on her heels as I mumble, "Did they send you because you're the only one not terrified of Jude?"

The barest grin along Ona's lips makes me laugh for the first time in a while.

***

Dread greets me like an old friend as Ona and I fall into our dwindled group of recruits that form in the massive foyer leading to the parade deck.

The enormous, detailed fish tank that reaches the domed ceiling pulls my attention as I bump into someone.

Whirling around, the word *sorry* barely escapes out of habit before I realize it's Kole.

Those boyish eyes regard me like a wounded puppy as he reaches for me. In the same breath, he thinks better of the action, pulling back his hand as if I'm still on fire.

That's what the fuck I thought.

"Sor, I…woah. You look…amazing." Kole's gaze falls as he takes a step backward, offering me space while the other recruits buzz around excitedly, careful not to get too close.

I should smack that sorry ass expression off his face, but I can't afford to explode right now. These feelings are still too fragile, and I can't entertain even a hint of bitterness, or I may blast this entire foyer into an inferno.

Taking a deep, calming breath, I cross my arms, forcing myself to keep it together.

When I don't respond with violence, Kole seizes his opportunity to apologize, "Sor, I can't tell you how sorry I am. Truly. For everything. I never knew that… you and him, huh?"

His voice is pathetically envious as a familiar, rich laugh echoes in my mind.

"I'm loving this."

I grumble a curse at Jude as I try to keep my composure. I don't need commentary in my head when I'm trying to stay calm.

Sucking my teeth, I give Kole a firm nod, praying the anger stays contained, "Mhm. Me and him."

"You know, I never tethered,"

Kole lets out a miserable chuckle, hoping to melt the tension between us as he shifts his weight, "I went through all of this for *you* to become a captain. What were the odds, huh?"

My glare intensifies, "I'm not a captain."

Kole's brows knit as if I've just said something outlandish, "You're tethered to the captain. What do you think that makes you, Soria?"

"*I* think that makes her his little shadow. Or just another toy to fuck."

Sera's evil voice slithers over my shoulder like a snake as dark, pointed nails twist a strand of my hair.

"Sera." Kole tries to throw her off my scent, but I wouldn't *pay* that boy to fight my battles.

"That's my girl."

Sera loops an arm though Kole's as Brody appears by her side out of nowhere.

"*Loving* the new outfit, Zero. You must think you've already made it, huh?" Sera licks full lips, and I notice her features have changed as well. Those dark eyes are sharper and her cheek bones are higher, but no amount of power could rid her beautiful face of that hatefulness that lies within her soul. A hatefulness I'm trying desperately not to give in to.

Suddenly, a brilliant, gorgeous voice calls behind me, "Considering who she's tethered to, I'd say she's already made it." Grape lands by my side with a wink, giving me a quick once over as Merry meets my other side. She grips my hand with the biggest smile, and I'm elated to see her bouncy self instead of that freezing, withered version from the canyons.

I've missed them so much.

Sera *tsks,* her finger trailing up Kole's arm, "What an adorable family reunion. When are you going to stop letting these kids fight your battles, Zero?"

"Pyromancer, this one is aware of your elevated state."

Sicar warns me, and I grit my teeth, trying to focus on clear skies and stupid bunny rabbits to keep me from dipping into the boiling pot of anger.

"I feel hot, Sicar. What do I do?" My voice sounds raspy as I fire the words to the phoenix, but he's on top of it as he sends me peaceful images of a calming sea.

"Gather the feelings of wrath and lock them away somewhere deep within yourself. Destroy the key and do not unleash it, or you will be bound to wielding the anger in your veins." Sicar warns in his resounding, mythical voice, and I listen. It takes the deepest breath I can draw without my tethered, and I wrap a lasso around the bundle of fiery nerves within me, stuffing them into a wooden box as this base had stuffed me into. I will not succumb to the wrath.

"Grape, you better get this bitch," I snap, flexing my hands at my sides.

As if following an order, Grape steps in front of me immediately, whipping out a dagger from his back, ready to launch into Sera.

Before all hell breaks loose in front of the fish tank, Director
Boz shouts above the rising chaos, "Recruits! Player style!"

Without question, each person abandons the fight lingering between sides as they fall into formation, and I take my place near Grape and Merry in the back, noticing *player style* has changed since I've saw it last.

In the very front, all recruits not tethered stand in single file, Kole hovering with slumped shoulders in the middle. The rest take their place beside their tethered with tilted chins and incorrigible grins.

They've waited for this moment their entire life.

Boz addresses our group with a rare smile, dressed sharply in Bachalorian blue with a myriad of pins across his chest, and I notice Neera is nowhere to be seen, "You've earned this moment. So whatever happens out there, know that you have done your best, and I am proud to say I have trained you all."

In the next breath, Boz turns in his neatly pressed uniform, making a grand motion with his arms to push open the wooden double doors with his delta.

"Here we go." Grape mumbles nervously, and I squeeze his hand next to me before shifting a foot over, prepared to march.

"Echo Company!" Boz shrieks at the helm as the winter sun nearly blinds me, "Forward! March!"

To my surprise, every last snowflake has been cleared from the parade deck, and a crowd awaits our arrival.

Everyone on the base lines the parade deck—from infirmary nurses and groundskeepers to directors and team administrators—dressed according to their roles, in everything from traditional Bachalorian blue to work tunics, suits, and day gowns.

They've arrived to see the best of the best. Now the best stares us down as we march in practiced unison to the commands of our director.

In perfect pairs, countless people stand saluted, spaced evenly across the parade deck in their own large formation. I don't have to look twice to wonder who they are. The unmistakable blues and ethereal beauty give everything away.

It's the players. There must be over one hundred of them.

Our company is halted, pivoted, and aligned to face the saluting players across the parade deck. My breath suddenly doesn't come so easily when I can't find Jude, but before I have a chance to scan every face in my field of vision, the murmurs cease in the distance as the President enters from the right.

A team of officials who create President RoBjorn's cabinet caravan in their perfectly pressed jumpsuits that represent our nation's colors. In unison, they flank their leader's side, taking the wide space between the players and us, ready to pass judgment once and for all as every gaze falls to their authority.

An uneasy wave of anxiety caresses my brain, telling me agony will soon rise if I'm apart from my tethered for much longer as I search for him desperately, but to no avail. I need to know where he is.

"I'm right here, Love."

Heavy shoulders dip in relief to hear his voice in my mind, and a brilliant grin reaches my lips as I watch Jude stride across the parade deck, unaccompanied, and completely unbothered.

Jude wears a typical midnight suit with flawlessly trimmed hair, styled neatly in an expensive manner. Black shades conceal that beautiful gaze as he strides with hands in his pockets toward the center, but he doesn't stop in his spot.

He keeps walking without stopping straight toward me.

Of the hundreds of individuals present for this monumental display that only happens once a year, Jude makes them all wait as he cuts through the formation of recruits on a mission. A mission for me.

When the captain's hand laces around mine, he pauses for a heartbeat, giving me a once-over behind those shades. I know now that's his chosen mask, but I see through them. What I see is a man who could not be blessed with any more beauty that tethering brings because he possesses it all.

"You're stunning." Jude tosses me a devious smirk with a subtle head jerk, *"And if I were you, I'd be* very *afraid to be left alone with me again."*

"Why's that?" I chuckle in my mind as the captain guides me to his position before the company of players. *My* new position.

"Because even though that uniform looks ravishing, I prefer you in nothing. Don't forget I'm a man who gets what he wants."

I bite my lips together, hoping my cheeks stay a neutral color as the deliveries begin to unfold, promising Jude to revisit the sensual images he's sending. I just hope I can focus.

RoBjorn stands stiffly as the winter's cold breeze rushes past, and Director Boz steps forward to greet his leader professionally.

"Director Boz Ojer," the President grumbles as the parade deck and every spectator falls in silence, "Before these witnesses and by the Aegis ordinance, do you swear you have trained these recruits to the best of your ability, so help your soul?"

Boz raises his right hand as he repeats, "Yes sir. I swear I have trained these recruits to the best of my ability, and I do recommend every last one for player promotion, so help my soul."

The President grants Boz a firm nod, straightening long arms to his side as he dismisses the director from his sight.

"What happens now?" I ask Jude as he sends a deep breath down my throat that I didn't know I needed.

"Now the tethered pairs present what they can do," Jude responds as the first line of pairs are motioned forward,

"Their final performance to show they're player material." Performance. That sounds an awful lot like the auction.

With the looming formation of players behind our backs, I settle myself in, sending up a silent prayer for my friends to do their best.

The President motions for the first pair to come forward, and two young men known as Pit and Harrot put on an impressive act of speed and limited teleportation, earning mutters of approval from the distant crowd observing. They seem quite pleased with themselves as they fall back in formation, replaced by the next pair.

I'm less than surprised when Sera and Brody send a ripple of applause across the parade deck with their routine. Sera blinds every eye present, submitting our consciousness to an empty black hole while Brody quakes the earth where we stand, recreating fear from nightmares. The President loves it.

Ona and Phia's act is more than impressive as they work in unison to show how strength can create deadly, choking vines that spew from the plant mover's hands. They prove the most unlikely of couples are not to be dismissed.

One after another, each tethered pair submits their combined gifts for review until Grape and Merry finally take the spotlight, and my heart rate doubles in anticipation. They have both sacrificed so much to get to this point. They have outlasted and outsmarted the best, and they deserve this.

Dammit they *earned* this.

The crowd silences as we all observe the shapeshifter kneel behind the hyperacusian with outstretched arms, holding every captivated gaze in ransom as the silence stretches further.

It reminds me of the show Grape put on for the bidders, and I realize whatever is about to happen has my little friend's name written all over it. He's never been one for the mundane.

In Merry's next deep breath, she shudders, and her arms extend in length by several feet, contorting into white, shimmering feathers as the rest of her body follows suit. Enormous talons replace her scrawny legs and her neck extends in the next breath until she takes the full form of a massive, white eagle with a sharp, obsidian beak.

She's radiant.

Grape gives the crowd one last surprise as he fishes a thick red ribbon from his pocket, turning to the eagle that stands over nine feet tall. She dips her neck for him as he fashions the ribbon around her feathered head, blinding her completely. With a wink, Grape pivots to the crowd, revealing a second ribbon as he blinds himself.

"Of course you would."

I whisper softer than my own ears can hear, but the smirk on Grape's lips tells me he heard.

With the shapeshifter's wings outstretched and hovering above Grape, a low grumble vibrates within her throat just before she pushes off the ground, snatching her tethered from where he stands.

A surge of gasps billow across the parade deck as the eagle soars in a straight line above our heads, higher and higher with her tethered clasped between spears for talons.

I begin to wonder how high Merry will fly as they become more difficult to see, caught in the sunlight—until suddenly, those talons release. Grape plummets to the ground.

Jude's firm hand grips my arm, keeping me by his side as I watch my friend fall from hundreds of feet to his death.

After a few wingbeats from above, Merry shoots downward, beak first after Grape who falls at a speed faster than her. She'll never make it in time.

Raw, unmitigated fear pulses through my veins as Grape barrels towards the ground, and I wince with sobs at the ready.

Merry catches up at the very last second, snatching her tethered *inches* from the ground.

A trembling hand flies to my heart as the audience lets out their praise, and I silently curse Grape for raising my blood pressure so high.

Merry folds back into herself as they both take off their blindfolds, holding hands while bowing to their fans.

I swear I see a flicker of a grin on the President's leathery face, and I realize this is exactly what he's looking for. He is looking for crowd pleasers. Grape and Merry may not be as lethal a pair as Sera and Brody, but with that presentation, Bachalorians from every corner will come to watch them.

Grape's wide smile follows him as he takes his place back in the formation, and RoBjorn steps forward to examine the couples standing at attention, waiting for their future to be determined.

The President flicks his gaze over his shoulder to pin me with a glare, seeming to weigh his options. Before anything can be said, Jude's hand falls from mine to wrap around my waist in a response of his own.

RoBjorn's lips twitch ever so slightly before turning back to the recruits who await his decision.

Slow, easy steps echo across the black tar as the President walks with crossed arms, making quiet calculations until he lands before Sera and Brody.

I watch their chests heave just before the President shoots out his arm in a put-her-there handshake, and the crowd applauds the first named pair. The first evil pair.

Carefully and thoughtfully, the leader of Aegis selects his picks as I continue to hold my breath for my friends. When Ona gets chosen, I clap for her, fighting tears as she picks up Phia from the ground in elation. When the President throws out a hand for Grape and Merry, my chest nearly concaves in relief. They did it.

The President turns to face his council and the veteran players with steepled fingers. His voice bellows with steely rigor, "I have made my selections. However, seeing that my retainer has at last found a match to such… un*worldly* power, I shall now select a new retainer."

"Retainer?" I throw the question toward Jude, noticing the barest flicker of irritation cross his eyes.

"RoBjorn chose me four years ago to be his retainer since I didn't tether. It's his Hail Mary in the games, but mostly it's a publicity stunt."

"How is it a Hail Mary?" I watch the President with narrowed eyes as he stalks the long line of recruits who stand by no one. They are the seemingly forgotten.

Jude's voice wavers in my mind with a sigh, *"You read that when one dies, so does the other? Though the other might not have injuries, they succumb to death typically within seconds of their partner. So even though it's never been done before, RoBjorn has it in his mind that—"*

"That a retainer could save the healthy one by tethering." I finish his sentence, eyeing the President carefully as he inspects the single recruits one by one.

"Gorgeous and *intelligent. Don't let me forget—delicious."*

I send a subtle elbow into Jude's ribs, which doesn't move him in the slightest. But as quick as my smile appears, it departs as the President makes his decision.

"Kole Arnson, please join my team of players."

"You've got to be shitting me." My hands clench as irritated nostrils flare to watch Kole's stupid face light up, vibrating in joy as he strides to stand off the side with the selected pairs. Kole's obsessive grin sends a bout of rage up my spine. He doesn't deserve this. He has no right to wear the same uniform I do—not when I've suffered the wrath of every wicked person for his sake. When will I be rid of this sap?

RoBjorn motions for the remaining non-selected to come forward, but my attention shifts to Grape placing a kiss on Merry's forehead. A single tear drips down his face as he whispers something in her ear, earning a giggle from his tethered. In an instant all my miserable thoughts about my ex-lover cease.

I press into Jude as his hand squeezes my side in response. Minus not being rid of Kole and Sera's murderous band of brothers, everything's worked out. My friends are *players.* With me. We survived eight terrible months of hell and will finally reap the benefits we are owed. Nothing could ruin this moment.

"Soria... I need you to stay calm." Jude instructs me with a tone that leaves no room for argument.

I look up at him, confusion creasing my brow as his grip around my waist tightens.

"We salute our new Arena Thieves! May you become my champions for years to come, so help your souls." The President calls out, and the remaining members of our company, tethered or not, sigh in defeat, awaiting their new assignments that will not be part of the team. There must be seventy recruits that haven't been selected.

Confusion turns to concern as medics in their crimson cross robes line the right side of the parade deck. Medics that we've never been granted until this moment. They linger on the edge with bags and supplies at the ready, but they're not moving. Not yet.

"As for those not selected," President RoBjorn backs away from the formation of recruits, falling in line with his cabinet several yards away, "I wish you well, and peace be with your souls for such valiant efforts."

"What is..." my words fall short as a dark, hooded figure cuts through the row of medics, revealing a pale face and a familiar, fatal ambiance that can only be described as death in human form.

The reaper.

Sicar fills my brain with thunder, *"I know your heart, so listen when I say it is imperative you do not move, Sterling One. They are watching."*

My heart falls out of my chest as the heavens abandon the poor, unknowing recruits who silently tell themselves they may be able to see their families soon.

Silence lances the sky like the calm before the storm as the reaper raises his arm toward the recruit's backs. In the next second, that horrendous, ear-piercing noise fills my ears with no relent, and shaky palms fly to my head.

When a rush of air inflates shriveled lungs, I look up to find nothing but dark smatterings of soot in place of the recruits who stood there seconds ago, blending perfectly into the black tar parade deck.

CHAPTER 36: DEPARTURE

When I was younger and hardly able to grasp the fact that my brothers were destined for greatness, my father sat me down to instill a lesson.

I remember wondering why my mother was obsessing over my siblings after they had discovered their deltas. She had forgotten about me entirely.

"Soria, your mother is a delicate being," my father told me, though the image of him is so distorted in my memories. Considering he already had his bags packed to abandon us that night, recalling details of him has never been my prerogative.

"Why?" I had cried as jealousy rose to watch my mother bake a cake in honor of my brothers. That flour and sugar were supposed to last until the weekend.

"Because that's how she was born. She is delicate like glass. You, Soria Lilja Davidsdottir, are delicate too."

"I am?"

"Yes, sometimes I suppose all you women can be. But not like glass. You're delicate like a *grenade*."

That's exactly how I feel at this moment as Jude guides me off the parade deck with urgency. I could detonate with the slightest movement.

All other noises have shriveled to a ringing in my ears as time slows and I lock myself in grief for the horrendous act I've just witnessed. Medics in their pristine robes, accompanied by healers and doctors alike rush the parade deck, dropping everything to tend to the newest players after eight months of brutality. The recruits who never knew the title will never know medical treatment, unfortunately, not where they are.

"Get me out of here," I hiss at Jude, feeling the mother of all fires ready to erupt with nowhere to go. The anger. The betrayal. The grief. It's all too much with absolutely no outlet.

"I've got you," Jude promises, "Just hold it together a little longer."

Once we're out of view from the audience who were busy throwing a joyous fete for the newest players, completely disregarding the innocent lives that were taken. Jude takes off in a sprint with my hand in his, toward the sea.

Sicar rattles my mind with a severe warning, *"Do not open the box of wrath! Pour the hatred already forged, but do not draw out the rage, My Pride."*

Unsteady knees hit the snow-covered shore as vibrating palms dig into the sand beneath layers of frost, and I let go.

Earth-shattering flames spew from every extremity as I scream into the void with eyes slammed shut, disintegrating every flake of snow and sheet of ice within a quarter mile out to sea.

"Where was the *mercy?*" I scream as the burnt sand consumes the flames ricocheting off of me, "The ordinance said they were allowed to live!"

Though the wooden box of rage begs me to reach for my power, I pull away, finding enough mental fortitude to sink into grief as the alternative.

"RoBjorn always finds ways around the ordinance," Jude mutters, taking a knee before me as his fingers lift my red-hot face. His expression is calm, yet stern. Unmovable. Most importantly, *unafraid.*

Through exasperated gasps, I wheeze, "Did you know he would do that?"

Jude's eyes tell me the answer before his lips part, "The President's been killing recruits for decades. He lets on all the time about not being wasteful, but he sees no value in something that can't earn him money."

My heart aches to think my tethered, the man I *love* has known about this and never once tried to stop it. Do I know him at all?

"You've watched him kill those poor students for *years!"* I get to my feet, facing Jude with blurry eyes.

The captain raises his chin as he keeps his posture, kneeling in the sand, staring up at me, "Now, that's not fair."

"Not fair?" Trembling hands scour my hair, "What about the mothers that will never see their children again because some tyrant decided their lives were meaningless? *That's* not fair!"

Jude's jaw ticks as he shakes his head, matching my tone, "They knew the risks!"

"Did they?" I scream, forcing myself to take a step back as Jude finally stands, facing me with squared shoulders.

To my surprise, the captain's voice rids itself of all hostility as he closes the space between us, gripping my hands of flames without blinking, "Soria," he sighs, "I need you to hear me when I say this, because whether you're ready for it or not, you're *mine.* I need you to know that being mine comes with horrors of its own."

"I can handle your horrors," I spit through gritted teeth as the flames ebb ever so slightly between his embrace.

Jude's grip tightens, "Can you? Because you nearly wiped out everyone on this base watching the reaper do his job."

I try yanking my hands free at that comment, but Jude holds them captive, forcing me to meet his gaze, "No one's saying it's right. In fact, I've always found the act of killing disgusting. You need to realize it's about to get a whole lot worse. Your glowing friend, Depitrio, those recruits. That was just the beginning. The minute you step into that arena, you need to prepare yourself to lose everyone for the sake of our country."

Despair finally douses every flame like a freezing tidal wave, and my knees buckle at the release of power leaving my body, but my tethered catches me.

"I don't know if I can do this," I sob into Jude's shoulder as a firm hand strokes the back of my head, "I never wanted to come here. I didn't want to become this."

"I know," Jude whispers as his breath hitches against my ear, "I am so… *so* sorry… for buying you. I never thought that I could…"

Jude's words fall off, and I pull back with misty eyes and one hundred questions. I hold them back. I made him a promise. He'll tell me when he's ready.

With a deep breath that I draw from Jude's delta, I sigh, "I don't know if I'll ever be ready to carry the responsibilities that you do, but I chose you too. Even though this isn't what I wanted, I'm here, Jude. I'm not going anywhere. I *am* yours."

His eyes dart between mine, blinking as his hands move to cup my face, pulling my forehead to his as he whispers,

"You told me last night that you loved me."

Goosebumps prickle my arms beneath the diamond uniform, and I notice it sits completely intact from the assault of Sicar's magic through my veins.

Jude pauses, his thumbs stroking my cheeks as he places a gentle kiss on my temple, "I haven't… I've never…"

"You've never told anyone you love them." I finish his sentence, but once again, I'm wrong.

"No, I… I've never been told that."

"Not even your mother?"

I lean back as his palms drop to my waist, and I swear I can see the years of agony and heartbreak in those bright blue eyes, though his exterior tells the world a different story. Here stands a man whose body may be tough as nails, but his heart is still healing from the wounds of his past. I will never play with something as precious as a healing heart.

This time, *I* cup his face in my hands, standing on tiptoe to brush my lips to his as I wish to take away all the pain I know, and all the nightmares I haven't learned about yet.

"You don't ever need to say it back. Just know that I love you, Jude Blackwell. I will follow you to the ends of the earth if you ask."

The faintest smile breaches his lips as he sighs into my kiss, *"Will you? Because as of this morning during my emergency meeting, the games have been moved up. We board the trains tonight."*

***

From what I'm told, there's usually a grand party that lasts several days after deliveries. The novice players go through rounds of drunken initiation rituals decreed by the veterans, typically ending in embarrassing stories that haunt people for life, but there's no time for parties tonight. Not when the entire base rushes around madly to load the trains on standby.

My bags are already packed to my surprise. I spend the rest of the evening following Jude like a lost puppy as he clears wings, barking orders here and there to players who aren't moving fast enough.

The entire training building is in *chaos* after receiving the demand to board ships for the games. Rightfully so. Everyone thought we had weeks yet to prepare, but the only explanation the President gave was that the north declared this, and we had no choice.

As we round another hall that leads down a massive corridor of players' chambers, I try my best to keep up with Jude. It becomes difficult as he's moving with purpose as he catches a pair arguing instead of sprinting.

Before I pass the first room, someone familiar catches my eye with a rusty mop pail and damp rags tucked between his belt.

I halt in my tracks, backing up with a wide smile to see my friend, the janitor, wiping down a bedside table with a hunched back and shaky hands.

I look back up to realize Jude's already on the other end of the hall, knife-handing players who nod feverishly at his commands.

Slipping into the room, I approach the old man who hums a little tune while he works.

"I wanted to say thank you," I murmur to Ivar, making the poor man jump in his boots.

He whirls around with a hand over his heart, smiling with wide eyes, "You've nearly made me faint, Love!"

"I'm sorry," I wince, realizing I stand several inches taller than him now, "I didn't mean to scare you. Do they have you cleaning the empty player chambers?"

I ask, glancing around at the giant room, but it's not nearly as big as Jude's.

Like the captain's chambers, this one holds a single bed but sheets are torn from the corners, ready to be washed. Off to the left is a miniature kitchen with Aegis paraphernalia hanging from the walls above, reminding me of the dormitories I've read about in the King's universities.

Ivar rolls a tired shoulder as he says, "Aye, it's custom to clear the first ten rooms as you lot leave. Whoever dies won't be needing it anymore, I suppose."

"Oh," I mutter, glancing around at the room that's probably held thousands of players, hosting them in a lavish manner as they await their inevitable death before a crowd.

Brushing off the death that continuously consumes my thoughts, I change the subject, "Well, I just wanted to let you know how much I've appreciated your help. I wouldn't have survived if you didn't find me more incense."

Ivar drops his rag to clutch my elbow with a proud smile, "It was my pleasure to assist the underdog. I am *so* proud of you, as I bet your folks are."

I swallow the pain of remembering my mother. I have no idea where she may be now. I force an uneasy smile, "I'd like to think they are," I lie, and those familiar, cloudy eyes look like they want to say more before flicking past me to the massive captain looming in the door frame.

I glance over my shoulder at Jude to find him pinning Ivar with a glare that seems… more than predatory. *Homicidal.* Ivar tilts his chin, leveling Jude with a stare that portrays something I can't comprehend.

To clear the sudden and obvious tension lingering, I try to make an introduction, "Um, Ivar, this is Captain Blackwell," "Blackwell, huh?" The janitor sighs.

"Yes…" I pause, "And Jude, this is—"

"We're leaving now." Jude orders, holding his hand out for me while keeping his eyes on Ivar and his mop pail.

"What's the matter with you?" I ask, but Jude doesn't answer me. He just keeps staring down Ivar with a stance prepared to fight.

"Anyway, thank you for everything." I smile weakly at Ivar as he nods without words, turning back to his chores as if threatened otherwise.

I push past Jude with a look that demands an answer for his blatant rudeness, and he follows behind me as we head toward the train platforms.

"I don't mean to sound this way, but... it's going to sound this way." Jude rumbles in my mind as I turn to him with confused eyes, *"I want you to stay away from that man."*

"What? Why?" I ask as we round another corner that leads to the stairwell.

"Because," Jude says as we descend the stairs with haste, *"There's something I haven't told you. When I took the auction stage, I gave them a different last name to leave my past in the past. The world knows me as Blackwell."*

"Are you saying Blackwell isn't your last name?"

"No. It's Ivarson."

I nearly trip over the last step, but Jude sends his hand out and a rush of wind balances me on my feet.

With wild, unbelieving eyes, I turn to him whispering, "As in… *son* of Ivar?"

"Correct. And because I care for you with my life, I'm begging you to keep your distance."

CHAPTER 37: ALL ABOARD

"Drop those packs and get your sorry asses in formation! Attention on deck!" Some director with too much supremacy screeches across the train platform as Jude and I arrive to apparently do headcounts.

I have no idea what my new role in his world is. I just try to keep up while following a man I apparently know nothing about.

"You know me." Jude responds in my head, and I curse him for having free access to my stream of consciousness that he doesn't allow me.

"Apparently not if I don't know your real name."

"You know it now."

I shoot the captain an exaggerated eye roll as we take the front of the formations, and Jude gives the row of directors nods to continue their counts.

Besides the glow of the moon above, the platform is pitch black in the dead of night.

It was like the first day I arrived here, except this time there are no recruits. Only the lethal, hardened, and *beautiful* players.

Aegis' best, face my tethered and me in their perfectly pressed dress blues. Silent, stern expressions sit like a disguise over every new and familiar face, ready to move on command as Director Boz squints angry-eyed at his scroll of names. I feel myself shrink before their gaze, moving a step behind Jude as the human weapons consume my field of vision with intimidating power. I don't belong at the helm the way Jude does.

With a subtle head jerk, Jude beckons me to follow him as he dismisses his players to obey Boz and the other directors. Each and every last one cuts their hands across their chest in response, saluting their captain with the utmost respect.

"They're saluting you too now, Love."

"No they're not. And don't change the subject," I bark at him, trailing his footsteps up the long and dark platform, *"Why is your father here? Did he know you were here?"*

These days my questions are piling up without answers, and it's becoming increasingly difficult to wait for the truth.

Jude leads me to the very front of the train as the rest of the players wait to be dismissed aboard, turning to me with a lowered voice, "We don't have time to get into every detail. I only told you that so you'd promise to stay away from him."

Ripping my hand from Jude's, I throw a finger in his face, "It seems like I'm the one making you a lot of promises when all you do is order them. I'm not one of your players, Jude. If you want me to trust you, then you need to start answering me."

With soft eyes, Jude wraps his hand around my fingers, pulling them to his lips as he sighs, "You already said you trust me."

"I do. But trust is a very fragile thing, and if you expect me to keep following you blindly, then… the least you can do is
throw me some damn crumbs!"

"Name the crumbs," Jude takes my other hand, those eyes locking on my mouth, "But I'm letting you know right now, we need to be focusing on staying alive in that arena, and speaking about that man will do the opposite to me."

I can't decide on embracing him or recoiling, because I just can't figure out how to feel. I know I'm in love with him, secrets or not. We're tied together regardless.

"Fine. I won't ask about Ivar." I give in, but before Jude's thankful smile reaches his eyes, I step backward, "But if we truly need to focus, then I'm not riding in this train alone with you."

"I don't like that," Jude flicks his wrist out and a gust of strong wind pulls me back to his chest, "I don't want you apart from me. Once we arrive at Ol'Reyka we need to appear as one entity."

I plant warm palms into his chest, pushing off with a scornful huff, "Well get used to it, *Captain.* After we win the games, it'll be a whole lot of alone time until you figure your shit out." I toss him the slightest grin as I turn on my heel, heading toward the last car that I know my shapeshifter and hyperacusian will board.

Jude clicks his tongue as I turn my back on him, *"Tell me what I have to do to get you back in my cabin, Soria. I had plans for our long trip that involved your gorgeous thighs wrapped around my neck."*

I force myself to keep walking, though my body tells me to turn around immediately, *"You can start with a crumb." "Name it."*

I chuckle to myself, throwing him off with the first question that comes to mind—something easy for his dark self.

"What's your favorite color?"

"You."

I roll my eyes, disappearing into the crowd that loads into their cabins with impressive speed. Even though every player moves like the train will leave without them, not a single digit touches me as I pass through. As if they'd been directed not to.

"I do love watching you walk away. But come back, please." Jude whimpers in my mind, but I'm already boarding the last cabin with a chuckle, wondering if he can hear my laugh.

"Give me crumbs and I'll think about joining you on the ride back." I mutter, knowing we won't return to Aegis for over a month, *"How about your favorite animal?"*

"Easy. Wolf."

I snicker at the captain's whiny tone, pulling my friends in for congratulatory hugs as they board our cabin, *"How about your favorite food?"*

Jude is quiet for several minutes in my mind as I settle next to The Beast, half-listening to Grape and Phia argue about the kind of five-course meals they'll serve the players in our quarters.

Finally, the captain responds, his voice velvety, *"Onions."*

"Onions? That's your favorite food?" I nearly snort, but Jude responds confidently.

"When you ate dinner for the first time in the chow hall, I was there. Watching from the shadows. The others left you with the scraps but that's just a tactic we do the first week. The cooks purposely set out less food to create divide."

"I knew it!" I shout through my mind.

Jude goes on, *"I watched you stuff all those cracker packets in your pocket, but I almost gagged when you ate an entire onion like an apple."*

"No one wanted it," I sigh, *"And food is food."*

"That's right," Jude says with praise as the train doors shudder to a close, signaling we're about to move out, *"Ever since then, anytime I thought of onions. Every time it showed up at meals. Whenever it was mentioned, even the smell, I thought of you. After that it became my favorite."*

My cheeks flare, and I almost wish I hadn't left the captain's embrace. I make a silent note to thank him with my lips for that delectable crumb.

"I'll be thinking about your lips this entire ride."

I can't help the war my mind is raging as the train doors close in place. Something utterly primal in my bones tells me two days without seeing my tethered, touching him, making sure he's safe and sound will drive me mad. Can I truly go that long?

"If you join me, I'll make it worth your while, Darling. But I know you need your rest."

"You know what I need?" I ask him, and instead of a response, my tethered sends me an image cultivated from our sweaty bodies a few evenings ago. Time moves slowly as his rough hand slides over my breast, a bead of sweat sliding down my sternum as my own moan sounds like a heavenly haze in the foreground.

I wonder how many times he's revisited that memory.

"Every five minutes. Now come here." Jude growls.

"I can't just let you off the hook so easily for being such a mystery all the time. I demand crumbs." Even my own voice doesn't sound convincing as I weigh the options, trying not to give in to what my body craves.

Him.

"I crave you all the time. But I respect your choice. Even if it's a stupid one."

I curse Jude playfully for reading the thoughts I don't send, wondering if there's a way to silence them before my subconscious omits something embarrassing by accident.

Rumbling from a different part of my mind in solitude is the ancient voice of Sicar, *"Pyromancer, should you desire, I can close the captain off of your free-flowing thoughts. Your inner monologue is a precious gift and I will protect you at all costs."*

His voice wraps around a part of me that I know Jude can't hear, and I contemplate the action.

Sighing, I respond to only Sicar, my words flickering the bright red string that belongs to him, *"No, it's alright. He wants trust, so I'll give it to him."*

Sicar tells me to give the word and he'll separate our minds, as well as promising to meet me at Ol'Reyka 'when the time is right' as he loves to cryptically say.

A horn from the very front of the train bellows, and a sudden odd surge of panic lights an invisible blaze along my spine.

Two days is a long time.

My eyes dart to the door, and I weigh the options, and quickly before I run out of time.

Stay and hold my ground? Or give in to what I really want.

Before I have the chance to decide, Grape catches my gaze, which is probably giving too much away, and he snickers in response to my internal conundrum.

Grape grins, his head ticking to the door as he mutters, "Go get him, girl." And I do.

Just before our cabin door locks into place, I hurdle over Ona and Phia, slamming the entrance wide to the night's freezing air. A lightning bolt of pain shoots up from my ankles as I land hard on my new legs, taking off in a mad dash as the train begins to heave forward.

I gain more speed as my feet fly. My friends hooting and yelling their elation from the very back cabin as I sprint like a horse in the ring, bounding toward the one I can never get enough of. Because at the end of the day, secrets or not, he's mine. I'll never give him up.

The adrenaline kicks in overdrive as the train's weight picks up more speed, matching my pace, and I haul ass to make it to the very first car.

Why did he have to be in the very first car?

My lungs threaten to shrivel as directors on the platform yell at me, and I pump my arms faster, finding my new length in leg carries my strides farther than ever before, but it might not be enough.

It has to be.

An eerie melody of my violin music dances in my skull as I push away every physical pain and will myself to outrun the train. I will beat it. I will make it to him.

With every ounce of energy I have left in me, my legs soar.

With a perfectly timed and deer-like leap, I slam into the door of the first, holding myself up by the long bar perched above the frame.

Instantly, the door slides open to reveal shocked, bright baby blues. Those strong arms don't hesitate to wrap around my back and pull me inside, making that terrible sprint all worth it. He's worth it.

"I didn't hear you decide to join me." Jude mutters in my head, crushing me against him in a relieved hug.

"Looks like we have company." A large man grins from a cushioned seat on the opposite side of the captain's luxurious cabin, holding a woman's bare feet hostage as he rubs them expertly. His dress blue jacket drapes over the familiar redheaded beauty like a blanket as she studies me with a smile, running a finger along her tethered's dark, muscled arm, swathed in black-ink tattoos.

The man regards me casually, as if he's known me for some time as he twists a long, thickly braided lock behind an ear. I recognize him around base, never two feet from the breathtaking metalist, Marble.

My eyes flash to Jude with a weak giggle, just before he sends me a soothing breath and grumbles in my mind, *"They joined me last second when I thought you weren't coming. I can make them leave."*

I stifle an audible laugh, imagining Jude forcing his players to crawl alongside the moving train at its top speed because these cabins aren't connected from the inside.

I shake my head, planting a modest kiss on Jude's cheek before our audience of two, *"It's alright. I just couldn't be without you."*

"I'm going to make them leave."

I slap a firm hand on Jude's chest, tossing his absurdity out the window as I take another deep breath from his delta, settling into a soft, velvet seat facing our train company. But I nearly lose my new oxygen as I realize who I've just plopped next to with no regard for his own space.

My heart rate doubles as a bead of fear-laced sweat falls down my back, knowing there's only one beast that can strike this much fear in my heart without a single blink.

I half expect the massive wolf to rip my head off for sitting so close on the bench that *clearly* belongs to him, but I'm met with something more terrifying than a bite to my jugular.

Fenrir opens his dripping jaw to reveal a tongue, bright pink against his midnight fur.

And he licks me.

Not a slobbery, constant, drool-filled slobber. A single, small lap against my bare hand that shakes by my thigh before he stretches back out on the velvet bench, taking up three-quarters of it. And the entire cabin is mesmerized.

"I told you he likes you," Jude grins, giving Fenrir a nod.

The enormous man shifts beneath the metalists' feet, raising a brow at Jude as he takes a seat next to me, probably wanting to ask a million questions about Fenrir and I, but knowing he can't. Hell, *I* wish I could ask a million questions about the acolyte next to me, like what magic does he possess? How can he turn into a puppy?

What other forms does he command? But I know that's not for my knowledge, just how Jude respects the bond Sicar and I have.

"And our bond is a millennium stronger than that of a measly canine and his master." Sicar grumbles in my head, and my own laugh floats down the string that ties him to me.

Scooting as far away from the wolf as possible to allow him his space, my attention shifts to admire the shimmering glass windows, plush pillows, and gold accents that complement every beautiful detail of this grand and spacious cabin. I suppose it would have been nice to have this space all to ourselves, but Jude and I will have plenty of time to remake those sweet, sweaty memories.

If we survive the games.

"We have forever."

Before my tongue twists with the three words I wish to blurt every time Jude makes me swoon, the behemoth of a man adjacent to us speaks up.

"Well?" The tattooed player grunts at Jude, "Are you going to introduce us to your bride?"

Immediately, my cheeks flare a shade brighter than Marble's hair, and I expect Jude to either laugh hysterically or slam his player's head into the wall. But neither happens.

I don't dare look at Jude directly as he answers this incredibly forward and awkward question, keeping my gaze on his reflection in the glass straight ahead.

To my surprise, the corner of my captain's mouth tugs into a devious smile as he laces a hand around my leg, tugging me to his hip.

"Someday soon, but for tonight, this is Soria Davidsdottir. Love, you remember Marble, and this is her tethered, Anders—a massive pain in my ass."

"A pain you couldn't get rid of since grade school." Anders spits with a deep, hearty laugh, and for the first time, I recognize the same subtle dialect in Anders' voice that I've come to obsess over in Jude's. They must be from the same eastern region in Bachaloria. There's still so much I don't know about him.

Marble pulls a filled chalice from the corner table, sipping with elegant, full lips before telling me, "It's great to finally meet you. Especially you know, when you're not headed into the hydra's jungle and all."

Before I can respond, Anders' eyes widen as he slaps a meaty hand on his seat, nearly tossing Marble's drink, "That was badass, by the way! The way you spent hours creating that huge vine-web. We thought you were boiled when we saw you had picked those bloody bells. But you have a pretty big brain, don't you, Soria?"

I try my hardest to contain the grin, because these two beautiful, beaming players remind me of my own friends. I never expected to be accepted by the elite so soon.

I sigh, "Well, I—"

"And then the *phoenix!* The way he burst into the sky with—"

"Are you going to let her respond?" Jude growls playfully, earning Anders a flick to his forehead from Marble. He shoots her a sheepish grin with a chuckled apology, and I can hardly hold my own laugh. This strong, intimidating and dangerous looking player is brought to a timid blush beneath the gaze of a slender woman half his size.

I brush my hands together nervously, hoping his people don't suddenly sprout claws as I decide to open up, "I don't know about *big brain,*" I giggle, feeling a squeeze from Jude for reassurance, "I may have snuck into Dr. Gencavage's auditorium to do some digging about which monster we would face."

"Like I said," Anders nods, tapping a finger to his skull, "*Big. Brain.*"

"In our year, we broke every rule to see the next sunrise, isn't that right?" Marble flashes a look between her tethered and mine, earning deep nods from both.

"Blackwell and I would raid the cooks' storage bins and hide the loot in a bunk, shaping the pile into a sleeping recruit with a blanket tucked over a mound of food!"

Anders tips his head in a roar of laughter, making Jude pinch the bridge of his nose in a beautiful chuckle.

I love his laugh.

My captain catches his breath, "That worked for one day until we pulled the blanket back to find a bed full of roaches and rats, you ass."

Marble joins in on the teared laughter, snorting in between wheezes as she adds, "And then you both threw that rat-infested mattress out the window, landing it in the courtyard. The directors were so fucking confused."

The cabin fills with laughter over the next hour as all three players share their memorable stories of life as a recruit just trying to survive another day. My heart swells another size bigger for Jude as I position the smallest puzzle pieces into place about who he is. A leader. A prankster. A teacher. A lover. A friend.

Dinner is split between us in the form of pre-packaged, canned meals that are enough to last the journey to Ol'Reyka. I finish every last morsel, but this time, slower than I had my first train ride.

Anders releases a terribly loud burp that earns him an elbow in his ribs from Marble as he laughs, "Well, enough stories for me. We all deserve a decent rest for what Seyka will have in store for us."

"Hopefully we all come back," I mumble, pulling my knees to my chest as Jude wraps me up in his arms.

Anders shoots me a narrowed look as Marble falls asleep on his chest, sticking a thick finger in my direction, "You have nothing to worry about, you know. Not with a power like that."

"He's right. Nothing to worry about. I've got you." Jude's voice touches my mind like a heavenly kiss, but it doesn't pull away the worry. Not all of it, anyway.

As if my new friend Anders can register the concern on my features, he yawns from the opposite side of the cabin, stretching as Marbles shifts on his chest, "Soria, have you ever heard the story of the lion and the lamb?"

I huff a single laugh through eyes that continue to heavy as Jude wraps a knotted blanket around me, "Let me guess," my eyes close completely, "I'm the lamb?"

Jude sighs in my mind as Anders answers sternly, "No. You're the lion."

My sleep-laden eyes squint open as the candle lights above flicker their last breath of smoke, and Anders nods to me, "The world is waiting to finally meet you in that arena. With the power you possess, you're the lion to take charge of that terrain. And the rest of the Bachalorian players are your lambs."

His words stick with me for a lot longer than I anticipate, and I roll them around in my head like a poem to be solved. An oracle that may have some meaning. But it doesn't. It can't.

I'm not special enough to hold the importance they think I own. The power isn't even mine, after all.

Before I have the chance to decipher Jude's soft, argumentative words in my brain, I slip into a deep sleep without another thought.

Our trains, packed to the brim with Bachaloria's finest, lurch into motion as their engines roar, carrying us through the winter night toward the Enemy In The North.

***

Forty-eight hours pass faster than I could ever have imagined, mostly taken up by sleep. And when we weren't sleeping, we were eating, then sleeping some more. Anders and Marble would share the occasional story about their time as recruits and how they always knew there was something special between them.

I suppose I know the feeling.

As the train sounds its horn for arrival, I roll sore shoulders, ready to accept a greatly needed break from this cabin.

We hadn't been allowed to know our location at any point, so every window was kept dark to induce confusion, but more importantly, much needed rest for most of us. I certainly relished in my uninterrupted sleep pressed against Jude's chest.

Now the beautiful dreams are over, and the real nightmare begins.

I follow Jude off our cabin and onto a pristine white platform that glistens in the afternoon sun.

My neck arches to take in the elongated glass dome that envelops the secluded station and the sparkling details carved into stone pillars. We've definitely arrived to Ol'Reyka—better known as The City of Diamonds.

I'm less than surprised to watch Fenrir leap out of the train on paws bigger than my face, stretching violently as enormous hackles rise to the sky. He releases a soft howl that shudders the glass above, raising the hairs on my neck, just before stalking through the station on a mission.

"Where's he going?" I ask Jude, bracing my arm on his to crack my back with a yawn.

"Probably to hunt. Most likely to do a lap around the city. He loves reconnaissance." Jude says as I watch the crowd create a berth wide enough for an elephant for the creature. They are right to fear him.

I take Jude's outstretched hand as he nods his head for us to follow Marble and Anders down the platform.

"You look well rested," I chirp, admiring his shiny dark hair that's slowly transitioning into raven black. His arms even appear a touch longer as his sleeves peel back with no more room, and a new sparkle in those swirling blue oceans for eyes reveal the subtle magic settled within him. *Our* magic.

Damn. I didn't know my tethered could get any hotter.

As the station becomes infested with Aegis players yawning and stretching long, inhuman limbs, Jude's gaze is lassoed tightly to me, and me alone.

"Take my hand, Love. We have work to do."

I do as I'm told, and Jude guides me through the company of players as they part like the Red Sea for us, saluting much to my discomfort at the notion. One of them even shouts, *Long live our captains!* And I stuff that insinuation far away, refusing to deal with a title I do not own.

"The rest are going to be escorted to their suites," Jude mutters as we reach the front of the train and cross a metallic bridge leading to a wide set of double doors in the distance, "But you and I have an interview first."

"What?"

My grip constricts around his hand as the doors obey his winds, revealing a familiar group of people in a quiet rotunda with only one other exit.

Marble straightens her tethered's collar as we cross the checkered, stone floor toward the small gaggle of people.

Off near the other set of doors stands the President, along with his entire cabinet who tend to every dire need, brushing off his shoulders for any stray specks of lint and mumbling things in his ear. His indentured servants.

"What are we about to do?" I whisper with new nerves for the unknown swirling in my stomach. Why didn't he prepare me for this on the train ride?

Jude ignores my question, *"I'm sorry for this next part. RoBjorn ordered them to be a part of the interview."* Jude sighs in my mind, his hand squeezing twice.

Before I can ask, two identical men with white hair and broad shoulders step out from behind Marble and Anders, and I nearly choke to see them in the flesh.

They're taller now, *much* taller with arms that go on for miles and bright eyes that I don't recognize. Their skin tones are a touch darker, more golden as if crafted by the very sun from the heavens while bright white teeth flash with every word spoken between them.

"Why are my brothers here?" I tremble in my mind.

Jude doesn't have time to answer before we reach them, earning everyone's gaze as the rotunda falls silent.

Jon, the older by three minutes, wears his long pale hair in his typical fashion, thickly braided down his back while Kiersik's sits shorter, tucked behind pierced ears and neatly combed. My brothers have always strived to be as different as possible, loathing the act of being compared so heavily. When their shadowed gazes meet mine, all reminiscing ceases. All I see now is pure spitefulness behind those eyes.

The sound of my boots meeting the stone floor is the only noise as we lock in a firm staring match, and no one speaks to remove the stress lingering.

Pursing my lips, I draw in a deep breath from Jude as Jon finally breaks the silence.

"You look… *different*, kid."

My palms heat the fabric on my arms as Kiersik nods slowly in agreement, "Yeah. You look tougher. Meaner."

"That's all you have to say?" The words fall out in a whisper as Marble and her tethered take a step back, but Jude doesn't leave my side. "You only care about what I look like?"

Kiersik, who's always had the shorter temper of the two, shakes his head at my question, "What else are we supposed to say to you?"

And I watch his eyes quickly flick to the captain at my side.

Without asking, Jude removes himself from the conversation, taking a spot closer to Marble as I seethe where I stand.

"Oh, I don't know. How about, 'Hey Soria! I've missed you! How's mom and the house?' Oh wait, you've never given a rat's ass!" My hands flex at my sides, flickering against my better judgment.

"Heated One, find peace." Sicar rumbles in a warning.

I try to heed his words, but when Kiersik retaliates in a heavier tone than mine, all thoughts of calming down disintegrate as flames drip from my fingertips.

"We didn't give a rat's ass? Look who's talking! You abandoned mom to run away with that pissant of a fuck who had you twisted around his finger. Did you think we wouldn't find out?" Kiersik spits as Jon grips his arm in silent warning.

"Abandoned mom? You left *us* alone and couldn't bother to send a single *krona* of your precious pensions! I had to eat *garbage* to survive!"

Dangerous flames trail up my arms in response, as I wield my words like weapons, my voice finding an octave so low I hardly recognize myself, "And I *know* you knew what was happening to me ever since I was bought. And neither of you did a *thing* to stop it."

My brothers' expressions harden, Kiersik's gaze flicking to Jude as they brace to retaliate, but the President clears his throat, dousing the anger in my body and replacing it with dread.

"Children, please do not make me pack up the fine glass, or do you forget that you are *not* in your own home?"

He walks between us with arms folded behind his back, shooting a scowl to all six players who stand before him, "If you desire to kill each other on my clock, so be it. But do this after we determine who's left standing. For all intents and purposes, the games begin now, so get yourselves together." He spits, laying a low warning to keep any embarrassment to ourselves.

Jude sends me a calming wave of oxygen and I swallow it with a sigh, trying to let go of the years of hatred for the ones who I still care for. My brothers do the same, blinking and shifting their focus on the President as we follow him toward the double doors that lead to heavens-knows-where.

"Chins high, my little Arena Thieves." The President growls, making Marble turn to me with darting eyes, gesturing to Jude about my hair.

He turns to me, cocking his head just before twirling a finger, and light tendrils of air swoop strands from my face, twisting them away with ease as if we're about to put on a show.

"You don't have to speak if you don't want to," Jude's hand laces around mine as the President inhales deeply before nodding to his cabinet members to open the doors, *"But they're going to hit you with the hard questions after hearing about you."*

"Who will?"

"The tellers."

Before confusion can burrow any deeper, the doors open to reveal a bright sun that blinds me, but more importantly, a *herd* of people before us. They leap to their feet, cheering and shouting while straining to get a glance at something.

"Not just something," Jude's voice floats across my mind as my posture stiffens, *"At you."*

CHAPTER 38: THE TELLERS

The sun beats down on my forehead mercilessly, and I grip Jude's hand tighter to keep mine from shaking before the masses.

I'veneverbeeninfrontofacrowdofthismagnitudebefore, much less behold their attention as they shout praises to the sky for our arrival. Even the auction doesn't compare to this ravenous sea of people.

Men, women, and children of all shapes and sizes wear the Bachalorian navy blue, bundled in winter coats with bright red cheeks and boots to the knees. Even though the light snow falls from above, it doesn't bother a single soul as they wave their banners, throwing fists to the air with elated smiles as we pass through.

The President leads us behind his cabinet members, nodding with a fake smile to the eager mob. A row of King's Guards lines a narrow walking path, keeping the public from touching the pride of Bachaloria. It's all too overwhelming. *"Jude,"* I whisper, pressing into him like he's my lifeline.

"Just ignore them. Look forward and focus on breathing." His voice soothes me as it falls over every nerve like a warm veil, and I do what he says, praying for this walk to be over as quickly as possible.

Marble is a natural as I watch her blow kisses to the audience who scream her name, begging for her attention. Her tethered, Anders, also plays the crowd, throwing a salute here and there, oozing charm as we descend the path toward a grand building made of red brick and mortar. One glimpse of the city beneath this snowy hilltop has me startled in my tracks.

The cottage fields are laughable compared to the City of Diamonds that sparkle back at me.

Adorned by a thin blanket of white along each rooftop and rounded dome sits the glistening city made of every jewel imaginable. The onyx streets are paved, lined with glimmering crystals and clear rubies to decorate even the smallest detail. Only the wealthy politicians of King Ragnar's court reside within this city, but I imagine they've never faced a day of unhappiness when such a beautiful view greets them every morning.

With a sigh, I give the city a nod of respect, humbled to stay in its presence for the next five weeks.

After what feels like the longest walk of my life, we push through the entrance of the new building, guided by the President's cabinet down a dim hallway to reach a nightmare I thought I had escaped eight months ago. A stage.

The audience that fills every last seat in this dark, unwelcoming amphitheater does not cheer as the sound of boots hitting hollow wood is way too loud. The silence cast from the tellers is deafening as every eye follows our movements like we're beasts to be studied.

Jude pulls my chair before a metallic table that stretches for miles, and we sit in our row silently as the many seats on the opposite end wait to be filled. I realize the captain has sat me at the end, perhaps for a quick escape should this so-called interview end in flames.

"That's right. Say the word and we're done here. But..." Jude pauses in my mind, wrapping a firm hand around my knee as he settles into his chair that's a little small for his frame. *"But it would be best if I stayed... right?"*

Jude shoots me a look that I understand. Whether I like it or not, this is my job now. To attend these meetings, nod and play the part. I suppose that's the assignment of the captain's right hand.

Jude's palm tightens slightly around my knee as his voice grumbles in my mind, *"You are not my right hand. You are my partner. My everything."*

My gaze shoots to the ground, hoping to keep blushing cheeks hidden as the tellers shift their weight with parchment and quills, waiting for this interview to commence. In my entire life, I never thought a man could make me feel this way. The ones I knew made it clear they had positions in life that I would never be a part of.

I lace warm fingers around Jude's, *"Thank you."*

"For what?"

"For believing I could do it. Kole never..." I halt those irritating thoughts of my ex-lover, knowing Jude probably doesn't care to speak of the one we both despise. But to my surprise, my tethered unlaces our hands, folding his palm behind my neck as he pulls me close.

Those delicious lips graze the shell of my ear as Jude whispers, "Kole wanted to hide you from the world. I want to present you to it."

Before I have the chance to pounce on my captain right in the middle of this stage, a ripple of murmurs from the audience snatches our attention.

To the far left, several new faces file in, marching stiffly in a perfect row as the crowd falls silent in their presence.

There must be a dozen of them, all dressed in uniforms of maroon-colored leather that wrap around rigid necks, cloaking perfect postures in a skin-tight fabric while long legs bear blades of all types. Their country's symbol of the poisonous rex-scorpion sits plastered across every chest as I study my enemy carefully.

Thick combat boots match their identical, raven-black hair combed into slicked-back, braided buns, sitting high on their scalps. Bright crimson paint drips from dark eyes, trailing down every face like blood, and it's only at the note of their intricate hair that I realize something about the Bloodletters as they take their seats in solitude, represented by no leader of any kind.

Seeing them for the first time piques my curiosity as I ask Jude, *"Are they all women?"*

"Yes. They pride their gender for being the warriors of their nation," he answers hesitantly, and as the enemy takes their seats on the far side of the table before the crowd, I notice something else that makes me feel uneasy.

Each face, though ethereal with the beauty that tethering brings, holds an innocence behind rounder cheeks and wider eyes.

They're young. *Much* too young to sit here, covered in blades with faces painted bloody in intimidation.

"Are they... children?" I ask Jude as the tellers shift, ready to begin their questioning.

"Some are. They've run out of adults with deltas, so they turn to the younger of their country."

"I can't fight kids!" I shout at him, feeling more than horrified as the oldest of them, who looks to be a few years younger than me, clears her throat to answer the first question.

"Speak. Up." The girl with a bloodied face growls at the teller in the middle of the crowd.

He swallows, straightening his tie as he raises his voice, "Apologies, Captain Lin Feng. I said, the public wants to know if you have any new players we can be excited about."

The girl, who must be their captain, bares her teeth in what appears to be a malevolent grin. The slightest difference between her and the players on her left comes in the form of a jagged scar along her nose and the number *8999* woven across her shoulder in black lettering.

The gaze of my enemy flicks down our row to find mine at the very end. Her eyes fixate like the insect predator ornamenting her chest, darkening with intrigue as fear snares me in wrought iron chains.

Lin Feng's groan is sinister as she answers the teller slowly, choosing every word carefully, "I have a few secret harpoons up my sleeve, but nothing like the beauty that Bachaloria has discovered. We thought pyromancers to be extinct. Too… *unpredictable,* as our new queen would agree."

"We did too, Captain Lin Feng," the President takes over from the center of the table, offering a smile to ease the tangible hostility between sides, "But that's what keeps the games interesting. Always some surprises in the mix."

And with ease, President RoBjorn hands the conversation back over to the tellers.

An hour of listening to the political banter between sides has me yearning for a time when all there was to do was bask in the peace and quiet, until one female teller directs a question my way.

"Miss Soria, is it?"

"That's *Player Davidsdottir,* to you." Marble barks.

"My apologies," the teller grimaces, her pale curls bouncing with the movement, "Though that reminds me, *Player Davidsdottir*, what was it like growing up with siblings that were always better than you? The sons of David have had our hearts for the past few years, but you're new to the spotlight.
Are you following in their famous footsteps?"

My breath escapes me as the teller waits patiently for my response, her gaze darting between my brothers and me.

Silence stretches on for too long before Jude cuts in, "No relevancy. Next."

The teller is insistent as others lean to the edge of their seats for my response, "I don't mean to pry, but the world is astonished by you and your story. We've heard very little from bystanders at your base, but it sounds like you are one in a million. Are you? One in a million?"

My mouth goes dry as every eye lands on me, and I have no words for them. I'm certainly not.

"Of course she is," Jude growls as his hand slides over mine, "Do you think I would tether with anything less than the best? I've waited my entire life for her." his hand squeezes mine with reassurance, but it doesn't save me from the jaws with quills.

"That's sweet," the teller says dryly, "But it's just hard for the public to believe a deltaless, young woman was plucked from the masses only to gain a supernatural gift unknown to man. Now she finds herself tethered to that team's captain." "What are you insinuating, teller?" The President takes over because Jude will not be the one to ask questions. I've gathered my tethered is a *suffocate-first-ask-later* type of man.

RoBjorn pins the young woman with a challenging glare, "Are you implying we do not breed authenticity? That Player Davidsdottir's gift is a sham? Because in thirty-five days we will show you all what our pyro is capable of."

I fight the urge to tremble where I sit as the teller doesn't back down, "I'm not saying she isn't capable of mass murder with a gift like that. I'm saying it is *awfully* convenient that Player Davidsdottir finds herself here without bending a few laws. Would you agree?"

"I most certainly would not," the President argues, but I know the truth. And so does Jude.

Captain Lin Feng turns in her seat to face me down the row, seizing her opportunity, "Player Zero, may I speak to you directly?"

Maybe it's the ebbing vibrato in her voice, or the fact that this girl terrifies the living shit out of me, but I brace every muscle, nodding to my enemy down the row.

Lin Feng's eyes dart with purpose around the amphitheater as she takes her time to speak, "Are you aware of what will happen to my people if we lose the diamond game this year?"

Her question takes me back, and I school my expression as the room bows to Lin Feng's authority.

When I don't respond, she says, "Your men teach that we will pillage and murder if given the chance. That we are the Bloodletters, always seeking to destroy. What they do not teach is that my people suffer stricter sanctions with each game lost." Lin Feng cranes her neck, gesturing to my row, "This year, after we have taken your players' heads and still lose, my people will have no choice but to sell their flesh in order to pay you."

My brow puckers as Jude fills my mind, President RoBjorn steering the room to his own will, *"Don't believe a word she says. Her delta is mental manipulation, and she's working outside the rules at your expense."*

"Then none of that is true?" My voice quivers, but before Jude can answer, Lin Feng interrupts RoBjorn to send one last statement my way.

"Player Zero, you do not strike me as an incapable woman. Our new queen—hallowed be her name, believes you possess a wonderful ability. I only hope the sins of our ancestors keep

you unbiased should you escape my blades."

Without so much as a blink, the terrifying captain finds her feet, and the rest of her players follow as she faces the audience with clasped, gloved hands.

"My empire will rest now to prepare for tomorrow's coin toss."

In that moment, without permission, our bloody-faced rivals turn in unison, marching off stage to the calls of their leader in a maroon tide.

In this moment, I prefer the enemy I know over the one I don't.

CHAPTER 39: THE SUITES

"You did the best you could," Jude assures me as we reach an elegant building that looks similar to King Ragnar's many chateaux.

Though the living quarters on Aegis are more than hospitable, Bachaloria spares no expense when it comes to hosting their beloved players during the Diamond Games.

Every level holds ten suites on either side, with a grand staircase cutting through the center. Black granite floors sparkle while diamond pillars line every wall, illuminating wealth like no other. I suppose if a number of players are headed toward their deaths, the least their country can do is shine the floors in their honor.

I squeeze my tethered's hand as we ascend, heading toward our suite that I've deduced is on the top floor of this enormous castle of a hotel.

"What's the coin toss?" I ask Jude, trying to make a mental note of where my friends could be as we reach the crescendo of the staircase. I should be surprised to find the entire floor belongs to Aegis' captain, but I have more on my mind than wondering how many krona were spent on these luxuries.

Jude pushes open the doors with a flick of his wrist, those strong gusts of air revealing a room three times the size of his on-base, and the view nearly takes my breath away.

A massive living space sits beneath an alabaster ceiling that extends for miles. Sheer curtains drape gracefully over a silken armchair, pulled back to unveil an enormous window presenting the starry night of Ol'Reyka and all it beholds.

Every piece of furniture, slabs of counter and decorative pieces of art represent the riches that every Bachalorian strives for but will never obtain. Everyone but us, I suppose.

I still can't believe eight months ago I survived on rainwater and scraps.

My fingers trail Jude's until I slowly leave his embrace, breathless as the window calls for me on the other end of the suite.

Darkness conceals what lies below, but I know buildings of magnitude sit beneath this wealthy, sleeping city, and the arena can't be too far either. Tonight, I will consume the darkness because it's all I can see. It's all I have the mental fortitude to handle.

The tension from the day melts as the captain wraps decisive hands around my waist, his enormous reflection crystal clear in the windowpanes before us.

Jude towers above me as a veiny hand drags my hair delicately, slowly, swirling blue eyes soften as his lips lower to brush against my ear.

"To answer your question, the coin toss determines a lot of things in the games. Who will go first." He plants a butterfly kiss against my temple and my skin prickles with goosebumps, "Who will play," those lips nip at my neck, "More importantly, the game itself."

Jude's hand flexes along my hip as I press into him, shooting my arm up to tangle my hungry hand in silky hair.

I pull his head to mine, devouring his kiss with every intent to repeat what we did after bonding our souls for life, but a nagging part of me is a little more distracted by the dangerous events that I still don't know much about. I never expected to end up here. I need this distraction. Death is too haunting to think about.

What if my death is right around the corner?

Jude twists me to face him, pulling back gently as he holds my chin between two fingers, "Why are you thinking about dying?"

I can't help the purse in my lips as he reads my unfiltered thoughts, wishing to return to my evening activity of undressing my tethered.

Jude's eyes darken as he scoops me off the ground, walking us with ease toward a plush couch that goes on for miles, "Don't worry. We'll revisit that in a moment. Tell me what you're thinking about. Out loud."

Lacing my fingers around the captain's neck, I settle into his lap as my questions fall out hesitantly.

"Let's say we win the coin toss, then what?"

"Then we present our bill of demands."

I shoot Jude a look that requires further explanation, and he sighs, twisting a single finger around a lock of my hair, "Our bill will say who's playing, what we'll play, and what we get if we win."

"Is that bill already written?"

When Jude hesitates, I nod, realizing this must not be in our hands.

"You're right. It's not in our hands. The bill is written by RoBjorn and King Ragnar together. I have my input about which game, but that's mostly it."

"You mean the *King* has a say in this?" I almost laugh at my own question because it's obvious he would. Though very few have ever seen King Ragnar in person, it's common knowledge that his hand exists in every detail of Bachalorian lore. He's known to be a controlling type of monarchy, and it makes sense he would create the deals with Seyka himself. I begin to wonder if we actually do place such strict sanctions on them.

"Don't worry about that," Jude shifts beneath me, pulling me close below flickering candlelight that creates a deliciously inviting ambiance, "Your only concern is staying calm and keeping those fires under control. There are strict rules about when and where to use your delta. I've seen the administrators execute players on the spot for the most minor infractions."

"But what if I can't keep them under control?" My voice breaks, "What if… they find out about me? I don't even have training."

A whirlwind of emotions begged to ignite the flames boiling within my veins.

A delicate hand slides from my hair to my cheek, caressing me with a promise, "I will slice off any hand that touches you again, Soria. I promise to keep you safe until the day we both perish."

Jude's deep voice wraps a blanket of security around me, and I realize, besides my mythical acolyte who may be soaring through the clouds for all I know, my tethered is the one I trust the most in this entire world. He would never hurt me.

The captain beneath me suddenly shivers at my touch, and I pull my hands back, worry creasing my face.

"What's wrong?" I whisper, my eyes darting between his.

Jude inhales, pulling his arms between us as he unbuttons his shirt sleeves, slowly rolling the fabric to both biceps with a reluctant breath, "I know trust is important to you."

I watch Jude carefully as he extends his arms before me, and the air between us falls frigid, his voice rippling softer than a whisper.

"Do you remember what I said when you asked why I hadn't tethered to anyone?"

"You said you wouldn't be able to keep your secrets."

"I was wrong," Jude says, "I can keep ever secret of mine, but I don't want to. Not from you. So, here is my… crumb. Of trust."

Jude holds both of my hands with a steely mask across his expression, but I swear I can feel him quiver in my grasp.

Suddenly, as the air thins and silence fills my senses, the beautiful sun-kissed glow of Jude's skin fades in his fingers, trailing up to reveal pale hands, wrists, and forearms carved with so many scars I can't count. The faded Aegis tattoo bleeds against blatant scatterings from cigar indentations, bringing tears to my eyes as I discover numbers and tally marks etched into my tethered's flesh.

My jaw trembles. "Who did this?"

Jude's hand brushes a hot tear from my cheek as his smile only furthers the ache in my heart, "No one I care to speak of. But I'm showing you to earn your trust. Fully. Fenrir's magic allows me to hide what I want to, but I don't want to hide from you, Soria."

The way he says my name opens a beautiful door in my mind. A powerful door. I know it has something to do with the magic wishing to settle into a strong emotion. An emotion I know is right for it.

I pull Jude's scarred hand to my lips, brushing a kiss against the pain he carries as I ask, "Why did you let me see the scar on your mouth?"

Jude chuckles, "Oh, that was just to get you to stare at my lips."

I laugh into his kiss as he pulls me close, and I can't imagine a sweeter moment.

This. Right here. This is what magnificent dreams are made of. The games may beg to steal my soul, but I know I've finally found what I've been looking for. And it's all mine.

"And you're all mine," Jude mutters, his hands gripping my hips as I roll into him.

Giggling into his neck, I whisper, "So, you must have liked me from the beginning if you wanted me to stare at your lips."

"Something like that."

"It's too bad you *broke* my violin. You know. I could have played something pretty for you." My mouth trails his neck as a rich laugh vibrates from his throat, "Why did you break my violin, anyway?"

I can tell Jude doesn't want to answer my question by the way he pauses for too long, finally answering, "I...needed you to be focused. On training."

With a chuckle, I pinch open the top button to his dark dress shirt, feeling more than giddy to see him naked again in only a matter of seconds, "That makes sense, I guess. Did you know I'd be such a badass in the end?"

Jude runs greedy hands up my back, pulling me closer with a grin, "I had always hoped."

My mouth halts above his, and I pull back, my smile fading,
"What?"

Jude's jaw tenses, his heartbeat racing beneath my palm with an answer I can't decipher on my own. Those eyes search mine too carefully as we sit in this harsh silence.

"What do you mean, you had *always hoped?*" I repeat in a whisper, every word falling out slower than the last.

Pulling away, I stare back at my tethered who's all too quiet.

"Why… did you buy me?"

My question doesn't shock Jude, but his muscles go taut beneath me, shaking his head, "I told you… I just—"

"Why did you buy me?" I ask again, locking sad eyes with his, "You can tell me. I won't get mad. I just need to know." Every nerve wishes to bolt, but I promised I wouldn't anymore. It's him and I against our enemies, but I need to know. I deserve to know.

Jude takes my hand with eyes weaker than I've ever seen.

"Okay, Soria. I'll tell you why. But, let me show you the whole story. Please."

I give him a single nod as he beckons me to close my eyes, his grip tightening around my hands, as I can tell this is a lot for my tethered. Too much.

"I trust you," I tell Jude, knowing he's about to do something he's never done before, and give a piece of himself away, and this time, not from a distance. From his very subconscious.

I know what it's like to be this vulnerable.

Jude brushes a kiss to my knuckles with a sigh, "Do you love me?"

My eyes blur as I nod, "Of course I do."

"Please don't forget that."

In the next second, the air stiffens, my vision fades and the image of a young man with dark hair and swirling blue eyes comes into view.

CHAPTER 40: SECRETS TOLD

I decide to give the auctioneers a fake name.

I won't live my life attached to my father for one more minute, so Blackwell it is.

They're afraid of me, I believe; otherwise, I'm interpreting these intense stares as anger over fear. But I've always been good at distinguishing the two.

The recruits don't trust me, and they shouldn't. I don't trust them either.

Three months of working my ass off had me leading the pack on every training exercise with ease, though no one stands out to me. I can't keep up this charade for much longer without drawing attention to what I'm failing at. Tethering.

Every day, Captain Yessaro watches me with eyes like a hawk. Probably because I'm excelling faster than the others.

A dangerous rumor floats through the company about dying if you're not chosen to be a player. Most don't believe it, but I do. I've seen the way the President skirts around the ordinance, annihilating the weak and blaming it on the good of our country. I just hope I'm enough.

At deliveries, I'm hardly myself.

I haven't felt anything since phase two's mental torture, and I think I'm about to go mad, but I can't let myself. I have to remain calm—use this to my advantage, and hopefully it will wear off soon.

On a positive note, losing my sense of touch has made me *beyond* fearless. You can't harm what can't feel pain.

I stand in the back with the other untethered misfits, feeling frantic because the one I know I need isn't here. If I even have someone. Maybe I'm meant to be alone forever.

When the President announces he's choosing a retainer, hope strikes my heart as he shoots his hand out for me, whispering in my ear, "You will not embarrass me the way my current captain has, so help your soul."

I nod in silence, wondering why the ones above have chosen to spare me yet again. Surely my luck will run out soon.

The Diamond Games are approaching too quickly, but Captain Yessaro keeps telling me to stay by his side. His tethered won't speak a word to me, though she doesn't speak to anyone. I suppose it's better that way. I hear she has fangs for teeth.

"Don't mind Ellsbeth. She doesn't like anyone." The captain nods to me as we fall out of evening formation, re-twisting a dark braid down the center of his head. Our company has been given strict instructions to pack our belongings and board the trains for departure to Ol'Reyka.

"Does she even like *you?*" I mutter, and to my surprise, the captain elbows me in the back with a chuckle, tapping a finger to his temple.

"Oh, she'll get you for that later, Black."

I have no idea what the hell he's talking about. Nor do I care.

The captain doesn't leave me alone the entire train ride.

He forced me into his cabin, asking too many questions with too much interest. His smile seems genuine, but I don't trust it. I don't trust anyone.

Yessaro's mouth twists, long arms extending across the velvet seat as he stares me down across the table.

"I know you." He says.

My neck stiffens in response to danger, and the candlelight flickers in our cabin. The captain had made his tethered ride in a separate car, isolating me for this two-day journey with no way out.

But I'm not completely defenseless. He may have power over the mind, but using your delta becomes difficult if you can't breathe.

Yessaro sighs, "Are you going to stop worrying if I'll kill you? Because I won't be the one."

"Are you sure about that?"

"We don't have time for this, Black." The captain grumbles, pulling something from his breast pocket, but I react too quickly, blasting a warm gust of air into his chest. The motion infuriates Yessaro, and I can tell he's losing his patience for me.

"What did I *just* fucking say? We don't have time for this!" He snarls, pulling out a small notebook and ink quill, shoving it across the table, "Now, take notes, kid. We may be stuck in here for forty-eight hours, but it won't be long enough."

"For what?" I growl back, snatching the notebook. After everything I've witnessed on this corrupt base, anyone who proudly wears these numbers has an ulterior motive.

Yessaro rolls his eyes, "For you to learn how to become captain."

My breath halts in my throat. This must be some sick joke. He doesn't mean that—he *can't* mean that.

"What the fuck are you talking about?" I demand, leveling Yessaro with a stare that dares him to deceive me. The only way to become captain is to challenge the current role and take it by ending their life. However irritating Yessaro can be, I have no intentions of killing him or becoming the leader of an entire base.

The captain scrubs a hand across the side of his shaved head, "I'll get to reasons in a bit, but let's just say I've pissed off the wrong group of people. Now I'm about to pay for what I've done, but *you*," he nods to me, "There's hope with you, my successor."

My disbelief sends a laugh across the table, "You've got the wrong guy."

"I fuckin' wish I did, trust me," the Captain snaps, "But it's you."

"Why me? I'm not going to fight you, Yessaro. Wouldn't Ellsbeth die too? You must be on something strong if you think—"

A heavy fist slams onto the table before us, fracturing the wood as Yessaro shouts, "She knows the sacrifice she has to make! Now I'm warning you, we don't have time for this so pay attention."

The version of me months ago would have recoiled to his tone, but fear disappeared along with my sense of touch. Maybe it's the look in the captain's eyes, or the fact that I have no choice considering I'm stuck with the guy for the next two days, but I give in.

"Fine," I crack my neck. "What do I have to do?"

That familiar, genuine grin meets the corner of Yessaro's mouth, "Write this down."

***

I hardly notice how beautiful the city is as our company marches through, preparing for the coin toss. I'm not surprised we won.

RoBjorn decides on full-frontal capture-the-flag, declaring we expend fifty percent of our players for the same amount of the enemy's. He assures me I'll only compete if necessary, but I know something he doesn't.

I'll be *leading* that game. I've never felt so nervous in my life.

"You ready?" Yessaro brushes my shoulder, his tethered on his right as we lead the company to one of the many exhibitions before the administration. Daily, the Diamond Game officials demand every player on both sides present for body checks to make sure no one has been altered or snuck something illegal in the weeks leading to the game.

It's the perfect scene for a switch of captains. I just hope I'm strong enough to do it.

"Are *you* ready?" I whisper to Yessaro as we turn a corner, glancing at Ellsbeth to find her steely, cold mask in place. Dark, glowing skin matches the braids that swish against her back, unbothered in the least. Perhaps she's unfeeling as well.

The captain and I didn't sleep a single second of the train ride. Every word Yessaro told me was more than devastating, though cryptic in nature. It's going to take me ages to figure out what he means by some of these quotes, but I suppose I have time.

Yessaro has always excelled with mind manipulation.
Without moving a muscle, he's able to attack the brain from the inside out, igniting paralyzing migraines that would make death by a thousand cuts more enjoyable. But to RoBjorn, Yessaro's gifts are null and void after he committed treason. So, as his last act of defiance, he's choosing the next captain himself.

Yessaro told me that killing him is my job, and taking his place is my fate. I just don't know if I'm that ruthless.

"Just follow through."

Yessaro grunts as we create our formation in the snowy field, lining up player-style before the administration. RoBjorn and his cabinet are present, as usual, creating a cluster for this morning formality. Just the eyes we need.

Yessaro gives me the signal as the last of the players find their place, and with the deepest breath I can draw, I step forward.

The field falls silent as my boots crunch the snow beneath, telling myself I can do this. I *have* to do this. Yessaro told me if I don't, RoBjorn will force me to tether to the first valuable player that succumbs to their partner's death. No one has ever successfully tethered twice. No retainer has ever survived past the games.

Every fiber of my being tells me I can't do this. That I *shouldn't* do this. I know I have no choice.

Keeping my gaze lowered, I face the formation, my back to the officials several yards away.

"Player fifty-three, what's the meaning of this?" Some bureaucrat with too much authority calls over my shoulder, but I'm not answering questions.

Learning from Ellsbeth, I slip on a mask of lethargy, hoping no one sees through my act though I feel sick to my stomach.

The words I've been told to recite fall out.

"Player One," I shout, watching Yessaro brush his tethered's wrist in a silent goodbye, "During the hikes, you fall to the middle of the pack. In knowledge, you fail on too many occasions. In addition, concerning your delta, there are stronger gifts than the ones you possess. For these reasons," I swallow, forcing myself not to choke, "I believe the only place you are fit to lead us is an early grave. I challenge you for the title of Captain."

Almost immediately, the sounds of feet shuffling to create space fill my senses, but I don't dare take my eyes off Yessaro.

Without question, The Captain steps forward to face me with a vengeful glare, but it's all an act.

The air falls frigid as I draw in the breath to command the winds around us. Every person present is stiller than a statue, watching with disbelief, and horror.

This is what they'll call me. The evil one who murdered their captain right before the games. He was the one who trained with them for years to get them here. They *love* him. Respect him. Trust him. I'm seconds from taking that away.

I don't care if my odds of surviving the game as a retainer are zero. I can't be his executioner.

"Yes, you can, Black."

I force the mask of numbness on tighter as The Captain's voice fills my mind. I know he's skilled at attacking the mind, but how the hell is he doing that?

"A little perk of being Captain. You'll see." His laugh fills my head as his hateful glare tells our audience a ruse, *"I'm sorry for making you do this, and I hope someday you'll realize why."*

It almost hurts that I can't respond back, and I know my seconds of stalling are almost up as RoBjorn's cabinet begins murmuring behind us.

"Go ahead, Black. You can do this."

Before I lose the nerve, I raise my arms, drawing in the air around me, but more importantly, the air from Yessaro's lungs.

His glare falters, his hands clawing at his neck in response to panic that deflated lungs bring. I wish it were me on the other end. I don't deserve to take the life of such a leader who would sacrifice his soul for reasons I can't understand yet.

"You will make a great Captain," Yessaro's voice settles in my mind, and I swallow the emotion that begs to flee, *"I just hope one day you won't carry this anymore. For your efforts, I have a gift to leave you."*

Yessaro gags on the ground as his face pales to a terrible blue shade, but his voice is strong and confident in my mind.

Before I give in to the side of me that begs to save my own soul and release his, an eerie vision flashes before my eyes.

Something familiar, yet foreign at the same time.

A massive, black wolf stalks through the pines I recognize on base. A wolf with orange eyes and raised hackles that sew fear in his prey's chest. He's wild, *feral even,* but I know him in the fiber of my being. He's not just an animal. He's powerful. Magical. Best of all, he belongs to me.

"Your acolyte is waiting for your return." Yessaro murmurs, and the vision of the wolf fades, and a new one emerges, but it's not a beast. It's a girl.

She's beautiful in a delicate way. Long, golden hair falls over her collarbones as she folds a cloth in two, organizing a dusty shelf with all the time in the world. Time slows as her face becomes visible, and those soft, brown eyes colonize somewhere deep within me, defying every notion of logic and refusing to leave. The image shifts to her in a stunning, red gown, and I'm weakened by her presence, my body rigid at the sight of her beauty.

I need to know her. I don't even know her name, but in the pit of my stomach, I know she belongs to me too.

"And your tethered is waiting for you as well."

"What?"

Before I can retract the air I've stolen, the deed is done.

Yessaro lies still, his face peaceful against the snow.

Ellsbeth cries a terrible roar, clutching her tethered in her arms, but she doesn't bear those fangs my way. Instead, in her last act of defiance, she shoots rocks from the ground toward the President's cabinet behind me with every intent to kill.

Several chunks of earth meet their mark, striking officials in the throats as arteries spew red across the ivory blanket beneath us, but RoBjorn stops Ellsbeth before she can inflict too much damage.

With a grand, infuriated gesture, the President sends a spear of water through her neck, and she falls to the captain's side, quiet forever.

***

A year of searching for her has me losing my mind and questioning everything I know. If it weren't for Fenrir's magic of sending me her vision every evening, I would have gone mad long ago.

I praise sleep just to see her.

After my company returned victorious from the Diamond Games, everything changed. Many tried questioning my instruction during the game, but those who did had died. Those who followed now vow to follow me to the ends of the earth. Though, I never asked them to.

Everyone thinks I'm untouchable, especially with a powerful wolf at my disposal, but no one knows my real motive to get through each day. I care for my players' survival, but I care about finding her more than anything. It will mean Yessaro's life wasn't wasted.

Though unorthodox, I attend every auction. Every blonde female, red gown, and brown pair of eyes has my heart rate doubling, but I'm met with crippling disappointment over and over again. She has to be here somewhere. All deltas must be present for the auctions. I wonder what hers is.

I send Fenrir on scout missions with my best description, but he's never successful. It's only until I overhear the Davidson twins talking about their younger sister that my eyes open.

The twins were bought in my year, and even though it's a long shot, their pale hair could match hers. Maybe.

Silently, I listen to their conversations from afar about their family they left behind and their regrets. Kiersik says they had no choice. That this is where they belong, but Jon talks about being homesick and wondering how Soria's surviving.

Soria. A beautiful name. *If* it's her.

I collect information about the Davidsons over the next week, planning a trip for departure to the meadows that skirt Cerica. Players aren't permitted to travel over thirty miles outside base on the weekends, but I have no choice. I have to know if that's her.

I haven't slept in twenty-four hours as I pass the Black Top Cathedral, following the dust trail that leads to the cottage fields, courtesy of the jabbering Davidsons who never shut up.

The spring sunset casts a warm glow over the puny cottage that's falling apart. The roof alone holds more holes than I can count, and the well reeks of rotten algae. This space isn't even livable.

Creeping around the sides, I peer into the cobwebbed windows, hoping I don't get blasted to hell for intruding. The only one inside is a tired, drunk woman who rocks with a scowl, tracing the rim of a bottle as it hums to her.

Just before I give up and head back to Aegis, footsteps down the path send me hiding behind the nearest tree like a frightened youth. How can one girl instill so much fear?

The front door creaks open and I peek inside once more, and the years of hopeless searching have finally come to an end. I've found the face I've been looking for.

Her.

She's just as lovely as I remember.

A sense of peace settles the pit that's been sitting in my stomach ever since I took Yessaro's life. Though seeing her doesn't heal the wounds, it lessens the torment that gnaws at my insides.

I make it three months before deciding I have to see her again.

With help from Fenrir, I've begun to create my own cabinet within the players, testing the ones who show the most promise. More importantly, the ones who trust me blindly.

I've chosen to bring Marble and Anders into my plan. They vow to follow me without question, proving it countless times during training trials and games. I've known Anders for longer than I can remember. They keep my name a secret, along with the contents of my notebook as we solidify our elite skeleton crew. If there's anything I've learned from decoding Yessaro's words I have written, it's that I can't succeed alone.

The second time I visit Soria, I'm surprised to find she's in love with someone. It isn't me.

The third time, I find her crying on her front steps, playing a sad song on a violin. It's only with a roar from Fenrir in my mind that I refrain from comforting her as every unrecognizable nerve compels me to do, but I hate to see her so sad.

By the fourth time, I decide it has to be my last. Yessaro must have sent me on the world's most heartbreaking chase, because I discover Soria doesn't have a delta. She was never born with one, which makes tethering out of the question.

Rage fills my soul like no other upon my return as Marble and Anders try calming me down, but nothing helps. Yessaro was wrong. She's not mine.

"But what if she is?" Marble urges me as I pace my room, flexing ringed fingers and trying to search for answers, "Haven't you heard of late bloomers?"

"It's not *impossible*," Anders nods, but it's such a far stretch. For all I know, those visions were something I made up a long time ago. I have no way of knowing now that I've obsessed over the same girl for years.

Planting hands on my hips, I sigh, "No. She doesn't have a delta. It's over."

I forget about Soria. Or at least, I try my best, but she haunts me.

Every time I close my eyes, I see her. Every time I drift away from the present, I hear her instrument, perfectly tuned in every sweep of her bow. Her voice keeps me up at night as I pray to hear it again.

I give in. If she was never mine, I just have to see her one last time to bid my goodbyes and leave a fortune at her doorstep. She doesn't deserve to live like this.

It's the middle of the night when I arrive, cursing the trains for halting for maintenance. I have minutes with her instead of hours as usual, but a minute is all I need.

She's sound asleep in a moldy cot, her violin at her feet, golden hair tangled as her sweet breaths drag with a noise I'll never forget.

Standing over her, my winds silence my presence as I observe the gentle rise and fall of her shoulders beneath a raggedy blanket. After tonight, I won't let her live like this anymore, but I'll never see her again.

Against my better judgment, I brush a strand of hair from her peaceful, sleeping face, but the act sends a jolt of electricity up my arm.

I *feel* her.

Years of feeling nothing and I… felt… *her*. This can't be by mistake. This must mean…

In my delirium, my back hits the wall with a *thud,* and she stirs, but I'm out of there faster than my wolf's ever run. And on the train ride back to Aegis, I curse myself for departing in such a hurry, forgetting to leave the case of krona.

Marble and Anders construct a plan—a terrible, horrendous plan to ignite the delta Soria must not have developed yet.

"It's in her somewhere. We just have to get it out. The fastest way for a delta to be born is through rage. She needs to get angry."

Marble tells me as I pack for the auction. I haven't seen Soria in several months, but soon she'll never leave my side.

I'll make sure of it.

"How are you going to get her to the auction?" Anders asks, picking at his teeth with a knife, "It's not like they'll let her on stage without a delta."

"Don't worry. I have a plan," I mutter, hoping the hydromancer I've been observing will take the bait.

The directors and I are put up a few miles outside of the cathedral, and I sneak out to set my plan in motion.

The sun sets on the grassy hilltop where I watch from a distance, listening to a conversation between a girl in love and a boy who's forever chasing a new high. I know the type.

He should be easy enough.

The hydromancer promises to meet Soria at his house in the morning, but he won't be waiting there for her. Not if I have anything to do with it.

Soria sprints home as I head for my target. Darkness covers the wooden porch as my winds slam the door open, and I can tell my presence strikes paralyzing fear into Kole's heart. His mother takes one look at my attire and offers me something to eat.

"No, thank you. I'm here for Arnson." I nod toward Kole, and it takes everything in me to keep my composure.

Kole's eyes widen as a shaky hand flies to his chest, *"Me?"*

"Yes, you. My name is Captain Blackwell, and I'm here to guarantee you a place with Aegis at the auction tomorrow. We believe your gifts could make for a powerful player."

Kole's lip trembles as tears well in his eyes. He nods feverishly through the mist, "I accept, Sir! What do you need from me? Anything!"

The hydromancer practically kisses my feet, forgetting about the girl he promised to run away with in seconds. If I were presented with the same opportunity, they would have to drag my bones away from her.

"Just be dressed and first in line at the auction tomorrow." I command and leave without another word.

Tipping off the King's Guards with false information about Soria harboring a powerful delta and hiding at Kole's address makes me feel queasy. I feel like I'm betraying her, but it's necessary. She's mine, and this is the only way.

When she stumbles on stage with a scarlet red dress and eyes like saucers, I'm speechless. This is the moment I have been waiting for.

In her presence, I can hardly think.

As she plays her violin with palms that quiver, that familiar melody nearly sends me into an oblivion I can't escape. It entrances everyone else in the room as well.

She's terrifying. *Mesmerizing*, and if I only have one prayer to send to the heavens, it's that she shatters me when she's done. I never want to know life without her, but I would be the worst type of predator if I follow through.

The type that snatches souls.

She's too pure. Too electric for me to steal. If I bid on her, she will have to face trials I wouldn't wish on my worst enemy.

I can't do that to her.

When the auctioneer sends her off the stage, the image of Yessaro writhing on the ground wages a war in my mind. I have to do this. By his instruction, I have to be tethered for his treason to come to fruition.

Before I can think, I've shouted: *ten krona.* And her fate locks into place with my bid.

Nerves of glass threaten to crack as I brace myself at the cathedral door frame. I have to do the opposite of everything I want.

When she looks up at me for the first time with those eyes I want to dive into, I nearly melt. But instead of embracing her, I decide to snap her violin in half. The look on her face hurts worse than any physical pain ever could—to feel like I've clipped an angel's wings—but there's anger boiling. I just need more. Pure, unfiltered anger digs out a delta faster than any other method.

I should know.

My invitation for these bloodthirsty recruits to do their worst has me disgusted for weeks as I watch her take unrelenting beatings. It's excruciating to watch a piece of your heart, tender and fragile, face torment under your own command.

No. Not excruciating.

Unbearable.

It takes Marble holding me at knifepoint every single night to stop me from saving her. I've forced Anders to cast a subtle shield across her body when she eventually sleeps, doing what I can from the shadows. As I always have.

"She still feels pain, but its intensity is lessened for minor wounds." Anders nods as we head toward the parade deck, "But I'm not excluding her from the mental warfare. She just needs to get mad enough."

"But what if I'm doing this to her for nothing?" I whisper.

"It won't be for nothing. She'll get there, she just needs time," Marble smiles.

It isn't until I watch Soria dart across the jungle floor with vines to create a snare that I realize she'll make it. She's more than just a beautiful face. She's wildly intelligent, passionate, and strong. To my surprise, she's found herself attached to an acolyte I didn't even know existed.

Soria may be the Pride of the Phoenix, as my players are whispering, but I know her. She's my tethered, my reason and the love of my life.

I only hope she never asks for the truth because she will finally realize what I am.

I am the villain in her story.

CHAPTER 41: HURT

My gasp floats between us as I pull back from Jude. Every nerve pulsates with raw, terrible fear as the memories sink in, plunging deeper into my subconscious as the puzzle pieces fall into place.

Jude's visions finally give answers to the questions that have burned holes in my brain, and as I stare back at those nervous eyes, I realize something terribly profound. Something horrifying and tragic.

I have no idea who this man is.

"You know me," Jude whispers, holding my hands hostage as his body goes rigid, knowing one wrong move will set me off. I'd need ten pairs of hands to count how many times I've been lied to. The pain from his memory begs to take me under as the rage knocks on the wooden box I've crammed it into.

Yanking my arms away, I push off his chest with quivering palms, creating distance as quickly as possible. I'm furious with him, but I'm afraid I may hurt him with the almighty fury boiling beneath my skin.

Jude's air fills my lungs as I turn my back on him, bending at the waist as the information plays on repeat.

"How could you…" My voice cracks as tears slowly paint my cheeks, and I can tell Sicar is trying his best to push down the anger, replacing it with heavy misery.

But I can't shake the betrayal.

The one I was supposed to trust most in the world had controlled my suffering from the shadows.

"Soria," Jude whispers behind me, and I can hear the plea in his voice. He's asking for mercy. But where was my mercy?

My tone finds a dangerous octave as emotions contend for control, "How *could* you?"

"I had no choice."

"You're supposed to protect me, and you fed me to the wolves!" My abdomen is ready to convulse as flames trickle up my arms, tasting the diamond uniform beneath its heat against my will.

This isn't me. This isn't how I feel.

I can't give in. Anger is too unpredictable. Peace strengthens bones and wrath destroys cities.

The pain in Jude's eyes begs to ignite a piece of that wrath as he crosses the living room.

"*Don't* come any closer." I snap, feeling the flames engulf my neck, "You stole me from my home. Ordered Sera to torment me all so I could… what? Tether to you? To make you stronger?"

"You know that's not the reason." Jude's expression softens and I can tell he's fishing around my unfiltered thoughts, "I couldn't stay away from you. I tried."

"You didn't try hard enough!"

The flames catch my hair, tossing strands behind me feverishly as I fight to keep the box closed.

"Please," Jude begs, reaching for me with those arms that
a piece of me wants to fall into, but the magic won't allow room for forgiveness.

I retreat with a snarl I don't recognize, feeling like a beast who's finally been let out of her cage, "You told me over and over again to trust you. To follow you blindly and give in. It turns out you've been the puppet master this entire time."

"I'm so sorry," Jude's miserable gaze is haunting as I wrestle the acrimony in my soul. "You have every right to hate me. Strike me. Torture me, I can take it. I deserve it. Do whatever you want but please don't run, Soria."

"How dare you ask anything of me." I spit, clocking his scarred hands, and my next words fall out with every intent to hurt him the way he's hurt me, "You're selfish. I won't waste my time torturing you the way you did me. You have enough wounds for the both of us."

My own words sting as I watch Jude's eyes vibrate, and I hate myself for saying them. I hate who I am right now.

Tears born of every emotion implore me to fall apart as I watch Jude's pale arms change hues in seconds. That sun kissed glow from Fenrir's magic drops over the captain's exposed skin like a veil, and every imperfection melts away. Along with every scar.

The captain's voice quakes as I reach the door, but I can't be here. I need time.

"Soria, I lo—"

"*Don't,*" I whisper, my hand clutching the golden door handle as flames create a protective barrier, "You told me to trust you, and I did. The last time a boy told me to trust him, it earned me a brand." My gaze falls over the tattoo reading *Aegis,* and the flames crackle along my collarbones as I breathe, "You might think you had better intentions, but you're no different than Kole."

With all the force I can muster, I throw open the doors, leaving a trail of fire in my wake as Jude begs for me to stay.

But I can't stay.

I can't face my tethered knowing what he's done. He *betrayed* me. Yet I love him so much it hurts. But *he* hurt *me.* If I stay, I may hurt him with a power I have no idea how to harness.

"Sicar!" I scream for him, rattling the bond that links us as my boots fly down the stairs.

I can't be here, but I can't leave. The administration will execute anyone not in their respective building at this hour.

It's not like I can escape this life even if I try.

"Soria!" Jude calls behind me at the top of the stairs.

Whirling around, I pin him with a glare that makes him falter in his steps, "Jude, stop!"

"Please don't leave. I know you still love me, and I'm asking you to stay with me. We have no choice." Jude's voice floats through my mind like a warm invitation, but I know my body right now, and his words are only adding fuel to the fire.

"Get out of my head!" Angry fists ball as I shriek for my phoenix once more, "Sicar!"

"I am here, My Pride."

"Tell me what I have to do to make this right," Jude says, "We can't afford to be divided right now. Seyka will destroy us piece by piece if they know we're not on the same page."

The flames take his plea as an appeal to forget what I've seen, and they rise in response, "You need me to put on a show for you?"

"For everyone," Jude sighs, "I told you a long time ago we have to stay together. This truly is life and death. If you let the world know we aren't madly devoted they'll rip us limb from limb where it matters. You'll never forgive yourself."

I open my mouth to protest, but Jude stops me with words more important than my own rage, "If you let this eat you alive and your friends pay for it in the arena, you'll become someone you hate."

"Like you?"

Jude doesn't miss a beat as his glare intensifies from the top of the staircase, "I know you love your friends, but I don't. I'll sacrifice every last one of them for you."

"What are you saying?"

"I'm saying, you may hate me right now, but you need to stay here. You must stay with me and work this out so our players don't pay the price."

The flames lose a hint of their heat as I follow the clear path in my mind, forged only by anguish for the fantasy I had created out of bliss. The romantic story that my love had only the purest explanations.

With a whisper, I welcome the navy blue, shimmering wave that caresses my skull like a heavenly kiss, and I know it's Jude's doing as his essence feels weakened through our tethered bond. As the anger dissipates, sadness enters, and my voice hardly reaches my own ears, "If you care for me the way you say, you need to leave me alone."

Jude's body language tells me he's doing his best to obey my boundary as he nods, *"If you want space, it's yours, Soria."*

My blurry gaze finally meets Jude's as I realize he's extracted a heavy piece of his delta just to calm me down, and my words are a pitiful whisper, "Someday you'll get tired of pulling me out of the fire."

Those swirling blue eyes are terrifying as he growls, "I would have drank the Elijahn sea to find you, Soria. Against your will, I'll pull you out of the fire every day if it keeps you with me."

Before I give in and throw myself into the captain's arms, I find it in me to tear away, bounding down the stairs in search of the ones I need right now.

I won't be a servant to these incredibly heightened emotions, but I'm afraid I won't ever forget what Jude's done.

I don't know if I love him more than I hate him.

My voice cries down the red string that belongs to Sicar, *"Cut him off."*

"Done."

***

My back aches as I stretch in the full-length mirror, cursing Merry's enormous, flared wings that dug into my back all night. I had asked to sleep in Grape's bed, but the little diva told me, Captain's tethered or not, he needs every inch of his mattress to sleep, considering that was our first night in the luxurious beds gifted to Bachalorian players.

The diamond uniform slips perfectly back into place after a hot bath, and I braid the hair framing my face as usual, noticing the white seeping from my roots has bled further into the blonde strands.

Curious eyes examine longer limbs and sharper features, blinking at the golden flecks in my once brown irises, and trying desperately not to think of Jude. I wonder what he's doing right now.

No. I don't wonder. He hurt me, and I won't let anyone hurt me again.

I find Sicar's string in my mind, following my friends down the stairs as we've been ordered, *"Where are you?"*

The phoenix doesn't respond as our company creates a formation outside our residential building, and I begin to worry until he finally answers, *"I am en route to Ol'Reyka."*

My brows pinch, *"Where have you been?"*

Sicar pauses in my mind as a muted yellow hue lines my vision, and his ancient voice echoes with sovereignty, *"It will not benefit you to question my actions, Golden One. You have relinquished trust in the Aeromancer, but you will not lose it in me."*

Sicar knows my own thoughts before I do, and he's right. The anger in me hasn't died completely, and it searches for a source to cling to. But I won't let it take my acolyte.

"Very good. Now that we have that resolved, one would be wise to recall their proficiency on the coin toss." Sicar chuffs in my mind.

Filtering through the formation, I find my place at the front where Jude waits for me with an outstretched hand and encouraging eyes that dart all over my face. He wears a suit of the deepest black, and the shoulders lightly sparkle with a dust of diamonds. I know he's picked this ensemble to match mine. Like we're the perfect team.

Before I slap his hand away, my tethered sobers my irritation, *"I know you don't want to, but you have to take my hand. We need to appear united."*

I stifle the curse in my throat, balling my fists before forcing my hand slowly into his. I'm just glad he doesn't have access to my free-flowing thoughts anymore. Otherwise it would be too easy to release every sour curse I have.

"That wasn't so bad, was it?"

"You better fucking watch it."

Jude runs a thumb over my wrist as we move, *"I hope you don't stay mad at me for too long, Love. I miss hearing your thoughts."*

"I'll let you back in when you do." My nails dig into his palm as a pathetic form of payback. But when Jude purses his lips in response, I nod, *"That's what I thought."*

Our company presents to the administration for our first round of body checks, then it's a two-mile march through the snow-capped city for the decider of everyone's fates.

As we approach the amethyst-crystal observatory, a row of officials in walnut-colored robes line our walk, leering beneath frosted covers as we enter the gates.

I reach for Sicar in my mind, bypassing Jude's string that hums against my skull, *"What were the rules to the coin toss?*
Isn't it just a... toss of a coin?"

"If only," Sicar huffs as our company files into the grand observatory, *"The country who wins the toss bears responsibility for many decisions."*

"I know—like what game and who plays and everything."

"And the option to oppugn."

Questions pile up as I follow the captain's lead ahead of our formation, and we take the right half of the observatory as our enemy files in, assuming the other side with plenty of space between us.

"What's oppugn?" I ask Sicar, squinting through the morning sun that casts a fatal light from the domed, glass ceiling above. My eyes threaten to seize as they adjust, and I focus on Seyka's players shuffling into position at the shrill command of their leader. They wear the same maroon leathers with bloody face paint, their gazes hungry with animosity as I behold every last body who means me harm.

Sicar answers as Lin Feng takes the front of the formation, and an impossibly tall player with a shaved head assumes her right side, *"It is an aged custom that has not been acted on in decades. The coin toss is not meant to be a deadly affair, but to oppugn would give an overwhelming advantage to one country."*

"Would people die?" My own voice quivers as the robed officials file in, holding loaded crossbows at their sides and blocking any exit we could use to escape.

"Many would die," Sicar says, and I hardly notice Jude squeezing my hand in a silent request to follow him to the center, *"In the instance of an oppugn, three tethered sets will be chosen by the winner of the coin toss to immediately fight to the death. It is a tactical measure that most choose to bypass."*

"Because that's too risky," I breathe, balling my fists at my sides to keep from quivering as we meet Lin Feng and her frightening partner in the center, *"Why would a team chance six players when they've already won the toss?"*

"It is strategic on more than one level but certainly yields unpredictable odds."

I watch nervously as Jude pulls a scroll from his breast pocket, and Lin Feng's partner hands her a folded parchment. It's not until the entire room falls silent that I realize all the anger sizzling beneath my veins vanished and has been replaced by nausea born of fear. I want to throw up.

Harsh footsteps fill the silence as a looming presence waits patiently in my peripheral vision.

Jude's hand releases mine, and perhaps it's the bond strengthening every second between us, but I feel every muscle in his body tense beside me, though I'm not touching him.

Lin Feng's gaze narrows on the person to my left, and I follow her line of sight to find a man of lanky stature standing way too close.

He looks at me with dark, curious eyes, standing tall in a chocolate uniform that matches that of the administrators. Tan hair sits tied at the nape of his neck, and every intense trait reminds me of an animal I can't quite place as his smile regards me carefully. He's frightening as his presence radiates domination over the room. He's not as strong as Jude—that I can feel somehow, but he's fast and unusually intelligent. Do I know him?

The administrator arches a brow at me, "It's a pleasure, Player Davidsdottir. I've heard so much about you."

I resist recoiling into Jude, though I don't have to look to know he's leveling this man with the mother of all death stares.

In my confused state, all I know how to do is offer a nod as he gestures toward the other three players in our circle, "These folks have met me before, but I've never been as excited to meet a commodity as I have you. My name is Gamemaster Benedikt."

A gloved hand grabs mine with a shake, and I blink as he bends at the waist, placing a kiss on my wrist that reads *Aegis.* Jude's warning growl sends a knowing smile to the Gamemaster's thin lips as he releases my hand, and I notice the cherry-red box in his grasp for the first time.

"Ladies and gentlemen, shall we?" The Gamemaster winks at me.

I throw Jude a helpless look, but his gaze is filled with malice as he stares over my shoulder, handing in his scroll.

Jude clears his throat, addressing our circle as Benedikt reviews our scroll with a creased brow, "I am Player One, and I have authority to recite the bill of demands on Bachaloria's behalf. Should we win today's coin toss, we demand the following privileges."

A subtle gust of air fills my lungs from Jude's exhale, and I curse him in my mind for the gesture. He may breathe for me, but I still don't trust him. Not fully, anyway.

Jude rolls his shoulders, speaking directly to Lin Feng as he recites from memory, "The game will require sixty-five players of my choosing from either country. The game will be seize the banner, and the winner will be determined by a successful capture and deliverance of the flag. Should Bachaloria lose the diamond game, we forfeit the end clause in the bill of demands to the opponent's discretion. Should Bachaloria win,"

Jude pauses briefly, and the next words have an edge as he enunciates clearly, "Our country demands seven hundred million krona in five installments from our opponent, as well as keeping previous sanctions in place until payment has been met."

Lin Feng's dead smile drags across my face as Jude finishes, and I can tell she's already introducing me to the power she has over the mind. But I can't shake the feeling that we're asking for too much.

The Gamemaster clears his throat beside me, frowning deeply at our scroll, "As a formality, how do you plead regarding the administration rules and fines overseeing the Diamond Games?"

"We accept all rules and fines." Jude says through gritted teeth, and I can tell he wants this coin toss to be over with already. I do too.

"Do you accept responsibility for all Bachalorian players?" Benedikt asks.

"Yes."

"Do you have any additions to this bill as you see fit?"

"No."

"And finally," the Gamemaster flips our scroll, folding it away in his own breast pocket, "Upon winning the coin toss, do you wish to oppugn?"

"No." Jude cracks his neck as our enemy hands over their parchment, their leader rocking on her heels.

Benedikt asks her the same series of questions, in which she tells us their ridiculous demands will require every single player from both sides, which, according to the pissed aeromancer in my mind, is unheard of. The game is called Dor Eudora, whatever the hell that means in their world.

Lin Feng crosses her arms as she recites their bill, "Should Seyka lose the diamond game, we forfeit the end clause in the bill of demands to the opponent's discretion. Should Seyka win, all sanctions will be lifted and Bachalorian borders will be abandoned until the opportunity to establish them at the next diamond game."

The smile spreading across Lin Feng's bloody face makes me sick, and the murmurs behind me threaten to spill my breakfast.

"They ask for that every year. Don't be intimidated." Jude reassures me, *"There's a reason why we have an eighty-five-year winning streak."*

Without blinking, Benedikt goes through the same questions he had asked Jude, "Do you accept responsibility for all Seykan players?"

"Yes."

"Do you have any additions to this bill as you see fit?"

Lin Feng's mouth twitches as she enunciates, *"Yes."*

Jude's exhale beside me gives his irritation away as the Gamemaster raises an indifferent brow to the bloody-faced player, "What would be your addition, Captain?"

Lin Feng's neck cranes slightly toward the ceiling, gazing at the muddy clouds above as if she's bored and trapped in an aquarium as a spectator.

That deadly gaze finally shifts to me, and me alone.

"I wish to add the tier clause our opponents had added last year, but with a beast of my own choosing."

Behind us, I feel every veteran Bachalorian player shift as sighs and murmurs only add to Lin Feng's grin. She knows what she's doing.

Before I can shoot Jude a frazzled question, the leader of Seyka dips her chin with crossed arms, "Player Zero, I will save you from asking your tethered what he is not prepared to answer. You do know our country called the games early this year, yes?"

I hesitate from answering her, realizing not a soul in this grand observatory has the guts to stop her from speaking.

With a chuckle, Lin Feng goes on, running a long nail across her jaw, "You see, our late Queen, Monarch Pietch, was slain by a Bachalorian four months ago. In her place, our new Queen saved us from ruin by creating laws to unite us and calling the games early in humble honor of our wrongfully slain ruler. It is only fair we insist of the same tier clause your people mandated of us."

I swallow the nerves that beg me not to speak to the one who holds the floor, finding a deep tone that raises the brows of my enemy.

"Clarify." I demand. Short and simple. I've learned from my captain.

Lin Feng purrs like a jaguar who knows something her prey doesn't, "Your tier clause from last year required us to produce our country's sacred beast, the hydra, for one year to train your novice players."

Jude's hand brushes mine in a silent warning to stay standing as the information begins to hit me like a sea of stones.

"What we had not made known was that Halkiya belonged to Monarch Pietch, tethered by soul and blood."

My knees beg to cave as Jude sends me a rich wave of calming air.

"So, as the one who had slain our queen's hydra," Lin Feng cocks her head, her voice plummeting daggers into my heart without moving a muscle, "You have been named the one who has slain our queen. We *will* have a beast of our own should we win the Diamond Games."

Jude laces a gloved hand around my back, but I can't focus on anything other than the terrible words Lin Feng utters next to Benedikt. Words I want her to take back as a fever threatens to pitch.

"Upon winning the Diamond Games, Seyka will take the phoenix."

"No!"

My voice rattles for Sicar but every emotion gives way as Benedikt clears his throat, taking over the room of fluttering gasps.

"Finally, as the last formality, upon winning the coin toss, do you wish to oppugn?"

The silence stretches on for too long as the entire observatory waits for the captain of Seyka to respond. Or move. Or say *anything*.

It isn't until I make eye contact with the cracked crimson paint staining her cheeks that I notice her grin is more than devious. It's delusional as obsidian eyes flicker.

"Motherfucker." Jude hisses.

Lin Feng flashes sharp teeth as she finally answers, "Yes. We wish to exercise our right to oppugn if we win the coin toss."

Without missing a beat, Benedikt folds away her parchment, extending the box gingerly to reveal a large, silver coin.

"Previous winners call."

"Heads," Jude spits, and in a single second, the fate of everyone's lives is determined without question.

Lin Feng's smile reaches her ears as the coin's tail stares up at us.

CHAPTER 42: OPPUGN

"S*oria, I know you don't trust me right now, but I need you to listen to me,"* Jude's voice jolts my skull, *"No matter what, do* not *interfere."*

"You're right, I don't trust you!" Queasy gasps try their best inflate flimsy lungs, but I know I can't focus on Jude's never-ending betrayal right now. Even if he knew what I had done to their queen or not. Now, Sicar may have to pay the price of our country's revolting sins.

I won't let them. They'll have to rip me apart to take my acolyte.

"They would have to catch me first, My Pride. Now focus. Time is limited."

I want to scream at Jude for keeping me in the dark for so long, but I can't. Not when our lives are on the line.

Listening to Sicar, I find an ounce of peace to force the question, "*Are they going to make us fight them right now?"* Trembling hands withdraw to my back as we move to our company, watching helplessly as Lin Feng consults with her tethered—though their lips don't move an inch as their expressions give away telepathy. *"And what's Dor Eudora? Some hide-and-seek shit?"*

I try my best to send calming waves over the electric nerves firing up my spine, but the task proves more difficult by the minute.

As Jude urges me to face our company, who wait eagerly for the decision, I force myself to draw in the breath he provides.

"Lin Feng gets to choose who fights, but she would be stupid to pick us. She'll probably pair her strongest with our weakest." My tethered rolls his shoulders beside me, sending a silent message to our company to remain strong. He still hasn't answered my second question. It makes me nervous.

"Jude," I say his name nervously, *"What's Dor Eudora?"*

The captain hesitates in my mind, and when he doesn't look at me, I know it's something bad.

Jude hedges a snarl, *"In their native language, Dor Eudora means Kill the Captain."*

Ominous, unstoppable fear threatens to send me into panic as Sicar's words make sense. It's purely strategic, though risky if Seyka's six best could eliminate six of our worst. She would be doing her country a favor while simultaneously securing her own safety within the arena. Suddenly my mind fills with worry for Grape and Merry.

"She's going to pick the novice players!" I cry, and that sickening smile tells me I'm right as Lin Feng steps forward with hands behind her back. Her humble posture fucks with my head as she delivers death warrants with slow, articulate words.

"We choose the following from Bachaloria to oppugn," Lin Feng's gaze drifts across our company, "Player thirty and Player thirty-nine," I stifle the sigh of relief to watch the sand-bender and shadow-wielder step out of formation to meet the center of the observatory.

That relief changes to dread as I remember the diamond game we're about to play will require every single player, and I can't imagine we'd have an edge if we're missing six players.

The next tethered pair Lin Feng calls out has my stomach in disarray as Sera and Brody step into the center, and I swear I watch Sera's shoulders shiver. Even though I wish Sera the worst things in life, I have to hope her evil self pulls the weight she throws for all our sakes.

My heart throbs as Lin Feng crosses unnaturally long arms, scanning our company with wretched intrigue.

Fear shatters me to my core as I weigh her options. She could choose Jude and I but he wouldn't let her players take a step before siphoning the air from their lungs. She could pick Grape and Merry, and I would meet an early grave because I know myself. Jude would have to lock me in a steel box to keep me from saving them ten feet away.

Or she could choose another novice pair who's tortured me for months. I could live with that option.

It's not until her gaze moves behind me with a nasty leer that I realize who I've missed in my prayer to the heavens.

Lin Feng licks her lips as she names her pair, and my heart falls out of my chest as Ona and Phia take the last place.

Misery doesn't begin to describe the heaviness in my stomach as I watch my friend take the center, and she wraps a meaty hand around her tethered's entire hand in a silent promise to do her best. I think of her Bird. How small and fragile that owlet was and yet it gained the love and affection of The Beast. Much like little Phia.

I have to save them.

"What can we do?" I beg Jude in my mind, pushing aside the hatred because this isn't about my feelings. Novice players don't have nearly enough training to conduct challenges. I can't watch Ona suffer.

Everyone besides the players competing pin their backs to the wall as The Gamemaster recites the rules.

"There's nothing we can do now. It's not like they would accept us as a replacement." Jude sighs, brushing a hand to mine.

A light flicks on as his answer sinks in, and one look from those serious blue eyes tells me to tread carefully, but I've already made up my mind.

"If I die, you die, right?" I ask him with pleading eyes.

Jude nods as he takes my hand, and I don't pull away, *"You would risk both of us for them?"*

His question isn't fair, but I realize no matter how many times I run the options over in my head, I'll never feel right about sacrificing the ones I care about. I don't even want to sacrifice the ones who tried to kill me more times than I can count. But I know there's a chance with Jude in the ring. I can't stand by helplessly.

Out of nowhere, Sicar's voice thunders low and deep in the cracks of my skull, and the doorway creaks open for this gentle wave of power that considers taking permanence, *"You are evolving, My Champion."*

Squeezing Jude's hand, I ask him, *"Do you trust me?"*

One look from my tethered tells me all I need to know, and I'm glad he does. If there's any chance to repair the bridge he's torn down, it starts here. Our lives are in my hands, and so are our players'. *My* players. My people.

I step forward, interrupting Benedikt from his explanation of the rules, my voice dangerously calm, "I have a proposition, if the winners of the coin toss would accept." Lin Feng's brow arches with a colorless smile and I swallow the bile in my throat.

Summon confidence.

Ignoring Sera's evil glare, I pass her to stand before the row of novice players like a protective barricade, trying to summon every ounce of nonchalance and boredom that Jude commands as I throw my proposal in hopes to tempt the enemy.

"I will hear of your proposition." Lin Feng grins, rocking on her heels once more.

"Take the captain and I as a replacement."

She scoffs, speaking slowly and thoughtfully, "Who do you wish to replace?"

The names catch in my throat because I may not know my enemy, but I'd be a fool to underestimate her intelligence. If I tell her Ona and Phia, there's no way she would release them. If I say Sera and Brody, she would see through the charade by the hatred pouring off of them in a self-destructive wave. I am not sure if I can lie well enough to convince her I want to save the shadow and sand benders.

There are too many variables and no guarantee I can save my friends. But maybe I can save them all.

Thinking quickly, I force a yawn of fake irritation, planting hands on my hips, "I couldn't care less who we replace, but I think it would be interesting if we take the others out of it."

My proposition lingers between us as the observatory falls silent, and Lin Feng steps closer to meet me three feet away.

She flicks out a surveying finger, pointing to Jude behind me, "You wish to face my compatriot and I solo, Player Zero?"

"If you're man enough." I shrug, praying she falls into my trap the same way the hydra had. I would kill him again if it meant I could save Ona.

Lin Feng's sinister smile twitches as she sighs dramatically, lowering her voice to a tone I know I'll hear in my nightmares, "Then it is a good thing I am not a man."

My heart sinks as Lin Feng hauls her gaze from me to Jude with a factitious grin, contemplating, "But considering I hold the power in this oppugn, I will counter your proposal. The captain and his tethered will face three of my pairs."

"Two versus six?" I spit, wishing I had free-flowing access to Jude's thoughts to determine how he feels.

Lin Feng *tsks*, feigning anguish with a deep frown, "What?
Are you not *man* enough, Player Zero?"

I offer Lin Feng a smile of my own, mustering the *performance* everyone has begged me to put on, "I'd just love the opportunity to dance with you alone."

She chuckles, flashing devious eyes all over the room as she thinks, finally groaning, "I know you are protecting someone in this lineup, yes? But I cannot determine who it is. However," Lin Feng wags a finger, "Because I do not wish to play Dor Eudora quite yet, I will accept your proposal of an equal fight."

Something heavy lifts from my chest because I know the second the fight begins, Jude will render anyone immobile by the air he wields. He can take two players in his sleep. No matter their combined deltas.

Lin Feng retreats to her company as they part for her, and she pulls two players hidden from the very back. Cupping her hands to their ears, she whispers muffled orders as they follow her lead, taking the center before me without questioning their captain.

The heaviness crashes against my chest like an ironclad trunk to see who she's chosen.

In this moment, I have given up every last notion that our Enemy in the North have been mistreated by us. They deserve every disgusting nightmare that awaits them by the leader who commands their deltas.

Lin Feng is merciless as she shoves two girls who can't be older than twelve toward the center. Though they are obedient, they quiver where they stand.

I bare my teeth, backing away from the young girls who wear cracked face paint and uniforms that are too baggy on their small frames.

"Is there a problem, Player Zero? You wanted a fair fight, yes?" Lin Feng laughs wickedly as she joins her company.

"She's baiting you. Don't give in," Jude warns me as he joins my side, but I can hardly see straight. I always knew Seyka's people were a vile and evil sort, but I never knew they could be capable of torture like this.

"I can't kill children," My voice shatters.

"You won't have to."

"Because you will."

"Because I would do anything for you," Jude soothes my mind as our players recede to the company against the wall, and Sera's disbelieving gaze ignites something in my heart as I realize I've just sacrificed myself and my sanity for someone like *her.* This is more than just saving Ona. It's setting our country up for success.

When Lin Feng forces us to play Kill The Captain next month, it will require every last player, per her bill of demands, and I can't imagine we would have an edge if we lost six people from the jump. Jude may assure me every hour that we haven't lost the Diamond Games in eighty-five years, but these stakes are too high. If we lose, my life stolen or not, forget whatever sanctions we've placed on the

Bloodletters. We would be forced to abandon our borders and allow the enemy inside our homes. Who knows what evils they'll bring with them.

"We accept," Jude says, sending a deep breath to my lungs as Lin Feng returns a salute that flares my nostrils.

The diamond game hasn't even started yet, but we're already playing. Jude and I have to win. I just hope I don't carry this with me for the rest of my life.

"The goal of the oppugn is to defeat your opponents." The

Gamemaster tells us as I keep my gaze level with the ground, "Weapons are not permitted besides the weapon your delta yields. Once I say begin, you will not leave the center until one team is victorious. The oppugn is between you four players alone. Any outsider who interferes will be executed on the spot. Any strikes against players not participating will result in that player's immediate execution as well."

The clang of metal crossbows loading tangles me in worry as the administrators shift to bear arms, blocking any exit.

"No matter what," Jude warns me, *"Don't lose your temper. They'll kill us both if you light up this room."*

"I feel sick." I groan, and I can't even look at our opponents. How dare Lin Feng subject them to this. How dare she give us such a terrible ultimatum that will haunt us until the day we die.

Jude whispers in my mind as I fight tears for what we're about to do, *"When he says begin, I want you to turn around. You don't have to be a part of this, Soria."*

An enormous piece of my heart aches in response to Jude's words. Astoundingly, the anger falls away as I realize he is willing to sacrifice his soul for mine. I couldn't live with a horror like this.

I wrap my hand around Jude's, fighting the tears as I realize Lin Feng is playing the game on a whole new level. She doesn't mean to kill us like phase one had. She plans to torment our minds like phase two.

"Just do it quickly, Jude."

I glance over my shoulder to find Phia clinging to Ona, and she pushes aside a short, dark strand of hair, mouthing *this too shall pass,* and Ona gives me a grunt from afar. I'll never get over her simple manners.

"Players ready?" Benedikt asks, and we all nod, ready to be done with this torment, "Then you may begin."

Jude doesn't draw out the young players' sentences any longer than necessary as he plants his feet, flexing ringed hands before the two girls can move a muscle in defense.

Tears stream down my cheeks slowly as I keep my miserable gaze on the real enemy in the room, and she watches her young players with raised brows as they drop to their knees, clawing at their throats in response to lack of air.

I don't even know their names. It's horrific to think they will only be a pair of numbers, forever seared into my brain.

Their faces turn a horrendous shade of purple as one hits the hard deck first, the other wheezing in her final seconds.

My tears flow steadier as the smaller girl reaches a hand out, begging for mercy while her other fist balls on the ground. Her seconds tick as bloodshot eyes grow cloudy, and her outstretched hand glistens with a sudden, bright light. But I don't realize what she's really doing until it's too late.

"Soria!" Jude screams, and time cradles me in a heavy embrace as I realize I need to move.

I need to move *now.*

I dive to the ground, but the spear of lightning was never intended for me as it meets its mark somewhere else in our company.

Jude's hand twists furiously in the air as he sends deadly winds to snap the girl's neck, but the damage has been done. My cry bursts my own eardrums to see the girl has taken two of our players in one blow.

Brody lies still and ashen as Sera screams for her tethered, pounding his chest in a desperate attempt to bring him back. His body had been thrown several feet, and I know she has minutes, if not seconds left.

My heart nearly convulses seeing the small frame lying limp in Ona's arms.

"Phia." My sob cuts deeper in my throat as Ona cradles her lifeless tethered between her arms, sinking to her knees in defeat.

CHAPTER 43: SHATTERED GLASS

My ears vibrate with a severe ringing as I behold my friend with no one to save her. Ona is about to die. I can't let her.

I lunge for Ona with open arms, and my pounding heart is the only noise I can hear.

Not the exasperated shrieking from Sera.

Not the laughter from Lin Feng.

Not even the Gamemaker's instructions to leave the bodies for the coroners.

Nothing.

Grape and Merry beat me to her as they kneel down to the ground, Merry muttering a prayer over the chaos for our friends' souls to find peace in the heavens.

As I watch Ona's large frame heaves, clinging to Phia's small, leaden body, I decide I can't live with this. I can't wake up tomorrow knowing I didn't do everything I could for the one who saved me all those months ago in the bloodstained bathing chambers.

Before I can think, my voice shrieks, rattling the glass panes in the domed ceiling fifty feet up. "Kole!"

Jude meets my side, bending to a knee as he reaches for my hands. "Soria, she only has minutes."

Fury finds its way back into my heart as I shove him away, growling at Grape and Merry and anyone else in a ten-foot radius, "No! Get away!"

I rip Merry from Ona, tossing her away without thinking, and every rational thought melts away as Ona lets go of Phia, and she can hardly keep herself up as her heart begs to give.

"Pyromancer, The Beast has fought valiantly, but nothing can be done. Her tethered calls for her as their bond no longer exists on this earth."

"No!" I scream at Sicar, *"I won't give up on her."*

I catch Ona's broad shoulders as she falls backward, using every last bit of strength to hold her upper body against my chest.

"Kole! Get the fuck over here!" I scream, and my tears hit Ona's pale cheeks as she blinks up at me, her breathing beginning to slow.

This isn't fair. This isn't right.

"Kole!"

"Zero." Ona chuffs in her deep voice, and her darting eyes find mine.

"I'm here, Ona. I'm here. It's going to be okay. Everything will be okay." I stifle the sob that lodges in my throat, knowing if I release it, I've given up hope.

Ona coughs, and I twist violently to scream for Kole again, until I'm startled to find him hovering above me.

"I'm here," he whispers, watching with horror on his face, and I know he's aware of what I'm about to ask. No, *demand.*

He owes me for the misery he's put me through.

Jude's voice echoes in my mind, and I ignore the pain lining his tone, *"Don't do this, please. Let her go."*

"Everyone shut up!" I scream, desperately gripping Kole's leg, "This is what you were saved for. Tether to Ona right now or I'll fucking make you!"

"I'll do it," Kole nods feverishly, kneeling on my other side to lock arms with Ona, but she doesn't take her eyes off me.

"Zero," she wheezes, and her face begins to wash out as the vein in her forehead throbs. That stupid vein that only appeared when she was smashing skulls. Or talking about Phia.

"Shh, it's okay Ona. I'm going to fix you. I'm going to fix everything." Ona doesn't hear me as she grips my wrist, squeezing weakly with a rare smile.

She sighs, "Zero. Thank you."

The tears fall faster than I can stop them as I shake my head, my voice breaking, "For what?"

"For cracker."

A miserable laugh leaves my throat, shoving all of my hope into Kole as he takes her arms. Suddenly, he hesitates, slightly pulling back with a look I know all too well. A look that torches something horrifying in my gut.

He's weighing his options.

Sera's guttural wails fill the observatory from several feet away, and I suddenly know what Kole's deciding. I know him.

I've *always* known him.

"*Kole.*" My voice is filled with lethal vengeance as I promise to tear him limb from limb if he does what I think he's going to do.

His pitiful gaze slowly meets mine as Ona coughs in my arms and Sera's cries rattle the walls. "Kole. Don't you dare."

The traitor swallows as he slowly shakes his head, pulling away with despair in his eyes that I will never forgive. In the next second, he leaps from his feet, sprinting to Sera who writhes on the ground, cursing the world for taking Brody from her.

"No!" I drop Ona, who takes her last breath, pouncing for Kole like a jaguar ready to shred, but strong arms trap my torso, swiping me midair.

"Let go of me!" I screech at the man holding me hostage, tearing into his arms as Jude blocks my line of vision, begging me to stop fighting as my brother tightens his grip.

Jon grumbles in my ear as I watch Kole roll Sera to her back, locking his arms with her in a Hail Mary attempt to claim her as his own.

I wiggle one arm free and send a sharp elbow into Jon's jaw, and he releases me on impact. With all the strength I can manage, I make a break for it, but a firm hand grabs my wrist, jerking backward until I'm slammed into a thick chest.

Kiersik snaps in my ear, "You can't interfere!" The officials along the exits shift their weight, keeping trained gazes to my every move. Lucky for them, their training is about to be put to use because all rationality left me the moment that bolt met its mark.

I thrash madly in Kiersik's arms, flailing like a snake caught on fire, until suddenly, Sicar's deep, serious voice settles in my mind, telling me all hope is lost.

"It is done."

My heart sinks in my chest as Jude moves out of the way to reveal Kole panting, pulling Sera to her feet with an expression I don't ever care to decipher.

Against every natural law created by the heavens, they're both alive.

The observatory settles into a silent, eerie truce as every soul present realizes the impossible has just happened.

And my dear, beautiful friend who lies dead on the ground paid for their sins.

My gaze finds Lin Feng's. The blood beneath my skin boils to a temperature I've never known as the image of her whispering to those girls plagues my mind. This was premeditated from the start with no amnesty.

She did this. She took Ona from me, and by the wrath in my veins, I will wipe her from the face of the earth.

"Daughter of David, do not!" Sicar thunders in my mind as Kiersik cries behind me from the flames singeing the fabric against his chest.

My flames.

My body ignites with a holy, terrifying fire as the heat charges beneath my skin, and everyone hurtles away from the inferno I'm assembling.

Jude tries sending that shimmering wave to douse the anger in my veins, but I don't want it.

I am power.

Jude lunges for me but my hands think for themselves, blasting him with a fiery gust that renders him immobile for just long enough.

My tethered may be fast, but I'm angrier. Nothing surpasses the torment my rage will wield.

"Do not avenge yourself. Leave room for my wrath, for vengeance belongs to me, and I will repay in your sacred name!" Sicar orders as the crossbows raise, but I can't think straight as I open the wooden box, and the hatred spews within, filling the void and assuming control of this rare, deadly, and *powerful* delta.

I know what I'm about to do will be the stamp of my own demise, but a vow sinks deeply into my heart as I decide my last act will be just as vengeful as Ellsbeth in Jude's vision.

My survival be damned. I want blood, and I want it from the enemy.

Domineering rage fills my soul and every fiber of my being as flames erupt over my chest, trailing my neck until jittery hands ignite with the weapon I wield.

My furious gaze locks with Lin Feng as she floats to the center, daring me to take the shot.

Ignoring the cries of my players, my brothers and my tethered, a terrible war cry rips from my throat, and I send my arms forward, unleashing the fires from hell onto my grinning enemy.

Just as the flames leave my grasp, a loud crash echoes from above, and glass litters the air.

A second before my blow of fire and smoke reaches Lin Feng, the massive, burning Phoenix intercepts the blast with outstretched wings. His body shakes as his back absorbs every flame, taking the full brunt of my power as the observatory dawns with a frightening red blaze.

"Sicar!" I scream, and unbelieving sobs choke me as I fall to my knees, wondering what I've just done.

Before I can blink, my acolyte twists in the air, extending sharp talons as he draws the fire with him and shoots back toward the ceiling. He bursts through the glass as the windowpanes crumble above and disappears in the winter clouds.

"Are you okay? I am so sorry." I cry, and Jude picks me up, brushing off my shoulders as the flames die as if I hadn't unleashed my fire upon him seconds ago as well.

Sicar sounds winded as he answers, *"Pyromancer, my body could bathe in lava, and it would not affect me. I am well."*

There are too many emotions. Too many grievances as I try to wrap my mind around the medics cloaked in red cross robes bagging up Phia's body, and now Ona's.

I send a silent vow to my friend's corpse that I will make her killers pay. The anger swallows the promise like an offering to keep me standing. I'll make them beg for the mercy Ona was never given.

My fogged gaze rakes over the newest pair with disgust to see them both still standing. Though Sera appears healthier than she's ever been, I know something isn't right as four players work furiously to keep her from clawing Kole's eyes as Brody's lifeless body is dragged away.

While Bachaloria's gained a tethered pair by doing the impossible, I can't help but think Lin Feng has won as she dips her head, offering an eerie bow as if it's my move next.

***

The day is lost as I follow Jude around, feeling less than numb as we go through the motions of new paperwork for Kole and Sera, record changes for the loss of our three players and of course, a three-hour lecture from the Gamemaster on what to expect moving forward for the diamond game in five weeks.

Every word spoken to me falls on deaf ears as I slip further into despair, sensing the weight of a thousand-year-old magic dive deeper into the rage that fuels it. But there's nothing I can do about it now.

"Soria, stay with me tonight. Please." Jude whispers as we're released to our rooms for the evening, but I'm too exhausted to fight him. I'm pretty sure Grape and Merry would rather I never speak to them again considering I ripped them away from their dying friend.

My dying friend.

Silently, I follow Jude up the grand staircase, his hand holding mine captive as pretty words try their best to soothe the horrors of the day.

It's not until I glimpse the world's most ominous pair waiting patiently at the crescendo of the staircase that I finally feel something other than heartache and grief.

Raw, incapacitating fear lances through my body like a wildfire as the King of Bachaloria levels me with a stare more terrifying than RoBjorn's at his side.

I don't know a single person who's ever seen the King in the flesh, but the paintings don't do his beauty justice.

He stands taller than the President, but just below Jude in an expensive, three-piece suit complemented by white puma fur decorating his neck. The priceless crown I'd recognize in any portrait is absent, revealing dark hair cut in a high-and-tight that only the wealthiest of nobles wear. Emerald eyes clash beautifully against rich, walnut-colored skin as Bachaloria's holy majesty tilts his chin to take us in.

Through angry, pinched lips, the President of Aegis steps to the side, revealing the short, glaring director whose shoulders roll with a narrowed gaze.

My palms heat as Neera regards me as no more than an insect in her peripheral as she hands Jude a scroll, stroking his thumb in the process. Where the fuck did this bitch come from?

"Now what?" I ask Jude in my mind, but before he can answer, King Ragnar speaks up, his voice rich and proper as his words float with authority.

"Let us skip courtesies, shall we? It would behoove you to speak to me directly. I have no interest in deciphering your hidden conversations."

I swallow, forcing my gaze on the scroll as I take Jude's side. Before I read a word, my tethered crumples the scroll in one fist, showing teeth, like his wolf.

"No laws were broken. I won't let you subject her to this."

King Ragnar's eyes dance around Jude's face with fascination as he says, "It is a false dichotomy to assume I am here under immoral efforts. Do not mistake me as your enemy, Ivarson."

My veins freeze over at the sound of Jude's last name, but he doesn't act the slightest bit fazed, even though RoBjorn and Neera give silent tells that his surname is new information. I hate the fact that she's here.

The King goes on, "Her acolyte may have prevented her from kindling a war within the observatory, but in doing so, that phoenix revealed something very precious to me, and unfortunately, our enemy."

My head shakes defensively as I ignore the glares from RoBjorn and Neera, "Whatever Sicar did, it was my fault. I take full responsibility."

"Ah, but therein lies the predicament, my player." King Ragnar takes a hollow step toward us as RoBjorn eyes me like a meal, "For whatever reason, your acolyte has become quite interesting to our Enemy In The North. Ever since he claimed you, in fact. Though now that we share the same vicinity, I certainly understand the compulsive need to protect you, Miss Davidsdottir. You are a jewel in this sea of sand."

Tangible apprehension settles over every set of shoulders as I reach for Sicar, but he's silent. Listening.

I hardly notice the primal noise in Jude's throat as King Ragnar's gaze studies my face for a heartbeat before adding, "Upon further investigation, it is now known that the enemy has discovered you are only a pyromancer by the gift of your acolyte. You were not born with power, were you, Miss Davidsdottir?"

My cheeks heat with dread as Jude sends me a breath, challenging the King, "You already know the answer. She still hasn't broken any laws."

"To you, of course not. To them, she has broken a very sacred law, indeed. She will be tried for international treason and put to death for entering the games with a power that does not belong to her," King Ragnar says, folding dark, gloved hands at his pelvis. Though, whatever supremacy he holds in this grand hall before our suite doors does not match the power that Jude conducts under threat of harming his tethered. I can feel the potency of Jude's gift radiating like an explosive, waiting to be jostled. I wonder if he's as capable of mass destruction under soul-wrenching pressure as I was.

"They would have to go through me, my company and her phoenix before that happens," Jude growls, "You may as well dismiss the games right now if that's the case."

"I thought you might say that," the King purrs, "After all, I would expect nothing less from a man in love with his tethered. You would start a world war over this girl?"

"I would end the world for this girl."

King Ragnar nods once, his gaze flicking to me with intrigue as chapped lips part, "Understandable. Wars would not be interesting if they were waged over a woman. You should be thankful I only bend a knee to my players on occasion, because I do indeed have an alternative plan."

Neera presents a new scroll, this one on black parchment as the King folds his hands behind his back, "Since the beginning of the games, there have always been specific bylaws written and unwritten to keep each side… well, on their side. Within these ordinances there *is* a rule bendable to our liking. We shall just have to hope our enemy does not become privy to what we know."

"And what do we know?" Jude snatches the scroll from Neera, skimming the paper until his eyes widen at the words I can't read.

"We know that Soria Davidsdottir possesses the gift to exert fire, per her acolyte," the King says as I nab the scroll to read for myself, "but, we have been watching you. Ever since the auction, my people have felt something… *off.*"

"Off?" I repeat in a whisper, scanning the scroll in search of answers. If they know something about me, that would only make one of us wise to the issue.

The King steps closer, ignoring Jude's warning in his gaze, "Do you believe a young maiden from the cottage fields could render my reaper defenseless by a few strokes on an instrument?"

My voice quakes with the word, *No,* recalling the auction stage all those months ago and how my song had saved my life.

King Ragnar traces my forearm with a gloved finger, tapping the section on the scroll that holds the answers.

"Whether you were aware or not, my reaper's delta was stolen for many nights after his encounter with you on the stage. It was not until I stepped into your presence moments ago that my suspicions were confirmed, Miss Davidsdottir. You have a second delta. And it was born through your veins just as every delta ever naturally is bred. We only need to draw it out under discretion, and the little matter of your life shall be solved."

My palms go weak, and I drop the scroll where I stand after reading the line, "*She indeed possesses two deltas. The former*
is fire, but the latter is still in question."

"Jude," my lungs grow heavy as my tethered keeps me balanced on weak knees, and for once, he has no idea what to say.

"We are the strong, the chosen and tried,
Forged in the games where the bold survive.
But mark this truth when the war horns cry,
Fear the unseen, or even the mighty will die."

-Bachalorian Player's Hymn

CHAPTER 44: JUDE

Fate has a peculiar way of taunting me with her promises.

One moment, I'm thanking the heavens for finally giving me everything I've begged for. The next, I'm sending my wolf on an impossible mission for information to keep what I've found.

If there's even information.

"You would be wise not to question my council, Aeromancer." The demanding phoenix blurts into my skull, ruining my concentration. I discovered my new mind-mate the moment Soria's train arrived at Aegis, when he so confidently demanded I protect her at all costs. I had no idea who this mystic voice belonged to until he revealed himself at the crucible's end, but Fenrir and I had both followed the voice's orders, conversing on strategy to inch her closer and closer to that brink of rage. I had an suspicion he belonged to her, but I could have never anticipated her acolyte would be something as powerful as the phoenix.

Sicar, of course, didn't agree with my methods, but he and I both knew suffering to the verge of fury was the only way. He enjoys mentioning seeking vengeance for my methods, but the pain of what I did to her hurts worse than any lashing could.

"My master heeds your commands, Your Excellence. Do not mistake him for a commoner." My wolf argues in my defense, using my mind as a battlefield as they so enjoy doing.

"It is only because you served with me in the Serpent War that I allow your objections, Fenrir," Sicar retorts as I sigh, rounding a long hall in search of the pair of doors with the diamond emblem, *"But you should know you sound whiney."*

"Whiney? I am unfamiliar with the notion."

"Pay heed to how the humans speak, and you may learn a thing or two."

"Alright, everyone stop." I grumble, scrubbing a hand over my face, *"I need help finding the damn room."*

"Third door on the left." Sicar sighs as if the answer's beneath him.

I march down the hall, crumbling the note that instructs a time and meeting spot in my fist. He better have something worthwhile to say, considering I'm wasting precious time—time I could be using to figure out what Soria is.

A bead of sweat falls down my back, and I draw a deep breath at the entrance.

"Master? Your illness—"

"I'm fine, Fenrir." I snap, sending a rush of air into the doors.

An orange evening sun tries to blind me, cascading through a grand windowpane directly ahead in this small, neatly decorated room. The Gamemaker's office just *had* to be on the opposite end of Ol'Reyka.

"I see you got my missive." The Gamemaker turns in his chair, resting an elbow on the oak desk between us. I've seen RoBjorn display the same tactic. They think it's a power move to act casual and fearless behind a desk, but we both know the only purpose that flimsy piece of furniture serves is to act as a barricade.

I don't bother taking a chair, crossing my arms as I loom above the beady-eyed Gamemaster, his gaze calculating and cold.

"I would ask you to sit, but this won't take long," he says, offering a sly smile that I'd love to wipe off his face, "You and I go way back, Blackwell. Or should I call you Ivarson? I can never keep your lies straight."

"Get to the point before I—"

"Before you *what?*" The Gamemaker spreads his palms across the table, his grin vanishing, "Before you suffocate me? Steal my breath repeatedly like when we were kids? My sources tell me you gave your tethered the same treatment in attempt to relinquish her delta. You must enjoy torturing those you care about."

"I haven't cared for you since you sold me out to the auction, Benedikt. And if we're trying to keep track of lies, would *you* like to go by Baron?"

My brother's lip curls into a snarl, and I can see my father's rage skittering across his face. He turned into him almost overnight when we were young, waking from a three-day coma with a sneer after I swore I'd never wield air again. I nearly killed him with my gift.

And every day since, I wish I *would* have.

"You took everything from me." Baron seethes, his voice low and menacing, "I was meant to be powerful, and you *took* that away when you slammed me into that stump. And now," he pulls back in his seat, his hands clasping before him, "I'm going to take everything from you."

I know he's not bluffing, and I'll be dammed if I let this monster destroy the only piece of my heart I have left.

"She's mine." I roll my shoulders, daring him to say the wrong words.

"Is she? Because my dear friend, *The King of Bachaloria,* would disagree. She is property of Aegis, meaning property of the crown. And ultimately," that disgusting grin returns, "Property of *me.*"

Without moving a muscle, my winds whip through the room, slamming him and that ponytail into the window, tendrils of air pinning his chest to the cracking glass.

Fear lances through his face, but it's not stronger than the anger that threatens to destroy me when he has the chance. He's been working in the shadows for years to try and ruin my life, but thankfully, I've always been one step ahead.

The only reason I pull my winds back is to allow him to speak.

"I won't say it again." I growl, tucking my arms tighter to my chest as Baron pants, smoothing his hair with fidgety hands, "Get to the point."

His mouth twists into that grin again, his posture coming unraveled, "Very well. You were always an impulsive young lad, so humor me while I ask rhetorical questions."

His insolence begs to rip apart my control as that same, eerie shiver greets my neck, sending another ripple of sweat down my back. But I don't have time to address whatever infection has been trying to work its way in for the past week. I need answers.

Baron resigns his seat, standing to snake around the room with those twitching hands shoved into his pockets, "Let me ask, *when* did you first notice your tethered hates you?"

Every muscle in my body tenses.

"Was it when you told her you murdered Yessaro to take his place? She must have noted your mercilessness then. Or when you ordered the recruits to torture her because she's an *abomination?*"

That control begs to slip as Baron sidesteps around the table.

"Or how about when she realized you set her up in those canyons to tether? She must have put all the pieces together by now—how you contrived this entire disgusting plan to bind her to you—but that precious girl never had a choice."

"I *never* set her up." My voice bellows across the room, but Baron doesn't flinch, his sneer matching mine as he crosses the space between us.

His brows dip, his narrow nose half a foot from mine, "*You* set everyone up. You've had plans to bring down the administration for years, and I'm finally going to stop you."

"I will devour your kin should he make an attempt on your life." Fenrir roars in my mind.

I resist putting my hands on the Gamemaster, summoning what miniscule amount of control I have left.

"You'll never be able to stop me." I flash a grin of my own, satisfaction greeting me when Baron's eyes flare, "Because you and I both know who holds the most cards, *Gamemaster*."

He works for the very thing Yessaro gave his life to destroy, and I'll finish what he started if it's the last thing I do.

Baron hisses, "You may have a wolf, the right of Captain and Bachaloria's favor, but you're not untouchable, Jude. If I've learned anything from years of studying your actions, you have developed a weakness." He tilts his head, retreating to take his seat once more, straightening his taupe tie and ribbon that labels him part of the Diamond Game Administration.

He's always valued his title.

"If you lay a finger on her, I'll kill you without hesitation." I threaten, coming to terms that my brother only called me here to taunt.

"Do you truly not understand the situation you have placed that girl in?" Baron raises an incredulous brow, "You used torture to make her angry, resulting in a power forced into her that she *doesn't* own. Now, if she fails to produce her *true* delta by the games, she will be hung!"

"And as I told the King, I'll destroy his country before it comes to that."

"And I believe you *would!*" Baron shouts, immediately snapping his mouth closed as if forgetting himself, his tone a sudden whisper, "It is clear to me that we are on opposite sides of this feud, but I have a job to do." He straightens his spine, composure rushing across every coiled feature, "Albeit heinous, you were correct in using torture to relinquish a stubborn delta hiding beneath the surface. You just didn't push her hard enough."

"Baron." My voice drips with malice as I spit his name, challenging his next words.

The Gamemaster smirks, pushing a scroll on black parchment across his desk, "I have been given strict orders by His Majesty to take over the operation of delta extraction by… *any* means necessary."

If it weren't for Fenrir's magic dousing every inch of my body in a tidal wave, I'd tear my brother's head from his body. My acolyte doesn't often expel his energy to calm me, but when he does, it's only because he has no other option.

"You won't go near her." I seethe, my winds pleading to send this room into a fatal hurricane. Soria isn't the only one with anger issues, but I have years of experience harnessing the emotions that come with a powerful delta.

"We'll see about that," Baron sighs, eyeing me as if I might try to choke him where he sits, "But you should know, the only ones aware of our… *lineage*… are in the room. It would be advantageous of you to uncover this secret, but if you did, I would ensure you never set foot out of Madden Penitentiary. Do we have an agreement?"

"You are no brother to me." I say, my expression flat and unmoved as I note a broken quill on the far corner of his desk.

Funny. He used to break quills when he couldn't figure out the answer to a mathematics problem.

"Related or not, I have never been given a task I couldn't accomplish. Try as you might, I will be the one to successfully pull out Soria's delta. And who knows," he shrugs, "Perhaps her *true* delta will let her tether to someone more worthy than you."

His words spear through my stomach like a poison dagger, and a new fear settles in my stomach, sending another bead of sweat down my back.

What if she *does* find someone worthy of her? I certainly know I could never be. But that doesn't mean I won't give my life protecting her and the innocent citizens who have no choice, no matter where they live.

I turn on my heel, spitting over my shoulder, "You have no idea what game you're trying to play with me, Baron." Because he doesn't. I've held onto a thousand deadly secrets, waiting for the perfect moment to release them into a maelstrom of chaos.

"Oh, but I do, dear brother," he shouts as I charge down the hall, "I am playing the Diamond Games, and I am going to win."

CHAPTER 44: JUDE

Don't worry, my little Arena Thieves. I write fast.

Acknowledgments

Oh, where do I begin?

With any gift, I give thanks to the Lord for making this dream come true. Many know I had my very own cabinet who helped me pitch this story and I would be lost without their underlying, unwavering, and truly heavy impact on this book's life. Tal, the Jim to my Dwight. Shania, the one who made me kick my feet over your reaction to chapter 34. Cheese, the Godmother to my child and my ride or die. Missy, the artist who painted my very own map of Bachaloria that's framed in my room. And Bri, the Merry to my Grape. It was truly like Christmas morning watching you read the first draft, and that is something no tangible gift could replace. You made this story real.

For the people who may not know it, but who have impacted my road as an author, you need to know how you shaped my writing. To my sister, you molded this story simply by being you and I am forever grateful for who you are as a person. To my parents, your endless support and encouragement since the day I found writing built my creative bones and helped me to never cede to the impossible. To my grandparents, thank you for helping me become the person I am today and being the pair that cheers me along on the sidelines. (Whether or not I have instructed you to skip chapter 34… please.) To Baldoni and Levron, my friends from afar, thank you for being such important pieces of my life and braving boot camp with me. I could write fifty books about the chaos we went through and it still wouldn't do our lives justice. To Gibby, the fastest friend I ever made, I miss you all the time. To Zoe, my best friend who introduced me to the animal world, you've inspired so many characters that have yet to be written. I can't thank you enough for your love (Debby Ryan hair-tuck).

And finally, I have three very special people to acknowledge and two of them can't even read.

Dalton, words couldn't describe how important you are to me, our family, and anyone who has the pleasure to meet you. You're stronger than any rock and wiser than any book could teach. Thank you for holding my hand through years of writing, learning, failing, and succeeding. You've gotten used to my long stretches of silence when I would disassociate saying "Hold on, I'm in my other world." And you are truly the only person who would smile and understand. In sickness and in health, I know we would be tethered in any lifetime, Meme.

And to Mer and Adam, you're not allowed to read this book until you're eighteen, but until then, all those nights you thought you drained me as newborns, you never did, babies. I was writing in the dark the entire time, hoping to make you proud one day. I love you both to the moon!

About the Author

Madison is a fantasy author whose stories are shaped by imagination, resilience, and a lifelong love of storytelling. She grew up on a farm in Missouri, where quiet moments and wide-open spaces inspired the worlds she now creates. After serving in the United States Marine Corps and earning meritorious awards, she turned her focus to writing the stories that had lived in her mind for years. A devoted writer, reader and dreamer, Madison weaves rich characters and immersive settings, often influenced by her deep love of animals (who she wishes could talk!) When she's not lost in her own worlds, she enjoys the outdoors with her husband, son, and daughter—usually with their Saint Bernards by her side.

Instagram: Author.MadisonZehring
Facebook: Author Madison Zehring
TikTok: Author Madison Zehring
LinkTree: Madison Zehring

SNOW PAW
PRESS

www.ingramcontent.com/pod-product-compliance
Lightning Source LLC
LaVergne TN
LVHW100505110826
845146LV00002B/519